The Embassy Murders
and Hills of Death

TWO CLASSIC ADVENTURES OF

by Walter B. Gibson
writing as Maxwell Grant

plus THE GHOST OF LIN SAN FU
a Whisperer thriller by Alan Hathway
writing as Clifford Goodrich

with new historical essays by
Will Murray and Tony Isabella

SANCTUM BOOKS

This Sanctum Books edition is an unabridged republication of the text and illustrations of three stories from *The Shadow Magazine,* as originally published by Street & Smith Publications, Inc., N.Y.: *The Embassy Murders* from the January 1, 1934 issue, *Hills of Death* from the January 15, 1938 issue and "The Ghost of Lin San Fu" from the November 1, 1938 issue. These stories are works of their time. Consequently, the text is reprinted intact in its original historical form, including occasional out-of-date ethnic and cultural stereotyping. Typographical errors have been tacitly corrected in this edition.

International Standard Book Number:
978-1-60877-068-7

First printing: December 2011

Series editor/publisher: Anthony Tollin
anthonytollin@shadowsanctum.com

Consulting editor: Will Murray

Copy editor: Joseph Wrzos

Cover and photo restoration: Michael Piper

Published by Sanctum Books
P.O. Box 761474, San Antonio, TX 78245-1474

Visit The Shadow at www.shadowsanctum.com.

THE Shadow ™
Volume 56

CONTENTS

Two Complete Novels From The Shadow's Private Annals As told to Maxwell Grant

Thrilling Tales and Features

Cover art by George Rozen
Interior illustrations by Tom Lovell, Edd Cartier and Albert Micale

Great things impend. Nations convene and prepare for a tremendous task for world betterment. The stage is set for civilization's proudest moment—and then come

The Embassy Murders

to baffle the nation and the entire world—but not The Shadow!

From the Private Annals of The Shadow, as told to

Maxwell Grant

CHAPTER I
FOOTSTEPS TO CRIME

IT was midnight. From the brilliance of one of Washington's broad avenues, the lights of a large embassy building could be seen glowing upon the sidewalks of the street on which it fronted.

Parked cars lined the side street. One by one they were moving from their places, edging to the space in front of the embassy, where departing guests were ready to leave. An important social event was coming to its close.

The broad steps of the embassy were plainly lighted. Upon them appeared two men dressed in evening clothes. One was a tall, gray-haired individual; the other a stocky, square-faced man who leaned heavily upon a stout cane as he descended the steps. The two men paused as they reached the sidewalk.

"You have a car here, Mr. Rochelle?" inquired the tall man, as a uniformed attendant approached.

"No, Senator," returned the man with the cane. "It is not far to my residence. I prefer to walk. If you should care to accompany me—"

"Gladly," interposed the gray-haired man. "Your headquarters is on the way to my hotel. The night is mild. We can talk as we stroll along."

The pair headed from the direction of the avenue. Side by side, they followed the route that Rochelle indicated. The embassy attendant watched them as they moved along the street. His gaze centered upon the man whom the senator had addressed as Rochelle.

Coming down the embassy steps, Rochelle's manner of locomotion had seemed quite normal. Upon the sidewalk, however, the man who carried the cane formed an odd and conspicuous figure. Every stride caused his body to incline heavily to the right, where its sagging stopped by Rochelle's pressure on the strong walking stick.

Then came a momentary stop. Rochelle's right leg, swinging forward, resumed its pace. His whole body seemed to twist with the effort. The halting limp continued with regular precision; yet despite it, Rochelle kept pace with the man beside him.

The man with the limp!

The embassy attendant knew him by sight. He was Darvin Rochelle, founder of the International Peace Alliance. His halting, sagging figure could be seen at all the important functions which took place at foreign embassies, for Darvin Rochelle was noted as a student of international problems.

TURNING a corner, Darvin Rochelle and his companion arrived upon a well-lighted street. Their faces showed plainly beneath the shadowy criss-cross of broad-branched trees.

The tall, gray-haired senator was listening with dignified pleasure to the words which his limping companion uttered. Darvin Rochelle, his firm face gleaming with the fire of enthusiasm, was talking in modulated tones that carried real conviction.

"World peace!" Rochelle's declaration came with emphasis. "It is not a dream, Senator! It is reality. Look at the world today. Do you see war? Only in scattered portions of the globe. Peace is the predominating desire of our present era."

"Perhaps," maintained the senator dryly. "Yet the world has not changed. Nations—races—all have differences. War, despite its futility, seems to be the only choice when difficulties must be settled."

"Agreed," stated Rochelle, turning his head as he limped. "Next, you will point out to me the failure that seems to have gripped the League of Nations. I shall agree with you there. Nevertheless,

world peace can be maintained. To further it is the work that I have chosen."

"Commendable," remarked the senator. "Let us hope, Rochelle, that your plans will succeed. From what you have told me, I realize fully that your work is worthy of support. The International Peace Alliance is unquestionably a new idea."

"Yet a simple one, Senator. It seeks to produce international understanding. That is all. We have representatives in every country. All are pledged to throw their influence into the scale that will bring the balance in favor of worldwide peace. They are workers in a common cause.

"There are barriers between countries. Such barriers were natural once, but today, with international communication a matter of great ease, the barriers are falling. The International Peace Alliance has stimulated trade relations between different countries. That, more than any propaganda, is the first step to permanent peace."

"Certainly," rejoined the gray-haired senator. "When nations depend upon one another commercially, their trend will be away from warfare. Yet international trade is handicapped—"

"By language," interposed Rochelle. "More than by any other single cause."

"You are right," agreed the senator.

"Therefore," resumed Rochelle, "the International Peace Alliance has found the way to remove that barrier. We are preparing our new universal language, called Agro. With its completion, there will be a positive form of international communication."

"Will it work?" questioned the senator. "The same attempt has been tried before. Esperanto—"

"Esperanto?" Rochelle's question was scornful. "Bah! Esperanto was a poor attempt at an international tongue. It was launched before its time. It died a natural death. Today, however, when all languages are becoming modern, the time is ripe for a universal system. Agro will fill the need.

"Agro will receive endorsement in every land. It will be taught in elementary schools. Each year, its vocabulary will be expanded. Agro is designed to grow until it will predominate. Then, Senator, world understanding will be complete!"

THE two men had turned into another street. Rochelle's halting limp came to a stop. Resting upon his cane, the enthusiast waved his hand toward a pretentious building.

"My residence," he stated simply. "Also the headquarters of the International Peace Alliance. Will you come in, Senator?"

"I should be back at my hotel—"

"Step inside for a few minutes. I shall order my limousine to take you to the hotel."

The senator agreed. With Rochelle, he ascended

the stone steps. The door opened as the two men arrived at the top. A bowing servant admitted Rochelle and his companion.

"Order the limousine, Gaillard," instructed Rochelle. Then, to his companion: "Let me show you our arrangements, Senator."

There were two doors on each side of the hall. Rochelle led the senator through the door to the right. He pressed a switch; the light showed a room that was fitted like a museum. Shelves and show cases held specimens of curios and products that came from all the world.

"Our display room," explained Rochelle. "It familiarizes all visitors with the customs and products found throughout the world. This"—he paused as he opened a door at the rear of the room and led the senator into what appeared to be an office—"is where all our detail work is done. At present, we have but a small force. That is all that we can accommodate. Later, we shall take additional offices elsewhere."

Crossing to the left, Rochelle limped through a door that showed another rear room of the huge ground floor. This place was equipped with tables covered with magazines and newspapers; its walls were lined with books.

"Our international library," informed Rochelle. "Current publications from all the world. These"— he was pointing to the books—"will all be translated into Agro."

"A great undertaking," commented the senator.

"Yes," admitted Rochelle, as he led the visitor through to the front room on the left, "but a worthy one. Our publications will go everywhere. Here, Senator, is our meeting room."

They were standing in the front room. The senator stared at the walls. Beautifully decorated in many colors, they formed maps in mural style. The entire world was depicted. Darvin Rochelle smiled as he observed the keen interest which the visitor displayed.

The senator was still walking about the room from map to map when Gaillard entered to inform Rochelle that the limousine was in front. The senator heard the servant's statement. He glanced at his watch. He walked toward the hall.

"Sorry," he said, "but I really must get back to the hotel. When I have the opportunity, Rochelle, I shall come to see you. I want to hear more about your peace plans. You are here most of the day?"

"Nearly all the time." They were in the hallway, and Rochelle waved his hand toward a broad marble staircase that led directly to the second floor. "My private office is above. Call at any time you wish, senator. Good night, sir."

AS soon as the visitor had departed, Darvin Rochelle turned and limped toward the stairway. His halting stride ended as he moved up the steps. It began again when he reached the top.

The man with the limp opened a door and entered a large anteroom, where chairs lined the walls. He passed through to another door and stepped into an office that was furnished with expensive mahogany. Here, Rochelle seated himself at a huge desk near the center of the room.

Directly to the left of the desk was a huge globe of the world. It was more than three feet in diameter; it rested in a circular mahogany cradle atop a heavy metal tripod. Pausing by the globe, Rochelle rested upon his cane. With his free hand, he spun the big sphere and watched it revolve.

A strange smile appeared upon Rochelle's face. Here in the lighted room, his features showed a curious change of expression. From those of an idealist, they became the countenance of a gloating schemer.

The spinning globe slowly dawdled to a stop. Rochelle seated himself behind the desk. He opened a drawer and reached inside. His fingers found a buzzer hidden at the top of the drawer. Rochelle pressed the button and waited. He was looking toward a mirror at the right side of the room.

The glass showed the reflection of a doorway at the back of the office. While Rochelle watched, the door opened and a stoop-shouldered creature entered with stealthy tread.

The newcomer was a dwarf, twisted in body, vicious in face. An ugly smile was on the deformed man's puffed lips.

"Over there, Thurk," ordered Rochelle quietly. He indicated the opposite side of the desk.

The dwarf complied. He took his stand in front of his master. Resting both hands upon the desk, he formed a grotesque monster with long, scrawny arms and head that seemed too large for the skinny shoulders which supported it.

Wild eyes gleamed from Thurk's pasty face. Bloated lips moved while the hideous creature spoke in a harsh, strange tongue:

"Kye kye rofe kye."

"Sovo," returned Rochelle, in a quiet tone. "Reen kye kye doke?"

"Sake alta alta. Seek alta eeta."

"Kye kye kode?"

"Fee."

"Dake."

With this syllabic utterance, Rochelle arose from his chair. He walked directly to the door where he had seen Thurk's reflection. As the master limped in that direction, the dwarf followed with bounding steps.

BEYOND the door, Rochelle came to a spiral staircase. He descended, without the aid of his cane. Thurk continued, creeping downward, until they reached a small room at the bottom of the steps. Here Rochelle unbarred a steel door. He turned out the single light and opened the barrier amid darkness.

Rochelle limped out into the cool air of a walled courtyard. Directly ahead, showing dimly in the vague light that came from above, was an iron fence with a little gate. It formed the rear of Rochelle's property. Beyond it was the back of a dilapidated house, for Rochelle's mansion was on the fringe of a decadent district.

Through the gate, Rochelle unlocked the back door of the house in the rear. He entered and groped his way to a flight of stairs. At the bottom, Thurk, still following, could hear the click of his master's cane against the stone of a cellar floor. Rochelle turned on a light.

Lying on the floor was the body of a young man. The blood-encrusted front of a tuxedo shirt showed where a bullet had ended the victim's life. Rochelle sneered as he gripped a post beside him and used his cane to poke at the body.

Thurk, approaching his master, produced a large envelope from a pocket. He handed it to Rochelle and pointed significantly to the body on the floor.

"Rike zay folo folo," declared the dwarf.

"Sovo," returned Rochelle.

He took the envelope, thrust it in a pocket of his evening clothes and pointed to the body with his cane.

Thurk understood the gesture. He stooped; with a display of remarkable strength, he hoisted the corpse to his shoulders and carried it through an archway in the cellar. Rochelle, still gripping the post, was listening. He heard a splash as Thurk dropped the body into some hidden vat.

A soft, insidious snarl came from Rochelle's lips. Leaning upon his cane, the man with the limp clicked back across the cellar. He retraced the course that he had taken; back into his own house; up the spiral stairway to his finely furnished office.

There, he opened the envelope that Thurk had given him. Within it was another envelope which bore the typewritten statement:

South American Correspondence.

Documents came out upon the desk. With eager eyes, Rochelle began to study them. His visage showed an evil gleam, as he perused these papers which had been purloined from a murdered man.

Completing his inspection, Rochelle arose and moved to a safe in the wall. He turned the combination, opened the safe, then placed the papers within. He closed the door and turned to find that Thurk had come back. Rochelle dismissed the dwarf with a wave of his hand.

Alone again, Rochelle indulged in a fiendish smile that gradually faded from his lips to restore his benign expression. Then, with the aid of his cane, he clumped through another door at the back of the office.

The hollow taps of the walking stick faded. Darvin Rochelle had retired for the night. Yet the echoes of that clicking cane seemed to leave their mark.

Those clicks had told of the footsteps of Darvin Rochelle, a man whose life, presumably, had been devoted to ways of peace and friendship. Such, however, was a pretense.

The footsteps of Darvin Rochelle had led to crime. The man with the limp was a monster whose ways were those of murder!

CHAPTER II
WORD TO THE SHADOW

LATE the next afternoon, a man appeared upon the fifth floor of the old Wallingford Building. He strolled through an empty corridor until he reached a door which bore this title:

NATIONAL CITY NEWS ASSOCIATION
CLYDE BURKE, MANAGER

The visitor opened the door. Inside he found a young man seated at a desk. This was Clyde Burke, manager and entire staff of the National City News Association. The visitor grinned as Burke looked up.

"Hello, Burke," he said.

"Hello, Garvey," returned Burke. "What brings you here so late?"

"Nothing special. Just thought I'd drop in."

The visitor sat down. He watched Burke going over piles of clippings, while he puffed at a cigarette. The visitor lighted one of his own. Like Burke, Garvey was a freelance journalist who had chosen Washington as a place to make a living through news correspondence.

Several minutes drifted by. Clyde Burke, stacking clippings in envelopes, paid no attention to his visitor. That proved to be the best way to start Garvey talking. The visiting newspaperman gave up an attempt to blow smoke rings and began to drawl in casual fashion.

"Heard another hot rumor today," he said.

"What's this one?" quizzed Burke, in a matter-of-fact tone.

"Another attaché gone haywire," remarked Garvey. "Here in Washington yesterday. Not here today. That makes number five."

"And I suppose," declared Burke, "that he disappeared with important documents on his person."

"You guessed it," rejoined Garvey. "Same as the

others, Burke. Laugh it off if you want to—but I'm telling you this is no hokum. I know the guy's name—and I know what's missing."

"Yes? When did you begin to rate so high with the State Department?"

"Never mind that. I've landed some good stories. But it's always my luck to pick up something that can't be used. The fellow that's missing is named Glade Tromboll. The documents that he had were correspondence with South American countries."

"Is that all you found out?"

"All?" Garvey snorted. "Say—that's too much. What can you do with it? Nothing. Like those other birds that flew the coop, this one is being kept quiet. Boy! You can't touch a story like that without official permission. You know what would happen if I tried to get it?"

"Sure," responded Burke. "You'd find out that there never was anybody by the name of Glade Tromboll here in Washington."

"That's it." Garvey grinned sourly. "You're wise to the way things work in this town. Land something that looks real—you can't touch it. It's lucky that newspapers like feature stories on the extermination of Japanese beetles and construction of irrigation canals. If it wasn't for old standbys like that, I'd starve to death."

Garvey flicked his cigarette through the open window and strolled to the door. He waved good-bye to Burke and left the office.

AS soon as the door had closed, Clyde Burke reached for pencil and paper. He wrote out the information which the other newspaperman had just mentioned.

Unwittingly, Garvey had brought important news to Clyde Burke. Garvey was but one of many freelances who dropped into the National City News Association. Ever since he had opened his office, a few weeks previous, Clyde Burke had been buying news items from those who had them to offer.

Why a young man like Clyde Burke should have come to Washington to compete with other news bureaus in the already overburdened capital was a mystery that had bothered no one. Others before Burke had fallen for that same lure. Journalism had the mythical tradition that one might gain fame and fortune by opening a Washington news service.

Thus Clyde had been classed simply as another hopeful who was predestined to failure. Men like Garvey had not even attempted to veil their opinions concerning his enterprise. They had seen others of Burke's ilk come and go. They allowed the National City News Association a few months of existence—that was all.

Little did they realize the true purpose of Clyde Burke's presence in Washington! The answer lay in the quickness with which Clyde had seized upon the rumor which he had heard from Garvey. Facts like the disappearance of Glade Tromboll were what Clyde Burke was seeking!

Less than a month ago, Clyde Burke had been working as a news reporter on the staff of the New York *Classic*. While serving in that capacity, he had heard the rumor, whispered among newspapermen, that four men had mysteriously disappeared from Washington.

No names had been given. Two men, it was said, were minor members of South American legations. Two others had been government employees. Each disappearance had been a matter of serious consequence.

Rumors that circulate through newspaper offices are usually well supplied with background. These stories which Clyde Burke had heard while working for the *Classic* had not been printed. But to Clyde Burke, they had proven more important than the greatest scoop he might possibly have made. Clyde had sent them on to one who would find use for them.

That one was The Shadow.

A STRANGE being who dwelt in unknown surroundings, The Shadow spent his life fighting in behalf of justice. A sinister figure whose ominous power had spelled doom to ways of evildoers, The Shadow had gained an amazing reputation as a battler of crime.

Through agents—men who, though faithful, did not themselves know the identity of their mysterious chief—The Shadow kept his finger upon the pulsebeats of crime. One of his active agents was none other than Clyde Burke. Through Clyde, The Shadow had learned these rumors of mysterious disappearances in the national capital.

Clyde Burke had come to Washington at The Shadow's bidding. This office, in which he acted as a news correspondent, was a blind. It was Clyde's duty to learn more about the rumored disappearances. Until today, however, Clyde had uncovered nothing.

Another rumor! A new disappearance! This was a double discovery. To a clear thinker like Clyde Burke, it carried a special significance. Four men had previously vanished from view: two were government employees; two were attachés of South American legations.

This fifth case—involving Glade Tromboll—was a link between the others. Tromboll, according to Garvey, was a government employee; the documents which the missing man supposedly possessed were South American correspondence!

Seated at the desk in his little office, Clyde

Burke set his lips grimly. He realized that he had been negligent. In two weeks at Washington, he should have gained some data prior to the disappearance of Glade Tromboll. Instead, Clyde had learned nothing; now, while he was on the very ground, another man had vanished.

In fact, Clyde had come to believe that the previous disappearance had been mere matters of coincidence. He had said so in his past reports. This time he would be forced to retract his statements. His own inability to get past the fringes of rumor meant that there could be but one way of getting further. Clyde would have to pass his work on to The Shadow.

Taking a telephone book, Clyde Burke looked up the name of Glade Tromboll. He did not find it listed. He consulted other reference books—those which contained the names of government employees—and still found no mention of the man he wanted.

Clyde brought out a fountain pen. On white paper, he wrote a brief report in coded language. Oddly ciphered words appeared in ink of vivid blue. As the writing dried, Clyde hastily folded the sheet and thrust it in an envelope. Using another pen, he wrote this address:

Rutledge Mann,
Badger Building,
New York City.

RUTLEDGE MANN was contact agent for The Shadow. A message sent to him would be forwarded to The Shadow himself. The ink in which Clyde Burke had written his message was a special type of fluid provided by The Shadow. Its dried writing would vanish a few minutes after the letter was unfolded.

This meant that The Shadow alone would have opportunity to read the coded lines. Should it fall into other hands, the message would prove useless; it would be gone before a person could begin to decipher it.

Clyde placed a stamp upon the envelope. He left the office, dropped the letter in a mail chute and returned. He closed the news bureau and strolled from the building. A short walk brought him to the hotel where he was stopping.

Seated in a room high above the street, Clyde watched the glittering lights as they appeared below. Washington, of all cities, seemed placid and law-abiding. Yet Clyde Burke felt convinced that somewhere in the nation's capital lay a problem that would prove difficult even to The Shadow.

While he was staring from the window, a sudden thought struck Clyde Burke. The young man went to a table and opened a drawer. He brought out a neatly printed card which bore the legend:

Club Rivoli
Across the Potomac
Open All Night

This was a spot that Clyde Burke had visited shortly after his arrival in Washington. He had learned that it was frequented by attachés of various legations, together with persons connected with the government.

Clyde had seen nothing at the Club Rivoli to arouse his suspicions. He had made the acquaintance of the proprietor—a genial fellow named "Whistler" Ingliss. Tonight, however, with thoughts of previous negligence disturbing him, Clyde Burke decided that a new visit to the Club Rivoli would be wise. He realized that he must pass up no opportunity while waiting for new orders from The Shadow.

Clyde Burke felt elated as he donned a tuxedo for his visit to the swanky bright spot across the Virginia border. He had hopes that tonight he might uncover some bit of information that would furnish The Shadow with a clue when he arrived.

Little did Clyde Burke realize that he was proving every bit as negligent as before. That was because he could not foresee tonight's events. Had he been able to do so, Clyde would not have trusted to the written report that he had sent the Shadow.

Instead, he would have put in an emergency call to The Shadow in New York. For Clyde Burke, without knowing it, was starting for a spot where lurking crime awaited!

CHAPTER III
THE CLUB RIVOLI

IT was nine o'clock when Clyde Burke reached the Club Rivoli. Located several miles from Washington, the bright spot appeared to be a large but obscure road house. The expensive cars parked at the side showed, however, that the Club Rivoli must have some unusual attraction.

Clyde had come in one of the cheap taxis so prevalent in Washington. He paid the driver, then entered the front door of the Club Rivoli. A modestly furnished lounge showed on one side; on the other a small, deserted dining room.

Clyde kept on through the hall. He came to a door farther on and rang a bell. A little wicket opened. Clyde held up his card for the man behind to see.

Bolts grated; the door opened. Clyde Burke passed through a small room. The chatter of people; the clicking of chips—both greeted his ears as he entered a long and well-thronged room.

The place was a gambling hall. The patrons were dressed in evening clothes. Women as well as men were gathered about two roulette tables where croupiers were spinning the wheels and raking in stacks of chips.

IN THE SWIRL

DARVIN ROCHELLE

DARVIN ROCHELLE, the man with the limp, the man who was behind the International Peace Alliance, and the leading character in the great attempt to bring about greater amity and more commercial relations between two continents. But while Rochelle talks peace, death stalks the streets of Washington, enters into the innermost chambers of secret embassies, spreading fear and suspicion.

THURK

THURK, dwarfed servant of ROCHELLE, who knows only one law—absolute subservience to his master, and faithfulness unto death. Thurk's ever-watchful eyes and quick limbs prove invaluable to the apostle of peace around whom hover all the dangers of greed and intrigue.

OF THE CAPITAL

CLUB RIVOLI, a gambling resort of high repute, visited by the élite of Washington's social and diplomatic circles, is operated by WHISTLER INGLISS. What strange things go on in this resort, and how they affect the course of worldwide events, furnishes the meat of this thrilling yarn of intrigue and political plotting.

WHISTLER INGLISS

MAURICE TWINDELL, young-man-about-town of Washington, whose activities are worth consideration in this story. Together with ANITA DEBRONNE, here is a perfect pair of plotters, with the Club Rivoli, gambling spot run by WHISTLER INGLISS, as an excellent scene of operations.

MAURICE TWINDELL

The near end of the room was lined with slot machines which took coins of half-dollar size. Several players were squandering their cash in these devices. Along the other walls were little curtained booths to which busy waiters were carrying trays laden with food and drinks.

There was a single opening at the right. This, Clyde knew, led to rooms where poker players gambled for high stakes. The office of Whistler Ingliss, the proprietor, was located in that direction. Clyde, however, was chiefly interested in what was going on in the main gambling room.

The Shadow's agent was quick to note that most of the players were foreigners, with Spanish-Americans predominating. This was something that he had observed on previous visits.

Clyde knew that the Club Rivoli catered chiefly to legations and visitors from other lands. A Pan-American convention was beginning in Washington; it was only natural that many of the visitors had learned of the Club Rivoli.

Clyde made a particular study of the Americans who were present. Taking a vantage point between the tables, he studied his fellow countrymen one by one while he made a pretense of watching the roulette play.

WHILE Clyde was thus engaged, he became conscious of a soft, melodious whistling close beside him. The sound took on a symphonic trill. Clyde turned quickly to see a man in evening clothes standing a few feet away. He met the other's gaze and recognized the suave face of Whistler Ingliss, the proprietor of the Club Rivoli.

The recognition proved mutual. Ingliss smiled as he ceased his light trilling. He advanced and extended a hand which Clyde accepted. Ingliss, a tall, good-looking man in his middle forties, possessed a friendly personality that had accounted much for the success of his gambling club.

"Burke," remarked Ingliss. "That's the name, isn't it? I gave you a card the last time you were here."

"Right," agreed Clyde. "Thought I'd drop in and watch the roulette roll. Like most newspaper-men"—he was smiling wistfully—"I don't have much to gamble."

"Quite all right," assured Ingliss. "My friends are welcome here to watch as well as to play. We want everyone to feel completely at home at the Club Rivoli."

Conversation ended for the moment. Ingliss, watching with Clyde, began to trill a meditative tune. There was a charm about the soft music that came from the gambler's lips. It was this habit of melody making that had given him the sobriquet of "Whistler."

In fact, the tune was provocative of a soothing lull. Clyde Burke began to feel as he had felt on his other visits to the Club Rivoli: that the place was a mere pleasure resort which had no connection with any other enterprise. He turned to speak again to Whistler Ingliss. At that moment, there was an interruption. An attendant approached the proprietor and handed him a small envelope.

"What's this?" inquired Whistler.

"Card inside, sir," explained the attendant. "A gentleman came to see you—by the side entrance. He sent this in to you."

Clyde watched warily while Whistler opened the envelope. He saw a sudden frown upon the gambler's brow as Whistler removed and read the card. Clyde glanced away as Whistler raised his head.

From the corner of his eye, The Shadow's agent caught Whistler's quick look. Ingliss, apparently, wanted to know if his momentary discomposure had been noticed.

Seeing no indication on Clyde's part, Whistler calmly turned to the attendant. He began to tear the card and envelope into small bits which he dropped in his pocket. He told the attendant:

"Ask the gentleman into the office. I'll drop in there to talk with him."

The attendant left. Resuming his trill, Whistler Ingliss strolled from table to table. He had adopted a perfect poker face. He showed no signs of hurry. Glancing toward Clyde Burke, Whistler noticed that the reporter was looking at the other table. Strolling away, Whistler headed for the archway and passed slowly into the hall beyond.

THE gambler descended a short flight of steps. Here a passage went off to the right. Two doors—one in each passage—indicated Whistler's office. The gambler opened the one from the central passage. He entered a neatly furnished room. Seated beyond a desk was a languid-looking man; he rose to display his lankiness as Whistler Ingliss entered. The gambler closed the door.

"Sit down, Dolband," suggested Ingliss, in a cordial tone. As the visitor obeyed, Ingliss took his own chair and brought out a box of cigars. "Have a real Havana and tell me what's the trouble. This is kind of unusual—a Secret Service operative dropping in on me."

Dolband took a cigar. Whistler Ingliss eyed him as he bit the end. The gambler had met Carl Dolband in the past. He knew the Secret Service operative to be a cagey individual. The flicker of Dolband's match showed a white, intuitive face.

"Want to look at the cash in my till?" quizzed Whistler, in a crafty tone. "I've got plenty of mazuma—but I'll bet you won't find a queer bill in it—"

"I'm not bothering counterfeiters," interposed Dolband. "There's something else I want to talk about, Ingliss."

The gambler assumed a perplexed attitude. Carl Dolband, leaning back in his chair, spent a full minute in studying Whistler's face. Then, satisfied, he began to speak in a confidential tone.

"How's business?" was his question. "Good receipts? Lots of people coming in and out?"

"Take a look," returned Whistler, with a smile, as he pulled a ledger from a desk drawer. "If it's income tax you're checking on, this will satisfy you. I keep the books on the level."

"Don't worry about that," rejoined Dolband, as he studied the entries in the ledger. "Here—this satisfies me. Put the book away. The money is coming in all right—that's all I wanted to know."

"What's the idea?" asked Whistler, with a puzzled laugh.

"I just wanted to be sure," stated Dolband, "that your joint was bringing in the gravy. I see that it is. So far as your gambling racket is concerned, that's a matter for the State authorities. So far as I'm concerned, I wanted to make sure that your place was doing so well that you'd like to keep it going. The reason I say that is because I want your cooperation on a little matter."

"You mean—" Whistler paused with well-feigned indignation.

"A shakedown?" Dolband laughed as he completed the words that appeared to be on Whistler's tongue. "Not a bit of it. I don't work that way, Ingliss. I'm after other game—and I want to know what you know about it. Straight. Do you get me?"

"Spill it, Dolband," urged Ingliss. "Say—if there's anything I can do to help you on a job—"

"You can," interrupted Dolband. "That's why I'm going to give you the exact lay. Listen, Ingliss: I'm on the trail of a fellow who disappeared last night—a man named Glade Tromboll. Did you ever hear of him?"

"Can't say that I have." Whistler shook his head. "I'd know the name if I'd heard it, Dolband. Who is Tromboll?"

"A government employee," returned Dolband cautiously. "One who happened to have some important papers on him. South American correspondence, Ingliss. There's a lot of South Americans come in here, aren't there?"

"Plenty of them."

"Not only that. Glade Tromboll, the man who is missing, was last seen just before he came to the Club Rivoli."

"Last night?"

"Last night."

"I don't think he could have come here,

Dolband." Whistler again shook his head as he spoke. "No one gets in here without a card. If this fellow Tromboll cleared town, he must have done it before he headed for the Club Rivoli. Unless—"

"Unless what?"

"Unless someone brought him in. I give that privilege with guest cards."

"Listen, Ingliss." Dolband's tone was severe. "I've got every reason to suppose that Glade Tromboll was here last night. It's up to you to prove to the contrary. I want a close checkup—and you've got to get it for me."

"If I fail?"

"It may be bad for you. I'm trying to be friendly, Ingliss, but I've got to report what I find. If you can convince me that Tromboll wasn't here, I won't mention your place when I report. If he was here, find out what became of him. That will keep you in right.

"But a halfway answer won't help you or me. I've traced Glade Tromboll to this club. I'm going to trace him beyond. What can you do to help me—especially when you know that you may be in a fix if you can't aid the cause?"

"Hm-m-m." Whistler became speculative. "Have you got a description of this fellow Tromboll?"

Dolband tossed a photograph upon the desk. Whistler examined it and shrugged his shoulders.

"Don't remember ever seeing this fellow," he remarked. "If he was out here last night, though, I'll find it out. Things will ease off in the roulette room. Then I can talk to the attendants, one by one."

"Do you want me to be here?"

"Better not. Listen, Dolband, I'll do all I can to help you. I've got a good thing here; I don't want it spoiled. You're sure, though"—Whistler paused anxiously—"that you haven't mentioned the Club Rivoli to anyone—"

"To no one," interposed Dolband. "I'm working on my own, Ingliss."

"That's good. Where can I reach you?"

"Hotel Starlett."

"All right. Wait here about five minutes—until I'm back in the roulette room. Then stroll out by the side door you came in. By midnight, I'll be able to tell you all I can. If this mug"—Whistler had picked up the photograph and was pointing at it—"was here last night, I'll know it!"

Whistler turned and walked from the office. He closed the door behind him. He strolled toward the steps that led up to the roulette room. He was trilling a familiar tune as he walked along.

Whistler stopped moving just after he gained the roulette room. His whistle, however, trilled a trifle more loudly. The tune changed.

CLYDE BURKE, eyeing the doorway where Whistler stood, saw a motion at one of the curtained booths not more than ten feet from the spot that Whistler had chosen. Two men in tuxedos stepped out. Clyde could see the hardness of their faces. He knew the pair for ruffians.

Indifferently, the two men strolled past Whistler. The gambler did not appear to notice them. The two men went through the doorway that led to the cardrooms and to the office. Another pair—in appearance they matched the first duo—came from a second booth.

Whistler Ingliss was strolling to the roulette tables. He passed within a few feet of Clyde Burke. Whistler's tune had lessened; it still carried an intriguing obbligato. The men who had gone through the doorway did not return.

Minutes passed. Clyde Burke, feeling conspicuous, approached a roulette table. He took his stand close to the spot where Whistler Ingliss, now silent, was watching the play. Clyde produced a small roll of bills and joined the game. His luck was alternating.

Whistler Ingliss had strolled away. The men had not returned from the direction in which they had gone, although fully a half hour had passed. Clyde decided that they must have left the Club Rivoli by the side entrance.

Clyde left by the front. He called a taxi that was outside. Riding back to Washington, The Shadow's agent stared from the window. Almost unseeing, he viewed the glow about the dome of the Capitol building; with no impression he gazed toward the Washington Monument, which towered fingerlike amid its encircling illumination.

Beating through Clyde's brain was the lilt of that final melody that had come from the lips of Whistler Ingliss. Somehow, Clyde Burke attached significance to that tune which had throbbed simultaneously with the appearance and departure of four sturdy ruffians.

Clyde Burke vainly sought the answer. He had gained an inkling of the truth. The whistled tune had been a signal, of that Clyde felt certain; but the purpose had escaped him. He did not know that Whistler Ingliss, with his trilling lilt, had signed a death warrant for Carl Dolband of the Secret Service!

CHAPTER IV
THE SHADOW HEARS

ON the following evening, a tall, keen-faced man arrived in the lobby of the Hotel Starlett. A bellboy took his bags. The arrival registered as Henry Arnaud and asked for a room that fronted on the side toward The Mall. He was given Room 817.

When he reached his room, Henry Arnaud tipped the bellboy. He placed his suitcase upon the bed. A thin smile appeared upon lips that were firm beneath a hawklike nose. As soon as the bellboy was gone, Henry Arnaud turned out the light.

The room had French windows that opened on a balcony. Arnaud approached them in the darkness and drew the two sections inward. A dim glow came from the city; the rolling of traffic sounded from the street below. Moving stealthily through the semidarkness of the room, Arnaud reached the spot where he had placed the suitcase.

There was motion in the gloom. Black cloth swung like a shroud above a head. Something swished as a black-cloaked figure approached the balcony. A tall, silhouetted form appeared within the rail; its shape was no more than a vague outline of a broad-brimmed hat above a spreading cloak.

The Shadow had come to Washington. From the balcony on the eighth floor of the Hotel Starlett, he was staring across the open spaces toward the tremendous obelisk which forms the most conspicuous landmark in the national capital— the Washington Monument.

Shrouded in the darkness of the balcony, The Shadow turned his keen gaze directly upward. The balcony above seemed to lure him to a test. Long arms stretched upward; gloved hands gripped the projection. Invisible against the darkened brick front of the hotel, The Shadow swung outward, high above the street. His gripping arms were firm; his strong arms drew his lithe body toward the objective. A dozen seconds later, The Shadow was on the ninth-floor balcony.

A projecting cornice formed a line between this balcony and the next. The same arrangement continued along the entire wall of the building. Pressing close to the wall, The Shadow swung over the rail. With firm, sidewise step, he moved to the next balcony. He crossed it and continued to the balcony beyond. There his progress ceased.

A light showed beyond the curtains of the French windows. The Shadow's hand tested the barrier. Inch by inch the windows spread until they formed a crevice through which peering eyes could see.

The Shadow spied a rotund, baldheaded man seated at a writing desk. Beside this individual was an opened briefcase. A stack of papers were at the man's right hand.

THE SHADOW knew the identity of this man. That was why The Shadow had chosen to register at the Hotel Starlett, under the name of Henry Arnaud. The man at the writing table was Fulton Fourrier, a divisional chief of the Secret Service.

In response to Clyde Burke's report, The Shadow had come to Washington. Knowing, through

Clyde's statement of Glade Tromboll's disappearance that this was a case for the Secret Service, The Shadow had chosen to watch the man to whom operatives would report.

Long minutes passed. The Shadow's vigil went unrewarded until a telephone rang beside the writing table. Fourrier answered it. The Shadow heard him give instructions to come up to the room. The Shadow waited.

There was a rap a short while later. Fourrier arose and waddled to the door. He opened it to admit a stocky, heavyset man whose stolid countenance announced him as one who dealt with decisive action.

A soft, almost inaudible laugh came from The Shadow's lips. The watching phantom at the window had expected the very man who had appeared. The stocky individual was Vic Marquette, Secret Service operative.

Fourrier was brusque as he waved his visitor to a chair. The chief finished his reports; then wheeled and spoke to Marquette.

The Shadow viewed their profiles: Fourrier, though pudgy-nosed and concave in features, had a firm-set jaw; Marquette showed a straight line from forehead to jaw.

Words came to The Shadow's ears; it did not matter when the distant rumble of a passing vehicle drowned them. The Shadow's eyes were upon moving lips, reading them as plainly as though they had been speaking close beside him.

"So you haven't heard from Dolband?" Marquette was anxious in his question.

"No," returned Fourrier soberly. "I don't like it. He should have reported tonight. So far as I can learn, he did not return to the hotel last night."

"Carl should have reported, chief."

"I know it." Fourrier arose to his feet and stood with arms akimbo. "Vic, I shouldn't have put Dolband on that Tromboll case. I'm afraid I know what has happened to him."

"You mean—"

"The same thing that happened to Tromboll, whatever that is. The same that happened to the others. We haven't found a trace of any of them. There's murder in the wind, Vic.

"I gave Dolband *carte blanche*. I told him to work alone until he got something. That's where I made my mistake—sending Dolband out alone. Poor fellow; I'm afraid he's gone, Vic. It was a great mistake—sending him alone."

"Who should you have sent with him, chief?"

"No one."

"I don't quite get you, chief. You say first that you shouldn't have sent Carl alone—then you say that you shouldn't have sent anyone along with him—"

"I mean," interposed Fourrier soberly, "that I should not have sent Carl Dolband at all. It was a one-man job and he was the wrong man. I used Carl because he was a smooth operative. I know now that that was a mistake.

"This job requires one man, and it wants a chap who can take care of whatever comes along. There's just one man for it"—Fourrier paused emphatically—"and you're that man, Vic!"

THE operative stared. Vic Marquette had not expected this assignment. He was, in a sense, new to work in Washington.

Vic had dealt with the toughest of cases. He had landed Reds and counterfeiters. The work of secret assassins who struck from undercover was something that fazed him for the moment. Fulton Fourrier seemed to read the operative's thoughts.

"It worries you, doesn't it, Vic?" questioned the divisional chief. "Well, don't let it throw you, old man. You've dealt with cutthroats before. They're all alike—no matter how smooth they seem. At the same time, don't forget that it's a big job.

"You've got a great record, Vic. You've tackled them alone, out in the sticks, when all the odds were against you. But I'll tell you something right now: here in Washington, with thousands of people about you, with police as well as Secret Service men to aid you, you're going to be in the greatest danger you've ever faced.

"We've linked five cases. Bolero—Piscano—both of them were South American attachés. Their papers went with them. Rexton and Clifford—like Tromboll—were Americans. But all of them had documents pertaining to South America. It's part of the same plot—and we can't even guess what it is."

"Espionage," suggested Vic Marquette.

"It looks like it," admitted Fourrier. "Yet where's the game? Some important documents were stolen; but murder seems an overstrong measure to obtain them. The people behind this game are using measures that would have been alarming even during the World War!

"I'll tell you the nature of those stolen papers. They consisted chiefly of correspondence between South American ambassadors, our State Department and the official governments of the countries involved. Singly, not one document is worth a picayune. Assembled, they might mean calamity. That's why we know that the game is one and the same.

"Who's behind it? Don't ask me. I can only tell you that they're not through yet. If they're springing something, they'll have to get more than they have. If I cut loose to stop them, they'll close up like clams. The game will wait.

"That's why it's a one-man job. Dolband was

after it in the right way. He was due to get results. They got him instead. That's why it's your job, Vic. Frankly, I expect you to blunder. Dolband must have blundered. Any man I put on the job will blunder. You're the one man who can get yourself out of a jam."

Fourrier paused. He turned toward the French windows. He seemed to notice that they were ajar. He moved in that direction to close them.

THE SHADOW did not stir. Fourrier changed his mind as he neared the windows. He swung and pointed directly at Vic Marquette.

"Vic," he declared solemnly, "any man who goes into this is likely to get himself into a terrible situation. The man who gets into it—and out of it—will bring back the goods on the people we want.

"I'm giving you the same lead I gave Dolband. Get to the spots where you're liable to find South Americans. Not around the embassies, but elsewhere. That's how Dolband started. He never came back with his report. Is that sufficient?"

"That's plenty, chief," asserted Marquette, rising. "Dolband talked Spanish; so do I. I'll stay at the Hotel Darma, where I am now. You'll get my reports."

"I'm counting on you, Vic," nodded Fourrier. "Let me know any data you may need. I'll be ready to help out."

As Vic Marquette turned toward the door, Fourrier swung toward the French windows. He pressed the barriers tightly shut. He saw nothing amid the blackness beyond.

As the windows clicked, a form moved upon the balcony. It rose over the edge, followed the cornice, then swung from the edge of a balcony beyond. Swaying outward; then in to the wall, The Shadow loosed his hold. He dropped silently upon the balcony outside of Room 817.

A soft laugh sounded from the windows of the room which Henry Arnaud had taken. A weird, whispered tone, that laugh was carried through the cool night air. The strange mirth, restrained in volume, was as prophetic as the words of Fulton Fourrier.

Vic Marquette had started on a dangerous task. Alone, he was sallying forth to seek the answer to six mysterious deaths. He was taking up the task in which Carl Dolband had failed.

Yet in his task, Vic Marquette would not be alone. Paralleling the efforts of the Secret Service operative would be another investigator whose ways would remain unseen.

The Shadow, too, had taken instructions from Fulton Fourrier. Invisible investigator of the night, the black-garbed sleuth was faring forth in search of insidious crime!

CHAPTER V
BIRDS OF A KIND

THE next morning, a taxicab pulled up before the door of Darvin Rochelle's massive residence. A portly, red-faced man alighted and noted the banner which hung above the entrance. He recognized its odd insignia as that of the International Peace Alliance.

Ascending the steps, the visitor rang the bell. A servant admitted him. The man looked curiously about the pretentious hallway. He eyed the marble stairs that led to the second floor.

"I want to see Darvin Rochelle," he rasped.

"Very well, sir," returned the attendant. "Your name, please?"

"Croydon Herkimer."

"Wait here, sir."

The servant went upstairs. He rang the door of the anteroom. A buzzer clicked. The servant went through the anteroom to find Darvin Rochelle seated behind his office desk. The man with the limp was dictating letters to a stenographer.

"Mr. Croydon Herkimer is here, sir," announced the attendant.

"Ah! Excellent," exclaimed Rochelle. "Tell him to come up at once. Usher him here right away."

Rochelle nodded to the stenographer and motioned toward the door. The girl followed the attendant.

As soon as the door to the anteroom had closed, Rochelle pressed the secret buzzer. The door at the rear of the office opened. Thurk, the dwarf, bounded in.

Rochelle went to the door of the anteroom. He turned and spoke low, jargoned words, in the language which he used with Thurk. The dwarf nodded.

Rochelle opened the door of the anteroom and crossed the outer apartment. As he opened the door to the hall, Croydon Herkimer appeared at the head of the stairs.

"Welcome," declared Rochelle, extending his hand. "Come into my office, Mr. Herkimer."

HERKIMER received the handshake. Rochelle hobbled through the anteroom and leaned on his cane while he opened the door to the office. Herkimer entered. Rochelle followed and guided his visitor to a chair at the left side of the desk.

Thurk had disappeared. Rochelle, seating himself behind the desk, was alone with the man who had come to see him.

Croydon Herkimer was fascinated by the appearance of the office. He turned to eye the massive globe behind his left shoulder. His gaze roamed to the expensive mirror across the room. It finally reached the desk; then centered upon the benign faced man behind it.

"You like my furnishings?" questioned Rochelle.

"Yes," returned Herkimer. "This peace alliance business appears to be profitable."

Rochelle smiled at the slur.

"The International Peace Alliance," he declared, "has many worthy contributors. Ours is a philanthropic enterprise, Mr. Herkimer. At the same time, we have money to spend—for those whom we consider to be in accord with our motives. That, I hope, applies in your case, Mr. Herkimer."

"That's why I came to Washington," returned Herkimer bluntly. "I hope you remember the terms of the agreement that you sent me. Here is the itemized list for the goods on which I negotiated. I am to receive the five percent that you promised me as purchasing agent."

"Exactly." Rochelle smiled as he took the list. He checked item after item; then looked up with a quizzical expression. "Two hundred and forty thousand dollars?"

"That's the total," returned Herkimer.

"Quite odd," remarked Rochelle. He drew another list from his desk drawer. "I gave you this assignment, Mr. Herkimer, because I anticipated that you could obtain better prices in the Middle West. At the same time, I received estimates here in Washington.

"Flour for the Far East. Woolen goods to Turkey and Armenia. Machinery to South America. On all these items you are higher. Why, the total of my list is sixty thousand less than yours. I expected it to be twenty thousand more."

A stern look appeared upon Croydon Herkimer's bloated face. The portly man said nothing as he adjusted a pair of spectacles to his nose. He drew a paper from his pocket, unfolded it and began to read.

"This is your letter, Mr. Rochelle," he declared at last. "My lawyers in Chicago tell me that it constitutes a contract. Your International Peace Alliance will be liable to a lawsuit if it fails to go through with these purchases."

"A lawsuit?" quizzed Rochelle. "For what sum, Mr. Herkimer—the amount of your commission—twelve thousand dollars?"

"More than that."

"Naturally." Darvin Rochelle laughed harshly. "For the amount, I presume, that you intended to take as graft. I know your game, Herkimer!"

SEIZING his cane, Rochelle arose to his feet. With his left hand, he pointed an accusing forefinger at the man across the desk.

"One hundred and sixty thousand dollars," announced Rochelle, "should be the purchasing price that you require. Instead, you ask two hundred and

forty. That means a profit to you of eighty thousand—to say nothing of the exorbitant commission you would receive—twelve thousand against the eight which is your rightful due.

"I have your figures, Herkimer." Rochelle's teeth gleamed in a sudden, vicious smile. "They are all the proof that I need. They fit in"—Rochelle triumphantly produced a file of papers—"with these!"

Herkimer stared at the packet in Rochelle's hand. The man with the cane laughed in raucous fashion.

"Mr. Croydon Herkimer!" Rochelle sneered as he announced the name. "Wartime profiteer—the man who made half a million by swindling the United States government—then lost it through foolish speculation. I wanted to test you, Herkimer. I did. I have found you out. Herkimer"—Rochelle's tone was lowered—"I could send you to prison for life!"

Croydon Herkimer was trembling. Slouched in his chair, the portly man stared bewildered. He looked as though he wanted to snatch the file of papers from Rochelle's hand. Leering, Rochelle forestalled such effort.

"There are duplicates," he laughed. "The original portfolio is in my safe. Back to your old game, eh, Herkimer? You profited through war—now you seek to profit through peace."

Terror showed on Herkimer's bulbous face. Rochelle threw the file of papers on the desk. Dropping his cane, he squared in his chair and leaned both elbows on the desk while he tilted his head forward.

"I tested you, Herkimer," he said, in a new and confidential tone, "because I need you. Do you understand? I need you. Not for this list. Bah!" Rochelle tossed aside the tabulations that Herkimer had given him. "That is trifling. Take your eighty-four thousand and let the peace hounds pay for it. That is the blind for the real game.

"War, Herkimer! There lies the real profit. Millions, man! Think of this—a continent at war—munitions and supplies coming from a single source! You and I tapping the unending spring of wealth. Does that interest you, my friend?"

Herkimer's jaw had dropped. The man was gaping in profound astonishment. Rochelle arose, seized his cane and hobbled around the desk. Herkimer turned and watched him reach the big globe.

ROCHELLE spun the sphere, then stopped it. With his left hand he pointed to the enlarged map of South America.

"Here is my plan," he asserted with a gleaming grin. "Bolivia and Paraguay are at war. Why? Over a strip of useless land called Gran Chaco. A boundary dispute—which seems small to us here in the States—but it is only one of many that exist through South America.

"Let us start here with Colombia. That country has never forgotten Panama. Should Colombia begin a war, mediation from the United States would be of no avail. What has Colombia to gain? This portion of Brazil. See—the Colombian claims are here plainly marked.

"Ecuador, which adjoins Colombia, claims this portion of Peru. Suppose that those two nations should be stirred to work together, each to claim its own desired portion of another country. I shall tell you exactly what would transpire."

Rochelle's finger ran down the map to indicate a territory marked Acre, on the Brazilian side of the Peruvian border. He tapped that spot with significance.

"Brazil and Peru," he stated, "would settle their boundary dispute in amicable fashion, so that they could form a natural alliance to resist Colombia and Ecuador. Bolivia, who feels that Paraguay started the Gran Chaco dispute, would join the alliance. So would Venezuela, for that country claims a portion of Colombia.

"Four countries: Brazil, Venezuela, Peru, and Bolivia, forming a belt across South America. Listen to the next step. Bolivia and Peru, gaining tremendous power and backing, would seek to regain the territory that they lost to Chile during the disastrous War of 1879 to 1883. Bolivia would seek Antofagasta, the port that she lost. Peru would fight to settle the Tacna-Arica dispute once and forever!

"A continent at war! All except Argentina and Uruguay, with reason to suppose that they would become embroiled in conflict. In every country,

"Remember! I hold you helpless, Herkimer!" The speaker clenched his fist with a crushing motion.

Jingoists would rule. And I, Herkimer"—Rochelle swelled proudly—"control a secret cabal of Jingoism throughout the continent of South America."

Croydon Herkimer was gripping the arms of his chair. Darvin Rochelle's change from enmity to friendship had captured the profiteer's imagination. Herkimer was nodding like a toy figure, drinking in every word that Rochelle uttered.

"South America," resumed Rochelle, in a tone both confident and persuasive, "would become a vast empire. Only through that step could peace be guaranteed. Those out of power would come in— for official governments would break as they did in Europe."

"And then—" Herkimer's voice was breathlessly expectant.

"I shall be the emperor," announced Darvin Rochelle, in a solemn tone. "By proxy, perhaps even, if circumstances so decide, through my affiliation with different men who will rule portions of the continent. But whatever the ultimate outcome, I shall be the controller. I shall be heralded as a bringer of peace—I—the man who shall have brought chaos to a continent!"

TURNING from the spot where he stood, Rochelle gave the mammoth globe a parting spin. While the sphere revolved, the dreamer of empires stumped back to his chair behind the desk. Crouching there, he eyed Croydon Herkimer with challenging gaze.

"Remember!" Rochelle's tone carried a fierce warning. "I hold you helpless, Herkimer!" The speaker clenched his fist with a crushing motion. "I am giving you the opportunity to gain millions only because your past record shows you capable of playing the game that I have played.

"As soon as war is launched, we shall begin a tremendous scale of profiteering. By building fortunes while war is in progress, I shall be able to dominate when peace arrives. You will be rewarded for your part."

"I understand."

"Remain in Washington. While you are here, prepare a complete scheme for the furnishing of padded supplies to the nations which will be at war. When men fight, they forget expense. Munitions, tractors, field equipment, uniforms—everything, Herkimer, must be provided. You will be my appointed agent to handle the profits that will come through war."

Rochelle arose and limped to the front of the desk. He gripped Herkimer's arm and drew the visitor toward the anteroom. All the way to the marble steps, Rochelle was buzzing encouragement into his new agent's ear.

"The scheme is ready" was his final statement.

"I have gained nearly all that I require. The making of war is my task; the reaping of the harvest will be yours. But remember!" Again Rochelle's voice took on its tone of insidious threat. "One false step will prove your ruin!"

"I am with you," affirmed Herkimer, in a positive tone. "With you, Rochelle, to the finish!"

The man with the limp rested on his cane while he watched his portly visitor descend the marble staircase. Then, with a quick twist of his body, he swung back toward the anteroom, halting with each of his peculiar strides.

When the stenographer arrived in Rochelle's office, in answer to a ring, she found the head of the International Peace Alliance beaming benignly as he sat behind his mahogany desk. The mask of kindness had replaced the face of evil. Once again, Darvin Rochelle had become an advocate of world-wide peace.

There was no sign of Thurk, the dwarf. The monster who aided the fiendish master had departed. Schemes of murder were on the shelf. Darvin Rochelle, man of integrity, was ready to resume his day's routine in the cause of international welfare.

CHAPTER VI
AGENTS OF MURDER

THE brilliance of early evening had come anew to Washington. Darvin Rochelle's headquarters showed somber in the gloom of its side street when a young man, strolling from the bright lights, ascended the steps of the mansion.

He was evidently an expected visitor, for the door swung open as he arrived. The servant who served as usher bowed and indicated the marble stairs. The young man ascended. He pressed a button at the entrance to the anteroom.

A minute passed. The door popped open. Darvin Rochelle, leaning upon his cane, smiled a cheery greeting as he beheld the visitor.

"Maurice Twindell!" exclaimed the man with the limp. "Come in my friend. Come in."

Rochelle led the way into the office. He took his place behind the desk. The young man seated himself at the side.

In the light of the office, Maurice Twindell presented a gentlemanly appearance. His evening clothes were faultless. His face, friendly in appearance, was a handsome one. His only fault was a shiftiness of gaze—a habit which he seemed anxious to overcome.

"Tonight," began Rochelle in a quiet, but emphatic tone, "I want you to go out to the Club Rivoli. Play the part of a habitue of the place. That is all."

"There is no one tonight?"

"Yes." Rochelle smiled. "There will be a victim. I have arranged, however, for Anita Debronne to take care of him. An attaché of a South American legation."

Rochelle paused to smile.

"You have done your share, Maurice," he said reflectively. "Bolero, Rexton, and Tromboll. Anita, however, has figured in only two cases: those of Piscano and Clifford. It is her turn again tonight."

"Who is the victim?"

"A young chap named Lito Carraza. Anita arranged to meet him early. Hence, he has committed the folly of not going back to his embassy. He will have papers which he was supposed to copy. He does not know their value. That is fortunate.

"Tonight, Maurice, I want you to be cordial to any Spanish-Americans whom you may chance to meet. There will be convention delegates at the Club Rivoli. Make friends with any who may be of use."

The telephone rang as Rochelle completed his statement. Rochelle picked up the instrument. He listened to words that came through the receiver; then answered in his odd language.

"Key zay kire golo?" His tone was questioning. "Sovo... Fee... Kay zay rike. Kay deek rema... Fee. Alk fare kay ake robole gomo."

Rochelle hung up the receiver. He turned to Twindell, who put a casual question, pointing to the telephone as he spoke.

"Whistler Ingliss?" inquired Twindell.

"Yes," returned Rochelle. "Anita is out at the Club Rivoli. I told Whistler you would be there soon. Remember what I have told you, Twindell. Keep your eyes open at the Rivoli. So far, I have confined our work to definite tasks. Now, with the goal in sight, we may need special information; we may also be able to use other aides."

ROCHELLE was tapping thoughtfully upon the table. His conversation with Whistler Ingliss had brought a sober expression to his face.

"A few nights ago," remarked Rochelle, "Whistler was forced to dispose of a troublesome visitor. The man was a Secret Service operative. He came to the Club Rivoli to question Whistler regarding Glade Tromboll."

Maurice Twindell started in momentary alarm. He regained his composure and stared hard at Rochelle.

"Bugs Ritler was at the Club Rivoli," resumed Rochelle, "with members of his crew. Whistler gave Bugs the signal. Bugs did the rest. Whistler called me afterward, to tell me how he had acted. I commended him upon his promptness.

"That is why I phoned you, Maurice, and told you, in Agro, to stay away from here until this evening. The fact that a Secret Service man had gotten as far as the Club Rivoli made it advisable for us to be cautious.

"However, there has been no recurrence. Whistler is sure that Dolband—the Secret Service man—was working on his own. If another investigator should take up the trail, Whistler may be forced to act again.

"So be wary, Maurice. Call me before you visit. Use Agro as usual; and avoid mention of names over the wire. Initials—in Agro—of those whom we know will suffice; for strangers, spell the names in Agro letters."

Rochelle opened a drawer as he finished speaking. He pulled a stack of bills into view and tossed the money to Twindell. The young man's face gleamed. There was a thousand dollars in the bundle.

"Keep track of any losses if you play roulette," reminded Rochelle. "I shall make them good, as usual. If you win—keep the profits for yourself. But remember—do not play too heavily. It would not look well."

Maurice Twindell nodded as he pocketed the money. An avaricious smile appeared upon the young man's face. Rochelle noted it and repressed a smile of his own.

He knew Twindell's weakness. He had bought this man as he had bought others. Rochelle indulged in a chuckle as the door of the anteroom closed behind the departing form of Maurice Twindell.

Outside of Rochelle's mansion, Maurice Twindell strolled to the nearest avenue. There he hailed a taxicab. He ordered the driver to take him to the Club Rivoli, across the Potomac. The cab rolled along. Twindell, lighting a cigarette, stared from the window as the cab passed the Hotel Starlett.

ODDLY, a taxi parked close to that hotel had just picked up a passenger for the same destination that Twindell had chosen. The driver of the second vehicle, however, had not been hailed from the street.

His first inkling that he had a passenger came when a voice spoke quietly from the rear seat of the parked cab. A whispered monotone ordered the taximan to drive over the Potomac to the Club Rivoli.

The driver started his cab. He wondered, as he drove along, how that passenger had entered without his hearing. The cab driver had been quite alert, watching for possible passengers. Had he known the identity of the fare who occupied his cab, he might have gained the explanation.

The passenger was The Shadow. He, too, had chosen the Club Rivoli as his objective. The Shadow had divined the truth of Carl Dolband's disappearance. It had not taken him long to gain that trail.

Since his arrival in Washington, The Shadow had received a report from Clyde Burke. It had told of mysterious happenings which Clyde had observed at the Club Rivoli. The Shadow had spotted hidden crime.

Coupled to this was the talk that The Shadow had overheard between Vic Marquette and Fulton Fourrier. Clyde's report of a special visitor to see Whistler Ingliss; the departure of men who looked like thugs—these had been sufficient for The Shadow to assume that Carl Dolband had met with misfortune at the gay nightclub across the Potomac.

Moreover, the Club Rivoli was a logical spot. It was a meeting place that attracted many South Americans. This was not the first visit that The Shadow was making to the gambling hall run by Whistler Ingliss. He had traveled to the Club Rivoli each night since his arrival in Washington.

The Shadow's cab made a rapid trip. The driver pulled up near the front door of the Club Rivoli. A hand came through the partition and tendered a bill. The driver took it and began to make change. When he looked for his passenger, he found the cab empty.

Perplexed, the driver scratched his head; then pocketed the bill that he had received and started the trip back to Washington.

As the cab swerved in the driveway, its headlights threw a beam toward a walk that led to the little used side entrance of the Club Rivoli. Long streaks of shaded blackness showed in the gleam. The driver did not notice them. Mere shadows did not interest him.

When the cab had passed, however, there was motion at the spot where the driver had viewed nothing but blackened streaks. There was a slight swish in the darkness. A being who moved with invisible stealth was making his way to the side entrance of the Club Rivoli.

A SPECTRAL form reached a locked doorway. A slight click marked The Shadow's prying efforts with a pick. The door opened. The Shadow entered the little side passage that led by the office which Whistler Ingliss used.

Reaching the secluded door of the office, The Shadow performed another silent operation with the pick. The door opened inward, by inches. Peering eyes gazed into the lighted office. The room was empty. The door closed. The Shadow moved toward the main passage.

With ghostly strides, the mysterious visitant ascended the short flight of steps. He paused by a niche just before he reached the roulette room. Here, totally unseen, he watched, his tall, black-garbed form merged with the darkness of the niche.

The roulette room was well thronged. Yet The Shadow, with piercing gaze, singled out each person one by one.

He spied Whistler Ingliss, standing near a roulette table. Beyond, he saw Clyde Burke. The newspaperman was playing a cautious game of roulette.

Farther away, The Shadow observed a third man. It was Vic Marquette. The Secret Service operative was wearing a tuxedo. He was playing the part of a chance visitor to the Club Rivoli. A soft laugh came in an almost inaudible whisper from The Shadow's hidden lips.

Vic Marquette was playing a wise game. He was one operative who was not known in Washington. He had not made the blunder of announcing himself to Whistler Ingliss. Like Carl Dolband, Vic Marquette had picked the Club Rivoli as a spot to watch; but he was following a course that showed discretion.

New patrons were entering the club. The Shadow spotted them with steady gaze. One was a young man in faultless evening attire. It was Maurice Twindell. The Shadow's eye followed the direction of Twindell's gaze. He saw the young man stare toward Whistler Ingliss; he caught the gambler's return glance. That was all.

Then, with a quick turn of direction that seemed intuitive, The Shadow stared toward a booth on the other side of the room. A waiter was approaching with a tray that held bottles and glasses.

A curtain opened; The Shadow sighted two persons within. One was a woman, whose lighted cigarette formed a white streak before her handsome, dark-complexioned face. The other was a young man whose sallow skin and heavy black mustache identified him as a South American.

Once again, The Shadow caught a momentary exchange of glances. The woman's gaze went toward Whistler Ingliss. The gambler gave a nod that was barely discernible.

The Shadow had spotted Anita Debronne, the second of Darvin Rochelle's agents. A soft laugh came from The Shadow's lips. It stilled as Whistler Ingliss came across the roulette room, heading for the passage in which The Shadow stood. The gambler passed within two feet of the spot where the lurking watcher waited unseen. He continued toward his office.

The Shadow followed. Whistler had entered the office through the door from the main passage. The Shadow took the other way. He softly opened the side door and peered into the office. Whistler was seated at his desk, going over accounts. The Shadow watched.

Evidently, Whistler was here to stay a while. The gambler did not know that he was under observation.

He had no reason to be acting in other than natural fashion.

A clock on the wall beyond Whistler's desk showed twenty-five minutes after nine. Slowly, the door closed; its lock turned noiselessly. The Shadow's form dwindled as it moved toward the end of the passage, to the door that led outside.

A FEW minutes later, Clyde Burke strolled from the roulette room. He, too, had noted the time; he had observed the big clock in the gambling hall. Clyde was following instructions—a mysterious message which had come to his office from The Shadow.

Posted at the Club Rivoli, Clyde was supposed to stroll to the front veranda at half hour intervals from nine o'clock on.

Reaching the spacious veranda, Clyde extracted a cigarette from his pocket and placed it between his lips. Standing by a rail near the steps—beyond him darkness—Clyde felt positive that eyes were studying him. He looked about nervously; then thrust his hand into his pocket to obtain a match.

His fingers encountered an envelope!

Someone, from beyond the rail, had placed this message here during the brief interval between Clyde's removal of the cigarette and his reaching for the match. The envelope could be but from one source: The Shadow.

Clyde opened the envelope. He removed a folded sheet of paper. He brought a match from his pocket, struck it to light his cigarette, and at the same time unfolded the message. By the glare of the match he saw coded lines which he read as easily as if they had been in ordinary script:

> Watch people in Booth 6.
> Observe young man who entered at 9:15; now playing roulette at Table 1.
> Stocky man at Table 2 is Vic Marquette. Secret Service. Report his actions.
> Await call.

Vivid blue ink faded as Clyde finished his perusal of The Shadow's message. Puffing his cigarette, The Shadow's agent thrust the blank paper and envelope in his pocket, as he strolled back into the Club Rivoli.

Clyde Burke had observed all persons mentioned. He had suspected nothing regarding any of them. It had remained for the Shadow to discover the participants in the new drama of crime that was unfolding at the Club Rivoli.

The Shadow had departed—somewhere in the darkness. Clyde Burke, as his agent, was entrusted with the work of keeping observation until the master might return.

Agents of murder were at work. The hand of their hidden employer was concealed. The Shadow had found no lead to Darvin Rochelle. Yet The Shadow knew that any deeds of crime would begin here at the Club Rivoli.

It was his purpose to match the schemer's craft with his own. Before this night was ended, The Shadow would deliver the first counterthrust to the plotting of an insidious supercrook.

CHAPTER VII
TRAILS DIVERGE

NEW patrons were arriving in the roulette room of the Club Rivoli when Clyde Burke returned. The Shadow's agent noted a predominance of South Americans. He realized that more arrivals in Washington were paying a visit to the exclusive gambling place maintained by Whistler Ingliss.

Clyde quickly spotted the two persons whom The Shadow's message had mentioned as being at the roulette tables. Maurice Twindell—whose name Clyde did not know—was gambling heavily on the turn of the wheel. Vic Marquette, at the other table, was playing a conservative game.

Clyde drifted toward the booth which The Shadow had marked. As he neared that spot, he spied a newspaper correspondent entering the roulette room. Clyde waved to his friend; the other journalist approached.

"Hello, Burke," greeted the newcomer. "What are you doing out here?"

"Hitting bad luck," laughed Clyde. "Just about ready to try a sandwich. How about you, Logan?"

"I'm with you."

Clyde drew back the curtain of booth five. He found it empty. He invited his friend to enter. Logan complied. Clyde took the seat that adjoined booth six. He left the curtain of his own booth open so that he could watch what happened in the roulette room. Logan seemed interested in the gambling. Thus, as the two men awaited the arrival of a waiter, Clyde could overhear the buzz of conversation that came from the next booth.

A man and a woman were talking. They were speaking in English—the man, however, had a foreign accent. Clyde caught the name "Anita"; a few moments later, he heard the woman address her companion as "Lito"; later came the name "Carraza."

Clyde was making progress by the time sandwiches and cool drinks had arrived. He knew that a South American named Lito Carraza was in the next booth; his companion a woman called Anita. Moreover, from snatches of conversation, Clyde was sure that Lito Carraza was an attaché of some South American legation.

Thus Clyde was content to keep no more than an occasional watch upon the two men at different roulette tables. He knew that the more important quest lay here. He listened for any bit of talk that might give information. Bits of Spanish, intermingled in the conversation between Carraza and Anita, made the task quite difficult.

MAURICE TWINDELL was having poor luck at roulette. The tall dilettante stepped back from the table and strolled about in dejected fashion. He glanced at various players, nodded to occasional South Americans who seemed to be acquaintances, and finally moved over to the second table.

Here Twindell noted considerable commotion. Among the players was a tall South American who was leaning forward with a gleaming smile. The man's sallow face showed keen delight at the success which he was gaining.

"*Caramba!*" The exclamation came from a watcher. "The man has luck. *Diablo*! He has won a thousand pesos in less than a dozen minutes!"

"Who is he?" came a question.

"Alvarez Menzone." Twindell heard the name. "From the Argentine, they say. Each night that he has come here he has won. Follow his play if you wish luck."

Twindell studied Menzone. He knew that the shrewd-faced South American was probably a visitor who had come to the Pan-American Convention. The man had money; he was willing to hazard it. He was the very type of person whom Twindell was here to observe.

Edging close to Menzone, Twindell obtained a stack of chips. Menzone, clicking his own chips, began to set them in methodical fashion: some on the odd, others on the black; finally a stack of chips on the corners of four squares.

As the wheel began to whirl, Twindell duplicated the other's hazard. Menzone looked toward the American and gave him a gleaming smile. The wheel came to its stop. The ball was resting in a pocket that was odd and black; its number corresponded to one of the four that Menzone had chosen.

The croupier pushed chips across the table. Menzone collected his in matter-of-fact fashion. Twindell withheld his eagerness as he gathered up his own winnings.

"You share my luck, eh?" Menzone spoke in excellent, but accented English as he looked toward Twindell. "Well *señor*, let us try again. Two hundred pesos—one hundred of your dollars—upon the odd. One hundred pesos here"—Menzone's long-nailed fingers hovered above the squares—"upon the No. 13!"

Others, about to follow Menzone's bet, hesitated superstitiously at the choice of the No. 13. They were not willing to hazard their money on the doubtful odds offered by a single square. Twindell,

however, did not falter. He duplicated Menzone's bet. "*Buenos!*"

The exclamation came from Alvarez Menzone, as the wheel ended its spin. The ball was resting beside the No. 13.

Menzone had won more than fifteen hundred dollars on a single turn of the wheel. Twindell, by following Menzone's lead, had made an identical gain.

WITH eagerness unrepressed, Twindell awaited Menzone's next wager. The dark-faced South American glanced at the man beside him and laughed.

"You are looking for the next play, *señor*?" he questioned. "This is it!"

Menzone pushed his accumulated winnings toward the croupier, with a gesture that signified that he wished his chips to be cashed. The croupier was quick to comply. He had been wondering when Menzone's winning streak would end.

In fact, Whistler Ingliss had appeared, summoned by news that a lucky player had started out to break the bank. Seeing Menzone cashing in his chips; observing Twindell by the South American's side, Whistler strolled away, trilling a soft melody as he feigned indifference.

"We have been lucky, *amigo*," laughed Menzone, clapping Twindell on the back. "We must not expect luck to last forever. Another night, I shall try. Should you be here to follow me—perhaps you may win if I should win."

"Si, *señor*." Twindell paused as he was counting the money that he had received. Then, in Spanish, he added: "You have but recently come to Washington?"

Menzone's eyes lighted as he heard these words in his native tongue. He nodded in reply to Twindell's question. Twindell watched as he saw Menzone add his winnings to a large roll of bills—all of high denominations, all probably gained here.

"I have other friends from South America," purred Twindell, in excellent Spanish. "It is a pleasure to meet you. My name is Maurice Twindell—"

"And mine"—Menzone was receiving Twindell's handshake as they stepped away from the roulette table—"is Alvarez Menzone."

New players were thronging about the table which the two had left. Twindell and Menzone were forgotten by those who had watched—with the exception of one. That was Vic Marquette.

The Secret Service operative had kept his eye on Alvarez Menzone from the moment of the South American's arrival. He had watched Menzone win; he had observed the approach of Maurice Twindell.

Moreover, Marquette had heard the introduction which the two had exchanged. He knew their names; and he was convinced that of all persons at the roulette tables, these two—particularly Menzone— would bear further watching.

The two were strolling toward the front door of the roulette room. Warily, Vic Marquette followed. Clyde Burke, watching from his booth, felt a secret satisfaction. He could not follow Maurice Twindell and still remain here at the Club Rivoli. The fact that Vic Marquette was on Twindell's trail relieved Clyde Burke.

An odd culmination! To Clyde Burke, Alvarez Menzone was simply a man accompanying Maurice Twindell. To Vic Marquette, Menzone was the quarry with Twindell merely his companion.

WHEN the two men reached the driveway in front of the Club Rivoli, they hailed a taxi. There were several cabs in view, for this resort was a profitable place to pick up fares. As soon as the cab had started, Vic Marquette hurried from the veranda. He entered the second vehicle. He flashed a badge in front of the driver's eyes and gave this order:

"Follow the cab ahead."

The driver obeyed. In response to Vic's occasional growls for caution, he kept well behind the other cab until both cars had reached the Potomac River.

Bridge traffic became heavy as the cabs neared the glowing city. Near the long block of buildings of the Bureau of Engraving, Vic's cab closed in on the taxi ahead. When the glare of blue-lighted windows had been passed, the second cab was so close behind the first that Vic could distinguish the heads of Maurice Twindell and Alvarez Menzone.

The lead cab passed the monument. It threaded its way along cross streets until it reached one of the broad avenues that form the pattern of a spider's web upon the map of Washington. The cab swung along the avenue.

Vic Marquette, peering almost from the driver's side, observed that neither Twindell nor Menzone were conscious that they were being followed. Their cab took another side street. It pulled up near a secluded apartment building.

Vic growled to his own driver to slow down, then to stop. The Secret Service man alighted half a block behind as the first cab came to a stop.

Alvarez Menzone and Maurice Twindell appeared upon the sidewalk. The cab waited at Twindell's bidding while the two were concluding a conversation. Vic Marquette, approaching, could overhear their talk, which was in Spanish.

"Then you do not intend to return to the Argentine?" Twindell was saying.

"Not for some time to come." Menzone wore an odd smile as he spoke. "Perhaps not at all. I have found the United States to be a very healthy place."

"But you say you have chosen Washington—"

"Why not?"

"It is an expensive city in which to live; one that offers very little opportunity, except to those connected with the government."

"Expensive—yes." Menzone laughed. "My apartment on the third floor of this building costs much more than I ever paid in Buenos Aires. But there are times, *señor*, when extravagance brings return."

Menzone's lips were smiling as the South American placed a cigarette between them. Menzone applied a light; delivered some thoughtful puffs of smoke, then extended his hand.

"*Buenos noches*," he said to Maurice Twindell. "It has been a pleasure to meet you, amigo mio. Let me express the hope that we shall meet again."

"We shall," responded Twindell, as he turned toward his cab. "Buenos noches, *señor*."

Menzone, still puffing his cigarette, remained watching while the taxi pulled away. Then the South American turned and entered the apartment building. Hardly had he disappeared before Vic Marquette followed.

THE lobby was a pretentious one. It lacked attendants, however, and Vic Marquette strolled about for a few minutes, undecided whether he should pay a visit to the third floor. Finally, the Secret Service man decided to the contrary.

Leaving the apartment house, Vic stopped on the sidewalk and noted the name above the door. He drew pad and pencil from his pocket. Methodically, he jotted down the name: Athena Court.

Even then, Vic was loath to leave the vicinity. He went across the street and stared toward the third floor, hoping that he might be able to locate the apartment occupied by Alvarez Menzone. Failing to gain any clue, the Secret Service man stepped out into the street and whistled to a cab that was coming along.

"Hotel Starlett" was the order that Vic gave to the driver.

As the cab rolled away, there was motion in the gloom at the side of Athena Court. From a narrow, cement passageway that led toward a rear fire tower, appeared a figure garbed in black. Outlined by dim light, this figure watched the departure of the cab.

A soft laugh came from hidden lips. The Shadow had observed Vic Marquette's actions. He had heard the order given by the Secret Service operative. He knew that Vic Marquette did not intend to follow Menzone again tonight.

More than that: The Shadow knew that Vic had not concerned himself with the affairs of Maurice

Twindell. Should Vic, in the future, come to deal with Twindell, it would result because of Vic's keen interest in the affairs of Alvarez Menzone.

Strange trails had begun tonight. Clyde Burke, back at the Club Rivoli, was watching two persons in booth six. Vic Marquette had taken up the trail of Alvarez Menzone. The Shadow, too, had found a quarry. Unknown even to Clyde Burke, The Shadow had left the Club Rivoli with the express purpose of watching Maurice Twindell.

After Twindell's parting with Menzone, The Shadow's course had changed. His figure, moving swiftly away from Athena Court, was retracing his way to the spot where crime still hovered.

CHAPTER VIII
ON THE SPEEDWAY

CLYDE BURKE was alone in the booth at the Club Rivoli. Logan had strolled away to play roulette. Clyde had dropped the curtain. He had been listening intently to the conversation which he had heard from the adjoining booth.

"So sorry, Lito." The woman's voice was speaking. "I thought we could stay here for a few hours longer. I haven't played a single chip at the roulette table!"

"It is nearly eleven," came Carraza's reply. "I must go to the legation. I was told to be there by ten. It is important, *señorita*. I have papers—"

"Can you leave them there?"

"*Si, señorita*. They were to have been copied. I shall have to say that I did not have time."

"And then?"

"The papers will be placed in the safe. Perhaps I shall be told to continue my copying tomorrow. Perhaps the work will be entrusted to another. I cannot tell."

"Can't you return here?" Anita's tone was urging. "Leave the papers, *señor*. Come back to see me. I shall play at roulette while you are absent."

"Very well." Carraza's tone was one of agreement. "But I must go quite soon. A few turns of roulette; then I shall leave, *señorita*."

Clyde Burke rose from his seat. He opened the curtain and strolled toward a roulette table. He realized that a prompt report to The Shadow would be essential. The clock in the gaming room showed five minutes before eleven. If only The Shadow would be outside by the veranda at the end of his half hour!

THUS thinking, Clyde swung from the table and moved toward the outer door. An attendant was talking in a telephone booth; the man dropped the receiver and turned toward the roulette tables. At the same moment, he spied Clyde Burke.

"Ah!" exclaimed the attendant. "Mr. Burke! A call for you, sir, from the newspaper office."

"Thanks," returned Clyde. Entering the booth, he picked up the receiver.

"This is Burke speaking," he informed.

"Report." The word came in a weird, whispered tone. Clyde knew that this was not the voice that the attendant had heard. Used expressly for Clyde's benefit, this eerie tone was a token of identity. Clyde knew that The Shadow was on the other end of the wire.

"The roulette player left," began Clyde, in a low voice. "He was followed by Marquette—"

"The others."

"They have just left their booth. The man is Lito Carraza, attaché of a South American legation. The woman's name is Anita."

"Where are they now?"

"At the roulette table."

"Watch them." The Shadow's monotone was an order. "Tell me what is happening. Look all about. Report."

Clyde obeyed, half wondering. Suddenly, he caught the import of The Shadow's order. Something was happening within the roulette room—something which Clyde Burke alone observed.

Whistler Ingliss had strolled from the doorway at the side of the room. Clyde could see the gambler's lips pursed as they trilled a tune. Events of another night were undergoing repetition. Clyde was quick to whisper what he saw.

"Whistler is giving a signal," he informed. "Men are coming from the side booths. The same men that I saw here before. Two—four of them."

"Watch Whistler."

"He is looking toward the roulette table. He has caught Anita's eye. She is talking to Lito Carraza. The man is preparing to leave—"

"Report received. Off duty."

Clyde Burke stood dumfounded as he heard the click of the receiver at the other end. He hung up his own receiver and stepped from the booth. The reason for The Shadow's quick termination of the telephone call was dawning on Clyde Burke.

Lito Carraza, heading into Washington, was to become the prey of mobsters! Anita had lured the South American attaché into a trap. Whistler Ingliss, receiving a sign from the woman, had ordered thugs to action!

The Shadow must have called from the city. That fact seemed obvious to Clyde. Could he reach here before Lito Carraza had left? That seemed impossible. The young South American was already on his way to the front door of the Club Rivoli.

Clyde watched Carraza's departure. The attaché

seemed a trifle anxious; Clyde knew that his expression was brought about purely by the thought of the reprimand that might be awaiting him at the legation.

The door closed. Whistler Ingliss had retired to his office. The woman with whom Carraza had dined was playing roulette. The attaché's departure had been observed by no one except Clyde Burke. The Shadow's agent alone had seen a man start forth to doom!

OFF duty!

Such had been The Shadow's order. Yet Clyde felt worried. Following Carraza's path, he reached the veranda at the front of the Club Rivoli. The lights of a large, foreign roadster had been turned on; a man at the wheel was pressing the starter. It was Carraza, leaving. Clyde was tempted to leap forward and warn the man to stop. His confidence in The Shadow prevented him.

As Carraza's car began to roll away, Clyde realized a new angle to the situation. Men had been dispatched to attack the South American, but they would certainly avoid an encounter in the neighborhood of the Club Rivoli. They would try to get Carraza between here and his legation.

The Shadow had foreseen that fact! There lay the reason for his prompt action. The idea brought quick decision to Clyde Burke. Off duty, The Shadow's agent had become a news seeker. He would follow into Washington.

Clyde called to the driver of a cab. The taxi rolled to the steps. Entering the vehicle, Clyde told the man to take him into the city. He added that he was in a hurry. The jehu grinned.

"Wait'll we hit the speedway, boss," he said. "I'll show you some fast time."

"All right," agreed Clyde. "I'd like to see it."

The Shadow's agent knew that speed would be necessary to keep up with the pace that Lito Carraza could make in his foreign roadster. In this surmise, Clyde was correct. Carraza, leaving the Club Rivoli, had stepped on the gas with a vengeance.

Heading toward the broad speedway, the South American attaché was counting on a clear road for his quick trip back to the legation. The glow from the dashboard of his roadster showed his fuming lips. Carraza was annoyed because he had lingered so long at the Club Rivoli.

The roadster swerved as it reached the speedway. As Carraza pressed the accelerator, another car shot out from a side road. It was a rakish touring car. It took up Carraza's trail. From a hundred feet behind, the pursuing car began to lose ground as Carraza piloted his roadster at a speed of eighty miles an hour.

The attaché, eager to get back to headquarters, had figured that his position would serve him should traffic police observe his speed. The road ahead was clear. Beyond the bright lights that lined the Potomac was the glow of the city, dominated by brilliance that showed the Capitol building and the monument.

Carraza slackened slightly for a long turn. Then, as he pressed the accelerator for a straight stretch, he muttered angrily. An old sedan was backing crosswise to block the speedway. Its erratic motion, in the path of Carraza's blinding lights, was a signal for immediate caution.

There was time to avoid a collision, even at the speed with which the roadster was traveling. Carraza stepped on the brake. His lunging car swerved, but held to the road as it came to a rapid stop. Intuitively, the South American turned the wheel so that the nose of his car pointed at an angle behind the balking sedan.

A TONGUE of flame spat from the sedan. A bullet zimmed against the windshield of Carraza's roadster. The glass cracked, but did not shatter. Another flash of flame. Carraza flung open the door beside the driver's seat and leaped to the speedway, on the side away from the stalled sedan. His eyes opened wide with fright.

Looming down from the direction which he had come was a rakish touring car. Its headlights showed Carraza plainly. From the side of the approaching automobile came an opening shot that missed its mark, but battered the side of the roadster.

Caught between two fires, Carraza leaped frantically to the front of his car. As his cowering form clutched the radiator, another shot came from the sedan. Certain doom awaited the attaché. It would be but a matter of seconds.

Then came the interruption that neither Carraza nor his pursuers had expected. The roar of a powerful motor surged from the bend just ahead of the sedan. With terrific speed, a roadster of greater power than Carraza's came hurtling down upon the sedan.

Gunmen, about to aim at their prey, turned to see this arriving car. The roadster, bearing down at ninety, seemed driverless! Behind its wheel loomed a spectral shape that seemed like a monstrous creature of the night!

Death was the driver of that car. Death, in the person of The Shadow! The bark of a huge automatic was the answer to the gunmen's challenge. The puny spats of revolver fire, directed at a hurtling target, were wild attempts to meet the power of the automatic.

Hot lead seared into the midst of crouching mobsters. Hoarse screams were the replies as useless revolvers clattered to the concrete of the speedway. As deadly as a crushing Juggernaut, The

Shadow had hurled vengeance into the ranks of men who were here to murder.

As The Shadow's car swerved past the front of the sedan, men in the touring car opened new and closer fire upon Lito Carraza. The attaché screamed as a bullet clipped his shoulder. Blindly, he plunged forward, staggering directly toward the blocking sedan.

But for The Shadow's quick and precise action, Carraza's course would have led him to sure death. A few seconds before, the sedan had contained four men whose hands were ready with revolvers. That circumstance had changed. The Shadow's perfect shots had done their work. Not a single hand could rise to shoot down the victim who came staggering into the death trap.

The touring car had stopped. Gangsters, leaping from its doors, were on Carraza's trail. They swung as The Shadow's car swerved past Carraza's road-ster. Blindly, they fired into the glare as jamming breaks brought the car of vengeance to a stop.

Revolver bullets spattered against the wind-shield. They might as well have driven against steel as that thick, bulletproof barrier with which The Shadow's speedy car was equipped.

With left hand on the wheel, The Shadow answered with his right. His automatic, thrust from beside the windshield, picked out the ruffians who snarled before the brilliance of The Shadow's head-lights.

One ugly-faced ruffian sprawled. A second, firing vain shots, staggered as a bullet reached him. Another gangster crumpled. Two who remained took to flight.

They were too late. A timely bullet clipped the first as he dodged beyond Carraza's roadster. A second shot caught the second man as he sought to clamber back into the roadster. On the step, the gangster screamed, threw out his arms and toppled backward to the concrete of the speedway.

Only one of the would-be assassins found opportunity to escape. He was the leader of the two-car mob—the man at the wheel of the touring car. "Bugs" Ritler, trusted henchman of Darvin Rochelle, had sensed the presence of a mighty menace as he had seen his squirming minions fall.

Springing from the wheel, Bugs went through the door on the left as The Shadow was dropping the last pair of snarling rats. Without pausing to fire a single shot, Bugs took a flying leap over a fence at the side of the speedway and gained shelter amid a clump of trees.

To the ears of the terrified gang leader came the strident sound of a taunting laugh. It was a weird cry that sounded like a knell when it broke the silence which had followed the stilling of gunfire.

The laugh of The Shadow!

SINISTER, mocking mirth, it rang out as the token of swift triumph. In quick, emphatic seconds, The Shadow had spelled doom to men of crime. Single-handed, he had turned the odds in his own behalf.

From the wheel of his powerful roadster, The Shadow could see Lito Carraza. The attaché whose life The Shadow had saved, was clutching his wounded shoulder as he stood, white-faced, close by the sedan where bullet-riddled mobsters lay.

Carraza was safe. No one remained to make a new attempt upon his life. The Shadow, turning his gaze along the speedway, spied the lights of a taxi-cab approaching from the direction in which Carraza had come.

The big roadster moved backward. Its rear wheels gripped the dirt that edged the far side of the speedway. The car roared forward. Swerving a foot from the rear of Carraza's stalled car, it shot along the broad road, back toward Washington.

Above the roaring throb of the powerful motor came a final burst of mockery. The laugh was repeated, like a distant echo, as the big roadster took the bend. The taillight twinkled from sight, just as the taxicab rolled up to the spot where three driverless cars were stretched across the speedway.

The Shadow's hand had struck. His strident laugh had marked his victory. Triumphant, The Shadow had departed into the darkness from which he had emerged!

CHAPTER IX
MARQUETTE REPORTS

ON the evening following the affray on the Virginia speedway, Vic Marquette appeared in the lobby of the Hotel Starlett. The Secret Service operative approached a room telephone and called Fulton Fourrier.

Vic Marquette had a habit of noticing people everywhere he went. He also possessed the pecu-liar ability of spotting those who seemed to be worthwhile watching. He had used this propensity at the Club Rivoli when he had observed Alvarez Menzone. He looked about him tonight, as he passed through the lobby of the Starlett.

On this occasion, however, Vic's ability failed him. He saw no one in the lobby who impressed him as important. He stared squarely at a tall, thin-faced man whose hawklike nose and keen eyes gave him a dignified expression. But Vic saw nothing about that individual to make a second look necessary.

The personage whom Vic Marquette passed by was the guest who had registered as Henry Arnaud. He was located in the lobby for one definite purpose: to await the appearance of Vic Marquette.

As soon as the Secret Service operative had taken one elevator, Arnaud arose and entered another. Alighting at the eighth floor, he moved swiftly to his room. In the darkness, a black cloak swished. A weird, shrouded figure appeared upon the balcony and began its precipitous and sidewise ascent to the outside of Fourrier's window.

Henry Arnaud had again become The Shadow. Crouched on Fourrier's balcony, his gloved hands eased the trifling space that he needed between the doorlike halves of the French window. Peering keenly through the crevice, The Shadow again became a silent listener to what was passing between Vic Marquette and his chief.

MARQUETTE was making his report. Fourrier, seated sidewise at the writing table, was ready with his questions. The Shadow took in every word.

"The Club Rivoli," remarked Marquette. "Yes— I was there. I spotted a South American."

"Not Lito Carraza?"

"No. That's where I slipped up, chief. The fellow I picked is named Alvarez Menzone. He made friends with a young chap named Maurice Twindell. I trailed the pair to the apartment where Menzone is living—Athena Court. Twindell went on; Menzone turned in."

"And all this while," interposed Fourrier sourly, "crime was brewing out at the Club Rivoli. You've read the newspapers"—Fourrier picked up a journal and tapped it—"and you know what happened there. They tried to get Lito Carraza, an attaché who had important legation correspondence on his person. He's the man you should have been watching."

"I know it," admitted Marquette. "I might have been watching him—if I'd seen him. I picked another man, chief, and I think I've got a lead."

"Let us discuss Carraza first," decided Fourrier. "According to the newspapers, he was attacked by gangsters, purely as a holdup proposition. Carraza was driving an expensive car. He was coming from the Club Rivoli. They tried to kill him, but some other persons opened fire. The one explanation seems to be that gangsters battled among themselves.

"The first people to arrive were two men: a taxi driver and his passenger, a news bureau man named Clyde Burke. They took Carraza to a hospital. He refused to talk.

"That's why the real meat of the story was suppressed. The legation informed me of what had happened. I went over there; I kept the facts out of print and I listed them for reference. Here they are:

"Carraza was dining with a woman named Anita Debronne. He left her at the Club Rivoli. She evidently induced him to go there so that he would have to return alone along the speedway. I sent two men out to the Club Rivoli. They learned that Anita Debronne was known there; that she had been seen to leave shortly after Carraza's departure."

Vic Marquette stared. This was news to him. He realized now why Fourrier was disgruntled. Had Vic been on the job at the Club Rivoli, the sequel to last night's happenings might have been different.

"So here is the story," resumed Fourrier. "I've put more men to work. One is looking for Anita Debronne. Two others are watching the Club Rivoli. If that's where attachés have been going before they disappear, we're going to put a stop to it."

"You're not closing the place?"

"No. We're crimping it—that's all. We've got a lead on the Debronne woman. We've found a crew of dead mobsters. But we're no closer home than we were before."

"Thanks to me," observed Vic moodily.

"Don't take what I have said as a reprimand," declared Fourrier, in an easier tone. "On the contrary, Marquette, I am highly pleased with what you have accomplished."

Vic looked up questioningly.

"There is no doubt," announced Fourrier, "about one thing. You picked the Club Rivoli as a starting point. That's where trouble was waiting for Lito Carraza. I want you to keep on from there. I think you're the man who can trail it farther.

"I've had to put other men on the case. It's obvious that the attempt on Carraza's life is linked with the disappearances that we've been trying to trace. This is still your job; the other operatives are covering you. Find some new clues. Go anywhere— everywhere. Back to the Club Rivoli—to legations— wherever you choose. I'll fix all that's needed. But bring in results."

"Thanks, chief," said Marquette. "You can count on me. I'll follow the same tactics that I tried last night. All these cases involved South American activities. I'm watching South Americans. That's why I picked Alvarez Menzone."

"The wrong man—"

"I'm not sure about that. He's an odd customer. He left the Club Rivoli right while his luck was running good. I followed him last night. I dropped around at the apartment house this afternoon."

"What did you find out?"

"Nothing. Menzone has a Filipino servant— evidently one whom he hired here in Washington. The servant is dumb. Menzone was not at home."

"Yet you still think that he may figure in this?"

"I'd like to know more about him."

"That's simple. I'll get any information that's available. In the meantime, don't waste too much time on the man. Find others that may appear suspicious. We'll trace them all down."

"That's just what I intend to do, chief. At the same time, I'm going to keep my eyes open for this fellow Menzone. If he crosses my path, I'll give him more than just a once-over."

THERE was a pause. Fourrier was thinking. A frown appeared upon the divisional chief's forehead.

"There's one thing I'd like to know," declared Fourrier. "That fight last night was a mighty brief one. It left Carraza bewildered. All that he can remember was gunfire—from two sides. Then he heard a car come driving up—brakes grinding—more shots. He was clipped in the shoulder; but in the meantime, his rescuers mopped up the entire crew that had him trapped.

"The car must have made a quick getaway. Carraza heard it drive off; and he heard something else, too. He says he heard a laugh—a weird laugh—one that he will never forget. Some of these South Americans are superstitious, but when Carraza told me about that laugh, I knew he meant it—"

… He was attacked by gangsters, purely as a holdup proposition…

Fourrier paused. He looked with alarm toward Vic Marquette. The operative was staring at his superior; his face was rigid.

"What's the matter?" questioned Fourrier. "You look like you've seen a ghost!"

"I haven't seen one," responded Vic, in an awed tone. "I've just heard of one."

"Heard of one? From whom?"

"From you. That laugh you mentioned. Chief, I know what it meant. You're right that this affair is getting big. I know who it was who washed out that crew of mobsmen."

"Are you going to tell me it was a ghost?"

"The next thing to it. Chief, it was The Shadow who got those mobsters. He's the only person who could have done a job like that."

"The Shadow?"

Vic Marquette smiled grimly. He nodded; then began his explanation. Fulton Fourrier listened half doubtingly. His interest increased as Marquette continued.

"They know about The Shadow in New York," declared Marquette. "Who he is—what he is— that's a mystery. The point is that The Shadow battles crooks. The underworld is afraid of him— more than they are of the police."

"I've heard something of it," admitted Fourrier, in a tone of recollection. "But this isn't New York."

"It's a case involving gangsters."

"Yes. You're right on that. But the theory ends there, Marquette. If this fighter you call The Shadow is out to end gang rule, he's accomplished what he's after. Give him credit for wiping out that ugly band. But that ends his part."

"Not a bit of it." Vic's tone was emphatic. "Chief, you can believe me or not when I tell you that The Shadow has played his part in putting down some of the greatest crime that this country has ever known.

"I've taken credit for some mighty big jobs. I'll tell you, chief, that I'd never have come through some of them if it hadn't been for The Shadow. He's pulled me out of some tight jams."

"And yet"—Fourrier's tone was incredulous— "you don't know who he is?"

"I've seen him." Vic was speaking in a tone of serious recollection. "I've heard his laugh. He is a ghost—The Shadow—a phantom completely cloaked in black. He moves with incredible swiftness. He strikes without mercy. He leaves as he comes. You can't trace him, chief."

Fourrier's brow was wrinkled. Vic noted his chief's expression. He realized that Fourrier doubted these statements; that the chief was worried about his operative's sanity.

"I'm not dreaming," asserted Marquette, as he rose to his feet. "I'm telling you of things I've witnessed, under unbelievable circumstances. The Shadow is a power; and he fights for justice. If he is here in Washington, it's not to handle a bunch of imported gangsters and then quit.

"It looks to me like The Shadow was in this deal. He has agents, and I'm mighty sure I know who one of them is. Maybe I'll get a line on The Shadow while I'm working on this case. If I do, it's going to help.

"Chief, the break is coming. I'm convinced of it; and you can count on me. I'm starting out tonight with more confidence than I've ever had— and if you want the reason, I'll give it to you. It's because Lito Carraza heard that laugh out on the speedway."

Fulton Fourrier smiled indulgently. Marquette's determination had put his chief's mind at ease. Fourrier followed Vic to the door; there, he clapped his operative on the shoulder.

"I don't disbelieve you, Marquette," he declared. "Your record shows what you have done; and you wouldn't take credit from yourself if you weren't convinced that it belonged elsewhere. If you've received aid from some mysterious source and think you're going to get it again, so much the better.

"Don't worry too much about Alvarez Menzone. I'll look up the fellow's record. And don't bank too much on The Shadow. Maybe you have a trend toward exaggerating his prowess.

"Get results. I'm counting on you. We're going to get to the bottom of this plot that has taken off six men and failed only when it struck the seventh."

Vic nodded his agreement. He went out through the door. Fulton Fourrier closed the portal, then turned back to his writing table, shaking his head in new doubt. It was evident that Vic Marquette's talk of The Shadow had not been entirely convincing.

AT the writing table, Fulton Fourrier felt uneasy. He glanced back over his shoulder. He noted that the French windows were ajar. He went and closed them.

For one brief second, while his hands were upon the window frames, Fulton Fourrier was face to face with the very being whose existence he doubted!

Beyond those windows stood the black-garbed being of whom Vic Marquette had spoken. Fourrier, however, did not see the sable-hued form. Merged with outer darkness, The Shadow was a creature invisible.

Fourrier returned to the writing table. As he sat down, he started as a surprising echo reached his ears. It seemed like the faint, hollow tone of a whispered laugh. It reminded him of the mockery which Lito Carraza had described; of the mirth which Vic Marquette had corroborated.

Fulton Fourrier sat motionless. At last, he shrugged his shoulders. He attributed that weird sound to a touch of imagination. He decided to forget it.

Yet, as he studied report sheets, the chief could not shake off that haunting sound. It persisted as a chilling recollection.

Small wonder! That was a laugh which no one could forget. Fulton Fourrier, though he did not realize the truth, had heard the laugh of The Shadow!

CHAPTER X
BURKE'S INTERVIEW

ON the following morning, Clyde Burke entered his office to find an unposted letter in the mailbox. He opened it and scanned blue-inked lines that were inscribed in The Shadow's code. The message contained concise instructions:

Interview Alvarez Menzone, Athena Court. Suggest that he may become a man of consequence in Washington. Offer to obtain a competent secretary to handle his correspondence. Return to your office and await a call.

The name of Alvarez Menzone was not familiar to Clyde Burke. The newspaperman picked up the telephone book and looked for the name. He did not find it. He located the apartment house, however, and decided that a visit to Menzone's residence would be the best step.

Clyde picked up the paper which had contained The Shadow's message. The sheet had turned blank while Clyde had been consulting the telephone book. The Shadow's agent tossed the paper into the wastebasket. He took his hat and left the office.

Arriving at Athena Court, Clyde looked over the nameplates and discovered that of Alvarez Menzone. The apartment number was 3-D. Clyde entered the deserted lobby, took the automatic elevator to the third floor, and found the apartment that he wanted. He pressed a button beside the door.

A minute passed. The door opened. A dull-faced Filipino, clad in white coat and black trousers, stared at the visitor.

"What you want?" he asked.

"I have come to see Mr. Menzone," replied Clyde.

"Nobody is home," informed the Filipino. "Mr. Menzone, he is away."

The servant was about to close the door in Clyde's face when a voice called from an inner room:

"Who is it, José?"

"Man to see you, sir," replied the Filipino, in a dull monotone.

"Tell him to come in," repeated the voice. The accents showed the speaker to be a foreigner.

José complied. He stepped aside and reluctantly allowed Clyde Burke to enter.

THE newspaperman found himself in a well-furnished living room. As he stood within the door, a man attired in a dressing gown appeared from another doorway.

Clyde Burke could not repress a stare. He had seen this man before. He was the South American whom Clyde had viewed from the booth at the Club Rivoli—the one who had gone out with an American whom Clyde had watched—the one whom Vic Marquette had followed!

"*Buenos dios, señor,*" greeted Menzone, with a gleaming smile. "I am Alvarez Menzone. You have come to see me?"

"Yes," answered Clyde. "My name is Burke. I am manager of the National City News Association—a Washington organization that corresponds with journals in other cities."

"Ah!" Menzone's tone showed interest. "You have come to interview me?"

"Exactly," returned Clyde.

Menzone seated himself in an armchair and waved Clyde to another seat. He picked up a wooden box, opened it to extract a cigarette, and offered one to Clyde Burke. The newspaperman accepted.

"You must excuse my servant," remarked Menzone, as he was lighting his cigarette. "He is very stupid, sometimes. I told him that I wished to see no one until later. He should not have told you that I was out, however. Gentlemen of the press are always welcome.

"An interview." Menzone smiled reminiscently. "I have given many of them, *señor*, but always in South America. This is my first experience in the United States. I suppose you wish to know why I am in Washington?"

"Yes."

"I have come"—Menzone seemed very serious—"to aid in the promotion of international good will. I am an internationalist, *señor*, so far as South America is concerned. The entire continent is familiar ground to me.

"Ah! What a future lies there! Through peace and harmony, South America could lead the world. Communication. Better communication. That is the first step that we must make. Not communication, *señor*—that is not exactly the word I want. Let me see what—"

"Transportation?"

"That is it, *señor*! Transportation. Let me explain."

Menzone went to the corner of the room and brought back a huge stack of papers. He produced a large printed map of South America. He pointed to lines of different colors.

"Here, *señor*," he said, "are the railroads as they now exist. These—in red. Here are the ones that we should have. Those, you see, are in green.

"We have neglected this form of transportation. Why? Because each nation, if it builds a road to the border of another country, is aiding a different nation. Take this green line from Bogota, in Colombia. It would be a wonderful form of transportation if it went southward; but to be of value, it would have to cross Ecuador and pass into Peru.

"Who must begin it? Colombia. Then Ecuador must follow. Peru could start it if she wished; but again, Ecuador and Colombia would have to cooperate.

"You see the problem? International effort is the only answer. How can it be gained? Through American capital. The countries of South America would welcome railroads."

"Here in the United States," remarked Clyde, "rail transportation is meeting with heavy competition."

"Because you have highways," explained Menzone. "But they come after the railroads. Great profit is there, for those who are the first to seek it. Years and years of successful rail transportation lie ahead in South America."

MENZONE passed the map to Clyde. He produced mimeographed sheets. Some of these were statements; others contained statistics. They gave reports on existing rail lines of the South American continent; also the potentialities of others that could be constructed.

"This will make good copy," remarked Clyde. He nodded as Menzone passed him photographs of South American locomotives and other rolling stock. "Yes. Coming at the time of the Pan-American Convention, I can sell this as feature material. You intend to bring up this subject at the convention?"

"So I hope, *señor*. I shall visit the legations and discuss the matter. But I wish to do more. I want this information to be just so. I want it so it will interest North Americans. There is the trouble."

"In what way?"

"I think as we think in the South. My wording is not good. I need someone who can understand to put it in the style that is accepted here."

"Why don't you hire a competent secretary?" Clyde Burke was prompt with the question, when he had gained the wedge. "That is all you need, Mr. Menzone."

"*Buenos*," agreed the South American. "But where am I to find such a man? I am here in Washington. I did not see the difficulty until I arrived. I know how secretaries go. Some are good; most are bad. You understand?"

"Perhaps," offered Clyde, "I could obtain the very man you need. It would not prove difficult, since you speak English so fluently. You want a man to handle your correspondence in the United States—"

"Exactly, *senor*. You believe that you could do that for me? Do so, I beg you."

"You have a telephone," remarked Clyde, as he looked across the room. "Let me take the number. You will hear from me within a few hours."

Clyde jotted down Menzone's number. He folded the data which he had received and extended his hand to the South American. Menzone received it warmly. Impressed by Clyde's promise of publicity and aid in obtaining a secretary, Menzone was gracious to the extreme. He accompanied his visitor to the door and bowed as Clyde departed.

As he took the elevator, Clyde's last glance toward Menzone's apartment showed the South American still standing in the opened doorway. Menzone was smiling, apparently pleased because he had been interviewed. Yet there was something sardonic about his expression that made a distinct impression upon Clyde Burke.

The Shadow's agent, as he strolled from Athena Court, was convinced that Alvarez Menzone's interest in South American transportation was not the only reason for his presence in Washington.

There was a shrewdness about Menzone that was difficult to analyze. Among the pictures which Clyde had received was one of Menzone himself. Studying the photograph, Clyde could observe the peculiar, lurking smile that appeared permanently upon the lips of Alvarez Menzone.

Clyde had missed this out at the Club Rivoli. He had not seen Menzone closely there. Since his interview with the South American, however, Clyde was convinced of The Shadow's wisdom in covering this stranger in Washington. The photograph—Clyde studied it more intensely as he traveled toward his office in a cab—gave Menzone the sleek, crafty expression of a villain in an old-time melodrama.

AT the office, Clyde began to arrange his material for a syndicated story. This was Sunday feature stuff without question. The Pan-American Convention had not yet begun its preliminary meetings. This story would break before the subject of extended transportation would come before the members of the convention.

Clyde visualized graphic pages: Menzone's portrait—pictures of South American railway equipment—boxed tables of statistics—a huge map of South America with its dotted lines of proposed railway systems. His first task, however, was to prepare a news story that the Washington journals would gobble. Opening the case of a portable typewriter, Clyde began to pound the keys in two-finger reporter fashion.

The ringing of the telephone came as an interruption. Clyde lifted the receiver. He announced his name; also that of his news bureau. A single word, uttered in a strange, whispered voice, came to Clyde's ear:

"Report."

It was The Shadow! Clyde gazed toward the door, to make sure that no chance visitor was about to enter. Then, in brief, concise words, he gave the details of his interview with Alvarez Menzone. He stated that he had obtained a story which was marketable; he added that Menzone was ready to employ a secretary, if he could find the man.

"Call Menzone." The Shadow's order came in a sibilant hiss. "Tell him that you are sending him the man he needs. Harry Vincent—a friend of yours—recently arrived from New York."

Clyde's eyes opened wide. Harry Vincent! Clyde had not known that Harry was in Washington. Clyde had worked with Harry before; he knew Harry to be one of the most capable agents in The Shadow's employ.

The Shadow had foreseen the possibility of Clyde Burke making a successful suggestion to Alvarez Menzone. He had summoned Harry Vincent here to be in readiness!

"Place story immediately." This was The Shadow's added order. "Menzone's purpose in Washington must become known."

The receiver clicked as Clyde was acknowledging the instructions. Clyde hung up; he waited a few minutes, then called Alvarez Menzone. He heard the persuasive voice of the South American across the wire.

"This is Burke," informed Clyde. "I've found the man for you, Mr. Menzone."

"To serve as my secretary?" Menzone's question showed eager interest.

"Yes," announced Clyde. "His name is Harry Vincent. He'll be out to see you some time today. He's a man from New York. Highly competent."

"Excellent" was Menzone's rejoinder. The South American concluded the telephone conversation with effusive thanks.

CLYDE began to pound the typewriter. His story was shaping rapidly. The Shadow's agent remembered the instructions. He glanced at his watch; it was not yet eleven.

Dropping the story for the moment, Clyde called the office of one of the Washington evening newspapers. He was connected with the city editor. Briefly, Clyde sketched the story that he had obtained from Alvarez Menzone. He read the lead paragraph of the copy that he had already written.

"Great stuff, Burke!" came the city editor's commendation. "You say you're still working on the story?"

"Yes."

"I'll have a copy boy over to your office in fifteen minutes. Give him the story—and photographs. We're going to break this in the next edition. We want it as an exclusive interview. You understand?"

Clyde acknowledged. He smiled as he hung up the receiver and went back to his typewriter pounding. He knew what this would mean: a first-page story of timely interest. Coming on the heels of recent railroad legislation in the United States; appearing in advance of the Pan-American Convention, this interview with Alvarez Menzone would bring the South American's name into the limelight.

A new outlet for American millions! Clyde could see the editorial comment that the story would bring. The other Washington newspapers would pounce upon it. Alvarez Menzone would be interviewed by many before this day was ended.

Harry Vincent, already on his way to Menzone's, would have immediate duties as secretary to the South American. Clyde smiled as he pounded out the concluding paragraph of his story, to complete the article before the copy boy's arrival.

Alvarez Menzone was crashing the limelight. Why? Because The Shadow so desired. Somehow, The Shadow had foreseen this possibility. What was The Shadow's purpose? Only The Shadow knew.

Spiderlike, The Shadow was spinning an invisible web. Here, in Washington, the being who battled crime was meeting craft with craft. Some master plotter of evil was lurking in the background. The Shadow sought to bring him to light.

Through the exploitation of Alvarez Menzone, the South American who had gained the acquaintanceship of Maurice Twindell, The Shadow was tending toward his goal. Action on the speedway was being followed by undercover progress in Washington.

Through Clyde Burke, The Shadow had gained the points he needed. He was bringing Alvarez Menzone into prominence. He had placed his own man—Harry Vincent—close to Menzone.

The Shadow knew that this would bring results. The ultimate was something which The Shadow, alone, could foresee. The Shadow, master worker, was seeking to bring crime from its lair.

CHAPTER XI
ROCHELLE RESPONDS

DARVIN ROCHELLE was seated behind his

huge, flat-topped mahogany desk. His lips were firmly set. His gaze was harsh as his eyes turned toward the man who was sitting close to the huge globe of the world.

Rochelle's companion was Maurice Twindell. The habitué of the Club Rivoli was attired in a business suit; he still retained the debonair manner that was characteristic when he appeared in evening clothes.

"We have met with difficulty, Maurice," observed Rochelle. "The final goal was within attainment, until that trouble struck on the speedway."

"I didn't think Bugs Ritler would fail you," remarked Twindell glumly. "It was a setup—to kill Lito Carraza and get his papers. I don't see yet how Bugs missed out."

"I have the explanation," asserted Rochelle. "Bugs managed to escape. That is fortunate. He reported back to Whistler Ingliss—in Agro—and told him what had happened. Bugs knows who it was that broke up his mob so swiftly."

"Another crew of gangsters?"

"No. A lone fighter, Maurice. The one whom all mobsmen fear. The Shadow."

Twindell showed signs of bewilderment mixed with apprehension. Rochelle smiled.

"The Shadow, Maurice," explained the man with the limp, "is a power unto himself. His usual habitat is New York City, but he has frequently been encountered elsewhere. His pastime is to fight whole gangs; to down them single-handed. He has been despicably successful. That is why I state again that Bugs Ritler was lucky to escape."

"You mean," interjected Twindell, "that this one man mopped up a whole crew?"

"I did not say one man," returned Rochelle. "I said The Shadow. He is more than a man, Maurice. He is a phantom of the night. A ghost that comes to life. For months, my schemes have been marked by steady success. Months narrowed to days; days to hours; hours to minutes. Then, when seconds only lay between me and the culmination of my scheme, The Shadow intervened!"

"To destroy your plans?"

"To balk them. From now on, Maurice, my old methods will be useless. Had we trapped Lito Carraza, I would have needed nothing more. Now, however—"

The telephone bell interrupted. Rochelle picked up the instrument and spoke. He changed from English into Agro.

"Kye kye zo kire?" he questioned. "Kye zay voso... Voso voso... Bole zee thone... Fee. Thone thone... Bole vake eef... Alk beeta bole reen kye zee sovo... Fee. Rema."

Rochelle hung up the receiver. He turned to Maurice Twindell.

THE young man seemed to understand the reason for the annoyed expression which was on Rochelle's face. Agro was plain to Twindell. But he had heard only one end of the conversation.

"Whistler Ingliss," remarked Rochelle. "He tells me that Secret Service operatives were at his place last night. You heard my answer. I told him to be very careful. Things are bad, but I promised to let him know when all is well."

"With the operatives covering," observed Twindell, "it's a cinch you can't make a move from the Club Rivoli."

"Operatives?" Rochelle spat the question. "Bah! If another man should appear at the Club Rivoli with those papers that I want, I could snatch him out from under the noses of Secret Service men.

"It is The Shadow who could prevent it!" Rochelle pounded the desk emphatically. "He scents mobsters as a fox trails a hare. Gangsters cannot thwart him. What is more, Maurice, The Shadow is a sleuth extraordinary. It is on his account—more so than that of the Secret Service—that I sent Anita Debronne into hiding.

"That is where you are going, Maurice. Out of town, to await my summons. This is your final visit here until my plans have been completed."

"But how—"

"Listen." Rochelle held up his hand for silence. "I am changing tactics, Maurice. I have used direct tactics because they succeeded. I needed you and Anita to lure victims to their doom. Such mechanism is useless now. I shall reserve it for the final stroke—the deeds which will follow the gaining of the documents which I have not yet obtained.

"Stealth is required. Real espionage, the art at which I am so skilled. The correspondence which Lito Carraza carried is stowed away in safety—deep within the safe at Carraza's legation.

"Mob raids would be futile. I need a new instrument: one that I can use to full advantage. You, Maurice, have provided me with such an instrument."

"I?"

"Yes." Rochelle smiled with evil expression. "On the night of Bugs Ritler's failure, you met a man from South America. Alvarez Menzone. You told me about him—a man of wealth, here in Washington to promote American capital for rail development in the southern continent."

"Yes. He talked with me as we rode back from the Club Rivoli. I saw nothing of value, except that he had international experience."

"That was sufficient." Rochelle was tapping the desk as he smiled. "I have consulted my files, Maurice. I have learned facts that interest me concerning Alvarez Menzone. I saw how he might prove useful. There was only one drawback."

"What was that?"

"His nonentity in Washington. A man may be important in South America, yet remain unrecognized here. Conversely, certain men of little repute in their own lands may be feted and lionized in this foolish city.

"Publicity is the deity which Americans worship. Let a man reach the news—his reputation is established. Since your acquaintance with Alvarez Menzone, his name has come into print."

ROCHELLE reached to the side of the disk and tossed three newspapers to Twindell. The young man nodded as he noted Menzone's picture on each front page.

"I saw these," remarked Twindell. "Menzone has crashed the front page all right. You mean that this is to our advantage?"

"Positively. I should like very much, Maurice, to receive Alvarez Menzone as a visitor. Let me suggest that when you leave here, you call upon our friend from South America.

"Suggest that his scheme for continental transportation in South America is dependent primarily upon favorable international relations. Its success should, therefore, be greatly aided through cooperation with the International Peace Alliance.

"Give him a bit of information: namely, that the International Peace Alliance has begun a drive for millions of dollars to be spent on commodities that will be shipped to foreign lands. The lack of inland transportation is the one factor which may prevent South America from gaining the chief benefit of these funds.

"Our promise to ship steadily to South America, should rail facilities be provided there, will certainly be of interest to Alvarez Menzone."

Maurice Twindell nodded. He glanced at his watch and noted that it was half past five. Darvin Rochelle smiled.

"Try to get Menzone before dinner," he suggested. "Call there in person. Report to me by telephone."

Maurice Twindell departed.

Shortly before six, he arrived at Athena Court. He went up to the third floor and rang Menzone's bell. A young man of keen-cut appearance answered. It was Harry Vincent, Menzone's new secretary. Twindell inquired for the South American. Harry informed him that Menzone would not be in until half past seven.

Twindell promised to return at that time. He went down to the street, found a drugstore and entered a telephone booth. He called Rochelle and made a brief report.

"Kay zay eef kire," declared Twindell, in Agro. "Kay zee kire rema. Sake goda. Seek coda joda. Alk keed."

Twindell went on to a restaurant.

It was just half past eight when he returned to Athena Court. This time, Harry Vincent announced that Alvarez Menzone was at home. The South American was seated in the living room; he recognized Maurice Twindell immediately and arose to greet the man whom he had met at the Club Rivoli.

A few words passed in Spanish. Harry, partly familiar with the language, grasped that Twindell wanted to discuss some matter privately. Menzone ushered the visitor into a small room that served as his study. He closed the door.

HARRY, listening from outside the barrier, could not distinguish the low, buzzing words. He slipped back into the living room when he heard the scuffle of chairs. Menzone and Twindell appeared. They shook hands at the outer door.

"Tell him," declared Menzone, in Spanish, "that I shall call shortly after nine o'clock tonight—it is almost nine now. You are sure that the hour will not be too late—"

"No, indeed," interposed Twindell. "He will be glad to see you, *Señor* Menzone. *Buenos noches.*"

Menzone returned to the living room. He remarked to his new secretary that he intended to go out for a short while. He did not, however, mention his destination.

Maurice Twindell, when he reached the street, entered the same drugstore where he had gone before. He put in another call to Darvin Rochelle and this time reported:

"Alk oto kay. Kay deek exat vodo. Sake ita."

This done, Maurice Twindell strolled from the drugstore. He hailed a passing cab and ordered the driver to take him to the Union Station. In accordance with Rochelle's order, Twindell was taking a trip out of town.

Meanwhile, Alvarez Menzone was dressing for an evening visit. He called Harry Vincent and ordered the secretary to bring maps and mimeographed sheets. Harry left these on the study desk. Menzone appeared from his own room, carrying a bulky briefcase. Harry saw him thrust the printed data into its interior.

As soon as Menzone had gone, Harry sat at the desk in the study. Drawing a pen from his pocket, The Shadow's agent inscribed a coded message in blue ink. Sealing the message in a small envelope, Harry carried it to the hall outside of the apartment.

Beyond the elevator, at a corner of the stairway, hung a fire extinguisher. Harry tucked the envelope behind the big cylinder and returned to the apartment.

MINUTES passed. Blackness moved on the obscure and little-used stairway. A shrouded form appeared; a gloved hand that seemed like a thing of living blackness extended to the wall. It plucked the envelope that Harry had placed in readiness.

Shortly afterward, a cab driver pulled up at the curb near Athena Court in response to a whistle. He looked about for the person who had summoned him. He saw no one. He was startled, however, to hear a voice from the interior of the cab. He realized that despite his alertness, his passenger had entered without his knowledge.

The driver nodded, as a voice gave him an address. He started the cab. Paper crinkled in the rear as hands opened an envelope. Harry Vincent's message appeared between black-gloved fingers.

By the light of streetlamps which the cab was passing, The Shadow read the meager report which his agent had been able to obtain regarding Alvarez Menzone's visitor and the subsequent departure of Menzone himself.

The coded writing faded. The paper and the envelope fluttered from the window. Blackness shifted within the gloom of the cab. Then came a whispered laugh. It was a token of keen understanding.

The Shadow, despite the little that he had learned through Harry Vincent, seemed satisfied with the way affairs were going. The meshes of his web were strung. The unseen network was ready to ensnare its prey!

CHAPTER XII
THE NEW GAME

"BE ready, Thurk."

Darvin Rochelle uttered these words as his dwarfish servant came creeping through the door at the rear of the office. Rising, with a smile, Rochelle gave new instructions: these in Agro.

"Co kay dake." Rochelle was limping toward the anteroom as he spoke. "Bole zee fela. Bole teeba teen alk bata."

With these words, Rochelle clumped through the doorway. He crossed the anteroom, opened the further door and held out his hand as a man arrived at the top of the marble stairway. It was Alvarez Menzone.

"Señor Menzone?" Rochelle's welcome was a friendly one. Then: "Come in, señor. You are welcome."

Limping through the anteroom, Rochelle conducted his guest to the office. Thurk was no longer in sight. Rochelle motioned Menzone to the chair beside the huge globe of the world. Menzone, like every other visitor, seemed intrigued by the huge sphere with its large-scale map.

Rochelle seated himself behind the desk. Menzone, turning, picked up the briefcase that he had brought with him. From it he extracted his own map and its accompanying papers.

"My friend Twindell"—Menzone was using English, the language which seemed familiar to Rochelle—"has told me that your plan and mine have mutual points. Both of us are concerned with the creation of international good will."

"My plans are philanthropic, señor."

"And mine are commercial. That does not change the fact that they are very much alike."

Rochelle began to eye the plans which Menzone had shown him. He shook his head, half doubtingly. Finally, he faced Menzone and smiled as he saw a steady gleam in the South American's eye.

"Futile!" exclaimed Rochelle. "These plans could never work! The transportation facilities that you suggest would take rail lines to districts that will never thrive, even though developed. Millions would be lost through your plans, señor."

"You are wrong!" retorted Menzone, in harsh accents. "You do not know the facts, señor! You are not acquainted with the work that I have done!"

"No?" Rochelle's utterance showed contempt.

Rising from behind his desk, Rochelle limped in halting fashion to a large filing cabinet in the corner of the office. Menzone could hear him mutter as he opened a drawer.

"L—M—" Rochelle paused on the second letter. "M—E; M—E—N; ah, here it is, Menzone!"

ROCHELLE drew a file from the cabinet. He moved swiftly, despite his limp, as he returned to the desk. He threw down the folded file with triumph and showed elation as he stared at the perplexed South American.

"I say," repeated Rochelle, with emphasis, "that millions would be lost through your plans. I also maintain that I am acquainted with your work. Let me add: millions lost by some are millions gained by others. You, Alvarez Menzone, would gain where others would lose."

"You accuse me—"

"I have the facts." Rochelle grinned fiendishly. "This file, señor, is a complete record of your past. Let us see what Alvarez Menzone has done!"

Rochelle opened the file. While Menzone clenched and unclenched his fists, the man with the limp calmly proceeded with his denunciation.

"The great nitrate swindle," he remarked, "had its inception at Antofagasta, in 1919. A certain Alvarez Menzone was the originator of that hapless scheme. It passed into other hands—with profit to Menzone—who left Chile shortly afterward. The bubble burst; those who remained were the ones who took the blame.

"We turn to Bahia, in 1921. We find Alvarez Menzone engaged in the promotion of a steamship line for the Amazon River. This comes close to transportation, señor. Half a million was subscribed;

yet steamships were never purchased. The funds of the Amazon steamship line disappeared very mysteriously.

"The defunct airport at Asuncion, Paraguay. That was another scheme of transportation which failed in 1924. Presumably, the time for such development of airlines had not yet arrived. Actually, the failure of the Asuncion airport can be attributed to the scheming of its promoter—Alvarez Menzone."

Rochelle paused to study his visitor. Menzone's face was set. Rochelle waited.

"Continue," ordered the South American.

"Bogota, Colombia, 1926," read Rochelle. "An expansion of the traction lines, to develop the outlying sections of the city. That was a double swindle. Rusted tracks—vacant lots—those alone remain as testimony to the loss of many thousands.

"Lima, Peru, in 1929. A remarkable scheme to develop airlines radiating from the Peruvian capital. Such lines now exist, but they are not the ones proposed by Alvarez Menzone. The overthrow of the existing government in Peru was given as the cause for failure; actually, the swindling methods of Alvarez Menzone were responsible."

"Continue." Menzone's tone showed confidence.

"La Paz, Bolivia, 1930," remarked Rochelle. "You were there at that time, Menzone; but something went wrong with your plans. You appeared in Caracas, in 1931. You started plans for a coastal steamship line in the Venezuelan city. That, too, came to an unexpected conclusion.

"From then on—nothing until now. But I can fill the gap, thanks to our mutual friend, Maurice Twindell. He tells me that you have come from Buenos Aires. That is quite likely. Argentina would naturally have attracted you. It was one country which you had not favored with your swindling presence.

"Financial conditions have not been good in the Argentine. So we find you here in Washington, *Señor* Swindler, ready to start a gigantic project in a country where your ways are not known."

Rochelle rested back in his chair, when he had finished his impeachment. He was studying Alvarez Menzone as he had studied Croydon Herkimer. The swindler, however, was less perturbed than the profiteer had been.

"Your facts are interesting," declared Menzone. "What do you intend to do with them,*señor?*"

"That," returned Rochelle, archly, "depends entirely upon you, my good friend."

MENZONE appeared mildly quizzical. Rochelle chuckled. Menzone was the type of man whom he had expected. A swindler deluxe, unperturbed by thoughts of exposure: such was the surface impression. Yet Rochelle knew that his visitor was actually playing a bold, though losing, game.

"Perhaps," mused Rochelle, "I could find a way to endorse your present plans, *señor*. It may be that you are a leopard who can change his spots. Tell me—what has been your reception at the South American legations?"

"A welcome one," returned Menzone calmly. "In fact, *señor*, I can say that they are more friendly toward plans for commercial development than they are for proposals of mere peace.

"Perhaps—this is only a suggestion, *señor*—I might make the way easy for someone such as yourself. The legations, *señor*, do not have those files which you have showed me."

"But should they gain them," parried Rochelle, "your visit to Washington would be ended, *señor*."

Rochelle had struck home. Menzone knew it. The South American bowed. It was his signal of defeat. Rochelle understood the gesture. He arose and stamped around his desk. He came to a limping pause as he neared Menzone's chair. Leaning on his cane, he clapped his free hand upon his visitor's shoulder.

"Look!" he ordered.

Menzone turned in the direction of Rochelle's gaze. The man with the limp turned out his hand and pointed to the globe of the world. He gave the sphere a twirl; he stopped it so that the continent of South America was predominant.

"There," declared Rochelle, "is the empire which I intend to rule! Ah, *señor*. You are surprised! You do not see how a man of peace can gain a continent. That is because I have deceived you. I am a man who seeks war—not peace.

"You said that we had much in common. You were right—but you did not know that your pretended statement was a true one. Your game has been to talk of South American development while you pocket profits. My game has been to further international strife while I scheme for warfare.

"Look! You who know South America will understand. Paraguay has warred upon Bolivia, in hope of gaining Gran Chaco. Let us suppose that Colombia and Ecuador should ally to gain disputed territory from Brazil and Peru. What would then result, *señor?*"

"An alliance for defense," responded Menzone, with a leer that matched Rochelle's. "The Acre dispute would be forgotten."

"And Venezuela?" Rochelle laid his finger on the globe.

"Ah, *señor!*" exclaimed Menzone, in crafty delight. "I see it now! Bolivar freed Colombia from Spain. He was from Venezuela. His countrymen have not forgotten the land which they think is theirs. Venezuela would join with Brazil and Peru!"

Half rising, Menzone thrust a long finger forward and tapped the portion of the map which represented

Bolivia. A second finger extended widely, to rest upon Peru. Menzone's hand moved.

"An alliance here!" expressed Menzone. "Peru and Bolivia, to regain provinces wrested from them years ago by Chile. South America torn by war, *señor*!"

"Exactly," smiled Rochelle. "What do you think of Argentina, *señor*?"

"Neutral—for a time," returned Menzone. "The same with Uruguay. Buenos Aires and Montevideo are close, *señor*." He clasped his hands together in an indicative gesture. "But they will join, *señor*, on one side or the other."

"Good," decided Rochelle. "I value your opinion, *señor*. But I can tell"—he was limping back to the desk—"the question that is in your mind. A continent is ready for war. How will it start? Am I right? Is that your question?"

"*Si, señor*," nodded Menzone eagerly.

"There," declared Rochelle, "is the empire which I intend to rule!"

"The making of war," declared Rochelle, "is in my safe. Documents—chiefly correspondence—have been obtained to set a continent ablaze. Messages have passed between the governments of South American nations and their Washington legations. Other messages have come to the State Department of the United States.

"Singly, these documents are of little value. Released at once, in different capitals, they will create havoc. In preparation for the Pan-American Convention, the authorities of every South American country have expressed their views very plainly—too plainly—on the matter of boundaries."

"I can see," laughed Menzone.

"Yes," resumed Rochelle. "What, for instance, would happen in Colombia and Ecuador if the people of Bogota and Quito learned that Peru, in settling the Acre question with Brazil, should express a desire to extend northern and western boundaries into Colombia and Ecuador?"

"There would be excitement in Colombia and Ecuador," decided Menzone.

"Excitement?" Rochelle laughed. "There would be riot! Jingoists in Bogota and Quito would dominate popular thought. Those factions, Menzone, are waiting for my word. Only one step prevents the completion of my plan.

"A few nights ago"—Rochelle eyed Menzone narrowly—"the attaché of a certain foreign legation was attacked while on the speedway—across the Potomac River. I am speaking of Lito Carraza. You have heard the name?"

"I read about him in the newspapers, señor. In fact, I had passed the very spot not long before."

"You know the man I mean. That is sufficient. My plans, Menzone, have passed the mere state of creating havoc in Colombia and Ecuador. They are also ready to cause retaliatory measures in Peru, Brazil, and Venezuela. To reach perfection, they must justify Bolivia's entrance into the grand alliance.

"The correspondence which Lito Carraza carried would have created the result that I desired. The papers are now safely guarded—in the vault of Carraza's legation. To obtain them, I need a man who can gain access to that embassy: one whose craft is equal to the task of entering the vault unseen."

"Difficult," suggested Menzone. "You would need a man, señor, who could discover the combination of the vault."

"No. I possess the combination. My espionage has been far-reaching. But I am afraid to entrust the task to mere safecrackers. Failure would disturb my final plans. Suppose"—Rochelle was tapping the file on his desk—"that this information should be forgotten. Would that promise spur you to do the work I want?"

Menzone smiled broadly. This was an offer that evidently pleased him.

"I am at your service, señor," he declared. "But you have forgotten one thing. What good will it be for me to interest American capital in railways for the southern continent? If war is to break loose—"

"You are wise," interposed Rochelle. "But you need have no worry of the future. First, by working swiftly, you can start your scheme. War will end it; you will not be blamed when millions of dollars are lost.

"Then afterward—if you continue to serve me well—your opportunity will come. You will have a place in my empire, Menzone! Beginning with tonight"—Rochelle's tone brooked no opposition—"you are in my service. If you succeed in gaining the correspondence that I require, there will be further work for you.

"Your activities will be covered by your railway promotion, just as mine are covered by the International Peace Alliance. If you succeed, Menzone, you will become my chief aide. Then you will learn the secrets of my system. Do you accept?"

"Si, señor," responded Menzone, with a knowing smile.

"That is well," laughed Rochelle. He tapped the file in significant fashion. "If you had refused, the publication of the truth about you would be my answer. Remember, Menzone"—Rochelle was adopting the tone that he had used with Herkimer—"that you have no alternative. I hold you thus."

Leering, the limping fiend extended his left hand and clenched it like a fist.

AGAIN, Menzone bowed. His smile, however, showed that the arrangement was satisfactory to him. Rochelle gleamed with evil satisfaction.

"You are in my service." Rochelle reached into a desk drawer and produced a small pamphlet. "Therefore, you may receive communications from me. You may also be forced to talk with me, by telephone—or with others in my service.

"For this purpose, we use the rudiments of the new international language—Agro. You can learn it from this little book. It is simple and easily understood. Keep the pamphlet until you have learned its contents. Be sure that it reaches no hands other than your own.

"Between now and the night when I shall require your aid, you can master this simple language. When I give the word for action, you will obey."

"With pleasure, señor," declared Menzone, with another bow.

"Come." Rochelle arose. "Our meeting is ended. Remember its details, Menzone. You can come here, when necessary. Our pretended activities in the cause of peace will be sufficient coverage."

Limping to the anteroom, Darvin Rochelle conducted his visitor to the marble staircase. Leaning on his cane, Rochelle watched Menzone's departure. As an attendant opened the front door, Menzone turned toward the stairway. At the top, he saw Rochelle, his left hand raised in token of farewell.

As Menzone gazed, Rochelle's clinging fingers formed a fist. It was a reminder of Rochelle's power. Menzone's answer was a glittering smile: the recognition of one schemer for another.

The outer door closed. Darvin Rochelle strode haltingly back into his office, to find Thurk, the dwarf awaiting.

"Sovo," declared Rochelle. "Exat vodo zo sovo sovo. Co kay zee toko, Thurk. Kay zay sovo sovo."

A pause; then with a wise gleam in his eye, Rochelle added, warningly:

"Alk alk zee thone, Thurk. Bole zee fela—foro."

The dwarf grinned and nodded. Darvin Rochelle, still thinking of Alvarez Menzone, clenched his left fist. Thurk copied the gesture.

Rochelle chuckled. His agents had never attempted to betray him, for he held them in his power. Alvarez Menzone would be like the rest. But should a final emergency arise, there was one upon whom Rochelle could rely without fail. That one was Thurk.

The evil-faced dwarf was completely the creature of the insidious fiend whom he served.

CHAPTER XIII
THE THEFT

THE lights of a large embassy were aglow. A diplomatic function of consequence was taking place upon this evening. Situated near a broad avenue, the building formed a spot of interest to people who were driving past in the direction of the northwest.

This embassy housed the legation of which Lito Carraza was a member. The gay function now in progress was a prelude to the opening of the Pan-American Convention, which was scheduled to begin upon the morrow.

The ambassador, a dignified, bearded South American, was attired in military uniform. Formerly a general in the army of his native land, he adopted this attire at important receptions. Kindly faced, this elderly ambassador lacked the warlike pose that might have been expected by those who viewed his medalled chest.

As proof that his thoughts turned to peace rather than war, the ambassador was listening with nods of approval to the talk of Darvin Rochelle. The head of the International Peace Alliance, surrounded by a lionizing throng, was beaming with good will as he discussed his favorite subject—that of friendship between nations.

"South America!" Rochelle was enthusiastic, as he leaned upon his cane. "One great country, gentlemen. A continent divided into separate nations, it is true, but all have the same purpose. All but one speak the same language; and that one has a kindred tongue. All are republics. It is the new world that shows the example to the old!"

Murmurs of approval greeted this statement. Most of the listeners were Spanish-Americans; diplomats, they understood the English phrases which Rochelle uttered. The spirit of good will seemed to prevail, with Darvin Rochelle as its sponsor.

Alvarez Menzone was present. A guest at the embassy function, the shrewd-faced adventurer was avoiding the limelight. Although away from the group of which Rochelle was the center, Menzone could catch the words that the other said. Also, Menzone was close enough to overhear the talk between two other men—Americans—who had drawn away from the group about Rochelle.

"Fine words," one was saying. "Rochelle is an idealist. That is all."

"They're drinking it in," commented the second American.

"What of it?" questioned the first. "It's the kind of talk they like. *Libertad*! Shout that word among a lot of South Americans and they raise a bigger cheer than a Japanese *banzai*. But when they come to settle things among themselves, nationalism runs riot."

"This Pan-American Convention is—"

"*Bah*! Soapsuds! It looks good because they're away from home. Wait until they get back where they belong. I'm giving you the truth when I say that the undercurrent of South American antagonism is tremendous."

The speakers moved away. Alvarez Menzone smiled. These Americans were discussing the very facts that Darvin Rochelle had mentioned. South America, like a volcano with a dozen craters, was ready for eruption.

MENZONE strolled past groups of courteous diplomats and attachés. Men in resplendent uniforms; others in evening dress; all were bowing and exchanging greetings. Spanish and English were intermingled languages.

Again, Menzone stopped by a spot where two Americans were speaking in low tones. He flicked his cigarette into an ornate receiver as he paused to listen.

"Do you catch the chatter?" one man was asking

the other. "Nothing about Bolivia and Paraguay. You'd think that Gran Chaco didn't exist."

"I heard Rochelle spouting peace and good will" was the reply. "It was going over big. Two thirds of the listeners were in uniform. That's irony, isn't it?"

"They like their wars in South America. Things have been too quiet there. Old-fashioned warfare was their business. Believe me, they're all watching modern methods in Gran Chaco. If they like them, it may be just too bad."

Menzone strolled onward. He reached a side room, and drew a cigarette case from his pocket. He extracted a cigarette, placed it between his lips, and looked for a match. He had none. Moving a few paces, he approached a stocky man who was staring toward the reception hall.

"A match, *señor*?"

The man turned at Menzone's question. His hand, moving to his pocket, stopped. Menzone's keen eyes met those of a firm-faced fellow, who could not conceal the sudden recognition that had gripped him.

The man whom Alvarez Menzone had accosted was Vic Marquette. In an instant, the Secret Service operative had recognized the South American as the one whom he had trailed from the Club Rivoli.

"A match, *señor*?"

The manner in which Menzone repeated the question showed apparent failure to observe the look of surprise upon the face of Vic Marquette. The Secret Service man produced a pack of matches. Menzone accepted them with thanks. He lighted his cigarette and returned the pack. He strolled onward. Vic Marquette watched him.

A thin smile crept over Menzone's lips. The man's sallow face seemed craftier than ever.

Menzone had been more observant than Vic Marquette had supposed. Placing his cigarette between his lips, Menzone puffed in thoughtful fashion as he returned toward the group with which Darvin Rochelle was stationed.

"It is late." Rochelle was beaming as he spoke. "I have a busy day tomorrow, gentlemen. I am preparing a copious report upon the subject of international relationship. It will be read in full at the Pan-American Convention."

Warm, enthusiastic handshakes were extended. All moved away with the exception of the ambassador. Side by side with Darvin Rochelle, the uniformed diplomat moved toward the doorway.

The pair paused close by the spot where Alvarez Menzone was standing. An attaché approached the ambassador. As the bearded man turned to speak to him, Rochelle edged closer to Menzone. He did not look at the suave South American; Menzone, in turn, was staring toward the door as he puffed his cigarette. The words that they exchanged, however, were audible.

"Alk kade," murmured Rochelle, in Agro. "Bole zee rike. Bole veek rema. Deek ake alkro gomo exat vodo. Bole reef folo folo."

"Fee," returned Menzone, scarcely moving his lips. "Alk zay fela."

Rochelle was turning to the ambassador. He limped beside the diplomat as they continued toward the door. Alvarez Menzone remained, totally indifferent to the passage of the pair.

NO one had overheard the conversation in Agro. No one would have understood the words had they been overheard. Secretly—yet with positive surety—Rochelle had told Menzone that he was leaving. He had instructed Menzone to remain at the embassy; to act later. He had added that Menzone was to come to his home tonight, bringing the papers.

Menzone, in return, had given an affirmative reply of understanding, with the added statement that he was ready.

Menzone's long fingers dipped into his pocket. Apparently, they were seeking a match or a cigarette. Actually, they were obtaining a most important slip of paper: the combination to the embassy vault.

Watching eyes were on Alvarez Menzone. They were the eyes of Vic Marquette. The Secret Service operative was peering from the adjoining room. He had not noticed the exchange of words between Alvarez Menzone and Darvin Rochelle. He was watching Menzone alone.

The tall South American strolled away. Vic kept him in sight. There was nothing in Menzone's actions that could excite new suspicion; yet Vic was determined to pursue his quarry. The longer he watched, the more decided he became.

The very fact that Menzone was moving about in purposeless fashion convinced Marquette that the South American had a special reason for being here. Vic was determined to learn that reason. He saw Menzone pass into a side room. Vic waited, then followed.

The Secret Service operative went by a huge curtain. He kept on. The moment that he passed, Menzone stepped into view and doubled on his tracks. Keeping to the wall of the reception room, the sallow-faced South American gained a hallway. He followed it and reached a door.

Slowly, Menzone turned the knob. He opened the door cautiously. He saw a heavy-browed attaché seated at a table, reading a Latin-American newspaper. With catlike stealth, Menzone crouched. As he launched himself for a spring, the attaché turned.

The man started to cry out; he was too late.

Menzone's swift attack bowled over the man and the chair in which he sat. So powerful was the sweeping spring that the attaché did not catch a glimpse of his attacker's face. A springing form that overturned him helpless, upon the thick carpeting. That was the only impression that the victim received.

Pinning his powerless opponent face downward on the floor, Menzone clamped the victim's hands behind his back. With a quick sweep, he snapped the man's belt buckle and whisked the belt away, His knee in the fellow's back, he bound the man's wrists.

The attaché started to cry out. Menzone flattened him and suppressed him with a firm hand. He used the man's handkerchief for a gag. Then, with snarled words in Spanish that warned his victim not to struggle, Menzone arose.

THIS room had heavy curtains. They were held with stout, ropelike cords. Menzone removed these and returned to the man on the floor. He completed the binding in expert fashion. Trussed hand and foot, the attaché could not escape.

All the while, the cowed captive had lain face downward. He had not caught an identifying glimpse of the attacker. Menzone, turning his eyes toward a huge vault at the other end of the room, saw that his coming work would give the prisoner a chance to observe him. With a slight laugh, Menzone settled that matter. He turned out the light, as he drew a flashlight from his pocket.

By the glimmer of a small torch, Menzone approached the vault. He drew forth the paper that bore the combination. Working smoothly, he turned the knobs. He swung the door open and focused his flashlight within.

The interior of the vault showed various compartments, marked with South American titles. Menzone found the one he wanted. He opened it and rapidly fingered sheaves of papers. He drew forth the packet that he sought.

A few minutes later, Alvarez Menzone appeared at the door of the darkened room. He regained the hall, made his way along it and reached the reception room. Pressing a cigarette between his lips, he plucked a match from a stand. The flicker of a flame showed a thin smile on Menzone's lips.

The South American strolled across the reception room. Vic Marquette, coming from a side room, suddenly spied the man whom he had been seeking. To all appearances, Menzone had not been out of the reception room. Yet Marquette had searched there, without finding him.

Chagrined, the Secret Service operative watched Menzone stroll about, then prepare for his departure. Vic, although his suspicions still persisted, decided not to follow. He had made one bull trailing Alvarez Menzone upon another night. He knew where the man could be reached. Vic remained as Menzone left.

TEN minutes afterward, an excited attaché appeared in the reception room. Most of the guests had left. Hence, the man's wild gestures were not noticed as he passed the word to another member of the legation. The second man gesticulated, motioning the informant away. Calming himself, the man who had received the news, started off to speak to the ambassador.

Vic Marquette hurried to the passage which the first attaché had taken. He saw a light from an opened door near the end of the hall. He hastened to that spot. He viewed two men: one the attaché who had brought the news; the second, a helpless attaché bound and gagged upon the floor. Beyond was an opened vault.

The ambassador arrived. With alarmed eyes, he stared at the two men; one freeing the other from his bonds. He saw Vic Marquette. The Secret Service operative showed his badge. The ambassador nodded. He made for the vault, with Vic beside him.

Scurrying attachés were entering. The ambassador addressed them in Spanish. He told them to go back to the reception room; to give no indication of the fact that trouble had occurred here. All left, save the ambassador, the first two attachés, and Vic Marquette.

As the ambassador began his inspection of the opened vault, a motion occurred at the end of the darkened hall. A window moved noiselessly upward. A dim form was outlined in the space. Silent footsteps approached the lighted doorway. Like a specter, The Shadow viewed the scene within the room.

The ambassador had turned to Vic Marquette. Soberly, the grizzled diplomat was announcing his discovery.

"Important correspondence has been stolen," he declared, in English. "It is serious, *señor*. Very serious."

The ambassador paused, then resumed:

"It is the correspondence, *señor*, which was carried by Lito Carraza, the night that men sought to kill him across the river."

"So they got it, eh?" growled Vic. "What's this fellow got to say?"

He pointed to the attaché who had been found on the floor. The ambassador quizzed his aide in Spanish. The man replied. Vic understood the words; the ambassador, not knowing this, went on to translate them.

"He cannot identify his assailant, *señor*,"

explained the ambassador. "He says that he was struck down suddenly. The man who opened the vault, turned off the lights. He used a little light of his own.

"*Señor* Fourrier must learn of this. We must notify him at once. Nothing must be said. Those papers are important, but their existence must be kept a secret. It would be a terrible mistake, *señor*, to let this be known just before the Pan-American Convention."

"I understand," nodded Marquette. "Do you suspect anyone of this robbery?"

"No, *señor*," returned the ambassador with a shake of his head. "It is incomprehensible."

Vic Marquette stood silent while the ambassador closed the vault. Evidently the head of the legation was anxious to suppress the news of robbery. It was Vic Marquette's duty to comply. Nevertheless, the operative could not restrain an assurance which he felt.

At the doorway of the room, he stopped the ambassador and made a cautious statement of the suspicions which he held.

"I was watching a man who was here tonight," explained Vic. "A South American—not connected with an embassy. He was out of sight a while before this happened. If he's the robber, you can count on me to get him."

"His name?" questioned the ambassador eagerly.

"Alvarez Menzone," replied Marquette.

"An invited guest," explained an attaché, who had overheard the name. "He is here to obtain capital for railroads in South America—"

"I recall him," interposed the ambassador. "I would not have suspected him of theft. Do you feel sure—"

"I'm going to trace him," interrupted Marquette. "I'll take the matter up with my chief. I simply wanted you to know that I'm starting with a clue."

They had reached the hall. The ambassador was nodding with a show of satisfaction. Side by side with Vic Marquette, the uniformed diplomat moved toward the reception room, with the attachés following.

DARKNESS moved in the hallway past the door from which the men had come. Keen eyes beneath a broad-brimmed slouch hat watched the departure. The quartet reached the reception room. The Shadow stood alone.

With piercing gaze, The Shadow stared into the lighted room which held the closed vault. Then, with a quick turn that brought a swish from the black cloak which shrouded his form, the mysterious visitor departed by the way he had come.

The window closed noiselessly. A figure glided through the gloom at the side of the embassy building. The whispered tone of a weird, knowing laugh came from concealed lips.

The Shadow had arrived after the theft had been completed. He had seen the ambassador's discovery that the correspondence had been stolen. He had heard the plans to keep the matter quiet. He had learned of Vic Marquette's new suspicions of Alvarez Menzone.

The Shadow's own agent—Harry Vincent—was covering Menzone. The Shadow, himself, had appeared in the vicinity of Athena Court. Yet The Shadow had not made his secret entrance into the embassy until after Alvarez Menzone had left, with stolen correspondence in his pocket.

Why had The Shadow failed to appear beforehand? What was the answer to the passive, hidden part that he was playing?

Only The Shadow knew!

CHAPTER XIV
THE CODE BOOK

ON the evening following the robbery at the embassy, Harry Vincent was seated in Alvarez Menzone's living room going over statistics which pertained to the South American's railway projects.

Menzone was also present. He had assigned this duty to Harry. Relieved of detail, Menzone was reading newspaper accounts that concerned the opening of the Pan-American Convention.

"Ah!" Menzone spoke to Harry. "Here is an account of the embassy affair. The one that I attended last night. It was very fine, Vincent. Sorry that I could not take you along."

There was a dryness in Menzone's tone that caught Harry's prompt attention. It seemed as though Menzone were enjoying a little joke of his own. Harry was unconvinced of Menzone's actions on the preceding night. Menzone had left early to attend the embassy function. He had returned about midnight. Harry, supposedly asleep, had heard him enter the study. Harry had sneaked to the door to watch.

He had seen Menzone studying a stack of papers. He had noted a gleam of satisfaction on the South American's face. Then Harry had dropped out of sight, to watch Menzone tiptoe from the apartment. It was after one when Menzone finally returned.

What was the purpose of these secretive actions? That was a question which baffled Harry Vincent. He had left a coded report for The Shadow, behind the fire extinguisher in the hallway. But there had been no word from The Shadow in return.

Working on statistics, Harry found his thoughts reverting to Menzone. He was convinced that the South American's railroad plans were a cover for some other operation. Yet Harry had discovered nothing concerning Menzone's secret business.

The telephone bell began to ring from the study. Harry arose from his chair. Menzone, also rising, waved his secretary back.

"Keep on with your work, Vincent," he said, in his peculiarly accented style. "Allow me to answer the telephone."

Was Menzone expecting the call? Harry decided that such must be the case. He saw Menzone enter the study. He saw the door close—but it did not fully shut. Laying his work aside, Harry tiptoed to the study door.

MENZONE was at the telephone. Harry could see him through the opened crack. The South American had drawn a small booklet from his pocket. He had it in readiness as he spoke.

"Fee," Menzone was saying. "Alk zay fela."

For a moment, Harry took the words for Spanish. Then the unfamiliar sound impressed him. Drawing a pencil and an envelope from his pocket, Harry jotted down the odd words that he had heard, spelling them in phonetic fashion.

"Sovo," Menzone was saying. "Bole bota atex vodo of alta... Alk rofe folo folo bole rojo..."

Menzone was listening. His smile increased as he thumbed the little book on the table before him. Then, in a tone of finality, he declared:

"Alk deek kire... Fee... Sake hoda. Seek alta eeta... Kye kye deek rema. Reen alk kode... Alk deek deek rema."

Harry was copying these words as the receiver clicked. He looked up hastily, just in time to see Menzone open a desk drawer and thrust the little book away. Menzone locked the drawer. This delay was fortunate. It gave Harry, still copying the final words, time to scurry back to the living room.

When Menzone arrived, Harry was back at work. The envelope was in his pocket. Menzone glanced at his watch. He noted the time as eight o'clock.

"I am going out," he announced. "I shall be back within an hour. Remain here, Vincent."

The moment that Menzone had left, Harry sprang to his feet. He approached the window. He saw Menzone arrive on the sidewalk below. The South American was carrying his briefcase of papers. Harry saw him hail a cab.

Apparently, Menzone was on his way to hold a conference with persons interested in his enterprises. Such would have been Harry's final decision, but for one fact—the oddly worded phone conversation which Menzone had held.

Harry realized that he had listened to an unintelligible language. The words which he had heard would prove useful in deciphering it; but they were comparatively few. The real key lay in the little book that Menzone had dropped in the desk drawer.

Hurrying to the study, Harry extracted a set of keys from his pocket. He found one that fitted the lock. He opened the drawer. He discovered the pamphlet. There was no wording on its paper cover. The title page, however bore this statement:

Rudiments of Agro.

On the next page, Harry discovered short explanatory paragraphs. They were followed by a vocabulary of words. Seizing pencil and paper, Harry began to jot down notes in shorthand, that he might copy the body of the pamphlet and leave the little booklet for Menzone's return.

These were specimens of the notations which Harry made:*

Agro, a phonetic language... Certain letters omitted... C, hard like K... Vowels pronounced as the letters themselves... Spelling "za" to be read as "zay."

Opposites expressed by a reversal of their syllables. "Doto"—"large." "Todo"—"small." Plurals, a repetition of the word... "Sak" - "hour"; "sak sak"—"hours"... Possessives, add "ro" before or after the word... Example: "Ki"—"they;" kiro"—"theirs."

Harry began to study the vocabulary. Here he found a list of words and began to write them as rapidly as possible. In capital letters, he noted the Agro words; after them, words in parentheses that were evidently the pronunciations as they would sound in English; these pronunciations appeared only where necessary:

all	OPO
always	FORO
at	OD (ode)
bad	VOSO
bring	RAF (rafe)
will bring	REF (reef)
brought	ROF (rofe)
careful	THON (thone)
come	DAK (dake)
will come	DEK (deek)
came	DOK (doke)
day	DOVO
do	VAK (vake)
will do	VEK (veek)
did	VOK (voke)
go	CAD (kade)
will go	CED (keed)

*Note: When he reached this point of his narrative, The Shadow supplied me with a copy of the Agro code book. It consisted of a pamphlet of some 28 pages, printed in small type. In preparing this chronicle, I have not attempted to provide the complete vocabulary as copied by Harry Vincent, as space would not permit. Instead, I have included only those words required to translate all the Agro conversations which appear in this story.   MAXWELL GRANT

went.................COD (kode)
good.................SOVO
have.................PANO
will have..........PENO
had...................PONO
heard...............TABA
will hear...........TEBA (teeba)
heard...............TOBA
hour.................SAK (sake)
house...............GOMO
here.................RIK (rike)
is......................ZA (zay)
will be..............ZE (zee)
was...................ZO
later.................REMA
minute..............SEK (seek)
no.....................EF (eef)
now..................GOLO
need.................RAJO
will need..........REJO
needed.............ROJO
night................VODO
paper................FOLO
ready................FELA
see....................ATO
will see.............ETO
saw...................OTO
second..............SOK (soke)
send.................FAR (fare)
will send..........FER (feer)
sent..................FOR (fore)
sooner..............AMER (ameer)
tell...................BATA
will tell............BETA (beeta)
told..................BOTA
then.................LOGO
there................KIR (kire)
this..................EXAT
that..................ATEX
to.....................AK (ake)
useful..............TOKO
when...............REN (reen)
yes..................FE (fee)

she...........KE (key)..........her
it..............KI (kye)
they..........KI KI (kye kye) ...them

one........... ALTA six........FODA
two.......... BODA seven......GODA
three........CODA eight......HODA
four.......... DODA nine........ITA
five...........ETA (eeta)zero.......JODA

more.........FO (foe)
less...........OF (oaf)

HARRY was impressed by the vocabulary, as he jotted down these words among many more. He noted how words were opposites: *dovo* and *vodo*—day and night; *rik* and *kir*—here and there. He was also impressed by the verbs; how the simple change of a single letter made the tense present, future, or past. While wondering about adjectives, he came across a notation which stated that the repetition of such a word gave it comparative or superlative degree. The example was "*voso*" for "bad;" "*voso voso*" for "very bad."

Then came the table of pronouns and numerals. These formed a simplified group:

I..............ALK..............me.
we...........ALK ALK..........us.
you..........BOL (bole)
he............KA (kay).........him.

Harry noted the alphabetical arrangement of the numerals. The entire pamphlet contained but a few hundred terms and he rapidly completed his copying. Then, with eagerness, Harry brought the jotted envelope from his pocket. He was anxious to learn what Menzone had said over the telephone.

"Fee. Alk zay fela."

Harry wrote this first in simplified Agro; then beneath it, the English translation, gained from a search through the vocabulary.

Fe. Alk za fela.

"*Yes. I am ready.*"

Harry continued:

Sovo. Bol bota atex vodo of alta.

"*Good. You said that night less one.*"

Harry pondered. The phrase "night less one" puzzled him. Then he caught the meaning. He inscribed, the corrected sentence: "*You said that last night.*"

Alk rofe folo folo bole rojo became: "*I brought the papers you needed.*"

Harry took the last phrases more rapidly:

Alk deek kire... Fee... Sake hoda. Seek alta eeta. Kye kye deek rema. Reen alk kode... Alk deek deek rema.

"*I shall come there... Yes... Hour eight. Minute one five. They will come later. When I have left... I shall return later.*"

Harry saw quickly that "hour eight, minute one five" simply meant fifteen minutes after eight. The system of notation, in Agro, was reduced to nine digits and a cipher, numbers being formed as one would give a telephone number in English.

He also observed that "*deek deek,*" literally "shall come shall come" signified "shall come back." The word "the" was not used regularly in Agro, but Harry found a notation that "co" meant "the" whenever necessary. A simple example was given: "*co ka,*" literally "the him" meant "the man." "*Co ki ki,*" literally "the them," meant "the men."

Harry deposited the code book back in the drawer. He knew that he had made a remarkable discovery. This unfamiliar language, Agro, was obviously the means of communication between crooks who were working toward a common cause. Alvarez Menzone was a member of that band. He was keeping an appointment at present—where, Harry did not know—with some other malefactor.

These facts must go to The Shadow!

Harry glanced at his watch. It was nearly nine o'clock. Menzone might be back at anytime. Harry began to fold the sheets that he had copied. He stopped, fancying that he heard footsteps in the hallway.

It could not be José. The lazy Filipino had retired before eight o'clock. Was Menzone making a surreptitious return?

Harry listened intently. He decided that his imagination must be working. He turned his gaze downward toward the papers that he was folding. Again the sound. Harry looked up quickly. The door to the room was open. Standing there, a revolver in his hand, was a stocky, hard-faced man.

"Where is Menzone?" came the rasped question.

A dawning recognition completed itself as Harry heard the words. He knew this intruder. It was Vic Marquette, of the Secret Service!

THE man at the door sensed Harry's expression. He advanced into the room. He eyed Harry closely. He lowered his revolver.

"Hello, Vincent," said Marquette. "What're you doing here?"

"Working as secretary for Alvarez Menzone," returned Harry promptly. "I've only had the job for about a week. Menzone is out at present."

Marquette became thoughtful. Harry Vincent was the man of whom he had spoken to Fourrier— the one whom Vic Marquette had good reason to class as an agent of The Shadow. Already Vic had come to a conclusion, namely that Harry's presence as Menzone's secretary was final proof that The Shadow was watching affairs in Washington.

Vic knew well that Harry would not—perhaps could not—make any statements that involved The Shadow's activities. At the same time, Harry Vincent could be sworn in as Vic's aide—and the Secret Service operative was ready to trust this man with whom he had teamed before.

"How soon will Menzone be back?" asked Vic.

"Any minute now." Harry's tone was anxious. "If he finds you here—"

"He's going to find me," interposed Marquette. "I'm going to nab that fellow, Vincent. What's more, you're going to help me."

Harry nodded. There was no alternative. The Shadow had given no instructions to cover an emergency such as this. On occasions where choice was needed, it was the part of The Shadow's agents to use their own discretion. Duty prompted Harry to side with Vic Marquette, in preference to Menzone.

"What's this?" Vic Marquette had spied the code book in the drawer. He brought it out. "Does this belong to Menzone?"

"Yes," returned Harry, seizing the opportunity. "Menzone is a crook—so far as I can see. He was talking on the telephone tonight, using an odd language. I unlocked the desk drawer after he had gone. I found the code book. I copied it in short-hand."

"Keep your copy," chuckled Vic. "I'm keeping the original. Say, Vincent—you've uncovered something. I know you're on the level. This is another time you'll be working with me on the showdown."

Harry produced the copy of Menzone's conversation. Vic Marquette chuckled and clapped his companion on the shoulder. He began to read Harry's translation. Harry watched him intently.

Neither man was observing the door. Neither saw the figure that appeared there, plainly framed: A tall, spectral form, clad in black cloak and hat. The Shadow, like Vic Marquette, had arrived at the apartment, occupied by Alvarez Menzone.

Watching with burning eyes, listening to the words that passed between his agent and the Secret Service operative, The Shadow was divining what had occurred. He heard Vic Marquette muttering the sentences which Harry had translated. As completely as if he had received a report from his agent, The Shadow was gathering the details that had brought about this scene.

"So that's the game, eh!" Marquette was saying. "No wonder those foxes have been dodging us. Agro—an international language. Say—I've run into some cuckoo lingoes, but this has them all stopped.

"There's a bigger bird in back of this, Vincent. This fellow Menzone is working for him. That's where Menzone has gone tonight—to see the big shot. We'll be ready for Menzone—you and I. When we meet him, we'll be on our way. We won't stop until we've met the big bird that's in back of him."

Vic Marquette arose as he spoke. The Secret Service man was ready to spread the snare for Menzone's return. The figure of The Shadow faded into darkness beyond the door. Silently, it issued from the hallway; swiftly it reached the living room and crossed to the outer door.

The final barrier closed behind The Shadow. The black form merged with the darkness of the stairs. Leaving Vic Marquette and Harry Vincent to trap Alvarez Menzone, The Shadow had left for the street below.

A whispered, sibilant laugh came from the darkness where The Shadow had passed, unseen.

CHAPTER XV
THURK STRIKES

DARVIN ROCHELLE was walking up the marble steps that led to the second floor of his palatial residence. He was carrying his cane; as he reached the top, he used it to aid his halting limp.

A smile beamed on the face of Darvin Rochelle. He had made his trip downstairs in company with Alvarez Menzone, after an excellent interview with that capable worker. He had spent a while on the ground floor; now he was returning to his office. It was nine o'clock and Rochelle was expecting another visitor.

Reaching the office, Rochelle found Thurk, the dwarf, crouching in a corner. Chuckling, Rochelle addressed his trusted minion:

"Kay kode. Kay zay sovo. Sovo sovo, Thurk. Alk rojo eef bole. Co kay atex deek golo. Kay zay voso. Alk rejo bole."

Rochelle's use of Agro displayed an interesting variant in the term, "*rojo eef.*" The use of the negative "*eef*" with the verb "*rojo*" signified "not." In English, the statement signified in full:*

"He has gone. He is good. Very good, Thurk. I did not need you. The man that is coming now. He is bad. I shall need you."

Thurk's eyes bulged. It was the dwarf's way of expressing eagerness. Crouching in his corner, Thurk's shape seemed monstrous. Long, thin arms, attached to a dumpy body, gave him the appearance of an octopus.

Rochelle returned to the door of the anteroom. He made a significant gesture and spoke the words:

"Bole kade golo."

Thurk understood the meaning: "Go there now." The dwarf arose. Rochelle continued through the anteroom and waited, steady as a statue, at the top of the stairs.

A FEW minutes passed. Rochelle saw his alert attendant step forward to open the front door. The servant below had spied someone approaching the house. Croydon Herkimer appeared as the door opened.

The bulky visitor saw Rochelle standing at the top of the stairs. He ascended to receive a welcome

*Note: Although Rochelle adapted English idioms to Agro, the language itself followed a form patterned after languages of Latin derivation. This was true of verbs. The word "bata," for example, could be interpreted as "come" or "is coming." Similarly, the past tense, "bota," meant "came" or "have come." Agro, as Rochelle himself stated, had not reached its completed stage. Rochelle had evidently postponed its further development while he used its simplified rudiments for the purpose of communication with his agents.   MAXWELL GRANT

greeting. Rochelle limped toward the office, with Herkimer following.

The man with the limp pointed to the chair at the side of the desk. Herkimer took it; Rochelle occupied his accustomed seat behind the desk.

"You have completed the arrangements?" he asked promptly.

"Yes," returned Herkimer. "Here is everything."

The profiteer produced a small portfolio that he had carried under his arm. He placed it upon the desk. Rochelle opened it. He began to go over sheets of statements. He chuckled.

"Companions in crime, eh?" he questioned. "The old guard—the others who shared your profiteering years ago. This is excellent, Herkimer. Excellent. You have done great work, providing me with these names."

"That was not my purpose!" exclaimed Herkimer in alarm. "I chose those firms because I knew they would work undercover—"

"You have simplified my task," interposed Rochelle serenely. "I can deal with them directly now. All that I have to do is study their past record. Then I can handle them as I handled you."

Herkimer showed repressed indignation. Crooked by nature, he was hypocrite enough to worry about his own reputation. He realized that he had played into Rochelle's hands.

"Do not be perturbed." Rochelle's tone was a suave purr. "All will go well with you, Herkimer. I am making matters easier for you. I shall reward you for your services. But first"—Rochelle was tapping on the desk—"I am going to take you into my confidence."

Herkimer shuddered as he met Rochelle's insidious gaze. He had a feeling that he was about to learn facts that he would prefer not to know.

"My plans are completed," declared Rochelle. "Six men have died, Herkimer, because I wanted them silenced. My only failure came with the seventh. I needed correspondence from a certain legation. I failed to obtain it through murder."

Again Herkimer shuddered. Rochelle continued:

"Then I obtained the services of a first-class lieutenant. Alvarez Menzone—a man from South America. He robbed the embassy vault. He gained the needed correspondence.

"I have sent the papers to the proper places. The first ones were of minor consequence. The final ones that Menzone brought were remarkable in their revelations. Their publication will create chaos—provided only that an act of violence is first committed.

"Tonight, Herkimer, I shall strike. I am assembling all of my minions. Each one will have an appointed task of murder. I shall depend upon my gang leader, Bugs Ritler, to show the way. He has assembled a crew of first-class cutthroats, Herkimer."

Rochelle drew a sealed envelope from his desk drawer. He flourished it before the eyes of his visitor.

"The names of nine men are in this envelope!" cackled Rochelle. "All are South Americans who at present are in Washington. Some are connected with legations. Others are here for the Pan-American Convention."

Rochelle's eyes steadied. His voice lowered to an insidious tone.

"All nine shall die tonight," he rasped. "Wholesale assassination. Their deaths will create tremendous indignation. Murder will be attributed to the agents of other South American nations. Then will come my revelations.

"You see the result, Herkimer? War—impending now—will be unleashed. Millions will be our profit. Millions, Herkimer! Wealth for you—an empire for me!"

Herkimer steadied his hands against the edge of the desk. He was gasping in horror.

"Not—murder!" Herkimer's voice showed fear of consequences. "I—I do not deal in murder, Rochelle!"

"What is warfare?" sneered Rochelle.

"Murder—perhaps," admitted Herkimer. "But it—it is not assassination. No—no—I cannot be a party to these crimes—"

"I talked with Menzone," remarked Rochelle quietly. "He left just before you arrived. He seemed pleased with my scheme. He will be here, with my other henchmen. When I choose men, Herkimer"—Rochelle's tone had hardened—"I pick those who prefer more than halfway measures.

"This is my ultimatum. You are with me—or against me. There is no middle course. Which is your choice?"

"I am against you!" exclaimed Herkimer. "That is my answer. You think that you hold me in your fist. You do—so long as you desist from your plan. If you attempt to expose my past, you will be forced to answer the charges that I bring against you."

"I shall deny them."

"Yes? I hardly think so. Your own activities will be curtailed. Your dreams of an empire will be ended."

ROCHELLE had arisen. He was leaning on his cane, as he glowered at Herkimer. The profiteer, encouraged by his own outburst, no longer feared the man before him.

"I shall make a bargain with you, Rochelle," he said shrewdly. "Give me back my list—give me the files which you hold concerning my past. Pay me a reasonable compensation for my silence. Then I shall do nothing to disturb your schemes of murder. Afterward, if your plans have succeeded, I shall be willing to deal with you—"

"Hypocrite!" snarled Rochelle. "It is not murder that repulses you. It is your own safety that you are considering. You want to make sure of profit—with no danger. You would like to hold the upper hand.

"You think that you can balk me. Try it. Compared to you, Herkimer, I am a benefactor of mankind. I cover my crimes, but I do not try to salve a selfish conscience. I refuse your terms. Again, I ask you for your answer."

"You shall get it," retorted Herkimer. "I have given you your last chance. You have refused it. I am leaving, Rochelle, and my first act will be to inform the Washington authorities of your insidious scheme. You have gone too deep to crawl out now. Try to expose my past. You will not be believed. That is my answer, Rochelle!"

Rochelle was gripping the desk with his free hand. He held his cane in his right. Herkimer, leaning forward, was watching it. Contemptuously, he was ready to risk a physical battle with Rochelle. It was in tune with Herkimer's character. Big and powerful, he was a coward at heart. A man of weak appearance—such as Rochelle—was the only type with whom he would seek a struggle.

Rochelle dropped the head of his cane against the desk. It seemed like a gesture of resignation. Herkimer laughed. He did not know that Rochelle had given an appointed signal. He did not know what was happening behind his back.

AS Rochelle's cane thudded against the desk, the upper hemisphere of the big globe opened. From its interior came the form of Thurk, the dwarf. The evil creature popped forth with the speed of a jumping jack.

In his long, scrawny hand, he held a long, thin-bladed knife. With only an instant's pause, Thurk swung forward and downward, to bury the death-dealing weapon deep between Croydon Herkimer's unprotected shoulders!

The profiteer sank without a gasp. His body crumpled to the floor upon a square rug that rested beneath his chair. Thurk leaped from the globe and scrambled forward to crouch above his victim. Rochelle stood with an evil smile upon his face.

"Bole voke sovo, Thurk," commended Rochelle. "Bole kade. Logo dake dake."

Properly interpreted, Rochelle had said:

"You have done well, Thurk. Go. Then come back."

The dwarf hoisted Herkimer's body upon his shoulders. Gleefully, he staggered from the room through the door that led to the spiral staircase in the rear. On the small rug where Herkimer had lain, a pool of blood remained as evidence of murder.

Rochelle went to a closet and brought out a rug of the same size, but of different pattern. He moved

With only an instant's pause, Thurk swung forward and downward.

the chair aside and placed the rug upon it. He went behind the desk. When Thurk returned, Rochelle pointed to the original rug with its blotting blood.

"*Alk rajo eef kye*," he said; in English: "I do not want it."

Thurk grinned. He folded the bloodstained rug and carried it from the room. The slight trace of crimson had seeped through. Rochelle covered it with the new rug and put the chair back in position. He closed the huge globe and resumed his customary chair.

The insidious leer on Rochelle's features betrayed the fiend's anticipation. To Darvin Rochelle, the violent death that Thurk had dealt to Croydon Herkimer was a mere appetizer to the feast of murder that was planned for this night of doom.

CHAPTER XVI
THE TRAP THAT FAILED

DARVIN ROCHELLE, most insidious of schemers, had laid a perfect death trap for Croydon Herkimer. Through it, the supercrook had dealt doom to a lesser exponent of evil. Herkimer had been willing to countenance death. His own demise was scarcely undeserved.

While Rochelle was still gloating over the crafty fashion in which he had disposed of the profiteer whom he no longer needed, another trap was awaiting a victim—elsewhere in Washington.

In the apartment on the third floor of Athena Court, Vic Marquette and Harry Vincent were lying in wait for Alvarez Menzone. Had Darvin Rochelle known this, his gloating would have turned to apprehension. Alvarez Menzone had become a most important cog in the criminal mechanism controlled by Rochelle.

Vic Marquette, swearing in Harry to service, had assumed full charge. Picking Menzone's living room as the strategic point, Vic had posted Harry behind a table opposite the door. In turn, Vic had chosen a corner by a bookcase. Vic had provided Harry with a revolver. Waiting, the pair was ready to trap Menzone the moment that he might appear.

Through the hush of the room came Vic's inquiring undertone—a question addressed to Harry Vincent:

"This Filipino of Menzone's—can he make trouble?"

"No." Harry's whisper was reassuring. "José is always asleep. We have not disturbed him. We can handle him easily if we raise a commotion in capturing Menzone."

"All right." Vic seemed satisfied. "I'm going to cover this fellow Menzone the moment he walks in. You back me up—and be ready to handle José if he appears."

"There's a back door," remarked Harry. "It leads to a hall by the fire tower. José could scramble that way; but he'll have to come into the passage from his room."

"Watch the passage then," ordered Vic. "After we bag Menzone, we're going to haul in the Filipino, too—even if he is stupid."

MINUTES ticked by. Vic had raised a window to a space of several inches. He heard a sound from the street. He motioned to Harry.

"Sounds like a taxi," warned Vic. "Maybe it's Menzone coming home."

"Listen for the automatic elevator," whispered Harry.

A minute; then came the dull, mechanical sound of the elevator. Both Harry and Vic were timing it. Both were sure that the elevator had reached the third floor when it stopped.

Had Alvarez Menzone returned? Or had some other dweller on this floor come up by the elevator? No footsteps could be heard. The answer depended upon whether or not the click of a key would sound at the apartment door.

A full minute. Harry and Vic decided that Menzone had not arrived; nevertheless, they were tense. Some trifling delay might have caused the South American to pause outside the door of his apartment.

Then came the unexpected. Harry Vincent, startled by the sound of a fierce snarl, turned quickly toward the opening to the passage that led by Menzone's study. Vic Marquette copied Harry's example.

Both men were staring at a tall, sallow-faced intruder who had appeared from the passage. It was Alvarez Menzone!

In his hand, the South American held a snub-nosed revolver. From his position, he had Harry Vincent and Vic Marquette on an almost direct line. The gleaming grin on Menzone's face; the fierce challenge that showed in his eyes—these were sufficient.

Helplessly, Harry Vincent and Vic Marquette dropped their revolvers and raised their hands. The trappers were trapped. Menzone's sneaking arrival had caught them unaware. The South American had entered from a direction that Vincent and Marquette had not considered.

"Ah, *senores*." Menzone's velvet tones showed hidden venom. "You have been awaiting me? Very kind of you. I regret that I was unable to oblige you by entering through the door which you were watching.

"Sometimes, *señores*, one remembers a trifling mistake that may cause trouble. Tonight, I recalled a little book which I had left in my desk. What if someone should have found it!

"Ah, *señores*, that is why I decided to come in from the back door, after I had ascended in the elevator. I was wise, eh? I have found a traitor and an enemy."

Menzone was moving into the living room as he spoke. An emphatic gesture of his gun hand brought understanding to Harry Vincent and Vic Marquette. With hands raised, the trapped trappers followed a beckoning motion. Menzone stepped aside and herded his prisoners toward the passage. Keeping them constantly covered with his revolver, he marched them into the study and forced them up against the wall.

Standing beyond the open door, Menzone uttered a sharp, hissing call for José. He repeated the cry. Its noise was penetrating. Menzone stepped into the study as José appeared. The Filipino entered, sleepily rubbing his eyes.

"Be ready, José," ordered Menzone, in Spanish. "I shall need you."

CALMLY keeping Harry and Vic covered, the South American seated himself at the desk. He called a number on the telephone. His eyes gleamed as he recognized the voice at the other end.

"Alt Mode," announced Menzone. These words, Harry recalled, were letter symbols of the Agro alphabet. A. M.—evidently an initialed proclamation of Menzone's identity.

"Boda co kye kye," stated Menzone. "Rike... Ode alkro gomo... Fee... Teeba alk alk kye kye?... Sovo... Bole feer co kye kye..."

Harry was grasping the meaning as Menzone hung up the receiver. The South American had been talking to his chief. This was the import of his words:

"Two men. Here... At my house... Yes... Shall we question them?... Good... You will send men..."

Vic Marquette stared blankly. He had not examined the Agro code book closely enough to gain even a crude understanding of the phonetic language. Menzone smiled. With a bow, he explained:

"You are fortunate, *señores*," he declared, in a sarcastic tone. "I have just talked with a man who is interested in your capture. He likes my suggestion that you be sent to him. He is making the necessary arrangements.

"You will have the pleasure, *señores*, of being present at a most important meeting that will be set for midnight. I shall be there—with many others. You will be questioned at that time. Perhaps, when persuaded, you will find it wise to talk."

He turned and spoke to José. The Filipino went from the study. He returned, bringing two lengths of rope, which Harry remembered having seen about a large, old-fashioned trunk in Menzone's bedroom.

Gripping José's right hand with his own left, Menzone drew it to his gun hand; with a deft movement, he passed the short-barreled revolver to José without uncovering the prisoners.

While José held Harry and Vic at bay, Menzone went to each in turn. With rapid skill he trussed the prisoners and left them seated on the floor. He whisked handkerchiefs from a desk drawer and used them as gags.

Vic Marquette recalled the bound attaché whom he had seen at the legation. He realized how cleverly the bonds had been applied to that man. He knew that Menzone was unquestionably the robber who had opened the ambassador's vault.

"Guard them," ordered Menzone, speaking in Spanish to José. "I shall leave the back door open. Men will come to take the prisoners. Remain here, José, until you hear from me. Be careful not to harm these prisoners. They will be needed later."

José grunted his understanding. Alvarez Menzone turned and leered viciously as he faced Harry Vincent and Vic Marquette; then his suave smile returned. The shrewd South American bowed ironically and strolled from the study, leaving José in charge. Harry and Vic heard the front door close, announcing his departure.

Vic Marquette's prediction was to be realized. Through an encounter with Alvarez Menzone, he and Harry Vincent were to meet the conspirator behind the schemes in which Menzone had played a single part. But they were not to meet that enemy as Vic had hoped. Helpless prisoners, they were to be carried to his domain!

Harry Vincent's thoughts were bitter. If only he had been able to notify The Shadow. Harry did not know that The Shadow had been here. He did not realize that he and Vic Marquette had been left to prepare their trap for Alvarez Menzone.

Two against one: snarers in ambush! The odds—seemingly—had been with Harry and Vic, yet the waiting pair had failed.

How much had The Shadow banked on their success? That was a question. The fact remained that Alvarez Menzone was unconquered.

Darvin Rochelle's lieutenant would keep the midnight meeting with his chief, despite the efforts of Harry Vincent and Vic Marquette. The two men upon whom The Shadow could most certainly rely had failed to ensnare Alvarez Menzone!

CHAPTER XVII
THE SHADOW WITHDRAWS

IT was nearly eleven o'clock. Clyde Burke was at the Club Rivoli. He had come here at The Shadow's bidding—in response to one of those mysterious communications that came at unexpected intervals.

Clyde's task tonight was a simple one. He had merely to keep an eye on events in the roulette room. Two men mentioned by The Shadow were under his observation. They were the Secret Service operatives whom Fulton Fourrier had placed at the gay nightclub.

Clyde had also looked for gangsters in the booths close by the side entrance from the roulette room. Those booths were empty. Clyde had decided why. Whistler Ingliss unquestionably knew that Secret Service men were on the job. He was not chancing gunmen in the place.

Whistler, himself, was free from surveillance. The Secret Service men had evidently passed him. Clyde Burke, however, had not. On two or three occasions, he had seen Whistler saunter through the opening toward his office. Clyde was suspicious of those trips.

The Shadow's agent had a hunch. Beyond the doorway at the side were card rooms. What if Whistler had a new crew of mobsters stationed in one of those rooms! Out of sight of the Secret Service operatives, the thugs would still be at Whistler's beck!

That was why, as eleven neared, Clyde Burke decided to end his passive observations. Although The Shadow had ordered him to remain in the roulette room, Clyde felt the urge to extend the field of his inspection.

Whistler Ingliss had gone to his office. Clyde Burke decided to follow. The roulette room was well thronged. Clatter of chips and cries of croupiers caused considerable din, broken by the exasperated exclamations of losers at the tables.

Clyde made an easy circuit of the room, reached the doorway at the side and stepped into the passage. He had hopes that he would gain some valuable information to give The Shadow, should communication with his mysterious chief be established at eleven.

Clyde descended the steps. He went by a side passage that led off to the side exit from the Club Rivoli. He noted a door that was ajar; light issued from within. Clyde peered inside.

IT was Whistler's office. The gambler was seated at his desk, telephoning.

"Fee." The words that Whistler uttered were in Agro. "Kye kye kode. Sake alta joda. Seek boda joda... Kye kye deek ake bole... Fee... Kye kye reef co kye kye..."

Clyde did not understand the strange jargon. Whistler Ingliss was reporting to Darvin Rochelle. The gambler was telling his chief that they—the mobsmen—had gone; that they had left at twenty minutes after ten; that they would come to Rochelle and would bring along the men whom they had been sent to get.

This meant that Bugs Ritler and his new squad of mobsters were probably at Athena Court, picking up Harry Vincent and Vic Marquette, the prisoners who had been trapped through the cunning of Alvarez Menzone.

Whistler Ingliss hung up the receiver. The gambler opened a desk drawer and removed a revolver which he pocketed. He was preparing to leave the Club Rivoli. He had not mentioned the hour of midnight over the telephone; but he had an appointment at that time. With the others of Darvin Rochelle's evil horde, he was due for the important conference.

Whistler was trilling a soft tune. Never perturbed, the gambler was as methodical and unconcerned as he would have been if starting to an ordinary social affair. A proof, however, of Whistler's keenness was already on the way. The soft lilt that he was trilling was but a covering for a suspicion which he had gained.

Dropping hands into pocket, Whistler stood in meditative fashion. Suddenly he wheeled. In quick fashion, he bounded to the door of his office; at the same time, he whisked his gun from his pocket. A second later, he had yanked the door inward and was standing with revolver pressed against Clyde Burke's ribs.

Clyde's hands went up. Gripping Clyde's shoulder, Whistler yanked The Shadow's agent into the room and closed the door. He forced Clyde to the opposite side of the desk.

"So you're a wise guy, eh?" demanded Whistler. "Snooping into my business. What's the idea?"

Clyde was at loss for a reply.

"I know your game," rasped Whistler. "You're no government dick, but you've been around this place too often to be on the level. I figured that the Feds weren't the only blokes on the job. Speak up. What do you know?"

"Nothing," retorted Clyde.

"Nothing, eh?" questioned Whistler. "We'll find out about that."

He glowered fiercely. Clyde Burke felt that his life was in the balance. Whistler seemed ready to loose the fire of his revolver. Yet the danger which Clyde sensed was purely imaginary.

The side door of the office had opened, silently, by inches. Peering into the room were a pair of blazing eyes; beneath them, the muzzle of a leveled automatic. Beyond that was blackness.

The Shadow had arrived. A hidden witness of this scene, he was covering Whistler Ingliss. Had the gambler sought to press finger to trigger, doom would have been his lot. The Shadow's automatic was ready to bark before Whistler could fire.

THE gambler's glare faded. Whistler laughed. He sat down at the desk. He lifted the telephone receiver. He put in a call. He heard Darvin Rochelle on the wire. In Agro, Whistler explained that he had taken a prisoner.

Rochelle's instructions were the response. Whistler checked them in brief phrases:

"Fee... Alk reef kay reen alk dake... Alk alk teeba kay reen kay beeta... Alk dake golo..."

Freely translated, Rochelle had declared:

"Yes. I shall bring him when I come. We shall hear him, when he will talk. I am coming now."

Whistler Ingliss arose. He made a gesture to Clyde Burke. The words that he uttered in English were a partial explanation of the instructions which he had corroborated in Agro.

"You're going with me," Whistler informed Clyde. "If you know what's good for you, you'll sit tight. You'll have a chance to do some talking where we're going. And listen, bozo—I'm a guy that's ready with the rod. See?"

Clyde saw. He knew that his only course was to do exactly as Whistler commanded. By such action, he would be safe—at least until he and Whistler had arrived at their destination.

Whistler approached Clyde and nudged him with the revolver. The Shadow's agent willingly complied with Whistler's order that they leave.

"We're going out the side door," stated Whistler. "No squawk out of you—see? Walk along like you were a friend of mine. Come on, now—this way—"

Whistler edged Clyde toward the door to the side passage. That door was closing. It locked. Whistler did not see the motion of the door nor did he hear the lock turn. The Shadow had withdrawn.

Producing a key, Whistler unlocked the little-used door with his left hand. With Clyde Burke at his side, the gambler pointed the way to the exit from the Club Rivoli.

He marched Clyde to a coupé. Taking the wheel, Whistler drove from the driveway, growling a warning threat that made Clyde rest motionless.

After the coupé had departed, a dim figure appeared in the glow that came from a side window of the Club Rivoli. A tall, spectral figure stood silent; then from hidden lips came a soft, weird laugh that was forbidding in tone.

The Shadow had seen all. Yet he had not moved to aid his captured agent! Instead, he had withdrawn from the scene! Clyde Burke had gone away a prisoner!

WHAT strange motive had withheld this king of action? The Shadow's failure to aid Harry Vincent and Vic Marquette was explainable: they had been capable of caring for themselves. But Clyde Burke had been entirely helpless.

Some answer lay behind this riddle. Yet it was strange that The Shadow should remain passive at the moment when pursuit of Whistler Ingliss would have led him to the secret gathering of minions of crime.

The answer was The Shadow's laugh. Eerie and unfathomable as it sounded in sibilant tones, that mockery carried an ominous portent.

The Shadow had withdrawn. His gliding steps were slow as they took him into darkness toward a parked cab near the front of the Club Rivoli. The whispered laugh had failed.

Darvin Rochelle—Alvarez Menzone—Whistler Ingliss—the lesser exponents of crime—all would be free to meet. The Shadow, in his dilatory appearance, could have gained but little inkling of what lay at stake.

Apparently, The Shadow had withdrawn. Why? Only The Shadow knew. The faint echoes of his laugh had been vague. Were they significant of hidden plans—or were they acceptance of defeat? That question could be answered by The Shadow alone!

CHAPTER XVIII
THE MEETING

DARVIN ROCHELLE was standing on the first floor of his palatial mansion. Three of his servants were close by. Rochelle was speaking to them in English.

"You are ready?"

Nods were the response. Each man showed a gleaming revolver. Rochelle smiled.

"Be on guard. Our meeting must not be disturbed. Two more are to come: *Señor* Menzone and Miss Debronne. Ring once when Menzone arrives; then send him up. Twice for Miss Debronne."

Chimes were tolling the hour of midnight when Darvin Rochelle turned toward the marble staircase. Rochelle limped to the steps; moved upward, then resumed his halting pace as he passed through the darkened anteroom.

The buzz of voices sounded as Rochelle entered his office and closed the door behind him. Seated about the room were trusted minions: Maurice Twindell, Whistler Ingliss, and the gang leader, Bugs Ritler. Two of Ritler's mobsmen were present as guards. They occupied a corner of the room toward the anteroom. Between them, trussed on the floor, were three prisoners: Vic Marquette, Harry Vincent, and Clyde Burke.

The gags had been removed. Yet none of the three captives attempted to voice an outcry. The presence of the mobsters, the handles of big revolvers jutting from their hips, were sufficient to command silence.

Darvin Rochelle was smiling as he sat behind his huge desk. All the gloss had gone from his sometime silky countenance. Darvin Rochelle was a fiend unmasked, gloating as he began to outline the way to final triumph.

"Two members of our band," declared Rochelle, "have not yet arrived. I shall reserve the details of our coming operations until they join us. A few preliminary remarks, however, may be appropriate.

"Tonight, we shall deal in wholesale assassination. Within this envelope"—he was holding up a sealed packet—"I have complete plans for the slaughter of nine prominent South Americans.

"Each death will be simple of execution. I have prepared all details and will appoint the proper workers. Moreover"—Rochelle's smile was broadening—"I have arranged for the planting of false clues that will place the perpetration of crime upon men who are actually innocent.

"After our instructions have been given, we shall proceed with another task. We have visitors tonight"—Rochelle was indicating the prisoners with a sweep of his hands—"who have responded to our urge to attend this meeting. Perhaps they may have statements of their own to make. Perhaps not. It does not matter. We shall dispose of our guests in fitting fashion whether they choose to talk or to remain silent.

"One is a Secret Service operative." Rochelle pointed to Marquette. "We have dealt with his ilk before. Another is a newspaper correspondent who showed overanxiety in his quest for news." Rochelle indicated Clyde Burke; then pointed to Harry Vincent. "Here we have a secretary who betrayed his trust. He tried to delve into his employer's secrets.

"Fortunately, his employer was my competent lieutenant, Alvarez Menzone. To Menzone, my friends, belongs the credit for the final step which brought us to this time for action. He gained the last papers that I needed. Tonight, we embark upon the slaughter that will throw a continent into chaos—that will make you, the companions of Darvin Rochelle, important factors in the building of a mighty empire!"

Rochelle pointed emphatically to the massive globe, upon which the conical outline of South America showed most prominently. While the fiend who plotted war was chuckling in unrepressed triumph, a buzzer sounded on the desk.

"Ah!" exclaimed Rochelle. "Menzone is here. He will be with us shortly. I left word for him to come directly to this meeting. You, Twindell, deserve credit for forming contact with Alvarez Menzone.

"The newest among us, Menzone has proven his competence. He will share in the deeds that I have planned for this night. We can count upon him—"

Rochelle paused. There was a rap from the other side of the door to the anteroom. Rochelle issued a friendly summons to enter. The door swung inward.

FOR a brief instant all within Rochelle's office stared blankly. Then came harsh gasps. The darkness of the anteroom was moving. Like a creature from some hidden vault of space, a form was emerging from blackness. While hushed fiends still gazed, the outline became clear.

A being clad totally in black. A form enshrouded by the folds of an inky-hued cloak; features concealed beneath the brim of a broad slouch hat. Such was the weird shape that Rochelle and his minions saw.

Beneath the hat brim were two burning eyes. Their fierce glare held a menace. From two hands encased in gloves of black projected mammoth automatics with tunneled muzzles trained upon the trapped fiends who shrank before them.

"The Shadow!"

The gasp of recognition came from Bugs Ritler. The gang leader had seen the destructive power of this mighty fighter, the night that Lito Carraza had been saved from death upon the Virginia speedway.

Then, The Shadow had met armed mobsters and had stilled their fire with slaughtering lead from his automatics. Now, The Shadow had come upon a group that was expectant of no danger.

Fiends sat helpless as The Shadow swept into the room. Circling toward the empty chair at the side of Rochelle's desk, The Shadow kept his guns trained on his clustered foemen. The mobsters who guarded the prisoners feared to move.

Each villain who viewed the muzzles of The Shadow's automatics thought that both guns were directed fully upon him. The black cloak swished; its crimson lining showed momentarily as The Shadow paused, just past the huge globe of the world.

From this position, The Shadow covered everyone with the exception of Darvin Rochelle. Yet the master plotter was afraid to make a move. Rising, he had gripped the desk with his left hand while he held his cane clutched in his right. Motionless as a statue, he stared toward The Shadow—so close that a quick swing of either automatic would mean prompt doom for the man with the limp.

"I have come," hissed The Shadow, "to end your schemes. You have prisoners. Release them!"

The command was directed toward one of the mobsters. Cowering, the man stooped and, tugged at the cords which bound Vic Marquette.

"Stand up!"

The mobster ceased his work as he heard the sibilant command. With hands above his head, he stood against the wall. Vic Marquette, struggling free from his loosened bonds, looked toward The

Shadow. He understood the order that showed in the glaring eyes. While helpless crooks watched, Vic released the cords that held Harry Vincent and Clyde Burke.

Three disarmed men were now at The Shadow's call. Guns were available, for they could seize them from the crooks. But as they waited for The Shadow's bidding, the sound of a creepy laugh made the released prisoners wait. Staring with the startled crooks, they heard The Shadow speak.

"You are awaiting Alvarez Menzone." The Shadow's words were directed toward Darvin Rochelle. "You might continue to await him forever. Alvarez Menzone is dead. He died in Caracas in 1931. That, Rochelle, is why your records ended.

"Alvarez Menzone was a murderer. He died at my bidding. His death was unknown. I, The Shadow, knew his past. That was why I, The Shadow, chose to resurrect the personality of Alvarez Menzone to gain access to your schemes!"

The Shadow's head moved upward. The folds of the cloak collar dropped away. The umbra from the hat brim vanished in the light. Darvin Rochelle stared aghast. The face which he and his minions were viewing was that of Alvarez Menzone!

THERE was no need for a further word. The truth had explained itself. Not once had The Shadow appeared while Alvarez Menzone was present. The briefcase which Menzone had carried— within its bulky interior had been more than mere papers. That portfolio had included the black garb of The Shadow!

Harry Vincent understood. When Menzone had returned to the apartment tonight, he must have come guised as The Shadow. There he had found Harry and Vic Marquette planning the capture of Alvarez Menzone. The Shadow had departed. Returning, as Menzone, he had easily trapped the trappers!

Vic Marquette understood. He realized that The Shadow, guised as Alvarez Menzone, had deliberately roused his suspicions to draw Vic on the trail of the plotters with whom The Shadow— as Menzone—had formed contact.

The capture of Harry Vincent and Vic Marquette had been essential, once they had pried into the affairs of Alvarez Menzone. So had Clyde Burke, spying on Whistler Ingliss, been taken prisoner while The Shadow stood by.

The Shadow, knowing that he would be present, had no fears for the safety of the prisoners. But he had not been willing to risk any step that might have caused Darvin Rochelle to postpone the meeting at which all the crooks were due.

Darvin Rochelle understood. As Alvarez Menzone, The Shadow had walked by the down-stairs servants, unmolested. Briefcase in hand, he had donned his black raiment in the anteroom.

But there was another question that lay unanswered in Rochelle's startled brain. As though divining it, The Shadow answered—not by word, but by action.

While his right hand automatic covered the crooks, his left arm rose to sweep the fold of the cloak collar about the false features of Alvarez Menzone. The left hand disappeared momentarily; it reappeared, carrying a white envelope with the automatic. The envelope dropped to the table.

"The stolen correspondence," hissed The Shadow, "is within that envelope. The documents that Alvarez Menzone delivered were spurious. They will be rejected as false when they reach South America. Your schemes, Darvin Rochelle, have failed completely."

Rochelle's left hand, gripping the desk, twitched itchingly. The master plotter wanted to grasp that envelope. He feared to do so. He stared at The Shadow. He saw the burning eyes—the leveled automatics beneath. Close by, Rochelle observed that the eyes which the others thought were everywhere, were directed upon him alone!

With a dejected leer, Rochelle let the handle of his cane fall heavily upon the surface of the desk. Feigning fear, he stared toward those blazing eyes, which seemed to be looking through and past him.

All eyes were upon The Shadow. No one realized that Rochelle had given a signal. Before a single crook could utter a gasp; before one of the released prisoners saw the danger, Darvin Rochelle's counter-thrust had come.

The upper hemisphere of the huge globe had opened. Bobbing noiselessly from its interior was Thurk, the hideous dwarf. Poised, the monster was beginning his downward swing to drive his wicked, long-pointed knife toward the unprotected shoulders of The Shadow!

CHAPTER XIX
THE STROKE OF DEATH

THE SHADOW'S body did not move. Beneath the descending knife of Thurk it remained a perfect goal for the blade. But The Shadow, his eyes still steady, performed a motion that was swifter than that of Thurk.

Although his back was toward the monster, The Shadow was ready. His right hand swung beneath his left arm. The right forefinger pressed the trigger of the automatic that it controlled. A burst of flame spat outward and upward, accompanied by the bark of the .45.

Thurk's forward lunge ended as a wild scream came from the dwarf's hideous lips. His ribs shattered, Thurk toppled backward in agony. His rebounding body thumped against the back-tilted top of the globe.

As the dwarf writhed, his weight upset the pedestal. Rolling from the opened, overturned globe, Thurk sprawled dead upon the rug beside the chair in which Croydon Herkimer had been slain.

The Shadow had met Rochelle's counterthrust. He had trumped the master plotter's buried ace. The laugh that came amid the echoes of the gun-shot brought a dawn of understanding to Rochelle's hate-racked brain.

The Shadow had spotted the huge globe as a death trap. His visits here, in the guise of Alvarez Menzone, had been accompanied by keen obser-vation. Had The Shadow stood on the near side of the globe, close to the chair where Rochelle guided visitors, he would not have seen the rise of Thurk.

But the Shadow had chosen the far side of the globe. His gaze, toward Rochelle, had gone beyond: to the mahogany-framed mirror on the opposite side of the room. In that glass, The Shadow had eyed the huge globe. He had chosen the very angle of vision that he needed to keep Thurk's hiding place in view.

Aiming with the mirror as his guide, The Shadow's shot had been no more than a simple test of his skillful marksmanship. His steady hand, diving beneath the upraised arm, had ended the evil life of Rochelle's murderous monster.

Yet even as The Shadow laughed, Darvin Rochelle performed an action of his own. The insidious plotter was demonish in his persistent attempts to thwart the black-garbed avenger.

The Shadow had turned one gun to finish Thurk. He had raised the other to keep the crooks at bay. Rochelle, momentarily uncovered, performed the one action which lay within his power.

LEANING forward with left hand on the table, Rochelle delivered a vicious, downward swing with his heavy cane. Had he aimed the stroke for The Shadow's body, the black-garbed fighter could have whirled away from it. But Rochelle, as he screamed an order to his minions, had chosen a more suitable objective.

His cane smashed against the automatic that bulged from The Shadow's left hand. It drove the weapon downward.

The effect of the blow was twofold. Not only did it clear the menace of that automatic, the downward drop of The Shadow's left arm clamped his second gun—the one with which he had slain Thurk.

Rochelle's quick action brought the momentary interval needed to swing his henchmen into action. As they heard their chief's cry and saw his deed, five men acted with single accord.

Whistler Ingliss and Maurice Twindell reached to their pockets for revolvers. Bugs Ritler and his mobsters shot their hands to hips. Guns flashed in the light.

The Shadow whirled. His swift turn swung him toward Rochelle. The master crook, sliding back with his cane, was about to scramble, crablike to the rear door of the office. Had The Shadow paused to end the fiend's life, it would have given the armed minions their chance.

Instead, The Shadow, swinging his unlimbered automatics, veered to meet the onrush. Tongues of flame belched from the mighty weapons. Caught within the echo-holding walls of the room, The Shadow's shots sounded a cannonade.

Bugs Ritler staggered. One of his gangsters loosed a shot. His bullet zimmed past The Shadow's head, then the mobsmen fell.

Vic Marquette was pouncing on the second mobster, who was aiming toward the weaving form of The Shadow. The bark of an automatic fore-stalled Vic and the mobster as well. Vic saw the gangster fall before he could grapple with the man.

Harry Vincent and Clyde Burke were alert. Each of The Shadow's agents had chosen a separate man. Harry leaped for Maurice Twindell; Clyde for Whistler Ingliss.

Twindell, thinking that the others could down The Shadow, wrenched away from Harry. Wheeling, he aimed his revolver point-blank between Harry's eyes. Harry sprang forward to forestall the shot. His effort was too late. Twindell was pressing finger to trigger.

HIS shot, however, never came. The Shadow had seen Harry's plight; a turn of his wrist with a trigger squeeze dispatched a leaden messenger to Twindell's skull.

Whistler Ingliss, fighting with Clyde Burke, delivered a glancing blow to Clyde's head. The newspaperman slumped to the floor. Whistler, his lips pursed for an imaginary trill, snapped his wrist directly toward The Shadow.

Gleaming eyes—a tongue of forking flame—these showed as The Shadow's gun barked in response to the cool gambler's calculating aim. Whistler Ingliss had delayed a split second too long. His lips widened; his hand went to his breast. Tottering, Whistler Ingliss wavered, then sprawled face foremost on the floor.

Vic Marquette had grabbed two revolvers from the floor. Plunging across the room, he caught Harry Vincent by the arm. Vic had seen the havoc of The Shadow's fire. He knew that the minions within this room were doomed.

"Come!" Vic was shouting the order as he dragged Harry along. "This way! That's where he's gone—

the big shot. Out through the way they brought us in!"

As The Shadow, now near the door to the anteroom, delivered his last deciding bullet, Vic Marquette and Harry Vincent gained the door at the back of the room. Harry was clutching a gun that Vic had given him. Together, these delivered prisoners were in pursuit of Darvin Rochelle.

The final echoes of The Shadow's gunfire were broken by a new and strident sound. It was a peal of taunting laughter, a burst of freed, triumphant mirth.

The Shadow had delivered doom to minions of crime. He, too, was ready to take up the search for Darvin Rochelle, the insidious master plotter who alone had fled!

CHAPTER XX
THE DEATH VATS

HARRY VINCENT and Vic Marquette were dashing down the spiral stairway. They knew the route, for it was through this way that they had been brought to Rochelle's.

"The house at the rear," panted Vic, as they clattered from the staircase. "That's where he's gone! Be ready, Vincent! There'll be other mobsmen there!"

The door to the courtyard was unlocked. Vic gripped Harry's arm as they reached the open. The two paused momentarily to listen. Sounds of gunfire were bursting from streets all around the area.

"The police!" exclaimed Vic. "Say—how could they have got here this quick? Come on, Vincent; this will help us. They're coming in from all sides. Our man is trapped!"

Vic and Harry reached the house in back. A dim light showed in a rear room. Vic spied a doorway. He opened it to show a flight of descending stairs. With Harry Vincent at his heels, the Secret Service operative led the downward dash.

A dim light showed in a cellar room; beyond it, another dimly lighted compartment. Harry Vincent clutched his companion's shoulder.

"Listen!" whispered The Shadow's agent.

Vic heard the sound. Within the stone walls of the cellar, it made a ghostly effect—a slow, steady tapping that was gradually drawing away. For a moment both men were startled by the uncanny noise. Then the explanation came in a blurted whisper from Harry's lips.

"The man with the limp! It's the tapping of his cane!"

Vic Marquette nodded. They had overtaken the villain whom they sought. Somewhere, beyond the narrow opening to the other section of this dim cellar, a fiend was seeking safety.

"Come!" Vic led a cautious advance. He and Harry crossed the first room swiftly, but with little noise. They gained the opening; off ahead, they could hear the echoes of the tapping cane.

Together, the pursuers moved foot by foot into the further room. Vic's eyes were straight ahead. Harry's wavered toward the floor. This was fortunate. Just as the tapping of the cane had ceased, Harry gripped Vic and drew him back.

The action was just in time. Vic Marquette's feet were on the edge of a stepping-off spot.

A rank odor surged to the nostrils of the pursuers. Their eyes accustomed to the gloom, Vic and Harry saw what they had just escaped. They were on the lip of a deep pit; several feet down in the uncovered hole was a murky, greenish liquid that filled the entire pit.

THEIR eyes traveled further. They saw a second pit separated from the first by a thin, dividing side. Beyond that, a gloomy wall, with a narrow edge of floor—

A chuckle brought eyes upward. With guns lowered, Harry and Vic were taken unaware. Their staring eyes saw the figure that they sought. On the narrow ledge beyond the further pit stood Darvin Rochelle!

The fiend was standing backed against the wall. His cane was in his right hand. His left was drawing it away. Before either watcher could recover, the cane had come apart. A hollow sheath was withdrawn from glimmering steel!

Up came Rochelle's right hand. Harry and Vic were covered by the strangest weapon that they had ever seen. The interior of Rochelle's cane had formed a long-barreled gun.

The portion where the handle had been now made a hand-grip with bulging chambers. The gun which Rochelle held was a revolver of small caliber, but with a rifle barrel that gave it power.

Covered by this weapon, it was futile for either man to move. Trapped by Rochelle, they could only hope to parry. The first words that the enemy uttered showed that no mercy could be gained.

"You shall die!" Rochelle's snarl ended in a wicked chuckle. "You, like others, shall end in my vats of death. Look before you—see where I have consigned the bodies of those whose murders I have ordered!

"Bolero—Piscano"—Rochelle was gleeful as he named the death list—"Rexton—Clifford—Tromboll—Dolband! All have been dissolved within the acid which those vats contain. They were murdered by Bugs Ritler and his mobsmen. They were carried here and dropped into the vats by Thurk.

"There was another. Herkimer. Thurk slew him and threw him into a vat as well. You wonder why I tell you this?" Rochelle sneered. "Because both of you, like the others, will meet with the same fate.

"No evidence will remain of my crimes. Speculation will exist; truth will be lacking. I shall depart by my secret exit; before I go, two more victims will be bestowed to their resting places. One for each vat of death!"

As Rochelle delivered a fiendish chuckle, Vic Marquette growled a quick command to Harry Vincent.

"Spread away" was Vic's order. "Open fire— both at once. Maybe one of us will get him—"

With simultaneous accord, Harry and Vic sprang sidewise, in opposite directions, along the edge of the nearer vat. It was their only chance. One was doomed, according to Rochelle's choice; the other had a slender chance.

Rochelle had divined the move. As the springing men swung their gun arms upward, the master plotter aimed first for Vic Marquette. All odds were in his favor. A quick shot with another rapid aim— both Vic and Harry would be doomed.

At that instant a shot resounded with a roar from a point directly in back of the spot where Harry Vincent and Vic Marquette had been standing side by side. The spreading action had cleared the way for a hidden marksman.

The Shadow! He had trailed the pursuers of Darvin Rochelle. He had heard Vic Marquette's order to Harry Vincent. A spectral figure, hidden from Rochelle's view by the men between, he had been ready with the needed shot.

THE roar of the automatic, enlarged by these confining walls, awoke staccato echoes. Darvin Rochelle's right arm was drooping. The sheathing cane slipped from his left hand and dropped into the vat before him. His long-barreled gun formed a pointer as its muzzle turned toward the depths of the vat. Like an omen, the gun slipped from Rochelle's hand. It dropped and sank into the simmering acid.

Rochelle's form was slumping. The villain's left hand was to his breast. His eyes were staring downward, bulging as they saw the fate that awaited him. His wavering body seemed to twist in a futile, convulsive effort to retain itself against the wall.

Then, as death followed the mortal wound, Rochelle's body took a rigid pose. It seemed to rise, almost as if alive. With a peculiar twist that formed a replica of Rochelle's halting stride, the body slipped from the ledge.

A splash came from the vat. A pungent odor arose as wavelets moved upon the greenish surface. The man with the limp was dead. His corpse, like those of his victims, was swallowed by the greedy acid in the vat of death!

From the archway to the outer chamber came the hollow tones of a weird laugh, that crept with ironical mockery above the vats. Even though that laugh had been uttered by their rescuer, Vic Marquette and Harry Vincent shuddered at its chilling tones.

The laugh reached a high crescendo. It broke with a shuddering gibe. Echoes rang from every wall—reverberations that seemed uttered by living, ghoulish tongues.

When the last note of that sinister taunt had died, a strange, predominating silence hung above the vats of death, where Harry Vincent and Vic Marquette stood motionless.

Triumphant, The Shadow had departed. His work was done. He had dealt just doom to Darvin Rochelle, the man with the limp!

CHAPTER XXI
THE FINAL REPORT

VIC MARQUETTE was in Fulton Fourrier's room at the Starlett Hotel. Wisely, the Secret Service operative was silent, as he listened to the commendation of his chief.

"I got your call, Marquette," explained Fourrier, "just before midnight. How you managed to get it through while those crooks held you prisoner is a miracle to me."

Vic maintained his silence. He realized that The Shadow must have called Fourrier just before coming to Rochelle's mansion.

"I went with the police," resumed Fourrier. "We got there and waited—surrounding the block as you had ordered. When those first shots came, we smashed through.

"We smeared those servants of Rochelle's. We got the gangsters piling out of the house in the back. But if it hadn't been for you, Vic, and that fellow Vincent you had with you, Rochelle would have made his getaway."

Fourrier paused to smile in elation.

"We nabbed the Debronne woman coming in," said the chief. "We're adding her confession to your report. With Vincent and that newspaperman, Burke, to add their details to your story, it will be the greatest thing in the annals of the Secret Service.

"The papers on Rochelle's desk. Not only his plot to kill nine South Americans, but that stolen correspondence from the embassy. You've proved to be an ace, Marquette!"

The chief paused to study a stack of report papers that Vic Marquette had given him. Vic had couched these in simple, unromantic style. Yet they showed the marks of a keen imagination.

For Vic Marquette had sensed The Shadow's wish. Wisely, Marquette had omitted all mention of the mysterious avenger whose lone hand had dealt every stroke of doom.

"No details of the fight," observed Fourrier. "Well, those aren't needed. The fact that you and the other prisoners got loose and polished off the gang is sufficient. Results are what we want in our report sheets."

Fourrier placed the report aside. He arose and clapped his hand to Marquette's shoulder.

"Your work is done, old man," he said. "I'm putting an international operative on the final job. A report came in on Alvarez Menzone today. The man was a clever swindler, last seen in 1931, at Caracas, Venezuela.

"He's probably headed out of the country. Maybe we'll get him—maybe we won't. It doesn't matter. He'll never trouble us again."

Vic Marquette smiled. He knew that Fourrier had unwittingly declared the truth. No one would ever get Alvarez Menzone, for Alvarez Menzone did not exist!

BLACKNESS moved on the balcony outside of Fourrier's windows. The barriers closed tight. A weird shape, crawling spiderlike, made its way to the floor below.

Ten minutes later, Henry Arnaud, bags packed, appeared in the lobby of the Hotel Starlett. This inconspicuous guest was leaving Washington. He paid his bill; his grips were carried to a cab.

As the taxi rolled along Pennsylvania Avenue on its way to the Union Station, a thin smile appeared upon the lips of Henry Arnaud. Eyes that flashed, were surveying the glittering boulevard. A soft laugh echoed from the lips beneath the bold, aquiline nose.

Washington seemed peaceful tonight. The lurking menace of insidious crime was ended. A monster of evil and all his insidious crew had been banished forever from the national capital.

The glow from the lighted capitol building revealed Arnaud's hawklike features as the cab swung toward the station. The lips were smiling still.

From them, again came that whispered laugh—an echo of the same weird tone that had reverberated in strident triumph at the death of a Darvin Rochelle.

The laugh of The Shadow! It was the token of the master who had played three parts in a grim, unrelenting game.

Deaths had been avenged. Lives had been saved. Justice ruled, with the threat of a continent in chaos safely ended.

These were the reasons for the triumph laugh of The Shadow!

THE END

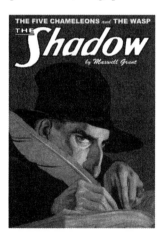

978-1-60877-072-4

Coming in THE SHADOW #57:

The Knight of Darkness battles supercriminals in two action-packed thrillers. First, The Shadow seeks to unmask *The Five Chameleons*, whose uncanny ability to blend with their surroundings rivals his own. Then, The Shadow feels the savage sting of *The Wasp* in his first encounter with one of his deadliest foes!

And in DOC SAVAGE #55:

Doc and Patricia Savage enter an Arctic abyss where dinosaurs and prehistoric humans survive, and race against Japanese agents to uncover the secret of *The Time Terror*. Then, a series of crimes by "graduates" of Doc's Crime College threaten to destroy his reputation. What is the sinister secret of *The Talking Devil*?

INTERLUDE by Will Murray

For this Shadow volume we shine the spotlight on Clyde Burke, who led a dual life as a crime reporter for the *Evening Classic* while being secretly in the service of the Master Avenger.

Burke was introduced in The Shadow's sixth exploit, *The Death Tower.* At that time, he was unemployed, thrown out of work when his former paper, the *Evening Clarion,* was absorbed by the *Daily Sphere.* During those early Depression days, New York's many newspapers were imploding into a smaller field, and men with Burke's background were a dime a dozen. As George Clarendon, an early false identity, The Shadow hired Burke to run a one-man clipping service. He joined The Shadow's group of secret agents in that story's sequel, *The Silent Seven.*

At the end of that case, the wiry newshawk got a job with the *Evening Classic,* one of New York City's numerous disreputable tabloids. Initially, he appears to be a special assignment writer, and sometimes continues to run his clipping bureau. In fact, Maxwell Grant sometimes seems confused about his actual role.

In *Mobsmen on the Spot*, he's freelancing. But in the next story, *Hands in the Dark*, he's on the *Classic* staff.

At the time of 1932's *Double Z,* while working as special assignment writer for the New York *Classic,* Burke is told to take over the crime column of a murdered reporter, but nothing more is mentioned of his "Wise Owl" column in succeeding issues. Also Burke appears to have gone back to freelancing at times.

Then in *The Golden Grotto*, Burke is working as a foreign correspondent in Europe but as a result of his activities is hired by the New York *Classic* as a special staff writer, where he remained, except for a period when he was fired for insulting new police commissioner Wainwright Barth and, on two occasions, following orders from The Shadow, he relocated to Washington DC to run a clipping bureau.

One assumes that the New York *Classic* is a renamed *Evening Classic.* But the odd reference to Burke reporting for the *Evening Star* suggests some early editorial confusion and perhaps these are two separate sheets. In any case, the *Classic*'s sleazy reputation and low-rent style allowed Burke wide latitude in serving the Dark Avenger yet still hold a job in those tough times. Maxwell Grant often describes Burke as a roving reporter. In one tale, *The Sledge-Hammer Crimes*, we are introduced to his city editor, Donney. According to 1942's *Legacy of Death*, Burke also did a column for the *Classic,* so he may have continued penning the Wise Owl feature.

Tabloids in those days were often distinguished by their garishly colored pulp paper—often dyed yellow or lavender. That is where the term "yellow journalism" came from.

If there was an agent of The Shadow with whom Walter Gibson could identify, it was Burke. For Walter had spent the decade prior to taking on The Shadow reporting for two different Philadelphia newspapers, the *North American* and later the Philadelphia *Ledger*.

Gibson drifted into the news business after a period of exploration:

> When I went to college at Colgate, I found out that the musical clubs would use a specialty act. So I went and did some of my magic. And they liked it. So I traveled with them as a magician.
>
> When I got out of college, I was after newspaper work. I had various jobs. Meanwhile, I would do private shows. Like club shows, sort of like a semi-pro. In fact, I had thoughts of getting up an act and going out on Chautauqua. At that time, there were a lot of Chautauqua magicians. I was figuring on that. But I also liked newspaper work. And just by luck I landed in a newspaper.

Walter started at the princely sum of fifteen dollars a week. This was back in the Roaring 20s, when Philly was an eight newspaper town. Competition for hot stories was fierce. The old-fashioned flowery style of newspaper writing, a holdover from the prior century, was fast being beaten out of young cub reporters like Walter Gibson by a new breed of hardboiled editor.

Early in his reporting career, a flood struck a part of Pennsylvania. Walter loved to repeat the tale of the journalist who sent one editor copy which began, "God sits in sadness above the town pondering the tragedy that struck...."

The annoyed editor wired back:

FORGET FLOOD. STOP. INTERVIEW GOD.

After losing out on a big story of a bridge collapse, Gibson's editor promised him the next scoop. It came when the telephone rang. President Warren G. Harding was passing through town on his way to Atlantic City and was open to an interview. Gibson got the exclusive story.

"I have a good feeling about President Harding," he recalled. "He was a newspaperman himself and owned a paper. So he understood reporters. I always thought he was a great guy."

In 1921, Gibson jumped over to the Philadelphia *Ledger*, where he earned twenty-five a week. He was resourceful.

Tasked to interview the great Opera singer, Enrico Caruso, who spoke no English, Gibson dragooned an Italian barber to translate for him.

Some of Gibson's reporting brought him in

Philadelphia *Ledger* reporter Walter B. Gibson in 1923

contact with Philadelphia's Prohibition-fueled criminal underbelly. After covering one gangland killing, he was forced to ride back to his beat, the Philadelphia Morgue, with the freshly killed corpse. With each lurch of the dead wagon, the dead man twitched in a macabre way.

Once, Walter found himself impressed into the law's service, an unfamiliar Colt .45 automatic clenched in his fist:

> I carried one once, when I was down in Philadelphia. This was before I did The Shadow. I was covering the Federal Building.
>
> I went into the Narcotics Squad and asked them if they had any stories. And the guy in charge said, "I may have a story for you right now." I said, "What's that?" "Well, some people who look to make a raid haven't shown up." Well, only a few weeks before, two agents had been making a raid in some place, and they found themselves covered by guns. But fortunately, somebody else had been heading for the same place too, and was supposed to meet them there. And when these people came, these other agents moved in, and they covered the people that had covered the agents! The first ones.
>
> So this fellow said, "Maybe there's a situation like that. So I've got to go out and check it. So you come along." He pulls two automatics out and handed me one, and said, "Here, take it." He deputized me in that office. And here was I, a mere reporter, going along with this guy! He said, "You know how to handle a gun, don't you?" Well, I hadn't fired one. So I said, "Yes." I didn't want to lose the story. He said, "Don't worry about it. The safety catch was on." And I thought, Oh, my God, where's the safety catch? I wanted the safety catch off. All I wanted in a jam was to pull the trigger!
>
> Well, when we got to the place and snooped around, it was all perfectly empty. And we found out that the other agents at Broadway, finding it empty, had headed on to some other place that they were supposed to check. So they had dropped in by the time we got back. But that was the only time I really carried one myself.

Walter always credited his inhuman ability to knock out two and even three 200 page Shadow manuscripts per month to his journalistic background:

> Well, basically because I had been a news writer. For ten years, I had been doing newspaper work. And mostly in the form of feature articles. I'd been writing for Houdini. I was writing for him at the time he died in 1926. That was five years before The Shadow. I wrote articles for Thurston, the Magician. The Ledger Syndicate in Philadelphia, which was owned by Curtis, used to put me onto assignments. I'd go out and meet a man who was an expert in aerial surveying, which was just starting. And I would write his story up. I made many interviews and things of that type.
>
> So I was very fast at descriptive writing. And stories of this sort, with The Shadow moving in and out of people's affairs, and fighting criminals and masterminds plotting, I was able to treat it in semi-factual style. So it was just like picking up the good old newspaper work.

Gibson was that rare species of reporter who adapted his journalistic skills to fiction. Many wrote pulp as a sideline, but few made a career of it.

CLYDE BURKE

"In the old days," he recalled, "a lot of newspapermen always wanted to write the Great American novel. But they were seldom successful because they were always too newsy; they didn't have enough depth. I would write The Shadow as if it were just happening."

Gibson rarely spoke of the origins of Clyde Burke, or any other character.

"A lot of them I would base on real-life characters, people that I knew." He once revealed. "For example I had a reporter, who was very much like a reporter that I knew. And there was always something generic with each one."

Gibson had another device he employed to generate character names:

> I found out my big problem was to suddenly have a story all ready. We'd need about seven or eight new characters. And where was I going to get

names? And say that I just didn't grab somebody's name at random. And maybe got somebody's name by mistake. A real person would say that "I didn't like it because they're all kidding me," and so forth.

So I would take a railroad timetable—a branch line—and take the names of the stations! For example, there's a branch line up in Massachusetts. You left out of Worcester, Mass., and the first station was Chatham. The next was Dawson. Then there was Holden. Brooks. Hubbardston. And Gardner. Hubbardston I cut down to Hubbard. Well, if somebody had said, Say, why did you put my name in—Brooks—and had me as a crook? "Well, you just happened to be station number 3 on this branch line."

Many of them I got in Florida, from the branch lines of the seaboard and the Atlantic coastlines. In those days in the '30s there were all these little branch lines, and I'd just go down and list them. It was easy to remember too. Often you'd get a character name, and decide to change it as you're writing and get confused in it. If I had the timetable to go to, why there it was. I learned all these little tricks.

A character like Clyde Burke would coalesce around an appropriate name:

Incidentally, I was talking about the character names, which I think is very interesting. Well, right from the very start I began trying to get character names that sounded real, but I could find some source for them. In other words, I didn't want to put somebody's name in the thing that was too common a name, because in that case the person with the real name might come in and say, "Why did you use my name?" On the other hand, I didn't want the name to sound too outrageous because it wouldn't sound real.

So I would take names—composite names—and really name them partly after people I knew. In the first Shadow, one chapter is titled The Tea Shop of Wang Foo. There was a magic dealer named Donald Holmes. And he put out tricks like the Tea Chest of Wang Foo. So that was where I took Wang Foo, for my first Chinese character. All little things like that happened along.

Harry Vincent I took from the Alger book. Cliff Marsland. In Florida, there was a man I knew who rented a houseboat named Marsland. I liked the name. Well, I'll take the "Marsland."

Clyde Burke. I knew a newspaperman for the Philadelphia *Ledger* named Clyde Rex, who later became the sales manager of the Ledger Syndicate. I took people like this. Then anyone who said it was their name or something, I could pull out the real prototype.

There were sound reasons for this practice. Street & Smith had lost a lawsuit when *Detective Story Magazine* writer Albert E. Apple, had made a villain of a Quebec attorney with a distinctive name. Coincidently or otherwise, there happened to be an actual Quebec lawyer by that very name. He sued. Street & Smith lost. Apple later committed suicide.

Another S&S contributor, W. Ryerson Johnson of *Western Story Magazine* and *Doc Savage*, ran afoul of the same awkward situation, but with different results, after his novel *The Branded Avenger* appeared in *Western Story* in 1937.

"Once I dreamed up a name I was sure nobody in real life would have: Wid Neff," Johnson recounted. "Wouldn't you know—someone named Wid Neff in New York City called me up, purporting to be greatly perturbed and transmitted a veiled threat of lawsuit for defamation of character. I went around to meet him. He turned out to be an actors' agent, and in the conversational exchange we developed enough rapport to go down and buy each other a drink."

Rumor has it that a real Dr. Clark Savage complained to S&S when *Doc Savage Magazine* first came out.

Our lead novel comes from the early phase of Clyde Burke's long semi-secret career. It was submitted to Street & Smith under the title, "The Man with the Limp" in June of 1933. As *The Embassy Murders,* it appeared in the January 1, 1933 issue of *The Shadow Magazine*.

Playing out against a background in the Chaco War then raging between Bolivia and Paraguay in South America, this story brings the Dark Avenger to our nation's capital for the first time. It's a city he will return to many times in the future, and there will come a day when Walter Gibson, growing weary of writing stories focused on New York's underworld, will consider relocating his mysterioso supersleuth to Washington D.C.

Here, Clyde Burke quits the *Classic* to set up the National City News Association. While it's not permanent, Burke will return in the future to reopen the wire service. But for this story, the intrepid reporter is a man without a newspaper, serving The Shadow in an entirely new capacity.

Vic Marquette of the Secret Service resurfaces, as he does periodically. The character of Secret Service agent Carl Dolband had previously appeared in *The Silver Scourge*, and returns here for his final bow.

On the other hand, *Hills of Death* was written in April of 1937 and printed in the January 1, 1938 issue of *The Shadow*.

Submitted under the title "Treasure Lodge," it presents the hard-nosed reporter serving as the proxy hero for this tale, which is why we chose it. Although a prominent Shadow operative, Clyde Burke did not often have the spotlight thrown on him. Here, he does—and he also shines. •

HILLS OF DEATH

Terrible death hovers over the hills of New Jersey, while The Shadow strives to break the grip of evil!

A Complete Book-length Novel from the Private Annals of The Shadow, as told to

Maxwell Grant

CHAPTER I
JERSEY MURDER

THE lights of the filling station were dimmed amid the drizzle, as the small coupé nosed toward them. It wasn't until the driver identified the round, dull glow of a gasoline standard that he was sure the place was actually a service station.

The discovery brought him satisfaction. Picking a way among the back roads on a hazy night was bad enough; it was worse when the needle of the gasoline gauge had wangled almost to the empty mark.

Pulling in between the gasoline standard and the shack that served as service station, the driver of the coupé honked his horn; then settled back to light a cigarette. The dim lights showed a wise face; eyes that were observant, but friendly.

Though young, the man at the wheel of the coupé had an oddish poise. His experienced air

caused many persons to class him as a newspaper reporter, which, in fact, he was. This traveler along the back roads of New Jersey was Clyde Burke, roving news-getter for the New York *Classic.*

Clyde was eyeing the service station as he lighted his cigarette. It looked like a one-man establishment; and the poorly painted sign above the door testified to that effect. It bore the name: "FRED'S SERVICE STATION," and the man who came from the little building was evidently Fred, himself.

He was the sort of service station proprietor that Clyde expected to see in a remote location like this. Fred was tall and lanky; he wore puttees, khaki trousers and an old sweater, topped by a black poncho. His face was dreary, weather-beaten; that of a man who had taken up his present occupation as a last resort.

There was something else, though, that Clyde noted instantly. There was a worried look on Fred's face as the fellow saw the coupé. He seemed to be expecting someone that he didn't want to see. His lips grimaced momentarily; then their expression changed. Clyde's car wasn't the one that Fred thought it was. That was why Fred gave his wan grin of relief.

"Fill her up!"

Clyde's brisk order brought a nod from Fred. Clyde's appearance added to the man's relief. That made the reporter more anxious to learn what was on the fellow's mind.

While Fred was busy at the gasoline standard, Clyde alighted from the coupé and strolled over to open conversation. His first words were a question:

"Do you have a telephone?"

Fred looked up suspiciously. He noted that Clyde was light of build, although wiry. He didn't seem the sort who would be making trouble. Nevertheless, Fred wasn't taking chances.

"Yeah," he returned, gruffly. "I got a telephone. Only it ain't a pay station. People don't use it, generally—"

"I want to call New York." Clyde produced his reporter's card. "The operator will give us the charges. I'll pay them."

Fred saw the reporter's card by the glow of the taillight. His expression showed a sudden eagerness. He wanted to talk to someone, and Clyde seemed eligible. Fred thumbed toward the service station.

"Will you wait inside, sir?" he questioned. "I'll pull your car around in back."

Clyde nodded. Fred's request told him exactly what he wanted to know. Fred was awaiting the arrival of another car. That was why he wanted the space clear.

Obligingly, Clyde went inside. He was seated in a chair by a battered desk when Fred joined him.

"TELL me something." Fred wasn't wasting any time. "Are you out here looking for a story?"

"In a way—yes." Clyde spoke frankly. "We picked up a tip, down at the newspaper office, that some New York mobbies were heading out this way. Just where they were going, and why, we don't know. So far, they haven't made any trouble."

Clyde was outspoken, because he was confident that Fred was no crook. What he didn't tell Fred was that the *Classic* knew nothing about the tip in question. Though Clyde was actually a newspaper reporter, he also filled another job. Clyde Burke was an agent of The Shadow, the superfoe to all men of crime.

It was The Shadow who had learned of gang car trips across the Jersey meadows. For the past four days, The Shadow had been watching a crew of hoodlums that he expected would start forth. Meanwhile, he had sent Clyde and other agents on tours of investigation, hoping that they might learn the probable destination of the crooks.

Clyde was thinking of those facts as he watched Fred. The man's eyes were staring out through the door, with a faraway gaze. He was nodding over what Clyde had told him. Suddenly, Fred voiced, in awed tones:

"Tonight's Wednesday!"

Clyde awaited an explanation of the statement. For a few moments, Fred hesitated; then broke loose.

"Listen, Mr. Burke"—Fred remembered Clyde's name from the reporter's card—"every Wednesday night he comes here, see? A fellow in a coupé; only it's bigger than your car. With Jersey license plates,

instead of New York. He never says nothing—just holds up his hand, spread like this, meaning he wants five gallons of gas.

"I've seen him close enough to guess what he is. He's a Turk, that's what! With a round face, yellowlike—and a mustache, like this." Fred drew his forefinger straight across his upper lip. "And he never smiles. Keeps his lips straight; just like the mustache."

Fred sat down. He watched Clyde, saw that the reporter was intent. That was because Clyde knew there must be more to the story. Filling station men didn't worry about steady customers having a foreign appearance and refusing to open conversation. Fred's next spell of hesitancy wasn't a long one.

"Here's what happens, everytime." Fred leaned forward in his chair. "The guy don't pull out right away, see? He smokes a cigarette—sometimes two or three. They smell like pure Turkish; I whiffed the smoke once, when I was close.

"Then, all of a sudden, a car goes by from the opposite direction. A sedan; but I never got its license number. That's what the Turk's waiting for, though he don't show it. Maybe he finishes his cigarette; sometimes he lights another, to bluff me. But he pulls out, circles back, after he's seen that car pass. And when he gets to the bend"—Fred pointed—"he stops to pick up something!"

Fred arose and paced the cramped floor, nodding wisely. He had told his story, and he considered it airtight. The tale impressed Clyde, too. Cars were infrequent along this lonely road. The fact that the Turk always waited until one had passed was sufficient proof that the mystery man was awaiting that machine.

"I shoulda called the State police." Fred glanced ruefully at the telephone. "It's too late, though. The Turk's about due. That means I got to wait another week."

"I have an idea." Clyde arose. "Don't call the State police at all; not until we know more about the case. Maybe I can find out something."

"How?"

"By getting down to the bend and seeing what the fellow does there. If he—"

A splashing sound interrupted. A car was wallowing in from the rain-soaked road. Fred pointed quickly to a little side door beyond the desk.

"It's him!" gulped the weather-beaten man. "Better duck out, Mr. Burke—"

CLYDE was off before Fred completed the hint. Once outside, he sneaked to the front corner of the little building. From his vantage point, Clyde saw Fred going out to a large coupé that had parked beside the gasoline standard.

The mystery car had arrived. Events repeated themselves exactly as Fred had described them. Clyde glimpsed a darkish face that moved back into the car as Fred approached. A hand showed at the window to gesture for five gallons. While Fred was putting gas into the tank, the man in the car lighted a cigarette.

Fred received his money and came back into the shack. The man in the car had finished one smoke. Clyde could see the tiny flare of a match, as he lighted another. Hurrying to the side door, Clyde opened it and beckoned to Fred.

"I'm going down to the bend," whispered Clyde. "If I don't come back, call this number. Tell the person who answers that you're calling for me; and give him the details."

The written telephone number that Clyde slipped to Fred was an unlisted one, important to The Shadow's agents. The man who would answer a call there was Burbank, The Shadow's contact man.

Fred put a question: "This number's the newspaper office?"

Clyde shook his head. He told Fred not to worry about it; just to call the number. Fred agreed; but made another proviso.

"Maybe I ought to call the State coppers, too?"

"Don't do that," interrupted Clyde. "If you've got to get in touch with the police, call Joe Cardona, the New York inspector. He knows me."

Leaving Fred, Clyde rounded the back of the shack and picked his way through the underbrush. His route was silent; for the ground was heavily soaked. Soon out of earshot from the Turk's coupé, Clyde found a sudden urge for speed. From down the road, he could hear the rapid rhythm of an approaching motor.

A sedan whizzed past, too swiftly for Clyde to do more than glimpse it from the bushes. It went by the service station; and by the time Clyde was near the bend, he could hear the coupé pulling away from Fred's.

Just off the edge of the road, Clyde waited while the coupé pulled up. It stopped some thirty feet beyond him.

Clyde watched the driver get out and use a flash-

light. He was looking for something just off the paving. Stealing out to the roadway, Clyde saw the flashlight glimmer on a muddy satchel. The man picked it up and came back to the coupé.

That was when Clyde performed an impulsive move. Behind the coupé, he was out of sight. There wasn't time to accost the mystery man; moreover, Clyde doubted the wisdom of seeking an encounter. He had time for something else: the right trick in this pinch. Tiptoeing along through the drizzle, Clyde reached the back of the coupé, just as the car started.

With a long grab, Clyde clutched the handle of the rumble seat and shoved one foot upon a bumperette. He gained another hold while the car was gathering speed. Clinging, flattened, the reporter was off on a trip that promised strange adventure.

BACK at the service station, Fred was listening to the last sounds of the coupé's departure. By the light of the gasoline standard, he studied the slip of paper that Clyde had given him. Memorizing the phone number, the fellow tore the paper to shreds. A look of suspicion came over his features.

Fred was thinking that perhaps Clyde had joined the man in the coupé. Maybe the reporter's visit was a trick to find out how much Fred knew.

With an ugly mutter, the lanky man went into the shack and picked up the telephone. He was about to call the State police, when he remembered something that Clyde had said, about calling Joe Cardona.

Just part of Clyde's bluff, thought Fred. All right, he would call that bluff. A chat with Joe would fix it.

Lifting the receiver, Fred told the operator to connect him with New York police headquarters. Fred grinned, thinking he would soon be exposing the methods of a fake reporter.

Fred's sudden mistrust was to prove his misfortune. He had trouble getting connected with Cardona; his call took longer than if he had telephoned direct to Burbank. That delay was to prove fatal, for Fred's own actions were putting him on the spot.

"Hello!" Fred was shouting at someone on the other end of the wire. "I want to talk to Inspector Cardona...Yeah. Cardona. I got some important news for him..."

Fred couldn't hear what was happening outside. A long touring car had slithered up to the front of the service station; men, peering from its interior, could see Fred at the telephone. A pair of huskies slid out from the car; muffling their raincoats about their chins, they sneaked up to the doorway.

"Hello, Inspector!" Fred was talking again, while the watchers drew revolvers from their coat pockets. "I'm a guy that's got a filling station, over in Jersey. I want to tell you about a car that stopped here...

What's that?... Say, I want to talk to Inspector Cardona! Get him on the wire..."

Fred turned, holding the telephone. He was muttering angrily, because of the wrong connection. His words were audible, until his eyes happened to gaze through the doorway. Then, Fred's lips kept moving, but they were soundless.

Goggle-eyed, the lanky man was staring into the muzzles of revolvers. He saw the intruders step through the doorway, their merciless eyes beady as they watched him. Fred clamped the telephone receiver to his ear; the horror on his face was proof that he could hear no one on the other end of the line.

The invaders didn't wait for Fred to get his connection. What they had heard was enough to settle their policy. This temporary interval was their opportunity. Before Fred had a chance to plead for life, the pair acted in concert. Stubby fingers pressed revolver triggers. Each weapon stabbed a single shot at six-foot range.

Fred's lanky body doubled. The telephone clattered from his hand and bounded on the floor. One second later, Fred's sprawling body thumped beside it. Ugly eyes watched the man's last squirm. Leering lips gave chuckles.

Killers had finished a man who knew too much. It had been easy to deliver cold-blooded death at this remote spot. This was one crime, they thought, that would never be traced. Their guess was a good one, so far as the law was concerned. But those killers were not considering another factor in the case.

Murderers were to pay for their deed, much sooner than they would have deemed possible. Speedy vengeance was due in this isolated place where men of crime had gained an evil triumph over a helpless victim.

CHAPTER II
CLUES IN THE NIGHT

THE sharp shots from Fred's shack were like a signal to other mobsters who waited in the touring car. One thug craned from behind the wheel, while two more sprang from the rear of the car. Reaching the door of the shack, the new pair was met by one of the murderers.

"We croaked the lug," growled a killer. "He was piping through a call to Joe Cardona! We'll listen to hear if Joe gets it. You guys take a gander in back of the shack. See if there's a buggy there."

The pair circled the shack. The killer in the doorway started in to join his companion, when he heard a warning *"Psst!"* from the driver of the touring car. The killer beckoned to his pal, who was listening at the telephone. The latter set the instrument on the desk and came to the doorway.

"Thought I heard a bus driving up!"

The warning words came from the touring car. The killers stared toward the roadway. They heard nothing, saw nothing. The *drip-drip* of the rain smothered the sounds that might have reached them. Hazy night added a blanket to obscure something that they might have observed.

A huge roadster was edging in from the roadway, coasting along with its motor stilled. The big car halted just short of being seen. From it emerged a shape that was lost in the darkness. Shrouded in night's blanket, an invisible arrival took stock of what he saw.

From his point of observation, that visitant spied the little side doorway near the rear corner of the shack. Clyde had left the door slightly ajar. Light gleamed through. Using that glow as an objective, a silent stalker approached through darkness.

One murderer was back at the telephone; the other was searching Fred's body when the door inched inward. A killer heard a slight creak; he whipped his revolver in the right direction as he stared instinctively toward the little door. The barrier swung wide.

On the threshold stood a shape of blackness—a cloaked figure that had materialized from night. Burning eyes peered along the line of a leveled automatic. That sight brought a hoarse shout of recognition from the killer's lips:

"The Shadow!"

HAVING trapped two killers on the actual scene of murder, The Shadow intended to hold them for the law. The telephone offered prompt communication with the authorities; and while the police were on the way, The Shadow would have opportunity for another task.

He could learn from his prisoners why they had come to this remote spot. The Shadow had a way of making ratty captives talk.

The murderers knew it. They recognized that The Shadow must have trailed them from New York. Only the foggish thickness of the drizzle had given them chance to lose The Shadow for short intervals. They were beginning to regret their hasty murder of Fred.

These thugs had some reason why they didn't want to talk. That was why they acted with sudden desperation.

One killer was crazed enough to open fire at The Shadow; a futile attempt, because the crook had no time for accurate aim. The other murderer chose a course that was equally unwise. He made a mad dive for the open doorway at the front of the shack, forgetful of the fact that The Shadow could easily drop him as he fled.

Luck favored the killers, where sense failed them. Without knowing it, the man who opened fire blocked The Shadow's aim for the rogue who was attempting flight. Rather than let one crook get away without punishment, The Shadow performed a sudden twist of tactics.

Instead of dropping the first crook with a point-blank shot, The Shadow wheeled out through the side door and cut for the front corner of the shack. The firing crook stopped short, gaping at the incorrect thought that his shots had driven off The Shadow.

For a moment, the killer was ready to follow; then he changed his mind. He ducked out through the front door, in hope of reaching the touring car.

Both killers were to learn their mistake, with promptness. The driver of the touring car saw them dashing toward him; he glimpsed The Shadow at the corner of the shack and gave a shout of warning. The murderers turned to deliver a hectic fire, that they began too late.

The Shadow's .45 spoke its own message. Two gun stabs were all that he required to stagger the fugitives. The first shot sprawled one thug on the running board of the touring car, where the crook clutched a wounded shoulder. The second bullet found the next man's gun arm. The killer dropped his revolver; he howled as he reeled toward the car.

The man behind the wheel had dropped low into the seat. He was sliding the car into gear, ready for flight, without waiting for his crippled pals to get aboard. That suited The Shadow.

The fierce laugh that shivered from his lips was an urge for the scared driver to hurry away and leave the actual murderers behind. That one fugitive could serve, later, to open a new trail to the big-shot who had sent this murder crew into action.

THE SHADOW'S policy was proof that he had made a miscalculation. He had not had a chance previously to learn the exact number of crooks in the touring car.

Arriving late, he had seen nothing of the pair that had gone to the back of the service station. They, in their turn, had not guessed that The Shadow was responsible for the firing that they had heard.

The pair had discovered Clyde's car. Starting the coupé, they came speeding around the corner of the shack just as The Shadow shifted off into the darkness. The glare of the headlights showed his cloaked form squarely in their path.

With raucous shouts, the thugs tried to take advantage of their lucky opportunity. The crook at the wheel tried to run The Shadow down, while the other leaned out with a revolver, to fire if The Shadow leaped away.

With split-second speed, The Shadow dodged the double menace. From his position, the gunmen expected him to dive to the right. The man in the driver's seat yanked the wheel in that direction, while his companion stretched wide from the window on the right. Both guessed wrong.

With a long bound, The Shadow went straight across the front of the oncoming car. He couldn't quite clear it with that spring; but the thump that he took from the left fender was a glancing one. Instead of rolling beneath the tires, The Shadow took a long pitch off into the darkness.

Flattening in the mud, The Shadow rolled over, in case his foemen had seen his landing spot. He came to hands and knees, still clutching his automatic. It would have gone badly with both crooks, had they stopped to battle further. They were wise enough, however, to keep on their way.

All that The Shadow saw of the coupé was the final twinkle of the taillight as it twisted past trees that lined the open road. He didn't even have time to recognize the car as Clyde's coupé. Coupled to that was another disappointment.

The coupé had cut across the touring car's path; in so doing, it delayed the touring car long enough for the crippled murderers to haul themselves aboard.

When The Shadow fired at the touring car, it was also on its way, blotted from sight in the haze. Both cars were in the clear, wheeling away in mad flight.

The Shadow remembered the telephone in Fred's shack. By a simple call, he could have the killers bottled. That would leave him free to investigate these surroundings, where valuable evidence might be found.

The telephone, itself, could be a clue, for The Shadow had noticed that the receiver was off the hook. There was still a chance to find out who Fred had been calling at the time when he was slain.

THE SHADOW hurried into the shack. He could hear *clicks* from the receiver before he reached it. Once the receiver was against The Shadow's ear, he recognized the excited voice that was coming across the wire. Joe Cardona had heard the shots over the telephone. The inspector was clamoring to know what had happened.

The tone that Cardona heard must have awed him, for Joe's babble ceased the moment that The Shadow spoke. In calm, whispered words, The Shadow announced his identity; then told Cardona exactly what had occurred. There was a short silence; after that, Cardona broke loose with a gruff-voiced thanks.

The New York inspector told The Shadow that he would promptly notify the New Jersey State police regarding the murderers. He added that the New York police would be on the watch, in case the thugs tried to head back into Manhattan.

Hanging up the telephone receiver, The Shadow stooped beside Fred's body and began a search. He found nothing in the way of a clue. Unfortunately,

Fred had torn up the paper that Clyde had given him. Those scattered fragments, lost outside, would have told The Shadow much of the entire story.

The call to Cardona was evidence that Fred had uncovered something that he thought the New York inspector would like to know. Whatever it was, it probably concerned some person unknown who had made a stop at the filling station.

That deduction was the reason why The Shadow went out to the gasoline standard and began examining tire tracks that he found there.

The Shadow saw marks that represented the touring car and the small coupé that he had not identified as Clyde's. Beside them were other tracks, that indicated a middle-sized car. The Shadow traced them; discovered that a car had pulled in from one direction and circled back the same way.

Entering his own car, The Shadow started along the road. He was using a yellowish foglight, tilted toward the hard surface. Rain had washed away the traces that The Shadow wanted, until he neared the bend. There, on the muddy shoulder of the road, were the same tracks that he had seen before.

Alighting, The Shadow discovered footprints. He recognized that the driver of the mystery car had stepped to the ground to look for something. The Shadow lost no more time. He drove along the road, his hawkish eyes on the lookout for more evidence.

THE trail was a blank one for nearly two miles. At that point, The Shadow saw a road that led to the left. It was a dirt road, muddied by rain despite the overhanging trees. Tire tracks showed in the mud.

On the ground, The Shadow examined the marks of the tire treads and made a careful measurement. They were the evidence he wanted.

The mystery car had gone along the dirt road. A map showed that the journey might prove a long one, for the road was poor and had intersections within the next five miles. There was a chance that the car might have stopped somewhere along this obscure road. It was also possible that if the car, had continued through, The Shadow might gain on it, during the five-mile course.

The Shadow was at the wheel. Gears meshed silently; the big roadster took smoothly to the dirt. The car gained speed along the lonely road. The Shadow was off on the quest that Clyde Burke had taken, a quarter-hour ago.

The Shadow's keen brain recognized that his trail might prove important; there was evidence to make it so. But The Shadow had gained no inkling that his agent was already involved. He was to learn of Clyde's part, later.

Finding an agent active on a trail was usually of advantage to The Shadow. This time, such a discovery was destined to produce disaster.

CHAPTER III
BROKEN STRATEGY

CLYDE BURKE had expected difficulty in clinging to the slippery back of the coupé. Instead, he had experienced no trouble. There had been a swift ride to the dirt road; after that, the car had rolled along at a very moderate pace. The man at the wheel was driving carefully.

The car had covered scarcely more than three miles in its quarter hour of travel, and Clyde was benefiting by the driver's care. He felt entirely secure on his perch; and with the gait no more than fifteen miles an hour, he resolved to break the monotony. There was a chance, Clyde decided, to learn more about the driver.

Gaining a good grip, the reporter pulled himself up to the rear window and looked into the interior of the car. Through the glass, Clyde could see the driver's wide shoulders and thick neck, but he couldn't get a good look at the mirror, which showed the fellow's face.

As he shifted his position for that purpose, Clyde happened to glance downward. What he saw, gripped his full attention.

The dashlight was a bright one. It showed the seat beside the driver. There lay the satchel that the man had picked up from the highway. The bag was a fair-sized one; it bulged so much that the clamp must have broken when it was pitched from the sedan that Clyde had seen go by the bend. The bag was wide open, its contents visible.

Clyde saw bundles of checks, that he recognized as the sort used in international exchange; bundles of currency, in American notes and bills of other countries. The bag was literally stuffed with wealth; but from the surface view, it was impossible to estimate the total.

Nevertheless, the sight held Clyde's eyes glued. That was why he failed to notice another pair of eyes, that peered suddenly toward him from the mirror above the windshield. Dark eyes, set in a flat, yellowish face; their sudden glint told that they had spotted the unwanted passenger on the back of the coupé.

Had Clyde looked at the mirror, he would have recognized that the driver of the car was actually a Turk, as Fred had said. But Clyde's opportunity went before he had a chance to take it. The Turk turned slightly so that his face could not be seen in the mirror. He was careful to give no inkling that he knew Clyde was on the back.

From that moment, the Turk began a cool campaign to lull Clyde into a false belief of security. He kept the car at its easy-rolling speed, picking the best spots of the road. When Clyde shifted back from the rear window, the Turk did not even notice it. He was confident that sight of the open bag would keep Clyde right where he was.

That was all the Turk wanted. It was the build-up for a coming stroke of strategy.

AT the end of a half mile, wheel tracks ran from the left of the road. They marked the entrance of a private byway that led through the woods. The Turk swung deliberately into the wheel tracks; brought the car to a stop in front of bars that lay between two fence posts. He opened the door beside him and stepped from the car.

This time, Clyde saw the Turk plainly; for the man made no effort to obscure himself as he walked into the path of the headlights. He took down the fence bars; carried them, one by one, to the darkness beside the rutty road.

Each time he lugged a rail, he paused to stack it before he returned. Those intervals—the first two—were the strategy that deceived Clyde.

Drawn high on the back of the coupé, Clyde watched through the window, expecting the Turk to come back into the light. Clyde allowed a half minute, because of the other delays. The thirty seconds had passed before Clyde suddenly suspected that something different had occurred. On a quick impulse, he shifted downward from the back of the coupé.

There was a splash, five feet away, just as Clyde's feet hit the ground. The reporter swung about, to see the Turk spring from a puddly spot. The yellowish face looked ruddy, demonish, in the glare of the red taillight. The fellow was coming for Clyde; the reporter's only course was to meet him.

Quick punches were Clyde's method. The Turk's big arms warded them off. The grab that he made for Clyde was the quick clutch of a wrestler's. Clyde tried to dodge, but he was backed against the car.

He stabbed a hard punch; it landed beside the Turk's jaw, but it lacked the weight to stop the fellow. A second later, Clyde's arms were pinned.

The reporter didn't succumb as easily as the Turk expected. Clyde was wiry, and proved it when his husky foe started to drag him from the bumperettes. A hard twist; Clyde was free enough to engage in a furious grapple.

He heard the Turk's breath hiss harshly, as though the fellow relished such a fight. Clyde found out why, when the Turk displayed more wrestling tactics.

Every clutch resulted in a fall for Clyde. The Turk threw him around the muddy road, off into the underbrush, with heaves that would have been knockouts on a wrestling floor. The soft turf was Clyde's salvation. Each time, he managed to be out from under, when the Turk came thudding upon him.

The finish came when the Turk finally missed a throw. The husky slipped on a patch of skiddy moss; went plopping backwards, hanging on to Clyde. Instead of wrenching away, Clyde saw a chance he thought would win the combat. He threw his own weight on the Turk, caught the man's neck and flattened the fellow's big shoulders on the ground.

There wasn't any referee to give Clyde the verdict; so it didn't count. Instead, the Turk's big hands smacked upward, took Clyde in a grip that nullified the neck hold.

Clyde twisted, writhing in a torturing clamp that would have done credit to a python. He felt himself roll over, to land on his back with a hard thwack. This time, he had no chance to get away before the Turk's full weight planked on him.

When the big man arose, Clyde was lying limp and dazed.

THE Turk grunted; picked up his prisoner and carried him over one shoulder to the coupé. With his free hand, the man put the opened satchel on the floor and sprawled Clyde in the front seat. He turned on the domelight, studied the face of his exhausted prisoner.

From a deep pocket, the Turk produced a small hypodermic syringe. He jabbed the needle into Clyde's arm. Circling the car, he took his place behind the wheel.

He watched the reporter for a few minutes; decided that the dope was taking effect. Turning out the domelight, the Turk started his car ahead. He did not stop to replace the fence rails.

Despite the rain, the Turk had the window open beside him. He was listening intently as he drove slowly along. At one place, the thickness of the overhanging boughs produced a hush despite the heavy rain. It was that quiet that gave the Turk his chance to hear a sound from behind his car.

The Turk had gained the sudden impression that another car had stolen into the woods behind him. Somewhere along this narrow, twisted road, a clever pursuer had doused his own lights, to creep up behind the coupé.

That, whether or not the Turk knew it, was a piece of strategy often used by The Shadow. Clyde's battle had given his chief a chance to close in on the trail. It was seldom that anyone detected The Shadow's ruse; but the wily Turk had done so, thanks to the intermittent behavior of the rain.

Just as he had trapped Clyde, so did the Turk prepare a snare for the unseen follower in the car behind him.

The coupé came to the end of the private road. It was simply a twisted crosscut through the woods, that terminated in another barring gate.

The Turk stopped; opened the door beside him. As he alighted, he drew Clyde over to the driver's

seat. The reporter hunched there; the dope had put him completely to sleep.

Leaving the door ajar, the Turk stepped forward. He took the fence rails one by one and pitched them from the road. The procedure was swift; the Turk was back to the car in less than a minute. As he arrived there, he paused. Giving the door a slight slam, he huddled low beside the fender.

The big rock ripped from the mossy soil, went crashing downward like a juggernaut. The Shadow went with it.

The trick was neat. Apparently, the driver had returned to his car. A few seconds more, the coupé would be on its way. This was the one chance to halt it. The Turk expected a challenge, and it came.

A tall figure suddenly blurred the window beside the wheel. A whispered voice spoke, as a gloved hand thrust inward with an automatic. An instant later, The Shadow's eyes saw the hunched position of the man at the wheel.

With an upward move of his wrist, The Shadow tilted Clyde's head backward. In the glow of the dashlight, he gained a startling sight. The Shadow was staring at the face of his own agent, gaining his first knowledge of the fact that Clyde Burke had first found this trail.

A BACKLASH was The Shadow's next move. He recoiled from the side of the car so suddenly that he was clear of the step when the husky Turk came hurtling from the darkness.

The Shadow had no time to aim. He was still twisting at the moment of the Turk's arrival. As big hands shot toward him, The Shadow let his auto-matic drop. His clamping fists hooked the Turk's forearms; halted them short of their mark. The fighters locked in a terrific fray.

The Turk had toyed with Clyde, during that earlier struggle, trying throws as the quickest method toward victory. With The Shadow he used headlocks, exerting a strength that had bone-crushing power.

The Shadow displayed the same tactics, meeting his opponent's efforts with equal skill. They wallowed through the mud; rolled to a grassy slope that lay between two big trees.

There, The Shadow took a deliberate sprawl, falling away from the Turk's hard lunges. Instantly, the Turk hurled himself upon his flattened adversary. Arms first, his hands going for The Shadow's shoulders, the Turk made an accurate plunge in the darkness. So accurate, that it served the very purpose that The Shadow had intended.

Hands, thrust upward, landed like steel clamps upon the Turk's descending arms. The Shadow's right leg, doubled upward, struck like a lever against his opponent's chest. An overhead kick gave impetus to the Turk's drive, sent the big man on a long somersault.

The Turk's spin was so swift that he never gained a chance to claw The Shadow.

There was a rolling clatter in the darkness. That stilled as The Shadow came to his feet and started to find his adversary. The Turk was sprawled beside a tree; close to him was a large rock, projecting from steep, slippery ground.

The Turk was groggy; but he rallied as The Shadow gripped him. He was ready for one last defiant effort.

The Shadow had another jiujitsu trick to take care of that. He twisted the Turk sideways; faded away to spill the fellow with a clipping scissors throw. All that The Shadow needed was a brace; he shoved his shoulders against the big rock.

The Turk lunged. The Shadow's legs clipped; his foe did a sideways tumble that ended in a helpless sprawl. But with it, the Turk was due for unexpected victory. All The Shadow's weight was against the big rock. That solid brace gave like a collapsing wall.

The rock overhung a gully. Its foundations loosened by the rain, the big stone was ready for a topple. It ripped from the mossy soil, went crashing downward like a Juggernaut, clearing a swath through the saplings that lined the edge of the steep ravine.

The Shadow went with it. The hole that the rock left was a large one; it swallowed him before he could clutch firm ground. The depths of the gully were like a vortex, that sucked its victim downward. The path that the huge stone cleared left nothing that could stop The Shadow's plunge.

THE groggy Turk heard the echoes from below; the clatter of the rock as it bashed the bottom of the gully. He came to his feet and crept to the brink, where he felt the sudden slant of the ground past the edge.

Echoes had stilled from the depths; but the Turk did not listen long to the patter of the rain.

Instead, he groped his way to the spot where his car stood. Pushing Clyde away from the wheel, the Turk took the driver's seat. He started the coupé out through the open fence. Once in the clear, he did not pause to bar the way behind him.

Again, the mystery driver was carrying Clyde Burke as a helpless prisoner, along with a satchel of wealth. This time, The Shadow was no longer on the trail.

CHAPTER IV
THE LAW'S SEARCH

A DOZEN minutes after the coupé's departure, there was a stir in the depths of the gully. A tiny flashlight flicked from close to the ground. On one elbow, The Shadow dully studied the rocky bed that had been his landing place.

The Shadow's fall had been a slanted one, a distance of some thirty feet. He had handled the spill with the skill of a professional tumbler; but a jolt against a hidden stone had stunned him at the finish.

He couldn't gauge how long he had lain there; but the steady sweep of the rain had certainly helped to revive him.

The main move was to get back to the roadway above the gully. The Shadow picked a path where small trees offered hold. He swayed dizzily at times, during the upward climb; but he was steady when he reached the top. Groping to the rutty road, The Shadow found his own car.

The big roadster was intact. The Turk hadn't wasted time to put the car out of commission. Chances were slight that The Shadow could overtake him. Nevertheless, with Clyde a prisoner, that was The Shadow's only course.

Discarding his cloak and slouch hat, The Shadow picked a raincoat from the rumble seat and slipped it over his water-soaked shoulders. He drove the roadster through the gate, came upon a dirt road like the one that he had formerly traveled. His foglight showed the coupé's tire tracks. The Shadow followed them.

Half a mile produced a narrow hard-surfaced highway. The Shadow saw tracks that told the coupé's direction. Those marks were to prove the finish of the trail. Within a half mile, The Shadow came to a crossroad, with a fork beyond it. There wasn't a mark on the macadam to tell which way the coupé had gone.

Consulting a road map, The Shadow made a choice and took that road. He came to another crossing; while he deliberated, he saw the lights of an approaching car coming from the right.

Before he could start, he heard a shrill whistle. The car halted beside The Shadow's roadster and a pair of New Jersey State police came from it.

One of the officers used a flashlight; it showed The Shadow's face. The police saw a thin, hawk-like visage beneath a felt hat; below, the collar and tie of a tuxedo collar that projected from the raincoat. They were impressed by the appearance of the roadster's driver; particularly, the quiet manner of his gaze. They asked for his license.

The Shadow produced it. The State trooper stared when he saw the name on the New York card. He looked at The Shadow's face, recognized it as one that he had seen in newspaper photographs.

"Kent Allard!" exclaimed the officer. "Say—you're the famous aviator, aren't you? The fellow who was down in Central America all those years?" *

The Shadow smiled as he gave a nod of admission.

"Sorry to have troubled you, Mr. Allard." The trooper returned the license card. "If there's anything we can do for you—"

"There is. I am trying to find the highway to Manhattan."

The State cop grinned. This was a good one: Kent Allard, the famous aviator, lost in the maze of New Jersey highways!

"We'll show you the way, Mr. Allard," said the trooper. "Better keep along with us, so other patrols won't stop you. We're covering all the roads tonight."

"How does that happen?"

THE officer explained. There had been a murder at a filling station. The victim had been calling New York police headquarters when he was slain. A New York inspector—Joe Cardona—had learned that Manhattan thugs were responsible. The Jersey police were looking for them.

"We've got those fellows bottled," declared the trooper. "Every main road covered. We're searching every secondary highway, on the lookout for suspicious cars."

Kent Allard became thoughtful. He remembered a coupé that he had seen a short while ago. One with a New Jersey license plate; he recalled the number in uncertain fashion, not quite sure of it.

The news impressed the troopers. They decided to report it, particularly when Allard said that the car had cut in from a dirt road.

The Shadow had named the license number of

---

*See *The Shadow Unmasks*, reprinted in *The Shadow* Volume 15.

the Turk's coupé; and his uncertainty was merely a pose. He had spotted the number, figure for figure, during his approach in the darkness.

Following the patrol car to the main highway, The Shadow decided that he had taken the only feasible method to aid Clyde, for the present. A search of his own would be impossible, with patrol cars all about. It was best to let the law do the work.

They were hunting for thugs, but they would certainly halt the Turk's coupé if they saw it. The fact that the number had been reported would force a questioning of the driver and whoever happened to be with him. That could produce Clyde's rescue.

LESS than two hours later, Kent Allard strolled into the exclusive Cobalt Club, in Manhattan. He was dressed in fresh attire; he looked about in quizzical fashion, as if seeking someone.

An attendant approached, to inform him that Police Commissioner Weston was in the grillroom.

Going down a flight of steps, Allard saw Weston seated at a corner table with Joe Cardona. Both the commissioner and the inspector gave greeting when Allard joined them.

"Hoped you'd be here, Allard," announced Weston, briskly. Then, with a smile: "We've just learned that your memory isn't quite as good as it might be."

For a moment, Allard's face looked puzzled. Then, the answer dawned.

"You've heard from the New Jersey police?"

Weston nodded; turned to Cardona, with the comment: "Tell Mr. Allard the details, Inspector."

Cardona gave them, in methodical fashion. The Jersey police had finally caught up with two cars on a main highway. They had wrecked the first one, a touring car, with bullets, when the occupants had opened fire. The three men in it had been killed. They proved to be New York gunmen; but they had given a surprisingly poor battle.

Allard made no comment at that point, but he could have explained a detail that Joe hadn't heard in The Shadow's telephone call. The murderers had been more effectively crippled than Cardona supposed. The Shadow's bullets were responsible for their inability to put up a hard fight.

There was another car, Cardona added; it was a coupé that had made a getaway, heading for the Jersey hinterlands. The State police hadn't managed to get its license number.

"Too bad," remarked Allard. "It may have been the suspicious car that I sighted on the back road. I reported that number, you know."

"We know," nodded Cardona, "but this wasn't the car. From what the State police did see of the license, they decided it was a New York plate. The car you saw had a Jersey tag, Mr. Allard."

"Quite true."

"And it hasn't been seen. The State highway department checked on the number. Your guess wasn't right, Mr. Allard. The number you gave them belongs to a car from Atlantic City. It's owned by a real estate man; he's at home and the car's in the garage where it belongs."

Allard chuckled at his own supposed error. He saw a road map on the table and began to study it. Cardona had marked it with a pencil. He explained that the marks represented spots where the Jersey police had barricaded the roads.

"They're still looking for a coupé," reminded Cardona, "and they may pick up the one you saw. Only, the tag won't have the number you thought, Mr. Allard."

ONE hour later, Allard left the Cobalt Club, after Commissioner Weston had received another report from New Jersey. Nothing had been seen of either coupé. Allard had received that news in an indifferent fashion, but it meant much more to him than Weston supposed.

Soon, a light came on in a darkened room. Ghostly, bluish rays provided a strange light upon a polished table. Hands crept beneath that glow, long-fingered hands that moved like creatures with a will of their own. From one hand glimmered a deep-tinted gem, a rare girasol of ever-changing hue.

The Shadow was in his hidden sanctum. Above the light was the burn of keen eyes; the air was tinged with the strange whisper of an inimitable laugh. The hands spread a map upon the table.

Fingers gripped a pencil, to mark the network of New Jersey roads with barriers identical to those that Joe Cardona had indicated for Kent Allard.

The Shadow was considering the mystery of the vanished coupés. One car was easily explained. It was Clyde's car, with a New York license; the machine that thugs had stolen from in back of the service station.

When that car had fled, The Shadow had logically supposed that it belonged to Fred, the service station man; for The Shadow had not had a chance to spot the New York tags. From Cardona's report, The Shadow had later learned that Fred, living alone at the service station, was unprovided with an automobile.

The riddle involving the Turk's coupé required another answer. The news from Atlantic City gave it. The Turk was driving a car that had counterfeit license plates. That fact was most important, for it enabled The Shadow to carry his analysis further.

Anyone driving a car with false license tags would be due for trouble, if he encountered police at anytime. Though The Shadow had not seen the satchel on the floor of the Turk's car, he knew that the man must have been bound on some important errand; he also surmised that the trip had not been the first that the Turk had made to Fred's service station.

The risk of a meeting with the law told two things about the mystery car's journey. First, it could not have come far; second, it must have kept exclusively to side roads.

That accounted for the car's later disappearance. The Turk had been lucky enough to reach his destination before patrollers met him. That left a limited area where the fellow's hideaway could be. Chances were that the Turk had taken Clyde to the same place, within the cordon that the New Jersey police had so promptly formed.

The Shadow studied the map, looking for loopholes. There were none. With the point where he had fought the Turk as a central spot, The Shadow found that all side roads had been barricaded where they met main highways. The one difficulty was the size of the space between.

It formed an irregular area, shaped roughly like a long diamond. The nearest point, a crossing of two main arteries, was only twenty miles from New York. But the far point of the diamond, another highway junction, was more than twenty miles west of the first one. From north to south, the space measured about twelve miles at the widest, tapering sharply as it neared the east and west extremities.

Roads were numerous in that area, and the State police had confined their search to those byways. A more extensive search was necessary—one that must be undertaken by picked men, working in systematic fashion.

It might require a week for an undercover crew to complete the scouring of that district; but there was a chance that some member of the search party would happen upon the objective soon after the hunt began.

THAT possibility decided The Shadow's next move.

Hands reached for earphones. A voice came over a wire:

"Burbank speaking."

The Shadow's hand marked sections on the map, as he spoke orders to the contact man. The Shadow was sending word to all his agents, through Burbank, assigning each man a section of territory to be covered. With those orders, The Shadow added details regarding contact between the searchers. All reports were to be relayed to a central point of the area.

The map looked like a patchwork design, when The Shadow had finished his instructions. Gaping from the exact center of the marked area was the largest block of the lot: a diamond that formed a core of the entire territory. That space was significant. It was the ground that The Shadow had chosen to search in person.

The bluish light went out. Deep stillness existed in the thick blackness of the sanctum. The room seemed empty, until a sibilant tone told that a presence remained there. That tone was a sinister laugh, mirthless in its rasp, foreboding doom to men of crime.

That laugh left shuddering echoes. When those reverberations had faded, the sanctum was actually deserted. The Shadow had departed to resume his quest, aided by a full quota of trusted agents. Efforts would be ceaseless, until Clyde Burke was found.

The law's search had ended. The Shadow's hunt had begun!

CHAPTER V
THE HIDDEN STRONGHOLD

WHEN Clyde Burke awakened, he found himself in surroundings that seemed singularly pleasant. That was due to the dreams that he had experienced. His brain teemed with a medley of fantastic images, produced by the dope that had quieted him.

Clyde was stretched on a divan, in a room that was lavish with rare furniture and expensive Oriental rugs. Soft light glowed from an ornamental wall bracket. Clyde saw a large door that looked formidable; he noticed suddenly that the room was windowless.

That accounted for a constant coolness that filled the place. Clyde realized that the room was air-conditioned, and in that state, it was entirely cut off from the world. He was in a veritable prison cell, despite its de luxe appearance.

A chaos of bewildering nightmares still troubled Clyde. He could picture hideous, fanciful creatures that had surrounded him. They seemed to people this very room, as if ready to spring forth and begin new torment. Clyde felt an irresistible desire to be gone from these premises.

He sprang for the door, to stumble before he reached it. Regaining his feet, Clyde rattled the doorknob. The door wouldn't open. It was locked and its bulk made it impregnable.

The spasm of horror passed; Clyde collected his scattered impressions and managed to reach a chair. He noted his attire; it was real enough. Clyde was wearing his own clothes, except for shoes, coat and vest. Those garments were resting tidily upon a chair.

Clyde managed to grin. At least *he* was real, even if the place wasn't.

Clyde's first act was to search his own pockets, to see what they contained. They proved empty;

someone had rifled them of their entire contents. That didn't worry Clyde; he couldn't think of anything he carried that would connect him with The Shadow.

Tracing the past, Clyde assembled sensible thoughts from his confusion. He remembered the drizzly drive along the New Jersey roads; the stop at Fred's filling station. He recalled the trip on the back of the coupé, with the struggle at the finish.

All during those recollections, Clyde fought to discard thoughts of nightmarish faces that kept cropping up from his dreams. Sometimes, those impressions gripped him so strongly that he could scarcely resist them.

Clyde remembered the sinister mustached Turk who had battled him; he identified the fellow among the faces from the nightmare. The whole room seemed to cloud; Clyde shut his eyes as he gripped the arms of his chair.

With his eyes shut, the room seemed whirling. Faces tormented him; dancing figures gestured and pointed. Clyde could fancy the babble of jeering tongues. Tilted in his chair, he lost his balance; he felt himself falling, as he actually was. But that short drop to the floor was like a plunge into a limitless abyss.

Clyde felt his final thud. He was surprised that it was such a light one. The jolt cleared his thoughts; the vicious faces faded. Then came hands, that raised him. Strong arms, but easy in their lift. Clyde felt himself settle back into his chair. He opened his eyes.

THE stare that Clyde gave was as fixed as a hypnotic gaze. He was looking squarely at a face that he remembered from that last chaos of thoughts—the one face of the lot that actually existed. The man who had raised him from the floor was the flat-faced Turk who had conquered him in last night's battle.

Oddly, sight of the man in the flesh was something that steadied Clyde's broken nerves. If any of the other faces had proved real, Clyde would have gone berserk. But this one, actual and alive, drove away impressions of the others. It brought back Clyde's sane thoughts. His lips smiled relief as he settled back in his chair.

The Turk spoke placidly, in English, but with a slow, choppy accent. His query was a careful one, tinged with concern:

"You feel better?"

Clyde nodded. He tried to answer, but his voice was choky, inarticulate.

"I am Yakbar," spoke the Turk. "You come with me?"

The last sentence sounded like a question; but Clyde realized that it was probably an order. Finding his voice, Clyde parried:

"Where do you want to take me?"

"To see the master," returned Yakbar. "He has said that I must bring you."

The Turk's tone was firmer. Clyde decided it best to visit the master mentioned by Yakbar. He started to get up from his chair; he would have tumbled but for Yakbar. The fellow caught Clyde and guided him to the door. This time, it stood open.

There was a trip through a short passage; a turn into another, with doors along the way. At last, they reached the end of a short corridor. There, Yakbar knocked at a final door.

A deep voice gave command to enter. Yakbar opened the door and urged Clyde through.

Clyde saw a room much larger than his own; but it, also, was windowless. It was furnished like an office; behind a big desk, Clyde saw a man of impressive appearance. He was elderly; his tight-skinned face denoted that, as did his shock of pure white hair.

But there was power in the long, scrawny hands that lay upon the desk; persuasion in the challenging, blackish eyes that glittered from the old man's countenance.

As Clyde stared, the white-haired man arose; he extended a hand for a shake across the desk. Clyde felt a powerful grip; he heard the boom of heavy-toned words, that were repressed with a peculiar effort of the old man's lips, so that they became a drilling purr:

"Good afternoon, Mr. Burke! I am Doctor Nicholas Borth. It pleases me to welcome you as my guest. Be seated, I request you."

CLYDE took a chair that Yakbar offered him. All the while, the reporter retained his stare toward Borth. Clyde had met men of many nationalities, and thought himself an expert at placing any foreigners; but Nicholas Borth baffled him. Either Borth was a man who had no country, or he was one who was at home in any land.

Doctor Borth seemed to relish Clyde's bewilderment, for his smile was an indulgent one. There was something friendly in the old man's manner—enough to make Clyde ask:

"How did you learn my name?"

"From these." Borth produced an envelope and slid Clyde's belongings to the desk. "You may reclaim them, Mr. Burke, for they are your property. But wait"—Borth raised a restraining hand—"I have not yet finished with introductions."

Borth gestured to his right. Clyde looked, to see a girl step from beside a filing cabinet. Her eyes met Clyde's; with that glance, Clyde felt a pleased impression.

The girl's face had a loveliness, along with a

frank expression. Her eyes had a sympathy, that was shown also by her lips. She was a blonde, and Clyde was positive that she was either English or American.

"This is Miss Delban," introduced Borth; then, as Clyde came to his feet: "Be seated, Mr. Burke. Miss Delban is my secretary. She has much to do here. For the present, however"—Borth's smile was a dry one—"she will join us."

With that, Borth turned to the girl and indicated a chair. He added the comment:

"Have your notebook ready, Diane."

Diane Delban. Clyde intended to remember that name, as well as the girl to whom it belonged. Diane's manner, the open look that she gave were meant to tell Clyde that he had one friend in these strange surroundings.

Clyde was prompt to catch that expression. With it, he sensed a warning that was easy to understand.

It would be best for Clyde to comply with any request that Doctor Borth might make. The piercing eyes that shone from Borth's withery face were the sort that could harden if they found occasion. Clyde felt sure that Borth was capable of dealing harshly with any person that he considered an enemy.

As for Yakbar, Clyde had already encountered the Turk's methods. The bone-crushing wrestler might prove murderous, if it came to a struggle in Borth's headquarters.

Clyde's speculations ended as Borth purred a question. The restrained rumble was a demand for information.

"YOU are a reporter, Mr. Burke," declared Borth. "Tell me, just how did you happen to embark on your present adventure?"

"I was lost in the back roads," replied Clyde. "I happened to stop at a filling station. I was there when Yakbar's car arrived."

"And then?"

"Yakbar waited. I wondered why. I saw his face; I wondered why a Turk was in New Jersey. Just on a crazy impulse, I climbed onto the back of his car."

Clyde's story was a partial statement of fact. He was intimating that his purpose was to obtain a newspaper story. Just how far Borth believed it, Clyde could not tell. The wise-faced doctor eyed Clyde steadily, but showed no change of expression.

"I shall give you a story, Mr. Burke," announced Borth, "and it will be a very good one. Provided that you do not make it public until a future date that I shall specify. Is that agreeable?"

Clyde decided that it was. Borth leaned across the desk; resting his chin in his hand, he spoke emphatically.

"The location of this headquarters must remain a secret!" declared Borth—"for a very simple reason. I am the representative of certain wealthy Europeans

who were forced to flee from their homelands, because they were persecuted by tyrannical governments. They found refuge in England, bringing fortunes in jewels.

"Even there, they feared spies. They decided to convert their wealth into money, by sending the gems to America. They entrusted me with the task of selling the gems—for which I receive a nominal commission, which will amount, however, to more than a million dollars.

"In order to protect myself, I have operated from this hidden stronghold; and that policy has proved wise. Criminals in this country have learned of my possessions, and are seeking to acquire them."

The story sounded plausible; Borth's convincing tone gave it a true touch. There was one point, however, that didn't click with Clyde. Borth must have guessed it, for he promptly covered the detail.

"Last night," he stated, "Yakbar made a regularly scheduled trip to pick up funds that were due from the sale of jewels. While I employ many selling agents, none know the location of this headquarters. Trusted persons bring checks and cash at stated intervals; but they always drop them at a place where Yakbar finds them."

That explained the matter of the satchel. Cannily, Doctor Borth had taken it for granted that Clyde had seen the money bag. He added a final statement:

"I have told you the whole story, Mr. Burke. If you wish, I shall have Miss Delban support my testimony." He turned to Diane. "Have I included every point, Diane?"

For a moment, Clyde saw the girl hesitate. She looked toward Clyde; then turned her eyes in Borth's direction. It was to the doctor that Diane said:

"You have given the facts, Doctor Borth."

THERE was a pause, while Borth stroked his tight-skinned chin. He was thinking about Clyde's presence here. When he spoke, his tone was smooth.

"Yakbar feared that you might be an enemy," Borth told the reporter. "That is why he brought you here. I am quite willing to release you, with the proviso that Yakbar take you, blindfolded, to a place some distance from here. Afterward, you will be free to relate your adventure here, for I shall soon leave this headquarters and return to Europe.

"Unfortunately, my plans are still uncertain. I might find it impossible to communicate with you at later date. Therefore, I suggest that you remain here for a few days. If you do"—Borth's tone was like a promise—"I might furnish you with more facts. Are you willing to remain, Mr. Burke?"

Clyde caught a nod from Diane. It indicated that there was actually but one choice: that was to accept Borth's invitation. Clyde did so, but with reservations.

"If I remain," he asked, "will I be a guest or a prisoner?"

"A guest," assured Borth. "Your room will be unlocked. I must specify, however, that if you come from your room, you must remain on this floor, exclusively!"

Clyde was about to ask what penalty would follow if he failed to abide by the terms. He decided to omit that question; but Borth again caught the thought and gave the answer.

"Should you take unfair advantage of my hospitality," the doctor added, "your status will become that of a prisoner. Those terms are fair, Mr. Burke. Do you accept?"

"I accept."

Doctor Borth bowed when he heard Clyde's reply. Rising, the doctor again indicated the objects that belonged to Clyde. While the reporter was pocketing them, Borth ended the interview with the abrupt declaration:

"Yakbar will conduct you back to your room. We shall dine in half an hour, Mr. Burke."

As Yakbar held the door open for Clyde's departure, the reporter looked back toward Doctor Borth. Past the elderly man, Clyde saw Diane. She was holding the notebook in which she had copied shorthand notes of everything that Clyde and Borth had said. For the first time, the girl was entirely clear of observation by either Borth or Yakbar.

Diane's lips framed words that she could not utter aloud. Clyde was unable to catch their import, but Diane's expression told him much. Her face was eager; tinged with anxiety. She was beseeching Clyde to be careful; at the same time, she was making it plain that he must somehow manage to talk with her alone.

That, Clyde decided, was something that he would accomplish at the first opportunity. No matter how hazardous the quest might be, it might produce facts that Doctor Nicholas Borth had craftily refrained from mentioning to his guest.

When Clyde finally left this hidden abode, he would carry more news than Doctor Borth expected. Clyde intended to have a complete report for The Shadow.

CHAPTER VI
CLYDE GAINS NEWS

ONCE back in his room, Clyde began to examine the articles that Doctor Borth had returned to him. Such an item as his New York reporter's card had served him in good stead. Whatever enemies Borth avoided, reporters certainly could not be classed among them.

After pocketing his belongings, Clyde noted his watch. It showed the time as half past six; Clyde thought the watch was stopped, until he saw the second hand moving steadily. That made him remember Borth's greeting.

The doctor had welcomed Clyde with the words "Good afternoon"; and, later, he had mentioned dinner.

This wasn't Thursday morning, as Clyde had first supposed. It was Thursday evening. Clyde had slept all through the day. No wonder he had awakened dopey! Yakbar must have given him an oversized injection.

While Clyde was thinking about Yakbar, there was a rap at the door. It was the Turk, himself, announcing that dinner was ready.

Clyde took that news eagerly, for he foresaw another meeting with Diane. He was disappointed. Yakbar led him to a dining room opposite the office, and there Clyde found Doctor Borth alone.

The dry-faced doctor gave no explanation for Diane's absence. He simply chatted with Clyde on other subjects, while Yakbar served an excellent dinner.

Borth mentioned a point that he had forgotten. He thought it best that Clyde's office have some explanation for the reporter's absence. Clyde agreed with that; when Borth supplied him with a telegraph blank, Clyde thought a while, then wrote out a message.

He didn't have a chance to code anything into the wire; he simply stated that he was seeking a special story and would return before the end of the week.

That apparently satisfied Borth. The doctor said that he would have Yakbar send the telegram from a nearby city. That left Clyde completely in the dark. Judging from the hours that he had slept, Clyde believed that he might be as far as five hundred miles from New York.

With Borth chatting about everything except the subject of his guarded gems, Clyde began to feel the aftereffects of the dope. He was almost asleep, sitting up, when they had finished dinner.

Borth suggested that his guest take another rest. Clyde went back to his room, alone; once there, he stretched on the divan and went to sleep.

Whether or not Clyde had used good judgment in letting Borth send the telegram was something that only the future could tell. As he slipped into his drowse, Clyde decided that the doctor could have sent one anyway, with Clyde's name on it; so it didn't much matter.

Somehow, this hidden lair, with its lavish furnishings, constant coolness and unchanging light, was a place where worry could not come until something happened.

IN fact, Clyde had gained the feeling that time stood still in the abode of Doctor Borth. It wasn't the dope that caused that peculiar sensation, for Clyde experienced it again when he awoke, this time without the troublesome recollection of hideous nightmares.

Fishing his watch from his vest pocket, Clyde noted the time. The timepiece said quarter of twelve.

Was it still Thursday evening; or did the watch signify the close approach of Friday noon?

Puzzling over that question, Clyde realized why he had gained the odd impressions about the passage of time. Daylight never penetrated to these windowless rooms. In such a cavernous dwelling, even a watch could not be called accurate.

There was another problem, Clyde had a distinct idea that something had awakened him. He groped for a recollection of a noise that he must have heard. While he was trying to place it, the sound came again—a soft, hasty *rap-tap* at his door.

The knocks ended, as though frightened away. When they did not recur, Clyde decided to investigate.

He found the door unlocked as Doctor Borth had promised. The corridor was lighted, but empty and profoundly silent. Clyde closed his door behind him; he stole along the corridors, the tufted carpeting stilling his footsteps.

He was puzzled about the doors, until he reached the one that opened into Borth's office. Clyde tried that door; it opened almost at his touch.

The office was empty. Once inside, Clyde decided that he had not violated Borth's terms. The white-haired doctor had simply specified that Clyde remain on this particular floor. That proviso itself was a puzzler. Picturing this as an underground abode, Clyde wondered how other floors came into it.

Looking around the office, Clyde gingerly tried the drawers of filing cabinets; he found them locked. The same was true of the desk drawers. Clyde's only discovery of any interest was a clock on the desk, its dial marked with twenty-four hours instead of only twelve.

Clyde knew that such clocks were sometimes used in Europe; and evidently Borth had brought this one with him. It was most useful in a place like this; and it had a space below the dial that showed the date.

From it, Clyde learned that his recent sleep had been a short one. It was still Thursday evening, although midnight was very close.

There was a door in a corner alcove. Clyde tried it, found it unlocked. He saw a circular stairway, leading farther underground. That explained Borth's warning regarding the limits to which Clyde could go. The opportunity, however, was one that Clyde could not let pass.

Dim light glowed from the bottom of the staircase;

those metal steps invited Clyde's descent. With no one about, a trip below seemed worth the risk.

CAREFULLY, Clyde went to the bottom of the steps; built solidly, the staircase gave no *clangs.* Below were short passages—a maze resembling the one above, but without doors at the sides.

Stealing along stone floors, between close-hemmed walls, Clyde at last saw a door ahead. Sight of it brought a quick intake of his breath.

The door was a bulky barrier of steel, with a combination like that of a vault. Beyond it could lie the treasure store that Doctor Borth claimed was in his keeping!

Clyde hadn't estimated how much that wealth might be; but from Doctor Borth's mention of commissions, Clyde figured that the total value ran into millions. It didn't seem likely that the vault door would be unlocked, but it was worth a chance to try it. First, though, Clyde stole back to a passage and listened to make sure no one was on his trail.

He fancied that he heard a stir from a side passage, where someone might have stopped at the sound of his return. Complete quiet followed, and Clyde was reassured. He decided to have a quick look at the vault; then return upstairs. He started boldly on his mission.

A dozen feet short of his objective, Clyde heard an excited whisper that struck a warning to his brain. He turned half about; before he could take another forward step, hands seized him. Clyde looked into the anxious face of Diane Delban.

"No farther!" exclaimed the girl. "I feared that you had come down here. You must go upstairs again, at once!"

Diane's tone told of real danger if Clyde advanced toward the vault door. But her anxiety for him to return upstairs was less important. Clyde leaned against the wall; he smiled slightly as he studied the girl's face. He saw a chance to learn new facts by continuing the girl's alarm.

"Tell me," questioned Clyde, "was it you who tapped at my door?"

"Yes," replied Diane. "I wanted to talk to you. I couldn't stay long at your door. I might have been observed there."

"By Yakbar?"

"Yes. Or by the others."

"The others? I thought that Yakbar was the doctor's only servant."

"There are others," declared Diane. "Many others! Like you, Mr. Burke, I once believed that Yakbar was Doctor Borth's only servant. That was when I met Doctor Borth, in London, where he told me the same story that you heard this evening.

"I came to America with Doctor Borth. For a while, we stayed at a hotel in New York. Then he spoke of enemies; we moved here"—Diane paused—"wherever this place may be. But it was just before we came here that I learned what his real business was; and who the enemies were that he feared."

Diane's eyes met Clyde's. Her hands pressed the reporter's arm. Steadily, the girl stated:

"Doctor Borth is a counterfeiter! He finishes work in one country, then goes to another. He floods every land with false currency, and departs before the law can apprehend him!"

CLYDE recalled recent reports of bad money in New York. He hadn't thought it a serious wave, because "queer" money peddlers were always starting anew, after one batch had been suppressed. But in this case, Diane's revelation pointed to a gigantic swindle. Managed by Doctor Borth, from a stronghold such as this, a counterfeiting enterprise could give the law a long run.

"Doctor Borth tested some of the false money in New York," explained Diane. "I had some with me; I was questioned by government men. I promised them I would learn where it was manufactured. At last I know"—Diane pointed—"for I have seen beyond that door! But there is no longer a way for me to communicate with the authorities."

Clyde considered all that Diane had said. The ring of truth in her story was definite; but Clyde decided that he could prompt new recollections if he seemed unimpressed by the girl's story. With a shrug, he remarked:

"Perhaps you have misunderstood Doctor Borth. You may have mistaken certain facts—"

Diane's eyes interrupted with an outraged gaze. She lost none of her loveliness when she gave that silent challenge. On the contrary, the look gained Clyde's admiration. He recognized the girl's bravery, although he tried not to show it.

Diane was wearing a dressing gown of navy blue. From a pocket of it, she produced a slip of paper that looked like a newspaper clipping. She gave it to Clyde.

"Read this," urged Diane. "Then tell me if you can trust Doctor Borth!"

The clipping was from a morning newspaper, that had evidently been delivered sometime late in the day but prior to Clyde's interview with Borth. Clyde read startling news: a complete account of the murder at the filling station.

The exact time was mentioned. Clyde recognized that Fred's death had taken place soon after his own departure. Mention of a telephone call to New York police headquarters told Clyde that Fred must have called Cardona instead of Burbank.

The kill was attributed to New York mobsters, who had fled in two cars. One was obviously Clyde's; but there was no mention of The Shadow. Clyde did not guess that his chief had arrived to wage battle. To Clyde, there was one pressing problem that concerned the present.

That was to escape the toils of Doctor Borth; to contact The Shadow and bring his vengeance upon the conniving fiend who had come from overseas. With that escape, there would be rescue also. Diane must be brought in safety from this abode where she was as much a prisoner as Clyde.

From that moment, Clyde resolved, no time could be wasted. Every thought must concern the vital issue. Clyde and Diane would be fighting for a common cause: the ultimate overthrow of the nefarious Doctor Borth.

CHAPTER VII
THE LOWER DUNGEON

THE clipping clenched in one fist, Clyde held up his other hand in warning. He and Diane listened, to make sure that they were not overheard.

Satisfied that they still had time together, Clyde gave the clipping back to Diane. As he did, he gritted the question:

"Did Doctor Borth try to explain this to you?"

"He did," returned Diane. "He said that it was proof that he had enemies."

"Proof for you—but not for me!"

"That is exactly what Doctor Borth said. He told me that it would not be good policy to show you the clipping. You might—as he put it—misunderstand the facts. He reminded me that you were a newspaper reporter; that you would twist the facts if you knew them."

Clyde's look was quizzical, as if he wondered whether Diane had felt the same. The girl's smile proved otherwise.

"I saw through the sham, Mr. Burke," declared Diane. "When I agreed with what Doctor Borth said, it was purely to keep him unaware of what I knew. Those enemies, as he calls them, were killers in his own employ. They weren't seeking a trail to this place, and, therefore, anxious to murder a man who might have spoken and spoiled their game. They killed to keep the law from learning anything regarding Doctor Borth himself!"

Diane's hands became limp. There was a choke to the girl's grieved tone, as she added:

"If I could only have sent word! The government men are waiting to hear from me. But it is impossible for me to leave here. I would be missed immediately."

"How about the servants?" undertoned Clyde. "Are there any who can be trusted?"

"Two, perhaps. But I have not sounded them. It would be useless, since their position is the same as mine."

There was no use in debating the Borth question any longer. Clyde knew that he had heard Diane's full story. The proposition was to find a way whereby this place could be revealed. Clyde started a suggestion.

"If I could leave here," he began, "without Borth knowing all that I have learned—"

Diane interrupted with a headshake.

"Doctor Borth does not intend to release you, Mr. Burke. He said as much tonight. Still, there might be a way—"

The girl paused, her forehead furrowed. Again, her hand pressed Clyde's arm. Her tone was an earnest one.

"If you were imprisoned," she told Clyde, "as Doctor Borth threatened, I could release you. I know a route by which you could leave!"

"But if Borth knew that I had gone from—"

"He wouldn't know. He would appoint a guard to watch your cell. I am sure that there is one, at least, who would report that you were still confined."

The idea sounded good. Clyde's nod told that he was game. Diane insisted, however, upon one provision.

"You must carry my message directly to the government men," said the girl. "I promised them a confidential report; I even memorized a code that I am to use. They are the only ones who could surely trap Doctor Borth. Any false step could mean escape for Doctor Borth; and if he should learn—"

"Your life would be at stake," finished Clyde, solemnly. "I understand"—he paused; then added the name—"Diane. I promise that I will carry your message, without visiting either the police or the newspaper office."

DIANE rewarded Clyde with a trusting smile. She did not know that Clyde's promise excluded the matter of contact with The Shadow. If Diane had heard of that mysterious being, she had not connected Clyde with him.

There was no time for Clyde to mention The Shadow to Diane. A plan had been arranged; the one course was to put it in operation.

"I've got to cross the old doctor," declared Clyde, grimly. "Suppose I let him find me down here, Diane. That would get him sore, wouldn't it?"

Diane nodded. Before she could speak, her ears caught a sound. It came from a distant passage, somewhere near the stairs. Diane's ears were keener than Clyde's, for she whispered a prompt warning before he heard the muffled approach.

"It may be Yakbar!" exclaimed Diane. "We must make him think that I have trapped you! He is one rogue who would never desert Doctor Borth!"

Hurriedly, the girl moved to the outer end of the passage. Clyde saw her draw a small revolver. She was watching for Yakbar, intending to cover Clyde the moment that the Turk arrived close enough to see her stage the act.

Clyde remembered a detail of the past. To help the cause along, he again started to approach the vault door.

"Stop where you are!" Diane shrilled the order in a tone that carried anguish. "Instantly or I fire!"

She shrieked the words at Clyde; he didn't realize that it was thought of his safety that impelled the sudden cry.

Before the girl could speak, her ears caught the sound of a muffled approach.

Blundering, Clyde would have gone still farther toward the vault door, if Diane had let him.

Quick-witted in emergency, Diane added sting to the needed threat. She tugged the revolver trigger; a bullet ricocheted from the wall beside Clyde's ear.

Astonishment brought Clyde to a standstill; he took a back step as he turned about to face Diane. For a moment, he thought that the girl had turned against him; an instant later, he saw that Diane had saved him.

The floor was sliding open between Clyde and the vault. Split halves were slithering beneath the wall, leaving a gaping pit below. That last step had put Clyde upon a trap; his withdrawal, thanks to Diane's shot, was all that rescued him.

Yakbar arrived to find Clyde faced about, his back to the blackened hole. Clyde's arms were raised; he was pale as he looked into the muzzle of Diane's gun.

The girl's features were also pallid; her hand was trembling. Yakbar took it for excitement at bagging a prisoner; he did not guess that the girl was actually concerned for Clyde.

Nor did Doctor Nicholas Borth guess the truth. The eagle-eyed old man appeared less than a minute later; he came from within the vault itself.

At sound of Borth's booming voice, Clyde looked around, avoiding the pit as he did so. Lights were out within the vault; but it looked deep, fitting Diane's description of a counterfeiting den. Clyde realized that the place must be air-conditioned, like the rest of this underground lair. Borth must have caught an automatic signal from the moving floor.

"So, Mr. Burke"—Borth's tone was cold, showing a harsh irony—"you have violated the hospitality that I provided! Perhaps you have forgotten our terms?"

Clyde did not reply.

"*We* have not forgotten them," resumed Borth. "I call upon Yakbar and Miss Delban to bear witness. You were to remain upon the upper floor. You failed to do so; therefore, you become a prisoner instead of a guest!

"You came to see what lay below"—Borth supplied a deep chuckle—"and you have seen. Not only this floor, but one that lies still lower down." Borth pointed to the pit, as he added: "Very well, you shall learn *more* of that lowermost floor!"

WITH a nod of approval, Borth motioned for Diane to put away the revolver. He beckoned to Yakbar; the Turk came toward Clyde, with big hands extended. Diane tried to flash the signal that all would be well; but she was handicapped because Borth was watching her.

From the girl's grim look, Clyde misunderstood. He thought that matters had taken a bad turn that Diane didn't expect. Clyde thought that Yakbar was going to hurl him into the pit.

With a sudden drive, Clyde flung himself upon the Turk. They began a battle like the one of the night before; but, this time, Clyde knew something of Yakbar's methods. Driven to sheer desperation, Clyde fought Yakbar to the wall, gained a neck-hold that the husky could not shake.

Doctor Borth boomed a loud command as he witnessed Yakbar's failure. Proof of Diane's statement regarding many servants was the event that followed. Footsteps clattered from remote passages. Arriving henchmen threw themselves into the fray. Clyde was lost amid the tangle of glaring faces that looked like demon countenances.

They were nondescript butlers of many nationalities, nearly a dozen of them, all anxious to put across the stroke that would quiet Clyde.

As they hurled him toward the pit, Clyde wrenched away. A diving opponent tripped him; Clyde took a backward spill for the trap. As he fell, he expected to plunge down into darkness. Instead, he flattened with a terrific jolt upon the solid floor.

Looking up, Clyde saw the sardonic face of Doctor Borth. The old man had pressed a switch just inside the vault door. During the fray, the floor had closed to make a solid landing place.

As powerful arms plucked him, Clyde saw beyond hostile faces. He glimpsed Diane and saw the relief that the girl registered.

This was the finish that Diane had expected from the start: Clyde a prisoner in the hands of Borth's henchmen, but unhurt.

THOUGH Borth had closed the deadly pit, his threat of a lower prison cell was fulfilled. Jarred by his fall to the floor, Clyde could offer no more fight as Yakbar and four others carried him bodily toward an outer passage. They reached a corridor that ended in a wall; Yakbar pressed a switch that opened the barrier.

The captors descended a long steep stairway, to another floor of passages where they used flashlights to find their way. The length of the descent made Clyde glad that he had not fallen through the opened floor.

They reached a door that suited Yakbar. The Turk opened it; flickered a flashlight into a cell that was furnished with a battered cot, a chair and a table. Yakbar grunted words in a foreign tongue. Clyde's bearers shoved him through the doorway; laughed raucously as their prisoner went floundering to the stone floor.

Before Clyde could gain his feet, the door slammed shut. A huge key grated in a rusty lock. In pitch-darkness, Clyde could only grope to find the cot.

As Clyde sat down, his head was in a whirl; but, gradually, his thoughts cleared.

As he sat down, his head was in a whirl; but, gradually, his thoughts cleared. This lower dungeon wasn't to be the end of his journey.

Imprisonment was the route to freedom. In that blackness, Clyde could fancy he heard the earnest tones of Diane Delban. He knew that the girl would find an opportunity to release him, and send him on the way for aid. It would then be Clyde's turn to bring rescue to Diane.

Looking into the future, Clyde could almost hear the whisper of strange, sinister mirth, that would eventually ring its mocking challenge through passages that lay above.

Clyde hoped that he would be present when The Shadow finally confronted Doctor Nicholas Borth.

CHAPTER VIII
THREADS FROM THE PAST

ANOTHER day had passed; with it, public interest in the New Jersey murder had faded. With three crooks dead, it seemed that the law had dealt stern justice to the murderers.

There was one man, however, who had taken the whole case very grimly. That man was Joe Cardona, the New York police inspector.

Cardona felt that he was to blame because Manhattan hoodlums had invaded New Jersey without his knowledge. He didn't tell that to the reporters who thronged his office; instead, Joe kept a bluff expression on his swarthy, poker-faced countenance. But all the while, the ace inspector was counting on some break that would reveal the New York angle behind the New Jersey crime.

There was one reporter who didn't show up in Joe's office. That was Clyde Burke, the one news-hawk who was smart enough to ask bothersome questions. For a whole day, Cardona had been expecting Clyde to breeze in with the gang. At last, Cardona inquired where Clyde was.

One of the reporters said that Burke had wired from Trenton, saying that he had taken on a free-lance assignment, which was Clyde's privilege with the *Classic*.

That news troubled Cardona. It gave him a hunch that Clyde might have traced the two hood-lums that escaped after the filling station murder. It would be swell, thought Cardona, if Burke sudden-ly showed up with facts that the police hadn't been able to get. Swell, nix! That idea simply spurred Cardona to seeking facts in New York before Clyde could bring in hot news from New Jersey.

It never occurred to Cardona that Clyde might be in a plight of his own. That was something that only The Shadow knew.

The situation, however, was due to produce results, because of the way Cardona had taken it. All this day, Cardona was tapping the "grapevine," through the aid of stool pigeons. Every now and then, underworld rumors reached him from squeamish crooks who served as the law's spies in the bad-lands. It was almost dusk when a ripe one arrived.

A rat-faced stoolie was introduced into Cardona's office. He had a story that clicked.

"I knowed th' mugs that croaked th' fillin' station guy," informed the stoolie, "but I ain't got no idea why they pulled th' rub-out. Only, they wasn't th' only boids that was out in Joisey."

"Who else was out there?" demanded Cardona.

"Some guy that had a slick sedan," explained the stoolie. "He went out and they tailed along."

"To cover up," muttered Cardona, on a sudden hunch. "Say, why didn't you spill this sooner, so I could find out who the guy was?"

"That's what I was tryin' to find out," whined the stoolie. "I knowed what kind of buggy th' sedan was, an' th' garage where it started from. Only, th' bus didn't come back there until today. So I just got my chanct to find out th' moniker of th' guy it belonged to."

The stoolie produced a crumpled piece of paper on which he had scrawled the facts. He gave it to Cardona, who read the name of Kirk Barsley, with the address of a public garage.

Joe dismissed the stoolie and immediately set to work. It didn't take him long to find out who Kirk Barsley was. A phone call to the garage was the first lead; and others followed.

Cardona summed up his findings to a listening detective-sergeant.

"Kirk Barsley," declared Joe. "For ten years a traveling representative for wholesale jewelry firms. Chucked up a good job, a few months ago, saying he was going into business on his own, but he hasn't been calling on his regular trade.

"Sounds like a front for some racket, if you ask me! A guy can't manage a business in New York and be on the road, too. Barsley can't have much capital; and he hasn't been buying jewelry to sell out of town. I'm going around and take a look at the guy!"

OFTEN, when Joe Cardona set forth on odd expeditions, his moves were promptly known to The Shadow. Sometimes, a janitor named Fritz was on the job at police headquarters; and Fritz— unknown to Cardona—was frequently impersonated by The Shadow. On other occasions, Clyde Burke spotted Cardona's moves.

Today, The Shadow was searching for Clyde, who, in turn, was a prisoner at Doctor Borth's underground castle. Nevertheless, Joe Cardona was spotted outside of headquarters.

The man who noted him was a hunchy, wise-faced fellow who had a way of dodging out of sight. His name was "Hawkeye"; he prowled the underworld, seeking news for The Shadow.

Hawkeye had not been delegated to the search in New Jersey. He wasn't suited to such territory. Instead, he had remained in New York; and there, Hawkeye had spotted the visiting stoolie who went to Cardona's office.

Wisely, Hawkeye had remained outside, to be rewarded with Cardona's own trail.

It was nearly dark when Cardona reached an obscure office building in a dingy district. There was no elevator; Joe walked up rickety stairs to the third floor. There, he found a darkened office that bore the name of Kirk Barsley.

While Cardona was rattling the knob, a tired-looking man came from another office. Joe inquired about Barsley.

"Hardly ever see him," informed the tired man. "He's never around in the daytime. Once or twice, when I've been working late, he's come in around nine o'clock. Maybe he'll be in this evening."

Cardona decided that he would come back later. He followed the tired-faced man down the stairs. From a stairway to the fourth floor, Hawkeye listened until their footsteps had faded; then started to emerge from his hiding place.

Hawkeye had just time to duck from sight when he heard a door open. A squatty man, as stocky as Cardona, came from a darkened office and cautiously went downstairs. Hawkeye promptly took up the new trail. It led to a small but well-kept apartment hotel, west of Times Square.

There, the squatty man stopped at the desk and said that he wanted to talk to James Cleeve. From the darkened outer doorway, Hawkeye couldn't hear what the man said over the telephone; but he went upstairs afterward. Hawkeye was able to watch the elevator dial. The car stopped at the fifth floor.

It wasn't long before Hawkeye was on that floor himself. He found an apartment door, where he could hear the mumble of voices. It was the one he wanted; but there was no chance to listen in from the hall.

The turn of the corridor indicated that Cleeve's apartment opened into a courtyard. On that chance, Hawkeye decided to invade an apartment that looked empty.

The door of the vacant apartment was locked; and Hawkeye was no locksmith. He chose another mode of entry: through the transom. Inside, he sneaked to a window and opened it quietly. Thanks to the warm weather, Cleeve's window was open, catercornered across the courtyard.

Hawkeye saw a group of men; four of them. He could hear their conversation. Moreover, he identified the man who must be Cleeve. He was tall, straight-shouldered, with a blocky face that bespoke action. Above Cleeve's square chin were tight lips, a keenly pointed nose and heavy eyebrows that matched his blackish hair.

Cleeve was a leader; that was instantly evident. The others listened respectfully to all he said; gave nods when his sharp eyes stabbed in their direction.

"SO you're sure that it was Cardona." Cleeve was talking to the squatty man. "That means he'll be back! Somehow, he's figured that Barsley went over to Jersey, two nights ago. I'm wondering"— Cleeve paused, to chew at the end of a cigar—"if it matters whether Cardona pinches Barsley."

Some of the listeners started a protest. Cleeve silenced them with an impatient gesture.

"We know that Barsley ships the cash to Doc Borth," he affirmed, "but we've learned, too, that Barsley never sees the old doc. The girl told us that much. The best thing we can do is let Barsley go his own way. If that means he runs into Cardona— all right. He won't talk about Doc Borth."

That satisfied the hearers; perhaps that was why Cleeve began to change his own opinion.

"I wish it could wait, though," he snapped, "until we've heard from the girl. She ought to be getting word through anytime. Maybe it would be better if we dropped in on Barsley first. If he sees this"— Cleeve pulled back his coat—"he won't stick around after we've gone!"

Cleeve turned toward the window to flick cigar ashes over the sill. His coat was still drawn back; Hawkeye saw a badge beneath the knuckles that held the lapel. The little spotter recognized the emblem. It was the badge of a government agent.

A light dawned on Hawkeye. He began to piece a story; his conclusions were very close to the statements that Diane Delban had made to Clyde Burke. Somewhere in New Jersey was a man named Doctor Borth; he had received funds that Kirk Barsley had shoved through. The trouble was that Cleeve and these other Feds were after Borth, not Barsley.

Hawkeye saw the complications that Cardona's entry might produce, with Cleeve waiting to crack down on Borth. Hawkeye's own idea was that Cleeve's second opinion was the better one—to scare Barsley out of town before Cardona got hold of the fellow.

There were snatches of conversation that Hawkeye could still hear. Cleeve had walked away from the window and was out of sight; other voices weren't as plain as his. From the rest that he heard, Hawkeye added a few more impressions.

There was mention of a mob being around when Barsley showed up at his office. Cleeve came through with the remark that Cardona might expect a crew on hand, since there had been hoodlums over in New Jersey, after Barsley had gone there. There was talk about the possibility of Cardona finding counterfeit money in Barsley's office, and what Joe's reaction would be.

Cleeve summed up some of that discussion when he happened to come back toward the window.

"We don't care how much Cardona gets on Barsley," declared the tall man. "The more it fits, the better! It sizes this way: There was a murder over in New Jersey and Cardona knows Barsley was over there, besides the killers.

"If he finds Barsley trying to lam, with a mob on hand to cover him, that starts the police after Barsley. If Cardona uncovers queer money, he'll have that count on Barsley. When they catch up with Barsley, any talk he gives about selling jewels won't go over.

"Barsley can't lead the police to Borth, so that leaves us clear to handle the proposition our own way. I'm still betting that the Delban girl will get word to us—"

THAT was all Hawkeye heard. Cleeve had gone deeper into the room, with the others following. There were mumbles; finally, the lights went out. Cleeve and his squad were on their way.

It didn't take Hawkeye long to follow. Once out of the apartment hotel, he hurried to a telephone. He put a call through to Burbank; but it wasn't to a New York number. Burbank was over in New Jersey, along with the rest of The Shadow's agents and The Shadow himself.

Hawkeye gave his story. Methodically, Burbank told him to stand by. In less than ten minutes, Hawkeye received a return call, giving instructions. In accordance with those orders, Hawkeye headed for the neighborhood of Barsley's office.

He made a discovery as soon as he arrived. The squatty man was back at his post; others of Cleeve's squad were also on the lookout.

There were times, Hawkeye knew, when Feds had one job to do; the police another. This fitted with such circumstances. James Cleeve had good reason to move in ahead of Joe Cardona, for Cleeve was after bigger game than Kirk Barsley. Cleeve was after the man most prominent in all this chain of circumstance—a mysterious individual known as Doctor Borth.

Whatever the immediate future might produce, Hawkeye was confident that another being of mystery would enter into these affairs where Borth was absent.

Hawkeye was counting on The Shadow.

CHAPTER IX
FORCED FLIGHT

THERE was a singular lull along the street outside the old office building; it persisted for the better part of an hour. Watchers had stepped from sight, and were remaining undercover. Hawkeye saw no more of Cleeve's men, although he could guess their positions. They, however, had not glimpsed the little spotter at all.

Hawkeye was wise enough not to venture too close to the building. A convenient alleyway, half a block distant, was just the hiding place that suited him.

The break came when a taxi rolled along the stilled street. A passenger poked his head from the window, took a cautious look and said something to the driver. Alighting, the man paid his fare and the cab pulled away.

The arrival took quick strides into the office building, carrying a small satchel with him. Hawkeye knew that the man must be Kirk Barsley. As Cleeve had anticipated, Barsley had returned before nine o'clock, the hour when Cardona was due. It wouldn't be much longer, though, before Joe arrived.

Sight of Barsley had attracted the attention of all watchers. That was why no one, not even Hawkeye, observed another approach that came when the cab halted. In from the corner moved a shape of blackness, that became definitely visible when it passed a lighted stretch of pavement halfway to the old office building.

There, gliding silently, was a cloaked figure, outlined against a whitish wall. The Shadow had arrived from New Jersey; he had lurked out of view until the right moment for his advance. He had timed the move to perfection, for he was past the lighted stretch at the moment when Barsley walked into the office building.

There was no more signs of The Shadow when Hawkeye and the other watchers gazed along the street.

The ground floor of the building was lighted; but the glow came from the depths of the hallway. Moreover, there were steps leading up inside the door.

Barsley had stepped from sight when he went up that short flight. So did The Shadow. His entry, though, was somewhat slower, for he eased the door by degrees, so that its opening and closing were unnoticeable.

THOUGH The Shadow had lost ground on Barsley, he regained it on the way up to the third floor. The stairs were badly lighted; the sound of the man's footsteps were The Shadow's guide.

He heard Barsley stop at intervals, to listen for sounds from below. On such occasions, The Shadow cut down the intervening space, thanks to his soundless tread.

When Barsley reached his own office, The Shadow was at the top of the stairs. Peering from semidarkness beyond a corner of the hall, he saw Barsley unlocking the office door. The man entered, carrying his satchel. He closed the door carefully behind him.

That was when The Shadow performed a move that was as swift as it was silent. Quick, sweeping strides brought him to the door before it had fully

closed. His left hand had peeled the thin black glove from his right. Deftly, he poked the crumpled glove against the closing door.

The glove served as a timely buffer. The door did not latch.

The Shadow eased the door slightly inward, gathering his glove with his right hand as he controlled the knob with his left. He was peering through a tiny crack when he heard Barsley stumble against a desk. There, the man found the lamp he wanted and pulled its cord.

As the light came on, Barsley emitted a startled hiss; with good reason. He wasn't alone in his own office. Seated at the desk was a blocky-faced man whose eyes were cold beneath their heavy brows.

The Shadow recognized that visitor from Hawkeye's description. The man at the desk was James Cleeve.

The glow that showed Cleeve's face revealed Barsley's, also. Kirk Barsley was tall, stoop-shouldered, somewhat crablike in his crouch. His face was long, its cheeks hollow. The man had a sickly whiteness; but his restless eyes were shrewd. His lips, too, declared that Barsley could be crafty. They pursed into an odd smile.

"Rather curious," spoke Barsley, in a croakish tone, "finding a stranger in this office. I didn't know that I had left the door unlocked."

"You didn't," returned Cleeve, bluntly. "The janitor unlocked the door for me, when I showed him this."

Cleeve pulled back his coat lapel. Barsley saw the visitor's government badge. For a moment, Barsley fidgeted; then looked relieved. He planked the satchel on the desk; poked his hands into his trousers pockets and waited to hear what Cleeve had to say.

"MY name is Cleeve," informed the visitor. He produced a wallet and pointed to an identification card that bore his photograph. "I just dropped in to ask you a few questions, Mr. Barsley. They pertain to the jewelry business."

Barsley thrust out his lower lip, as if to stifle a smile. He spoke dryly when he replied:

"Let's have the questions, Mr. Cleeve."

"Just where do you buy goods wholesale?" queried Cleeve. "We haven't been able to learn that, Barsley. You're something of a mystery along Maiden Lane. Some of the wholesalers down there seem to doubt that you are in the jewelry business at all."

Barsley smilingly produced a black book from his pocket. He spread the pages in front of Cleeve's eyes.

"All out-of-town purchases," he explained. "I do all my business in the Midwest. Suppose you check with some of these concerns, Mr. Cleeve."

Barsley gave a sly look when he spoke. The Shadow noted it, although Cleeve did not. It was obvious to The Shadow that the black book was faked. Barsley was using it to stall Cleeve.

"I shall be in town a few days," added Barsley. "I always use this office when I am in from the road. After you have communicated with these concerns"—he pointed to the book—"drop back and see me again, Mr. Cleeve."

Cleeve nodded, as he copied some of the data on a sheet of paper. He arose and put the paper in his pocket. Barsley saw Cleeve glance at the satchel. Obligingly, Barsley opened it.

The satchel contained some blank checkbooks; a few bundles of receipts, with a small number of similar items. There was a bank deposit book that had some checks and currency tucked between its pages; but the amount was not large. Barsley demonstrated that, when he fingered the money under Cleeve's eyes. All the while, Barsley's spreading grin was a pleased one.

He didn't have enough cash with him to make his enterprise seem large. His limited funds fitted with the fake list of jewelry sales that he had entered in his little black book. Barsley was posing as a very small dealer, eking out a living through much travel and effort.

Cleeve seemed satisfied with Barsley's story. He reached for the bills that the stoopish man had counted, gave them an examination in the light. Returning them, Cleeve spoke both frankly and apologetically.

"We're looking for 'queer' money," said Cleeve, thumbing his badge. "Counterfeit stuff has been showing up a lot of places. That's why we've had to check on a lot of chaps in different lines of business. We picked you, Mr. Barsley; but you've turned out O.K.!"

THE SHADOW could see Cleeve's eyes while Barsley was putting back the contents of the satchel. It was plain that Cleeve knew exactly what the situation was, although he had hidden his thoughts from Barsley. The Shadow, too, had come to a definite conclusion regarding Barsley.

Whatever his game, whether legitimate or crooked, Barsley handled the collection end. Sooner or later, that satchel would be stuffed with funds that came from many sources. The Shadow was confident that Barsley had delivered one bagload of checks and currency somewhere in New Jersey, on Wednesday night.

Since then, the fellow had begun a new series of collections, but had only made small ones to date. That was why Barsley was pleased because Cleeve had chosen this particular evening to visit him. Barsley didn't care how many Feds looked into his satchel, while its contents were as slim as they were tonight.

One thing was evident, however, from Barsley's manner. The fellow tried to hide it, but didn't succeed. That was the fact that Barsley did not intend to return to this office again. He was very anxious to leave, and his curbed impatience betrayed it.

Cleeve stalked about the office a few minutes, remarking that he would like to look around a bit, just as a matter of routine. He opened a door, stared into an empty closet. There was a shelf above the level of Cleeve's eyes.

Rising on his toes, Cleeve took enough of a look to satisfy himself. He turned about; gestured a good-bye to Barsley. Cleeve came toward the hall door.

That was The Shadow's cue to ease away. His hand let the latch catch silently. The Shadow was merged with the gloom of a doorway farther along the hall when Cleeve came out. Watching Cleeve head toward the stairs, The Shadow saw him turn about for a last look toward Barsley's door.

It was good strategy on Cleeve's part—starting Barsley off for parts unknown, keeping things so that Borth would think himself secure. But there was just one hitch to the proceeding; it became apparent after Cleeve had gone.

Barsley didn't come out of the office; instead, he remained behind the closed door.

After a few minutes, The Shadow approached to listen. This time, the door was latched; but with his ear close to the woodwork, The Shadow could catch the tones of Barsley's voice.

The fellow was making a telephone call. All that The Shadow heard was his final statement:

"All right... Yes, fifteen minutes, since you can't get here sooner. Wait for me out front."

The receiver clicked on its hook. The Shadow heard Barsley sneaking toward the door. The cloaked listener was out of sight again when Barsley peered toward the stairs, to make sure Cleeve wasn't around. Ducking back into his office, Barsley waited there.

MINUTE by minute, the time ticked off; closer and closer came the scheduled moment when Cardona would appear. The approach of nine o'clock was injuring the calculations of both Cleeve and Barsley.

Cleeve hadn't figured that Barsley would linger; Barsley, in his turn, didn't suspect that Cardona was due. It was a slow-motion race against time, with a chance that Barsley might beat the dead line; for his quarter hour of delay would end a few minutes before nine.

The Shadow timed Barsley's actions almost to the dot. It was just four minutes of nine when the door of the office opened and Barsley stepped out into the hall. He was carrying the satchel; he tried to appear unconcerned as he walked toward the stairs.

That was proof that Barsley thought he was being covered by Cleeve alone. He was putting on an indifferent pose that he thought would satisfy any watchful Feds that Cleeve might have stationed downstairs.

Again, The Shadow followed Barsley. This time, the man showed none of his hesitating tactics on the stairs. His confidence seemed to increase, judging by his footsteps. The Shadow closed the gap; he was almost on Barsley's heels when they reached the final flight.

Because of the light in the lower hall, The Shadow waited on the last steps, watching from gloom until Barsley reached the outer door.

It was then that the climax struck.

Just as Barsley pulled the door inward, a man stepped through to block him. Barsley went back against the wall, the satchel dangling from his fist as he faced a stocky challenger. Again, Barsley was treated to the sight of an official badge; this one was the emblem of a New York police inspector.

Joe Cardona had arrived in time to halt Barsley's flight. New questions were due for Kirk Barsley— ones that he couldn't answer as easily as Cleeve's. Cardona was here to get present results, not future ones.

The showdown between Joe Cardona and Kirk Barsley was to have a silent witness in the person of The Shadow.

CHAPTER X
DOUBLED PURSUIT

"YOU'RE Kirk Barsley?"

Cardona gruffed the sharp question promptly enough to hold Barsley speechless. The stoopish man finally nodded, twitching his lips as he compressed them.

"I've got a few questions to ask you," Cardona growled. "I'm taking you down to headquarters."

Barsley started a feeble protest. He muttered something about false arrest; the indignity of a ride in a patrol wagon. The final mention brought a sarcastic comment from Cardona.

"We'll ride in your own car, Barsley," said the inspector. "It's on the way over from the garage. With a detective in the front seat with the driver."

"You were there at the garage?" gulped Barsley. "Waiting until I showed up?"

"Not exactly," returned Cardona. "We stopped there on the way over. Just when you happened to call up and ask for the car to be sent here. I came ahead, while the boys stayed to look through the car."

"To look for *what*?"

"Any evidence they might find, to prove that you drove over to New Jersey on Wednesday night!"

That worded jab hit Barsley hard. The fellow actually wilted. Cardona clamped a fist on Barsley's right arm; took a look through the front door.

As if timed to Cardona's gaze, a car pulled up at the curb. Cardona recognized Barsley's sedan; he saw the detective alight and walk toward the building.

"Come along, Barsley!"

With that growl, Cardona twisted Barsley toward the door. It was a bad move, for it placed Joe between Barsley and the watchful figure of The Shadow. Moreover, The Shadow had no time to shift his own position; for the move that Barsley made was a sudden one that didn't start until he was beyond Cardona.

As Cardona's free hand yanked the door inward, Barsley tugged away, took a long swing with his left arm. In his fist he held an improvised weapon: the small satchel.

Cardona made a quick parry. The satchel had a momentum, however, that Cardona didn't calculate. The bag thudded the whole side of Cardona's face with a terrific smack.

Cardona staggered, losing his grip on Barsley. The prisoner did an immediate dive down the short steps to the street.

There was a scuffle when Barsley met the incoming detective; but it didn't last long. Barsley's sudden bolt caught the dick off guard, for he thought that Cardona had Barsley in hand.

Barsley made another swing with the satchel; when the dick ducked to draw a revolver, Barsley beat him to that move. Cardona from the doorway, the dick in the entry were both menaced by the brandish of Barsley's quick-pulled gun.

It was lucky for Barsley that he didn't stop to fire. He never could have dropped either of his two opponents. Cardona was pitched suddenly aside, as a black-cloaked form swished past him. The gawking detective was bowled to a corner of the entry, only a split-second later.

The Shadow had arrived, swiftly enough to beat Barsley to the shot.

BARSLEY didn't wait for combat. He fled at the instant of The Shadow's surge. Long bounds took him to his own sedan, which had been parked just past the building. Barsley's angled flight took him temporarily from The Shadow's range.

The driver from the garage saw Barsley coming; knew that the waving revolver could mean business. The fellow dived through the door on the street side, letting Barsley gain the driver's seat.

The Shadow stopped before he reached the sidewalk. From a corner of the building entrance, he trained his .45 deliberately upon Barsley's car, which the fugitive was frantically trying to start. With a single bullet, The Shadow could have permanently halted Barsley's flight; but he lost the chance before he used it.

Cardona and the detective supplied the untimely intervention; their blunder helped Barsley instead of handicapping him. Together, they piled past The Shadow, trying to overtake Barsley. They reached the running board of the sedan, putting themselves squarely in The Shadow's path of fire.

Since they wanted to capture Barsley, The Shadow lowered his gun. But neither Cardona nor his sidekick were equal to their self-chosen task.

Barsley threw in the clutch just as they tried to board the car. The sedan whipped away; Cardona and the detective sprawled along the curb. First on his feet, Cardona shouted to the driver of a parked taxi. The cab wheeled up; Cardona and the detective jumped in, to begin a chase.

There were other cars coming along the street. Just as The Shadow saw the first of them, a revolver spurted from an alleyway. The Shadow recognized the signal instantly. It came from Hawkeye. The spotter had seen Cleeve and his squad go away; they had departed too early to witness the arrival of another group.

There were mobbies in the rakish touring car that was now coming into view. They had seen the start of Barsley's flight; also the pursuit that Cardona was about to stage. Their purpose was to cover Barsley's getaway. The muzzle of a machine gun was swinging toward Cardona's cab.

Hawkeye's hurried shot did no damage; it came when the touring car had passed him. It served well, however, for it speeded The Shadow's action.

The Shadow did not wait for the thugs to declare themselves; he had them labeled when he heard Hawkeye's signal. Sweeping both hands into action, The Shadow stepped from his doorway and blazed shots into the murder car.

The machine gun didn't begin its crackle. A crippled driver let the touring car slither to the curb. Hoodlums heard the sudden mockery of The Shadow's laugh, challenging from the spot where his big guns had mouthed their deadly hail. Abandoning their car, they dived for the street and went staggering for doorways.

The Shadow reached the wheel of the touring car, beckoning as he went. Hawkeye came sidling from cover and jumped into the back seat. Barsley had rounded the corner and was off to a good head start; but Cardona's cab could still be trailed.

The Shadow was entering the pursuit. He expected more trouble ahead; and it came within the second block.

Cardona's cabby had spotted Barsley's car taking another corner. The cab swung to follow; there was a sudden shriek of brakes. Another crook-manned car was bowling in to block the chase. The cab skidded, twisted toward the curb. Revolvers spouted toward the cab's occupants.

AGAIN, The Shadow drove in with needed rescue. There was one element of luck; these thugs were using revolvers instead of a machine gun. That break was all The Shadow needed to stem their attack.

His left hand used an automatic to tongue a withering volley, while his right managed the steering wheel. The Shadow's shots spread devastation.

Crooks were sagging before they could pick off Cardona and the detective. The driver of the thug-manned car wheeled from the scene of battle. The chase had changed. The Shadow was speeding after this new crew that had cut in to cover Barsley's flight, and the band that he pursued was crippled.

Cardona's cab was out of the chase; but another car had taken its place. Hawkeye recognized it, when he looked back. The car was a coupé that Cleeve had taken when he left Barsley's.

Though he had left the neighborhood when the first mob car appeared, Cleeve must have heard the distant shooting and recognized its cause. He had hurried for the scene, hoping to be of use.

Hawkeye gave that information to The Shadow, as they rounded a corner. The news meant very little, for Cleeve was too far behind to take a hand in matters.

In fact, the chase itself was proving fruitless; for within a few blocks, The Shadow recognized that Barsley had cut off in one direction, while the thugs were taking another. Failing in their cover-up job, they were at least capable enough to give a false trail.

The Shadow's chance to overtake Barsley was lost. He concentrated upon running down the carload of hoodlums, hoping that some of them might talk if trapped.

That also proved difficult. Choosing their own route, the crooks led The Shadow into a maze of streets near the river. Their driver knew those thoroughfares well. He made a series of twisty turns, gaining sufficient ground to be out of sight when The Shadow arrived.

Passing one turn, The Shadow ran into a dead-end street, where he was forced to back his car and turn outward.

Cleeve's car missed the turn entirely, it sped past the outlet of the blind alley, chasing after nothing. The Shadow, however, still saw a chance to track down the crooks.

As he stopped his car to look along side alleys, he ordered Hawkeye to go out to the street and watch for any sign of the missing car. If the mobsters were still twisting in and out the mazy streets, there was a likelihood that they might suddenly bob into sight.

In the interval that followed, Hawkeye decided that the chase was finished. He saw no traffic on the street; he turned about to rejoin The Shadow. Just then, there came a warning roar; a new car rocketed into sight, heading straight for the alley where The Shadow was located.

Instinctively, Hawkeye guessed the answer. Somehow, crooks had learned where The Shadow had stopped. This crew of hoodlums, new entrants in the turmoil, had headed in to trap The Shadow.

HAWKEYE got off a warning shot; then ducked beyond a stack of ashcans. The murder car occupants never noticed him. The lights of The Shadow's automobile were their guide.

They roared in upon it, opened fire with a machine gun that completely riddled the old touring car. Backing out from the alley, they sped away.

There wasn't any use for Hawkeye to fire after them. His only hope was that The Shadow might still be alive. Hawkeye dashed in to look for his chief before police arrived. He reached the inner end of the alley, stared into the touring car. His flashlight showed complete vacancy.

Staring blankly, Hawkeye suddenly noticed the wall behind the touring car. The facts dawned upon him. The Shadow had heard the warning shot; had recognized its import. With his own position spotted, The Shadow had chosen a new one, with remarkable speed. He had left the touring car and scaled the wall before the riddling fire began.

Scurrying away through a side alley, Hawkeye chuckled at the thought that the doubled trail had failed. Where The Shadow had gone and what his purpose would be were questions that Hawkeye could not answer. He would have been amazed, had he guessed.

Tonight's episode had brought new facts to The Shadow. Enough for him to let others handle events elsewhere, while he remained in New York. Though many details of crime would require later investigation, The Shadow understood the major game at stake.

Crooks, themselves, had flashed their message without realizing it. The Shadow would be prepared for moves to come.

CHAPTER XI
CHANCE MEETING

CONTRASTED to the swift events in Manhattan, time was passing very slowly in the buried cell where Clyde Burke lay prisoner. Night and day had passed; sleep had been Clyde's only solace in the pitch-darkness of the underground prison, except when Yakbar had entered to bring him meals.

Yakbar's appearance told Clyde why Diane had not come to aid him. The Turk had taken over the duty of watching the prison cell. Until Yakbar was relieved, nothing could be done. Clyde remembered that Diane had described the Turk as the one man who was utterly controlled by Doctor Nicholas Borth.

Clyde's luminous-dialed wristwatch showed ten o'clock. That hour meant no more than all the others that had passed until Clyde heard a scraping sound outside his door.

It meant that a key was in the lock; for Clyde had heard the sound before: when Yakbar brought the meals. This time, however, the scrape was cautious. Moreover, there was no reason why Yakbar should arrive at this hour.

A surge of hope swept Clyde. The interval before the door opened seemed longer than some of the wasted hours that he had recently experienced. When the barrier swung, Clyde saw the glow of a flashlight; it revealed the face of the person that he expected.

Diane Delban had come with her promised rescue.

The girl was not alone. With her was one of Borth's servants, who had been in the group that Clyde had battled the night before. He had a yellowish face, with flattish nose and puffy brows and lips. Clyde remembered him chiefly by a scar that ran across his chin.

Diane had done well in choosing this fellow as an aide. He was the sort that Doctor Borth would least suspect as one who had turned against him.

Diane beckoned. Clyde came from the darkened cell. The girl told the servant to lock the door and remain on watch. She started along the passage, whispering for Clyde to follow. They threaded twisty corridors; came to a solid wall like the one on the floor above.

There, Diane found the hidden switch. The wall slid back; the girl's flashlight showed a stone stairway that led farther downward.

Once past the barrier, they were free to talk. Clyde questioned Diane about the scar-chinned servant. She assured him that the man would prove dependable. He was one of a few who had become discontented in Borth's service; he had listened to Diane's offer of reward if he joined her cause.

ALL the while, Clyde and Diane were following a narrow tunnel that was hewn through rocky soil. Unlike Borth's underground headquarters, this passage had no concrete reinforcement. Workers had chiseled it roughly, picking their way through fissures in living rock.

At times, the passage almost doubled on itself.

In his talk with Diane, Clyde lost his sense of direction.

That did not seem important, as the passage had no side passages wherein a person might lose his way. Clyde's oversight, however, was to produce unfortunate consequences later.

They came to the end of the passage. Rough steps, nothing more than chunks of stone, led upward to a squarish slab of rock. Diane held the flashlight toward the barrier.

"That is the outlet," she told Clyde—"the emergency exit that Doctor Borth provided in case of invasion. After you are outside, you must remember its location and find your way from there. When you return with the government men, you can bring them through this passage. Doctor Borth will never expect a raid from below."

Diane lowered the flashlight. Paper crinkled as she gave Clyde an envelope. It was blank and unsealed, but Clyde could feel a message folded inside it.

"Take this to James Cleeve," ordered the girl. "You will find him at the Brayland Apartments, in New York City. This message will be the only introduction that you need. I have written it in the special code that he had me memorize."

Diane's hand held Clyde's arm. The flashlight's glow showed her eyes, large in their earnest expression. Her lips spoke the question:

"You will not fail me?"

"You can depend on me, Diane!" returned Clyde. "I haven't forgotten our bargain. I'll see Cleeve before I go to the office, or visit the police. This is a job for the Feds. I'll stay with them."

Diane smiled her confidence. She gave Clyde the flashlight; he held it toward the steps, while Diane found a lever. The stone slab moved; Clyde crept through, keeping his light close to the ground.

He crouched in a tangle of bushes, while Diane slid the slab shut from within the passage. Turning with the flashlight, Clyde caught a last glimpse of the girl's face; just before the slab went tightly shut.

THE thought that gripped Clyde was one of prompt action. Here, in the clear outside air, it was his task to make for New York with as much speed as possible. For the first time, he also realized the necessity of taking proper bearings. As a beginning, he examined his present location.

Like the stone slab in the ground, Clyde was shielded by a cluster of bushes on a steep hillside. Branches formed a slanting screen that ran to an overhanging ledge. This spot, nestled in the midst of a thicket, was a place where prowlers would not penetrate.

In fact, Clyde found difficulty in getting out of it. Brambles gripped him as he wrenched through, to reach the outer slope.

Dull moonlight showed the bushes. They formed a perfect coverage, like a scraggly layer following the slope to the jutting ledge. Nothing betrayed the hollow that lay within the brambles. The camouflage was another proof of the cunning methods used by Doctor Nicholas Borth.

The hillside was rocky and blackened with patches of trees, through which the moonlight trickled. Clyde chose a downward course into the valley, keeping his route as straight as possible. He noted conspicuous rocks; kept count of the paces that he took.

Two hundred yards brought him to an old road; there, his flashlight fell upon two battered posts that had once been a gateway. They made an excellent marker for future reference. Clyde followed the old road, still measuring the distance. After half a mile, he reached a narrow paved highway.

In the dark, Clyde tabbed his calculations on a sheet of paper, using his fountain pen that held the fading ink used by all The Shadow's agents. He folded the paper and tucked it in the envelope that Diane had given him. Striding along the paved road, he saw a highway marker. Its number told him the most important fact of all.

Clyde was in New Jersey, within fifty miles of New York City. This valley lay between the two ranges of rugged hills known as the Watchung Mountains. Again, Clyde was forced to admire the craft of Doctor Borth. No one who wanted isolation could have chosen a better district than the Watchungs.

Only one good road tapped the valley, and it was not much traveled. Often, Clyde recalled, fugitive criminals had fled to the Watchungs, where it had been difficult to track them down. Borth had gone such crooks one better. He had actually buried himself beneath this rocky terrain!

Borth's stronghold was an impregnable underground castle, tucked in a veritable wilderness, yet within an hour's ride of New York City.

There wouldn't be much trouble retracing the path to the secret exit. Clyde had valuable information; his job was to cover the few miles that would bring him to civilization, then hurry into New York.

CLYDE was speculating on that prospect when he heard a *thrumm* behind him. He didn't have time to duck before a car swung a bend. He was outlined in the glow of the headlights.

Clyde faced the car boldly, as it stopped. He expected Yakbar to pop out and challenge him; for Clyde feared suddenly that his escape had been discovered. Instead, Clyde heard a voice he recognized.

Two seconds later, he was aboard the halted car, shaking hands with the clean-cut driver who sat behind the wheel.

The man in the car was Harry Vincent, another of The Shadow's agents. The chance meeting marked the end of a long quest. Clyde Burke had at last been found.

It didn't take Clyde long to tell his story. For a finish, he produced Diane's envelope. Clyde brought out the paper that bore his own notations; he remarked to Harry:

"I'll read off the distances. Better copy them, for I used the fading ink."

Harry turned on the domelight. Clyde opened the paper. To his puzzlement, it was already blank. Clyde looked at his fountain pen and found the reason.

The barrel was broken; the ink had trickled out. That must have happened twenty-four hours ago, during his struggle with Yakbar and the others. Clyde hadn't learned it because the ink had dried on his clothes and then faded.

Harry's voice came quietly: "Give me the details from memory. I'll put them down."

Clyde complied. He wasn't quite sure, but he thought he had them right. Harry made two copies in pencil; gave one to Clyde. He asked to see Diane's note. Clyde produced it; the message was in code, as Diane had said.

Harry turned the car around and headed back for the dirt road that Clyde had mentioned. As they rode along, Harry suggested a suitable procedure.

"You take the car, Clyde," he said, "and drive into New York. You won't run into any trouble. I've been over these roads this evening, and they're all clear. Carry the note with you. Stop at No. 27 after you're through the Holland Tunnel."

By No. 27, Harry referred to a small eating place that specialized in fish and chips. It was just the spot where The Shadow could send Hawkeye, or a taxi driver named Moe Shrevnitz, to contact Clyde. Both of those workers were in Manhattan.

"All right," agreed Clyde. "It will take me nearly an hour to get in there; and I'll be a half hour longer, getting coffee and chips. Only, you'll have to contact Burbank; and with my taking the car, you'll be handicapped."

"I'll use shortwave radio," explained Harry. "The set's in the rumble seat. I'll keep it with me. Burbank can send somebody to pick me up later."

They had reached the old road. Harry drove as far as the ancient gateposts, to clock the distance. He headed the car around; then alighted and removed his radio equipment. Just as Clyde was ready to drive away, Harry asked him one question:

"What about that lower tunnel, Clyde? What direction would you say it went?"

Clyde studied the paper that listed his later bearings. After a short calculation, he replied:

"Northeast into the mountain side. But it isn't important. There's no turnoff in the tunnel."

Though Clyde didn't realize it, he had made a very bad guess as to the direction. He didn't think that it would cause any complication; but that, in turn, was another bad surmise. Clyde's mistaken statement was to cause grief for both himself and Harry.

AS soon as Clyde had driven away, Harry lugged his shortwave set a short distance up the hillside. Choosing a rocky spot, he set up the equipment. The job was so brief that an idea struck Harry. There was plenty of time to contact Burbank before Clyde reached Manhattan.

Time enough to check on some of those distances that Clyde had recited from memory. With that plan in mind, Harry shoved his radio set beneath a scrubby bush and went back to the gateposts. From there, he routed himself up the hill.

Everything checked as Clyde had given it. Harry reached the thick brambles beneath the ledge. He didn't look for the slab beneath the bushes; that would have been unwise. Harry decided to go down to the slope and send his message to Burbank.

He thought, though, that he could find a better path if he moved along the slope. Wisely, Harry took a westerly direction, because Clyde had said the tunnel went northeast. Because of that course, Harry thought that he was going away from Borth's underground headquarters. That was why Harry felt both secure and interested when he came upon a path among the trees.

A little higher on the hill loomed the squatty bulk of a deserted building. Harry approached; used his flashlight to see that the place was an abandoned hunting lodge. Harry noted a wide veranda skirting the building; a broad, flat roof above the one-story structure.

High steps led up to the front door, which was crudely locked and badly battered. Windows were boarded, but there were gaps between the slats.

Climbing the steps, Harry tested the padlock. When he tugged it, the hasp came from rotted wood. The door groaned on its hinges as Harry opened it.

This abandoned lodge could prove highly useful, Harry decided; that was why he chose to investigate it. He pictured The Shadow's coming campaign against Doctor Borth; realized that a squad of agents, or Feds, could be quartered in this forgotten structure.

Moving from room to room, Harry copied notes on his sheet of paper.

The main room of the lodge had a fireplace with a broad stone hearth. Harry studied it, then turned the flashlight around the big room. The glow of his torch still gave a view of the flat hearth; but Harry wasn't looking in that direction when the unexpected came.

Slowly, noiselessly, the hearth came upward on a hinge. Out from the depths peered a tawny face: the cold-eyed countenance of Yakbar!

Harry Vincent had found more than he supposed. Clyde had claimed that the exit tunnel burrowed northeast. Instead, it ran northwest. This hunting lodge was directly over Doctor Borth's underground castle. It served as the blind for that remarkable fortress.

Some signal had flashed below when Harry tampered with the broken door. Yakbar was on the job; and the Turk's moves were as calculating as ever. He showed no haste that would betray him; instead; he emerged steadily from the steep steps that lay beneath the hearth.

IT was chance alone that told Harry of Yakbar's arrival. Turning toward the fireplace, Harry saw the rising Turk. The powerful wrestler sprang from the top step; made a grab for Harry's arm before The Shadow's agent could produce a gun.

For a quarter minute, the struggle was a fierce, evenly matched one. Then, from the depths, came another pair of huskies. They soon pinioned Harry; wrenched him away from Yakbar.

Despite the odds, Harry was on the point of breaking loose, until Yakbar, freed from the grapple, produced the needle that he had used on a previous night.

The Turk jabbed the hypodermic into Harry's arm; then added his own weight to the struggle. Three against one, plus the dosage prepared by Doctor Borth, were odds that could not be offset. Harry's fight slowed gradually, to end with a complete slump.

Yakbar and the others carried Harry below. The stone slab lowered into place to show the barren hearth.

Doctor Borth had lost one prisoner, an agent of The Shadow, only to gain another!

CHAPTER XII
CLYDE'S CONTACT

THE sequel to Harry's capture came when Clyde reached No. 27, after an uneventful drive into New York. Seated at a corner table in the fish and chip establishment, Clyde kept watch upon the doorway while he drank his coffee.

There wasn't any sign of Hawkeye; nor did a cab pull up that might be Moe's.

It did not occur to Clyde that Harry had encountered trouble, for Harry had said nothing about making a closer approach to Doctor Borth's preserve. Reasoning things over, it struck Clyde that the lack of contact was simply a token that he should go through with the mission that he had promised Diane.

The girl had stated that James Cleeve was the head of a squad of government agents, secretly operating in New York. Clyde had passed that information to Harry. Under such circumstances, Diane's message could be classed as a report from one government operative to a superior; and its main purpose was to properly introduce Clyde to Cleeve. There would be no reason for The Shadow to intercept a bona fide message of that sort.

From that, Clyde drew the obvious conclusion that The Shadow expected him to visit Cleeve and make a later report. Finishing a second cup of coffee, Clyde left No. 27 and took the wheel of Harry's coupé.

Driving uptown, Clyde decided to leave the car in its usual garage and take a cab from there. He did so, and arrived on the secluded street that Hawkeye had visited earlier.

Alighting at the Brayland Apartments, Clyde entered and inquired for James Cleeve. The clerk called the apartment; after a short conversation, he received word that Mr. Burke was to go up to the fifth floor.

As he entered the elevator, Clyde happened to glance through the door to the street. He thought he saw a man slide out of sight; but he decided that his guess was wrong. Clyde had looked over the front of the building when he arrived, and had seen no prowlers at that time. He figured that he had simply caught a glimpse of someone who was shuffling past the doorway.

When he reached Cleeve's apartment, Clyde saw a peering eye through, the crack of the partly opened door. He must have passed inspection, for the door swung inward promptly. Clyde stepped into the living room, to find three men waiting him.

There was no difficulty in recognizing James Cleeve. The tall man's square face and steady eyes marked him as the leader of the group.

"SO you are a reporter from the *Classic*." Cleeve's tone carried as sharp a stab as his eyes. "Perhaps you might tell me, Mr. Burke, just why you wish to interview me. It is rather unusual"— Cleeve's smile showed an indulgence—"for a newspaper to be interested in the activities of a group of salesmen. Particularly one like this. Our line is furniture."

"I'm not after a story," explained Clyde, "I have a message for you, Mr. Cleeve."

He produced Diane's note. Cleeve read it; Clyde saw keen eyes light beneath their heavy brows, Cleeve's smile became a tight one. He turned to his companions.

"It's all right, men," he told them. "Burke knows we're Feds. He's seen the Delban girl."

Despite the odds, Harry was on the point of breaking loose, until Yakbar produced the needle that he had used on a previous night.

Cleeve drew back his coat, to flash his badge. He waved Clyde to a chair. There was something more important that he wanted to know.

"Where did you come from?" he queried. "How far away is the hideout? Can you lead us back there?"

"Easily," assured Clyde. "Unless I made some slip-up when I took the distances."

He picked up pencil and paper, traced the complete route to Borth's. Cleeve's eyes gleamed, particularly when he learned that the goal was less than forty miles distant. He glanced eagerly at his watch; noted that it was almost midnight. After a short calculation, Cleeve shook his head.

"I'd like to have started tonight," he said, "but it won't do. It's pretty isolated territory out there; Borth might have lookouts posted. We could sneak in there early in the evening; but after midnight would be a bad time. We'll hold off the raid until tomorrow."

That decision pleased Clyde. It offered a chance for contact with The Shadow. Rising from his chair, Clyde remarked casually:

"I'd like to go with you, Mr. Cleeve. What time shall I come around tomorrow?"

"Wait a minute, Burke," laughed Cleeve, clapping a friendly hand upon Clyde's shoulder. "Where do you want to go now?"

"To the *Classic* office. I want to find out if Doctor Borth sent that telegram he made me write."

"All right, Burke."

Cleeve stood reflectively, as Clyde started for the door. A complication occurred to him; again he motioned for Clyde to wait.

"You can't let this story out, Burke," warned Cleeve. "That's for your own benefit, as well as mine, since you're going with us tomorrow night."

"That's agreed," returned Clyde. "I won't spill a word of it at the office."

"Good enough! There's another angle, though. Tonight, we traced a fellow named Barsley, who works for Borth. We figure he's the collector who chucked that bag of cash over in Jersey, for Yakbar to pick up."

"Then he's the fellow who had the mob kill Fred, the service station man?"

"Right!" Cleeve's tone was grim. "There was a crew covering up for him tonight, too; only we didn't know it until too late."

CLYDE was hearing interesting details. He wanted more; Cleeve decided to give them. He explained his purpose of letting Barsley get away to avoid capture and questioning by Joe Cardona.

Clyde saw the wisdom of Cleeve's policy, since it kept Borth uninformed that the trail was coming closer.

"Barsley gave the jewel-selling stall," stated Cleeve, "and I pretended to fall for it. The trouble was, Cardona must have shown up when Barsley was on the way out. I heard the shooting, but I took up the trail too late. The way things turned out"— Cleeve's tone was rueful—"I wish I'd grabbed Barsley when I had him."

"Here's the bad point, Burke." Cleeve's headshake was serious. "If that crew spotted me following them, they may have tracked me back here. Normally, they'd lay off Feds quicker than they would cops; but maybe Barsley didn't have a chance to tell them I was a Fed. So we're playing our cards close.

"We can't afford a run-in with a bunch of hoodlums while we're after bigger game. The information you've brought us makes it all the more important to lie low."

Stepping past Clyde, Cleeve placed his hand on the doorknob. When he beckoned, he indicated his own men along with Clyde.

"I'm sending these boys downstairs with you," said Cleeve. "You wait in the lobby while they take a stroll around the block. Don't start until they come back with the word that everything's clear, And remember—mum at the *Classic*."

WHEN Clyde reached the lobby, he had time for speculation while his two companions went out on patrol. He approved of Cleeve's tactics. Feds didn't leave matters to chance.

It was nearly ten minutes before the pair returned; each had circled the block in an opposite direction. One of them gave Clyde the route to the nearest subway station, four blocks distant. Methodically, the other reported to Cleeve on the house phone. The result was a nod for Clyde to start his journey.

A chance recollection struck Clyde after he was outside; something that he had forgotten to mention to Cleeve. He remembered the shuffler who had gone past the front door at the time of his arrival. He wondered if that prowler still happened to be about.

Scanning the street, Clyde saw no sign of suspicious persons. Even the cars that were parked along the street appeared innocent.

Nevertheless, Clyde could not shake off the peculiar strain that gripped him. Easing his footsteps as he neared a corner, he sensed a sound behind him. He had the distinct impression that someone was following, ready to come up and accost him in the darkness.

Without looking back, Clyde increased his pace. He made quick strides across the next street. On the far side, he paused to look back.

That was when he glimpsed a figure that shrank back from sight—a hunched, furtive man whose face Clyde could not see. The glimpse, though, provided another link. The hunchy man reminded Clyde of Hawkeye.

Whether or not it was Hawkeye who had shuffled past the Brayland Apartments, Clyde could not decide. He felt sure, though, that it was Hawkeye who had picked up his present trail. On that basis, the rest was plain.

Hawkeye wanted to contact Clyde; therefore, he had slid up closer in the darkness. Clyde's sudden quickening of pace had defeated Hawkeye's effort to reach him. The result put Clyde on one side of the street, Hawkeye on the other.

Clyde expected Hawkeye to cross and join him. Instead, the hunchy little man shifted away, going back along the street that he and Clyde had followed. That puzzled Clyde. It made him miss the idea entirely.

Assuming that the hunched man was actually Hawkeye, his departure was obviously intended to make Clyde continue along his route, probably to a meeting with The Shadow, farther on. But Clyde jumped to another conclusion. He decided that the shifty follower wasn't Hawkeye. So Clyde stood on the corner, straining his eyes back toward the other block.

The policy was a bad one, as Clyde was soon to learn. He was losing valuable minutes that he should have spent in continuing along his walk to the subway. When Clyde did turn to resume his way, he was one block short of the position that he should have reached. Others were to take advantage of that fact.

Just as Clyde started away, a touring car wheeled up to the corner and made the turn. The car was moving rapidly; but its speed changed when its driver saw Clyde. Brakes gave a sudden shriek; the automobile staged a dead stop at the curb.

Men in black were acting with the same promptness as the driver. The door was open; they were piling to the sidewalk as Clyde turned about.

There wasn't a chance for Clyde to dodge them. No doorways were handy along the street. Before Clyde could budge, a pair of thugs had him between them. Revolvers were prodding his ribs. An ugly growl buzzed in the reporter's ear:

"Come along, lug! You're taking a ride with us!"

CLYDE hesitated. He knew what the ride would mean: a one-way ticket with no return. He chewed his lips as he realized how he had dodged Hawkeye, back in the other block; Hawkeye, who wanted him either to wait or go ahead, not to stand and gawk from a street corner.

That was something Hawkeye had figured Clyde wouldn't do. That was why Hawkeye hadn't waited to watch.

The jab of a gun reminded Clyde that he could stall no longer. It told him also that his present spot was a bad one. This street was lonely; a muffled shot wouldn't be heard far. It would be easy for these thugs to shoot him, then haul him into the touring car, if Clyde refused to go of his own will.

In a pinch like this, it was better to take a chance on future luck rather than accept sure trouble for the present. Mechanically, Clyde nodded. He started toward the touring car, pressed by the guns of his captors.

At the curb, they shoved him roughly aboard. Clyde found himself between the deadly pair; he saw a leering hoodlum who sat beside the driver; that fellow was looking gleefully into the back seat, also ready with a rod.

Clyde Burke had met up with one of those roving bands of thugs that had earlier been on hand to cover the flight of Kirk Barsley.

Crooks of the sort who had murdered Fred. Killers who would dispose of any person who seemed to know too much. They figured that Clyde was such a person; and they were right.

As the thug-manned car pulled from the curb, Clyde Burke was gripped by the gloomy thought that this ride would mark the finish of his long service with The Shadow.

CHAPTER XIII
THE RETRACED ROUTE

THE touring car was headed in the direction that Clyde had been going; but that was small comfort to the prisoner. Whatever these captors intended, they certainly weren't offering a friendly lift to the subway station. They were headed for parts unknown, and Clyde was going with them. How long he would remain alive depended upon how long it would suit the convenience of his captors.

By the end of the block, Clyde had a good inkling of what was to come. He knew it from the way the driver brought the car to a cautious stop, to take a good peer along the avenue before he turned the corner.

That was the usual technique of the one-way ride. Pick up a victim; take him along at an easy pace, so as not to excite suspicion. Find the spot for murder; give him the works, then dump him. The speed always came when the killers made their getaway.

This ride wouldn't be a long one, Clyde guessed. There were plenty of miserable neighborhoods within a mile or two of this section. The crooks had probably picked the very alleyway that would be a suitable resting place for the victim's body.

The car turned another corner. Thugs were looking back; their pleased growls assured the driver that there was no one on the trail. The car threaded along a few more streets; as it passed one corner, Clyde looked to the left.

He gained an instant's elation when he saw a parked car, with its cowl lights glowing; but his enthusiasm was short-lived. Low conversation among the captors proved that they had expected to see that car.

These mobbies were working with a reserve crew. The driver had come past this corner so that the other band could follow along. To Clyde, that news marked the end of a frail hope that he had nourished. He had counted on making a bold break: a leap from the touring car, then a run for it.

Sometimes a surprise stunt like that could work. Not this time. Any such attempt would leave Clyde helpless, at the mercy of the second crew. As he shifted around, Clyde could see the lights of the trailing car, a block back.

"Gettin' scary, huh?" The snorted words came from the hoodlum on Clyde's right. "We gotta dose that'll end that! You'll be takin' it soon!"

The nudge of the crook's revolver muzzle told what the dose would be. Like the others, that killer was simply awaiting word for murder. He was right, when he said it would be coming soon. The car had reached an ill-kept street; from its slow progress, the driver was obviously looking for the proper alley entrance.

The thug on Clyde's left said nothing. He gave a contemptuous glance toward the reporter; then stared to the left. Like the driver, he was looking for the alley; but all the while, he was keeping his gun hard against Clyde's ribs.

The car took a jounce. There was a thump beside Clyde's right shoulder; a slight thud that Clyde thought came from the body of the touring car. The man on Clyde's right leaned forward; Clyde thought that he was trying to crane toward the left, so that he could look with the others.

There was something odd, though, in the way the fellow's chin settled against Clyde's elbow.

Crouched there on the running board, The Shadow had listened to all that was said.

Staring downward, Clyde realized suddenly that the thug was unconscious. Somewhere, out of darkness, a slugging blow had reached the side of the killer's skull. Before Clyde could fully appreciate what had happened, a low whisper sounded in his ear.

Clyde knew that voice. It was The Shadow's!

INSTANTLY, the situation was plain. Hawkeye had expected Clyde to meet The Shadow at the end of the block where the touring car had appeared. Clyde's own delay had led to his sudden capture. But when the car had reached the next corner, it had picked up another passenger.

All through this ride, The Shadow had been on the running board on the right side of the car. Crouched there, he had listened to all that was said. Out of sight of the car that held the other crew of gunmen, The Shadow had bided his time until the right moment. The opportunity had come. The Shadow had coolly taken one thug from combat.

He had a way to deal with the others. The Shadow's whisper told Clyde what to do. Tensely, Clyde restrained himself. They were at the alley; the car was swinging into it. The mobster beside

the driver was looking through the windshield; but he was just ready to turn about.

The car came to a stop. That was the moment for action. The preliminary move came when The Shadow released the bobbing thug who was on Clyde's right. The unconscious hoodlum flopped to the floor of the car. His sag gave Clyde space.

In accord with The Shadow's order, Clyde jerked away from the gun that poked him on the left. As he did, he grabbed for the muzzle, shoved the crook's hand upward before the fellow could fire.

The move was a complete surprise; for the man on the left didn't know that he alone was covering Clyde. All he could do was try and stem the reporter's attack; grapple to keep his own gun.

The thug beside the driver heard the scuffle; he swung about to aim, snarling as he came. He never had a chance to jab his gun muzzle toward Clyde's face. The Shadow was again in action, this time with a long, inward surge across the rear door.

Clyde missed that amazing move. The Shadow used his left hand to vault inward. His right fist sweeping ahead, seemed to haul him with its driving reach. Carrying a huge automatic, the gloved fist sped over the front crook's head; then came downward. It found the thug's skull in the manner of a grappling hook.

The stroke sank the aiming killer. More than that, it enabled The Shadow to haul himself completely into the car; for he kept that gun hold once he had gained it. Without a single revealing shot, The Shadow had gained control. The rest of the battle appeared simple.

With a side swing, The Shadow slugged the driver as that thug swung about. While the fellow was still settling over the wheel, The Shadow moved in to aid Clyde. The help was necessary; for though Clyde was still holding his own, he hadn't managed to wrench away the last thug's gun. With The Shadow smashing in, complete success seemed sure.

A bad break spoiled the victory.

THE SHADOW'S fist, sledging for the crook's skull, delayed as Clyde twisted partially into its path. Expertly, The Shadow completed the blow; but it was slowed, and the stroke was a glancing one.

The crook slumped; his revolver hit the floor. That partly deceived The Shadow in the dimness.

Settling in the rear seat, The Shadow fired shots into the upholstery. That was supposed to tell the crooks in the other car that Clyde had been given a dose of bullets. To complete the illusion, The Shadow opened the door on the right; he shoved out the unconscious gunman who lay on the floor.

From the mouth of the alley, watchers took the sprawling form for Clyde's body. As the stunned thug fell, The Shadow heard a motor throb. So far, the trick had worked.

It was then that the break occurred.

The last crook had recovered, still gripped by Clyde. Like The Shadow, Clyde thought that the fellow was completely out. He realized his error when the thug managed to clutch the door handle on the left.

The door gave; the crook's weight went outward. Clyde didn't have time to get loose. He went sprawling with the unarmed thug.

There were excited shouts from the other car. Sight of two more men spilling from the touring car told them that something had gone sour. There was a clatter of feet as rowdies jumped for the alley. A big spotlight gleamed.

Crooks saw Clyde, rising from beside the touring car. They knew him for the victim that they wanted. They aimed, so promptly that Clyde had no chance to get away. All that saved him was the promptness with which The Shadow diverted the aim of the killers.

With a strident laugh, The Shadow sprang from the door on the right. His mockery was a compelling challenge. His cloaked shape, outlined in the spotlight, was a target far more important than Clyde Burke. To a man, the cover-up crew aimed for that weaving figure in black, intending to finish their cloaked enemy forever.

They were to realize promptly how The Shadow had outwitted them.

The Shadow had not sprawled into the alley; he had sprung there. He was wheeling as he landed, ready for double action. He started a sidestep, away from the car; then faded back toward the vehicle itself.

Those shifts were possible, because crooks were changing their aim. The other phase of The Shadow's action was a prompt attack of his own.

His right hand was already opening fire with its gun. His left was whipping a second automatic from his cloak. His shots sounded along with the revolver fire of the thugs. Echoing in the alley, the blasts of his big .45 made the revolver shots sound puny in comparison.

Thugs dodged to escape those crippling shots. It was lucky for them that The Shadow held Clyde in mind. He was firing more rapidly than usual, in order to fully divert the enemy. That was why his fusillade clipped only one of the scattering thugs. They were making for the shelter of their car and the corners of the alleyway.

THE SHADOW was boxed, as he had been before. This alleyway was a clear one, going through to the next street; but a dash in that direction would be futile. It would do for Clyde; but not for The Shadow. Battle was his only chance.

Clyde had reached the front of the touring car; The Shadow saw him there. He pointed the reporter through; hissed a quick command for flight. As Clyde started, The Shadow turned about to meet a new fusillade that was starting from the alley entrance.

Clyde's reluctance ended when he saw The Shadow's tactics. With his first shot, the cloaked marksman drilled the spotlight that glared along the alley. With a shout of triumphant mirth, he zigzagged toward the crooks, using his automatics as he went.

Thugs were firing at the spurts of The Shadow's guns. He, in turn, was picking the flashes of their revolvers. But The Shadow was changing position, while they were stationary. That gave The Shadow all the odds.

Dashing through the alley, Clyde could hear the taunt of an evasive, quivering laugh amid the lessening fire. When he reached the next street, he heard the roar of a motor; as it faded, there was a final gibe of mirth.

Mobsters in the cover-up car had fled, leaving

the rest of their band to The Shadow. The cloaked fighter's victory was sure.

Clear of the alley, Clyde decided suddenly that he now had an opportunity to return there. Contact with The Shadow was possible, with the thugs banished. But before Clyde could turn about, he heard the whine of a police car's siren.

Sounds of battle had been heard. The law was approaching, headed for the very street where Clyde stood.

Explanations would be difficult, if Clyde had to give them. He didn't want to spoil The Shadow's victory by undergoing a police quiz. A lot depended on keeping facts unknown; particularly those that concerned James Cleeve. Clyde had already guessed that The Shadow must know a lot about those Feds who were quartered at the Brayland Apartments.

Taking it on the run, Clyde reached a corner before the police car arrived. He ducked through other streets, not caring where they led. At last, he reached a spot some distance from his starting point; he saw an avenue, with a cab parked near an elevated station.

A trip to the *Classic* office was out of the question. Clyde decided that as he entered the cab. He didn't know how to reach The Shadow, for the present; but he realized that there might be a chance to meet up with Hawkeye.

That was why Clyde gave an address where he thought Hawkeye might be; and where he felt sure that crooks had not returned. He told the cabby to take him to the Brayland Apartments.

ALIGHTING outside of Cleeve's, Clyde paid the driver and looked around for Hawkeye. He thought he could discern a shifting figure at a distant doorway; but before he could make sure, a man stepped from the entrance of the Brayland.

The arrival was one of Cleeve's operatives, the squatty chap who had watched Barsley's office.

"What's up, Burke?" The squatty man spoke in puzzled tone. "How did you get back from the *Classic* so soon?"

"I didn't get there," returned Clyde. "A mob tried to take me for a ride! I got away from them."

The squatty operative whistled. He looked anxiously along the street; then drew Clyde inside. He went to a telephone; as he picked it up, he motioned toward the elevator.

"Better get upstairs and talk to the chief. I'll tell him you're on the way."

Cleeve was waiting when Clyde reached the apartment. His eyes glittered beneath their heavy brows when he heard Clyde's story. Clyde was hazy when he described the part that The Shadow had played; he spoke as though his rescue had been a chance one. Cleeve accepted it as such.

"One of Barsley's crews got into trouble, earlier," recalled Cleeve. "I guess this mysterious rescuer of yours was in that, too. I've heard of him—The Shadow. He's done good work tonight! I don't think those mobbies will be back here.

"Still, we're taking no chances. You stay with us, Burke. Tomorrow evening, we'll head for Jersey. If luck's with us—and I think it is—those thugs will be thinking about The Shadow, instead of us. That will leave us clear to move in on Borth."

Cleeve showed Clyde to an interior room of the large apartment. He smiled when he saw the reporter sag wearily to a chair. Cleeve dropped his hand on Clyde's shoulder, with the comment:

"You're fagged out, Burke. Turn in and get a good sleep. You'll need it for tomorrow."

Alone, Clyde followed Cleeve's advice. When he had turned the lights out, he opened the window. Standing there, he stared into the darkened, silent courtyard. Off in a corner, Clyde saw the dim light of another window; he stared suddenly, as something streaked the dull wall within it.

Moving into the light, Clyde saw a singular silhouette: a hawkish profile, topped by the outline of a slouch hat. That token remained motionless, then vanished as a hand turned off the light from somewhere within the room.

Clyde grinned to himself as he stretched on the bed. He didn't have to worry about later contact with The Shadow. His chief had chosen another apartment, here at the Brayland. Evidently, The Shadow had spotted Clyde's room, and had waited to deliver his identifying signal.

Sooner or later, Clyde would have his chance to communicate the facts that he had learned. The Shadow, like James Cleeve, would be given the trail to the hidden citadel of Doctor Nicholas Borth.

CHAPTER XIV
CLYDE REPORTS

IT was early afternoon when Clyde Burke awakened after a long and much-needed sleep. The sound that roused him was an abrupt rap at the door; so sudden that it took Clyde a few moments to grope for a recollection of his present location.

When he opened the door, Clyde saw the squatty operative who was so frequently with Cleeve. The fellow had a grin; he held a watch before Clyde's eyes. Clyde blinked when he saw that it was almost two o'clock.

"The chief wants to see you," informed the summoner. "Climb into some duds. He's in the living room."

Clyde watched the squatty man walk along the hallway to the front of the apartment. There, he turned right into the living room.

Stepping back into his own room, Clyde started to dress; as he did, he remembered the courtyard. He looked across to the window where he had seen The Shadow's silhouette.

That window looked ordinary by day; so commonplace that Clyde began to think that his imagination had gripped him last night. His series of bizarre adventures had left him in one of those in-between states, where it was difficult to decide whether he had undergone certain experiences or had simply dreamed them.

Of one thing, Clyde was sure. The Shadow had rescued him from death last night. Whether or not The Shadow was still about was a question. Clyde didn't find any answer when he looked from his window.

That was because the answer lay elsewhere—at a spot where Clyde had failed to see it. The hall outside his room was darkened, for it had only one small window, near the rear. Hence, neither Clyde nor Cleeve's man had observed the figure that watched their brief interview.

Silently, unseen, The Shadow had entered Cleeve's apartment. Stationed at a spot where the hallway widened, in front of the living room, The Shadow was awaiting his chance to contact Clyde.

The squatty man had left the living room door open. The Shadow approached; peered through the crack to see Cleeve seated near the window. There was a road map on the table; Cleeve was marking it with a blue pencil while the squatty man watched him.

"HERE'S the last crossroad, Felkin"—Cleeve turned the pencil over, to use its red end, as he drew a circle—"after that, it's a five-mile ride without another turn-off."

"Except the dirt road," objected Felkin, pointing to the map. "You'd call that a turn-off, wouldn't you?"

"Yes, but it's not on the map. It probably lies about here"—Cleeve continued the blue line—"and it doesn't lead anywhere."

"Except to Borth's."

Cleeve chuckled when he heard Felkin's comment. The Shadow watched the keen-eyed man lean back into his chair.

"It starts us on the way to Borth's," agreed Cleeve. He dotted the end of the blue line. "Figuring this as the old gatepost, half a mile in from the good road, we won't have far to go up the mountainside. About a quarter mile, Burke said."

"That's what he said," nodded Felkin. "However, he *came* from the place; we've got to get to it. Maybe that won't be easy in the dark."

"We'll spread out for a starter; then close in. Anyway, we'll have Burke with us."

"You're taking Burke along?"

There was surprise in Felkin's question. Cleeve noted it; gave a simple nod as his reply. He was looking at the map again when the squatty man began a protest.

"Listen, chief. You told us this morning—"

"I know what I told you," interrupted Cleeve. "I figured we'd go without Burke. He'd be willing enough to stay here, on the promise that we'd let him have an exclusive story after we raided Borth's hideout. That is, Burke would listen to persuasion.

"But after what happened last night, we'd be taking a bad chance, leaving Burke behind. We don't know who might spot us going out. Anybody might barge in after we've gone. If Burke's with us, we don't have to worry about him."

Pausing, Cleeve tapped the red circle that marked the crossroad on the map.

"After we've passed there," he declared, "we'll have things clinched. "We'll move in on Borth, with our full force! That will give us big odds, according to the message Burke brought from Diane.

"Doc Borth will be due for a real surprise, especially when he sees Burke with us. That's going to be a swell showdown, Felkin; one that I wouldn't want to miss!"

THE SHADOW was moving away as he heard the finish of Cleeve's statement. There were footsteps in the hall; Clyde was coming from his room. The Shadow shifted to block his agent's path. Whatever surprises were due for the night, Clyde gained one in advance.

In the gloomy hall, Clyde felt a gloved hand grip his arm. He heard the whispered voice, seemingly from nowhere, that sounded in his ear:

"Report!"

The Shadow had moved deep enough into the hallway to intercept Clyde before he reached the living room. Neither Cleeve nor Felkin guessed that the reporter was already on his way. But before Clyde could speak, there was the sound of a closing door from a side hallway.

It meant that another of Cleeve's men was coming through the apartment. Coolly, The Shadow added the order:

"Later!"

An instant afterward, the gripping clutch was gone. Clyde blinked. He couldn't guess which direction The Shadow had taken. All that he heard was the approach of heavy footsteps from that side hall. Clyde knew that The Shadow didn't want him to linger while one of Cleeve's men came through. Promptly, Clyde approached the living room and entered.

"Hello, Burke!" greeted Cleeve. Then, to the man beside him: "Close the door, Felkin, while we go over the details."

Cleeve showed Clyde the map, with the route that they intended to follow.

"We'll leave here at seven-thirty," he added. "That will bring us to the crossroad—this red circle—by half past eight. We can close in on Borth about nine o'clock."

There was a pencil by Cleeve's elbow. Unnoticed, Clyde pocketed it. He broke the pencil; its muffled crackle was unheard. Gripping the stubby point, Clyde wrote on a slip of paper that was in his pocket.

All that he gave were the times that Cleeve had mentioned. They, alone, seemed necessary, for Clyde supposed that The Shadow had heard all other details from Harry Vincent.

The chat ended, Cleeve suggested that they have lunch. They walked from the living room; once in the hall, Clyde wadded the paper and flipped it from his pocket. Their route led toward the interior of the apartment; when they were gone, an event occurred that Clyde had expected.

A gloved hand plucked the wadded message from the floor. That was not all, The Shadow had his opportunity to learn more while he remained here. He entered the living room; studied the map that lay near the window. That done, he returned to the hall.

The way was open to Clyde's room; The Shadow went there and made a brief search. Finding no other message, he departed, silently opening the front door of the apartment.

HALF an hour later, The Shadow was in his sanctum. Clyde's terse message lay on a table beneath a blue light, along with a road map that

duplicated Cleeve's. Beneath the time schedule that Clyde had written was a penciled line. That meant the message was complete.

A low laugh pervaded the sanctum.

The brevity of Clyde's report explained much that The Shadow sought. Since last night, Clyde had known that The Shadow was at hand. Therefore, the reporter should have been prepared to deliver many facts when he gained a chance for contact. Instead, these meager items were all that Clyde had given.

There was only one answer to Clyde's seeming negligence.

Clyde obviously believed that The Shadow was acquainted with all required details, except the actual time schedule that James Cleeve and his followers intended to use when they invaded Borth's citadel.

There could be only one reason for such supposition on Clyde's part. The reporter must have contacted someone else in The Shadow's service, between the time that he left Borth's and arrived at Cleeve's. That gave The Shadow a much-needed link.

Long fingers drew a typewritten sheet into the light. It was a morning report, relayed in from Burbank, in New Jersey. It told of Harry Vincent's failure to make contact after midnight. During early morning hours, other agents had been scouring the Jersey hinterlands in search of Harry; but to no avail. Wherever Harry might be at present, he was in no position to report through Burbank.

The only conclusion was the right one. Clyde had met Harry; had given him extensive facts regarding Doctor Nicholas Borth. Some ill luck had prevented Harry from sending the word through. Clyde, however, had carried the facts to James Cleeve.

Cleeve's marked road map was the result. On his own map, The Shadow penciled a blue line, identical with the one that Cleeve had drawn. He even marked a red circle at the crossroad that Cleeve had designated as the last danger spot that the expedition would pass.

That done, The Shadow rested his forefinger at the end of the blue line; moved it slowly in a semicircle, to indicate the open space to the north.

Somewhere in that limited area lay the secret abode of Doctor Nicholas Borth. A place that Clyde Burke had left; a sector where Harry Vincent could have ventured. The fact that Clyde had returned safely from his imprisonment indicated that Harry likewise remained alive.

The Shadow's hand inscribed inked notations, that faded like passing thoughts. Piece by piece, he was fitting probable facts. When he had completed that survey, he snapped off the bluish light. Absolute darkness filled the sanctum. The only sound that stirred that blackness was the chilling tone of a laugh that trailed to nothingness.

The Shadow had departed. He had business in New Jersey before Cleeve and his operatives reached there. Secretly, alone, The Shadow would penetrate to the hidden citadel where Doctor Borth was master.

CHAPTER XV
DANGER BELOW

WANING afternoon brought gloom to that lonely dirt road along the Watchung mountainside. Storm clouds on the western horizon had completely blanketed the setting sun. Beneath the thick trees, The Shadow could scarcely discern the battered gateposts when he reached them.

This was the end of the blue-marked route. The Shadow had hours in which to investigate. The gloom was to his liking; it meant that he could search for Borth's hideout without being spotted by any lucky observer.

Driving his car between the ancient posts, The Shadow parked it out of sight. Alighting, he started through the underbrush, searching as he went. He paused at the spots where trickling daylight aided him. In gloomier places, he used a brilliant flashlight along the ground.

No chance prowler would have found Harry's radio equipment, for it was well buried in a thicket. The Shadow, however, was looking for such traces of his missing agent, and a broken branch gave him an early clue.

Pressing past the crushed bush, The Shadow uncovered the shortwave apparatus, set up for communication.

That discovery told its own story.

Harry Vincent had not been captured at this spot. Borth's men would certainly have dismantled the radio apparatus and taken it along with them. It was plain that Harry must have decided to investigate the mountain slope; that he had run into trouble farther up. That meant that he had gone to check on certain details that Clyde Burke had given him.

Moving upward among the trees, The Shadow took a semicircling route. As before, he was looking for traces of Harry, and he found them: deep prints in the turf, where Harry had gone from one rocky spot to another. Those footprints pointed to the left.

Observing from that spot, The Shadow saw the stony ledge to the right, where the prickly bushes so cleverly hid the hillside exit. Whether or not that secret opening could have deceived The Shadow was a question that would remain undecided. Having found Harry's trail, The Shadow followed it, instead of tracking back.

By night, The Shadow moved invisibly. Here, in this fading daylight, his figure could be seen. Yet only the sharpest eyes could have spied The Shadow's course.

Wearing his black cloak and hat, he moved with spectral glide. Every tree, every bush clump served as a shrouding cover. Only in the intervening spaces did The Shadow's cloaked shape show its full outline.

Streaked daylight indicated a clearing ahead. On the fringe, The Shadow saw the sprawling hunting lodge with its boarded windows. He chose a circuit; from the shaded side, he reached the veranda. Once over the rail, he was lost in the dullness beneath the porch roof.

THE cabin door was padlocked. The lock was new; not rusted, like the one that Harry had broken. Judging by the rusty nails in the boarded windows, The Shadow decided that someone had entered recently; that the door had been repaired afterward.

That was another clue to Harry; moreover, it indicated the mistake that the missing agent had made. The Shadow guessed that the door was wired, to flash a signal below.

The windows, too, could be fixed. That was why The Shadow chose the roof. Scaling the side posts of the veranda, he came to the flat top of the lodge. There, he found a broad expanse of weather-beaten tar paper. On hands and knees, he crept along the black surface, toward a raised space that proved to be a boarded skylight.

Flat on the roof, The Shadow noted other skylights. Like the windows, they might be wired; but The Shadow doubted it. Anyone trying to enter the old lodge would naturally try the windows before going to the roof. These skylights could be the one weakness in Doctor Borth's defense.

Carefully, The Shadow worked on the skylight beside him. It gave, under noiseless pressure. Raising the flat barrier on its stout hinges, The Shadow slid his body through. Hanging, he let the skylight settle on his fingers; then he dropped to the floor beneath. His landing was catlike in its silence.

Using a tiny flashlight, The Shadow searched the ground floor of the lodge. He came to the big living room. There, the search provided a new clue: a freshly splintered floorboard near the fireplace. That told of a struggle; a sliding heel that had dug hard into the board.

Turning his flashlight, The Shadow noted the broad stone hearth.

Boards had warped against the edge of the slab, enough for The Shadow's keen eyes to detect the crack of the traplike opening. Probing with a thin piece of flat steel, he was rewarded by the slight click of a hidden catch. The slab came upward under the prying force of The Shadow's gloved fingers.

Below, The Shadow saw steep steps: wooden strips that were like a ladder, tapering toward the bottom. He started the descent, letting the slab close above him.

When he reached the bottom, ten feet below, he tested the floor and found it solid stone. The space was cramped; it had no outlet. The Shadow brought his flashlight into play. The glow showed a solid steel barrier just opposite the steep steps.

The metal sheet was set in stone. Probing the edges, The Shadow found a crevice; worked with a long flat picking instrument to find a catch. That effort failed until he bent the metal strip, wedging it past the edge of the metal door.

When the catch clicked, it came with a sudden snap. The door slid a fraction of an inch; The Shadow was prompt enough to press it sideways before the catch could lock again.

Chilled atmosphere greeted The Shadow as he stepped into a dimly lighted passage. He had reached the upper floor of Borth's air-conditioned abode. Sliding the well-oiled door shut behind him, The Shadow started along the very corridors that Clyde Burke had followed, a few nights before.

The doorways, fortunately, were deep. When one opened suddenly, The Shadow had time to press into a recess that was diagonally opposite. The man who stepped from the open door did not see The Shadow; but he, himself, came plainly into the cloaked watcher's view.

The man was Yakbar, coming from Doctor Borth's office.

YAKBAR closed the office door and walked stolidly along the corridor. As soon as the Turk had made a turn, The Shadow followed. He saw Yakbar unlock a door and enter a dull-lighted room.

After a few minutes, Yakbar came out again. He returned directly to Borth's office; again, he failed to see The Shadow. The mysterious visitor was in a doorway before Yakbar arrived.

Once Yakbar had closed the office door, The Shadow approached it. The door was unlocked; its knob yielded under subtle pressure. In inching fashion, The Shadow worked the door inward, to get the view he wanted. At the desk, he saw the shock-haired figure of Doctor Nicholas Borth.

A question issued from the old man's lips.

"What of the prisoner?" demanded Borth. "Could he talk to you, Yakbar?"

"Not yet, master." The Turk's tone was apologetic. "He has awakened; but his stupor is not ended."

Borth showed annoyance.

"Your mistake was excusable with Burke," he said, testily. "Alone, with a journey ahead, you had need to use the hypodermic. But with this man, Vincent, it was unnecessary!"

"I am sorry, master."

"That may not help. This man Vincent may prove dangerous! He is not a reporter like Burke; whoever he is, he came here armed. We must learn his business; meanwhile, it would be folly to leave this stronghold. Yet, at times"—Borth stroked his chin—"I feel that it is folly to remain."

There was a stir from the corner of the room. For the first time, The Shadow saw Diane Delban as she stepped into his range of vision. The Shadow detected a look of alarm on the girl's face; but she suppressed it as she spoke to Borth.

"We are still secure," assured Diane. "Denovar tells me that Burke is still quiet in his cell."

"Burke does not matter," snapped Borth. "We can release him when we leave. But this man Vincent"—the doctor's tight fist pounded the desk—"may know much more than we suppose! It is unfortunate that he must drowse a few hours longer."

Borth looked at the oddly dialed clock upon his desk. After a short calculation, he added:

"Rouse him at twenty-one thirty, Yakbar."

The Shadow recognized that Borth was working on a twenty-four hour system; that twenty-one thirty would be half past nine. Harry's present status would continue until after the hour set for Cleeve's invasion.

That suited The Shadow's own plans perfectly. It meant that he would not have to make separate plans regarding Harry.

Borth arose from the desk; The Shadow heard him say something about a visit to the strongroom. He watched Borth go to the corner alcove; heard the sound of descending footsteps on the circular stairs.

Intent upon Borth, The Shadow momentarily forgot Yakbar and Diane. As a result, he was forced to an unexpected move.

The Shadow whisked from the doorway, not an instant too soon. Yakbar had approached, coming to the outer corridor. Deftly, The Shadow managed to close the door gap before Yakbar arrived; but the latch did not catch. Lacking time to attend to that detail, The Shadow whisked to the gloom of a doorway across the corridor.

THE office door puzzled Yakbar. The Turk was positive that he had closed it tightly when he entered, and he grumbled that fact to Diane.

At last, Yakbar shrugged his shoulders and went along the corridor; but he stopped at the first corner, to glare back in suspicious fashion. From the mutter of his lips, it seemed that the Turk intended to return after he had finished with some duty.

That was why The Shadow did not linger. Diane was looking in the direction that Yakbar had taken; her forehead showed the furrows of a worried frown. Moving from his doorway, The Shadow glided in the opposite direction, toward the passage that led back to the lodge.

Diane happened to turn as The Shadow went from sight. The glow of the corridor showed a moving silhouette along the floor; but that streak slid away as Diane stared. Simultaneously, Yakbar came back along the corridor; his eyes fixed steadily ahead.

Diane noted the suspicious expression on the Turk's face, but she said nothing. Instead, she stepped back into the office, to let the Turk pass.

The Shadow, meanwhile, had arrived at the steel door. On this side, it had a lever that opened it. Losing no time, The Shadow stepped through; the door was closing when he entered.

Through the closing crack, The Shadow saw Yakbar go past the entrance to the final passage. The Shadow was confident that he had managed an unwitnessed departure. He flicked his flashlight on the steep steps; began his ten foot ascent to the fireplace above.

Even during that brief climb, The Shadow was concentrating upon tasks that lay ahead; planning a surprise that would strike before nine o'clock. The Shadow had found his own route into Borth's domain; he could be there, in full control, when Cleeve and his men arrived.

Knowing only this one route, The Shadow could foresee difficulties for Cleeve when the latter invaded. The Shadow was taking that into calculations of the future.

The Shadow had almost forgotten the present. He was reminded of it, in startling fashion, just as he reached for the inside catch that held the locked hearth slab above his head.

Something clicked below. Turning his flashlight downward, The Shadow saw a change at the narrowed bottom of the shaft. The stone floor was sliding back beneath the wall, leaving a bottomless chasm four feet square!

Had The Shadow been on that spot, he would have had no standing place. His speedy climb up the ladder was all that had taken him from the sudden menace of that pit.

A whispered laugh from The Shadow's lips told that he felt himself secure. The mirth died, however, an instant after it began.

There was another *click*; it came from the steps themselves. In a flash, every step caved downward, hinging against the sharply sloping wall to form a solid slide, instead of a stairway. The Shadow's flashlight dropped from his hand as he made a wild grab for some hold in the darkness.

There was none. The flashlight was going like a plummet into the depths, blazing a course along which The Shadow followed, straight downward. Arms wide, legs stretched in the darkness, The Shadow was clawing nothingness when he took that fall.

The light of the tiny flashlight dwindled to a speck, then vanished, leaving no revealing signs of The Shadow's fall. A sharp click sounded as the steps came back in place; then a slithering rumble added its ominous tone.

That final sound was the floor of the shaft sliding into place. It moaned its echoes to listening ears that heard it from beyond the steel barrier. That rumble served as testimony that a hapless victim had gone to death below.

CHAPTER XVI
AT THE CROSSROAD

HOURS had passed since The Shadow's thwarted departure from Borth's; hours that had made but little change. Harry Vincent still lay in a stupor from the overcharge of dope that Yakbar had given him the night before. Clyde Burke was waiting with Cleeve, ready for the start to Borth's.

Oddly, thoughts of his agents were the impressions that first strummed through The Shadow's brain, when consciousness again was his. He sensed that time had passed; that his plans for others might be ruined. His own plight did not come to him with full force until after he had gathered those scattered details of the past.

Then, The Shadow was gripped by the incredible.

He was alive, despite the plunge that he had taken. A seeming impossibility, for he had viewed the depths awaiting him before he fell. Amazing

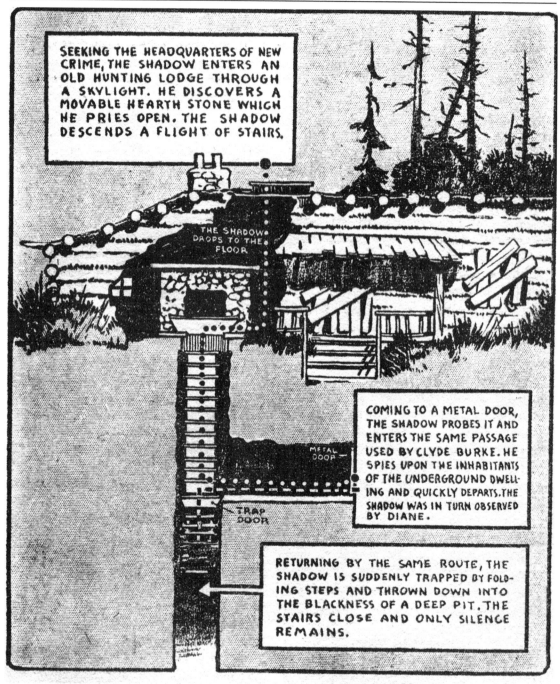

SEEKING THE HEADQUARTERS OF NEW CRIME, THE SHADOW ENTERS AN OLD HUNTING LODGE THROUGH A SKYLIGHT. HE DISCOVERS A MOVABLE HEARTH STONE WHICH HE PRIES OPEN. THE SHADOW DESCENDS A FLIGHT OF STAIRS.

THE SHADOW DROPS TO THE FLOOR

METAL DOOR—

TRAP DOOR

COMING TO A METAL DOOR, THE SHADOW PROBES IT AND ENTERS THE SAME PASSAGE USED BY CLYDE BURKE. HE SPIES UPON THE INHABITANTS OF THE UNDERGROUND DWELLING AND QUICKLY DEPARTS. THE SHADOW WAS IN TURN OBSERVED BY DIANE.

RETURNING BY THE SAME ROUTE, THE SHADOW IS SUDDENLY TRAPPED BY FOLDING STEPS AND THROWN DOWN INTO THE BLACKNESS OF A DEEP PIT. THE STAIRS CLOSE AND ONLY SILENCE REMAINS.

though some of his past escapes had been, this twist from death was too unbelievable to be actual.

The aches that ran through The Shadow's head were terrific, proof in themselves that he had come to a solid landing place. When he pushed his hand to the back of his head, his fingers dipped oozing blood that stained his cloak collar. That was real enough; but still it didn't fit the facts.

Memory of the abyss was too vivid. The Shadow recalled his last glimpse; it had satisfied him that he was due for a drop of sixty feet at least. No one could plunge that far, undeterred, to land on solid stone without a broken limb.

Apparently, The Shadow's skull had taken the jar, for his only injury was the one that had stunned him. Yet the force of the long fall should have bashed his head completely.

Still, he was alive; and badly cramped at that. When The Shadow tried to move about, he found himself jammed close against a wall. He remembered the flashlight; he began to grope for it, until he realized vaguely that the torch would be useless.

On hands and knees, he probed the stone floor about him, only to find the flashlight missing. That, too, was curious. Apparently, the metal flashlight had shattered into atoms while its owner remained intact!

One hand struck suddenly upon a ledge close to The Shadow's knees. As his fingers rested there, The Shadow realized slowly that he was clutching wood. He steadied in the darkness; breathed thick, musty air. He placed his other hand in front of him; it touched another ledge, higher up.

Slowly, thoughts connected themselves. These were not ledges that The Shadow clutched. They were wooden steps, rising at a sharp angle, like those in the shaft that led up to the fireplace of the abandoned lodge. This thick darkness, the murky air were the same that The Shadow remembered when he had started his final climb!

Pushing his arms sideways, The Shadow found them cramped by stone walls. Twisting, he found a steel surface behind him. His lips phrased a laugh that was no more than a repressed whisper, The Shadow had solved the riddle of why he was still alive.

FALLING, he had flung wide with his arms and legs. He hadn't gotten a grip, going headlong down the shaft; but his skull had thumped a wall before he reached the open trap at the bottom of the flattened steps. That thud had been a lucky one.

Sprawled, The Shadow had wedged into the narrow vortex near the bottom of the tapering shaft. Less than four feet square, the opening had not been large enough to let his long-limbed body through. An oversight on the part of Borth, or whoever had devised this trap; but one that had proven most advantageous to The Shadow.

No wonder he couldn't find his flashlight! It had gone to the depths below, while The Shadow had jammed in safety. Probably, he had been slowly slipping while he hung suspended; but he had stayed long enough.

The same hand that had opened the trap had closed it, satisfied that The Shadow had rocketed to the pit below when his wedged form had relaxed, The Shadow had simply settled upon solid surface.

The steps were back again. That was helpful. Scaling a sliding surface would be possible ordinarily; but not the way The Shadow felt at present. He swayed; lost his grip as he tried to make the climb. Only by resting at intervals did he manage to reach the top.

There, The Shadow's fingers fumbled nervelessly with the catch that held the hearth. When it finally released, he was barely able to push the hinged barrier upward.

Once he rolled upon the wooden floor of the living room, The Shadow was able to relax. The air was better here. Despite the steady throbbing of his head, he gained strength enough to reach for the skylight. His efforts faltered, until he found an old table stowed with some other rickety furniture. He managed to negotiate the skylight and flounder on the roof.

MOONLIGHT covered the Watchung mountainside. The storm from the west had drifted; both the hill above and the valley below were plain in the early evening glow. Night, however, made the whole scene a mass of trees, bleak sentinels of blackness; except where rocky ledges made shimmery streaks of silver.

Deep draughts of air revived The Shadow. He dropped from the low side of the roof; instinctively, he sought the shelter of the woods. Groping through the pitch-darkness under the trees, he stumbled over rocks and roots until he encountered the old dirt road.

After that, the route was easier. The Shadow paused at intervals to light matches and look for signs of the battered gateposts. At last he found them.

Leaving the road, he reached the bushes that hid the shortwave radio. A few minutes later, The Shadow was tapping out coded words to Burbank.

The Shadow's first question concerned the time; for he had smashed his watch in the fall. Burbank gave it as ten minutes after eight. He also reported that Hawkeye had seen Cleeve leave the Brayland Apartments at half past seven.

Cleeve was on schedule; Clyde was with him. They would reach the crossroad, red-marked on Cleeve's map, at half past eight. There was still time for The Shadow to be there first.

Pounding through The Shadow's mind were recollections of the plans that he had been making when he started his return trip from Borth's. He had intended to investigate further; to prepare his campaign exactly as he wanted.

There wasn't time for that. Preparations must be rushed. Afterward, events would snap into line.

To Burbank, The Shadow gave instructions regarding his agents who were scattered in the New Jersey hills. Marsland, "Tapper," others who had been called to search for Clyde were to converge as ordered. Crofton, a capable aviator, was to head for Newark Airport; then join the rest.

Never before had The Shadow sent such hectic instructions. Any recipient other than Burbank would have supposed that they were driftings from a jarred brain. But through the weave of The Shadow's orders, Burbank saw the connecting threads. He recognized that something must have happened to his chief; but he could tell that each disjointed order was leading to a common purpose.

BURBANK verified the instructions. The Shadow signed off; gathering up the shortwave set, he made his way to his car. Jouncing along the dirt road, he hit the paved highway and sped for the crossroad.

State police were absent along that intervening five-mile stretch; and it was fortunate. To The Shadow, the road seemed a blurred stretch of gray that flowed beneath the wheels of his speeding car. He kept to the wide ribbon, but his course was eccentric; bordering one edge, then the other.

The Shadow realized that his brain was swimming; but he maintained the mad pace, relying on sheer instinct to keep him on the highway. He was clocking the speedometer with kaleidoscopic glimpses, that told him when he neared the crossroad. There, The Shadow applied the brakes; took a wide veer to the left.

Even that calculation was a vague one. The right wheels of the car jounced heavily as they struck the edge of the road. Bringing the machine under control, The Shadow zigzagged for thirty yards. Picking an opening between the trees, he turned into it, giving the brake pedal a final shove.

The car crackled through the underbrush; its tires settled in the mud of a tiny gully. Turning off the lights, The Shadow rested in the darkness.

He was ahead of schedule; he could afford these few steadying minutes. The night was still; but The Shadow's ears were hearing the shriek of swift air, as a recollection of his speedy ride.

As that illusion faded, the croak of crickets came from the woods, as if timed to the racking throbs that still palpitated The Shadow's brain.

Alighting from the car, The Shadow made his way back toward the crossroad. At moments he listened, hoping for sounds other than the drilling cricket tones. At last they came—the purrs of approaching motors.

Close to the crossing, The Shadow stepped from the road. He was blended with trees and underbrush when the lights of the cars arrived.

The procession was Cleeve's; three cars in all. Cleeve was in the first one; when the motors stopped, The Shadow could hear the leader's words, addressed to the occupants of his own car.

"It looks clear here," spoke Cleeve. "Well, we've reached the jumping off place. Let's go ahead!"

The Shadow heard an objection, voiced by Clyde Burke: "Maybe somebody's trailed us from New York."

"We'll see about that," interposed Cleeve. He gave a low whistle, that brought a figure from the rear car. "Spot anybody tailing us, Felkin?"

Felkin's reply was in the negative. Cleeve decided to proceed. Starters grated; motors hummed. The cars headed for Borth's. From his hiding spot, The Shadow heard the motors die in the distance.

There was a whispered laugh from the hiding spot—low, steady, a sign that The Shadow's rest had brought a further restoration of his strength. That mirth betokened knowledge of the future. Despite Cleeve's assurance that his party had been untrailed, The Shadow expected others to arrive.

Brief minutes proved The Shadow's foresight.

HIS ears again keyed to their full ability, The Shadow caught the tones of new motors, coming from the east. The first car to arrive was a coupé that The Shadow recognized as the one taken from Clyde Burke on the night of Fred's murder.

The second was an old sedan, the third a low-built touring car. Both of those automobiles were geared for speed, despite their ancient appearance.

There was no doubt regarding the identity of the occupants.

They were thugs, the survivors of previous battles, gathered for this last expedition. The pair that had been hiding out in New Jersey with Clyde's coupé as a trophy, were leaders of the outfit. They were the men who alighted, to growl orders to their companions.

"This is where we cover, see?" The speaker was within a dozen feet of The Shadow. "We're waiting half an hour, just in case The Shadow—or any other smart guys—show up here! Then we're moving in. We know where Cleeve's headed. When we close in after him, he'll—

A sharp rasp interrupted. Thugs were listening; they had heard an increasing sound. The man who had been interrupted gave a hard laugh.

"Just one of them airliners," he said. "They're liable to bear over this direction, coming out from Newark."

"That ain't the noise I'm listenin' to," piped another interrupter. "I'm hearin' a car, comin' along the road Cleeve took to get here."

"Yeah," agreed the hoodlum, "it's a buggy all right; but it's rollin' along our road!"

"Wait! It ain't just one car! It's two, closing in on us!"

There was an order for the mobsters to spread; to cover both roads and intercept the approaching cars. Crooks had forgotten the rumble from the air. Viciously, they spat oaths that promised slaughter to the persons who were driving toward the crossroad.

Flashlights glimmered, as their owners looked for spots that would serve their ambush. The crooks were forgetful on one point only: the situation that existed in their very midst.

None suspected the shape that was creeping from the underbrush, approaching the pair of leaders who still remained close by Clyde's coupé. An arm swished downward through the darkness; the weight of a heavy automatic found the first leader's skull.

That stroke, the gasped groan that came with the hoodlum's fall were heard by the man beside him.

The crook turned, flicked his flashlight above the figure of his fallen pal. There, outlined in the glow, he saw the shape of a weird fighter whose name he had mentioned only a few minutes before. The crook voiced that name again; this time with a hoarse outcry, that brought startled responses from the spreading thugs about him.

Husky-throated, frozen-lipped, the mobster was giving a call to action when he gulped the name:

"The Shadow!"

Leaving the road, The Shadow reached the bushes that hid the shortwave radio. A few minutes later, he was tapping out coded words to Burbank.

CHAPTER XVII
SILENT STRATEGY

SILENCE had covered The Shadow's approach into the midst of his foemen. For the present, he was willing to discard such strategy. There was reason, too, for the change that came.

In the midst of a deadly horde, The Shadow needed every advantage that he could obtain. Seldom did crooks hold The Shadow in a cordon. He wanted them to overlook the temporary chance that had come to them.

A weird taunt burst from The Shadow's lips—a chilling, awe-compelling laugh that fitted his unexpected arrival. Ignoring the thug that stood at his very elbow, The Shadow swung about the circle of ambush-seeking thugs.

Big guns were looming from his fists. To each staring hoodlum, the muzzles were an individual menace. So was the mockery that The Shadow voiced.

Crooks dived, seeking distance before they opened fire. Their leader, gaping, realized that he was deserted. With a raucous shout, he tried to break the spell. He succeeded; but brought disaster on himself. His method was a lunge, straight for The Shadow, who was turned the other way. As he sprang, the crook came up with his gun.

The Shadow sidestepped; his twist took him from the focus of the crook's flashlight. The fellow stopped short; darting his head from side to side, he blasted shots from his revolver. With those reverberations, new mockery sounded from behind the crook's shoulder.

Holding his trigger finger, the thug wheeled. Again he saw The Shadow, almost beside him. The mobleader snarled as he aimed, confident that his next bullets would not be wasted. That shapeless, weaving blackness was The Shadow. He knew that much, but no more.

The Shadow's peculiar twist had ended in a lunge of his own. The arm that sideswiped from the darkness seemed to come from nowhere. Again, a sledging gun clouted a waiting head.

The crook's trigger finger tugged convulsively; his revolver spurted a final useless shot. He crumpled, with his gun and flashlight, the snarl dying on his lips.

Others heard the shot. They trained their flashlights. Instead of their leader, they saw The Shadow weaving toward the shelter of the coupé. As he turned, The Shadow opened fire; wildly, the outspread thugs returned it. The crossroad roared with battle's tumult.

Revolving in turret fashion, The Shadow was volleying a rapid fire that scattered his enemies farther. Self-preservation was more important than their urge to deliver death. Not one of the surrounding dozen could seize a chance for steady, calculating aim.

That didn't worry them. They thought they could outlast The Shadow. When his ammunition failed, he would be helpless.

They had forgotten a factor that they considered unimportant: the approach of the automobiles that they had heard. The Shadow, however, had remembered those arriving cars. He was timing his shots accordingly.

There was an instant when The Shadow's fire ceased. Crooks thought his guns were empty, and bounded from the underbrush. Then, as lights appeared around the bend, The Shadow tongued his remaining shots in quick succession.

Two thugs sprawled; others leaped away for new shelter that they failed to reach. Brilliant headlights blinded them; guns talked from the whizzing car that was bringing the first of The Shadow's agents. Another pair of lights gleamed from an incoming road. The harried hoodlums guessed that new aid was coming up.

Crooks leaped for their own cars; they started a mad flight, spurred by the pelt of bullets all about them. They abandoned Clyde's coupé, along with half of their crew. Only one road was open: the one that led to the north, past The Shadow's hidden car.

Mobsters took that route, and The Shadow's agents let them make their start. It wasn't luck that allowed that getaway, it was The Shadow's own design.

Off to the north, where the road ran through a gap in the Watchungs, those thugs would find a snare awaiting them. State police had already received an anonymous tip-off, stating that crooks would arrive at a given spot. The Shadow had purposely left that open path to the north.

THE cars that bore The Shadow's agents were moving from the crossroad. The Shadow sprang into Clyde's coupé and ran it into shelter. The crossroad lay clear in the moonlight, forming a mammoth X. There were moments of silence while watchers waited; then the silvery glow was blanketed by a blackish shape that settled silently upon the junction point.

A curious machine had reached the battleground, to make a perfect landing. It was The Shadow's wingless autogiro, piloted here at his order. The long, broad blades were spinning lazily as the pilot stepped from the ship to join the other agents. The Shadow came from the fringing darkness to take the giro himself.

The motor zoomed; the huge blades churned the air with blurring speed. Braking one wheel, The

Shadow swung the ship toward the eastward road, which had a slight downward slope. Rolling forward, the autogiro was lifting as it was swallowed by the blackness of the trees.

Watching agents still heard the motor's roar; they saw the strange ship rise suddenly above the woods and climb straight upward, dwindling in the moonlight.

As the giro diminished to a toylike size, the roar of its motor became a purr. Listening ears could easily mistake it for the hum of a distant airliner, fringing a range of the Watchung hills. Crooks at the crossroads had gained that impression. The Shadow was confident that Cleeve and his companions would do the same.

Therein lay The Shadow's strategy.

THE SHADOW had undertaken two tasks. The first was to cover the crossroad after Cleeve and his men had passed it; the other, to enter Borth's stronghold before Cleeve's invaders arrived there. Both of those aims accomplished, The Shadow could prevent trouble from the rear while he assumed control of the coming battle in Borth's citadel.

Earlier, The Shadow had planned to let his agents handle the crossroad, by waiting there until Cleeve had gone by. Circumstances had made it impossible for him to post the agents before Cleeve arrived; hence, The Shadow had gone to the road junction in person.

Thanks to the arrival of the autogiro, The Shadow still had time to accomplish his second task. Cleeve's schedule allowed a half hour before he closed in on Borth. It would take his squad some minutes more to work their way up the mountainside. The Shadow, meanwhile, had handled battle in a dozen minutes; another ten were all that he required for the flight by autogiro.

The impending conflict between Cleeve and Borth had all the elements of an equal struggle.

Cleeve was arriving secretly; he held the advantage of numbers. Depending upon a surprise attack, Cleeve felt confident of success. His chance of victory was a good one.

Borth, on the contrary, was crafty. His buried citadel was a house of tricks, where anything might happen. The wise old doctor was certainly smart enough to know that a calculating invader would use a surprise attack. Borth, therefore, might be ready for surprises.

A third factor was needed to swing the outcome. Only The Shadow could provide that service, through measures of his own preparation. Trusting upon his own devices, he intended to be on the scene when conflict came.

From a one-mile altitude, The Shadow looked down upon the moon-bathed mountainside. He could see the dull ribbon of the paved road weaving serpentine among the black-massed trees. Along a higher contour were tiny glints that indicated rocky spots.

Cleeve and his men were lost beneath the thick trees. If they had heard the autogiro, they could not see it. Once the motor's thrum ended, they would agree that it was a plane flying elsewhere.

The time for new silence had arrived. The Shadow stifled the giro's motor. His ship began a mile drop with all the stealth of a settling bird of prey.

Those windmill blades spun faster and faster as air whistled through them. Their noiseless resistance increased; the giro was literally hovering as The Shadow guided it. His full faculties restored, The Shadow was sighting for a landing spot much more difficult to detect than the crossroad where his pilot had first landed the ship. The Shadow was looking for the roof of the abandoned lodge.

In itself, that roof was impossible to find. It was covered with a black-tarred surface that rendered it invisible. But The Shadow had taken that into calculation. There was a clearing about the old building; and that open space was the landmark upon which he depended.

Though the woods seemed thick to persons on the ground, the aerial view showed several cleared passages. At half-mile altitude, The Shadow had no choice between them; but when the autogiro had dropped another thousand feet, he saw the marker that he needed.

One open space was centered by a blotchy square, that represented the old lodge in the center of its clearing.

The Shadow veered his descent. The autogiro parachuted at an angle; it straightened and settled squarely upon that blackish square.

The jar of its wheels against the roof was trivial; shock-absorbers took it, while the forward roll made the force a glancing one. Then came the brakes. The autogiro stopped, almost in the center of the roof.

Thanks to the broad expanse of the building top, the ship could not be seen from the ground below. Neither Cleeve, nor Clyde, nor any of their companions would learn that this ship of the night had arrived before them.

STEPPING from the autogiro, The Shadow approached the roof edge and listened. There were no sounds of approaching men, but his eyes detected the glimmers of flashlights among the trees.

One such glow appeared near the path that Harry had followed to the hunting lodge. The Shadow knew that it represented the flank of Cleeve's searching party.

Instead of moving toward the lodge, the light turned promptly in the opposite direction. The Shadow's laugh was low, significant. He had the answer to the last problem that had confronted him.

It hadn't seemed logical that Cleeve would adopt searching tactics to approach so conspicuous an object as the lodge that served as cover for Borth's underground abode. Nor would Cleeve consider entry easy if he expected to go down the shaft beneath the fireplace.

The Shadow had already considered the likelihood of another route into Borth's. The actions of Cleeve's crew proved there was another way.

Clyde had used that other route and probably thought it the only one. He was leading Cleeve into the hillside. Therefore, the invaders would come up into Borth's stronghold from below. That left The Shadow free to enter from above, with no others to follow.

Crossing the roof, The Shadow raised the skylight. Again, his laugh toned low. He was willing to risk the dangerous steps beneath the fireplace, confident that no one would suspect his new arrival. He had plenty of time to be deliberate; for he could picture Doctor Nicholas Borth still in his office, lulled by a false sense of security.

The Shadow could see no cause for complications that might produce unexpected trouble within the stronghold. That analysis was justified by The Shadow's own observation; but it happened to be incorrect.

Recent minutes had produced a change within Borth's citadel. Events were brewing there; events so important that they would have spurred The Shadow to absolute haste, had he known of their existence.

CHAPTER XVIII
ALARM BELOW

THE SHADOW was right in his picture of Nicholas Borth. The shocky-haired doctor was actually in his office; and he sat there unperturbed. He was glancing at his clock, allowing a half hour more before he ordered Yakbar to bring in Harry Vincent.

Yakbar, too, was in the office, stolid as ever. But there was a restless person present; the one who was to provide the shift of circumstances. That person was Diane Delban.

The girl was sure that Cleeve would invade tonight. She had every reason to suppose that Clyde had completed his mission. She was wondering, though, where Harry Vincent fitted in the picture. Diane wanted to find that out.

Finding a chance to leave the office, Diane made an excursion to Harry's room. She unlocked the door; looked in to see Harry seated on his couch.

He had awakened in a bewilderment similar to Clyde's experience.

Diane spoke in a low tone. Harry saw the girl; he blinked to clear the blur that bothered his eyes. Diane came tiptoeing into the room. She spoke a quick question:

"You've come from Cleeve?"

Harry didn't answer. He was a little puzzled about what to say. He knew that Diane must be the girl that Clyde had mentioned; but he remembered that Clyde had promised Diane that he would go directly to Cleeve's. Maybe it would be best, Harry thought, to claim that he was one of Cleeve's Feds.

While Harry was still undecided, Diane turned suddenly toward the door. The girl placed her forefinger to her lips. Stepping quickly into the corridor, she closed the door behind her. She didn't shut it all the way. A harsh voice stopped her, with the demand:

"Why did you come here?"

"I was passing," Harry heard Diane reply. "I heard the prisoner moving about. I was looking to see—"

"I shall look! It is my duty!"

The door opened. Harry saw Yakbar. The Turk entered; gripped Harry's shoulder and drew the prisoner to his feet. Yakbar spoke the simple command:

"Come with me!"

IN a dopey manner, Harry accompanied the Turk to Borth's office. Diane followed; her face was troubled. When Borth saw Harry, however, he was too interested to bother with minor circumstances. He started a sharp interrogation.

"Why did you come here?" he demanded. "Are you one of my enemies?"

Harry looked blank as he shook his head. He spoke as though connecting scattered recollections; and he did it well.

"The woods—the road"—Harry's tone was vague—"yes, I remember them. Then the cabin, or hunting lodge—whatever it was—"

"Where you were captured," snapped Borth. "With this in your possession, Mr. Vincent!"

From the desk drawer, Borth produced an automatic that Yakbar had found on Harry. Borth gestured with the weapon; flung it back into the drawer, as he questioned:

"Why were you armed?"

"The woods were lonely," volunteered Harry. "Sometimes criminals hide in the Watchungs."

Harry looked boldly toward Borth as he spoke. The doctor caught the inference. He indulged in a withering smile.

"I am no criminal," declared Borth. "I am a man

who has a mission: the protection of treasure and wealth that were entrusted to me. I intend to leave here tonight. If you are what you claim to be—a person who fell into chance misfortune—I shall release you.

"On the contrary"—Borth spoke shrewdly—"if you are an enemy, I shall hold you as a hostage! My enemies have been active lately. Look what they did in New York, only last night."

Borth picked up a newspaper; planked it before Harry's eyes. There, Harry read the news of Barsley's flight; with it, a piece of information that intrigued him. Joe Cardona, searching Barsley's office, afterward, had found a few thousand dollars in counterfeit money tucked deep on the closet shelf.

It happened that The Shadow, too, had read that news. Also that Cleeve had shown the news account to Clyde, at which time Cleeve had cursed his own stupidity for not searching Barsley's himself. Harry did not know those details; but the matter of counterfeit currency made him connect Barsley with Borth.

Perhaps the doctor noted Harry's interest. Borth's next statement indicated it.

"Kirk Barsley is my agent," declared the doctor, grimly. "His actual duty is the sale of jewels. He never handled counterfeit money in his life. The police have trumped a false charge against him."

Borth's gaze was narrowed, to see the effect of his words. Harry gave a nod, as though he agreed. Borth wasn't quite satisfied.

"I am a lenient man," declared Borth, crisply. "I am patient, even with my enemies. This citadel is filled with pitfalls; but only for use in emergency. I have never had to use them, and hope that I shall never have to do so.

"Therefore, Mr. Vincent"—Borth's tone took an a smoothness that sounded fatherly—"if you are an enemy, your best course is to confess it. I shall not be harsh; I promise you. I am always lenient, unless persons show themselves unworthy of fair treatment. For instance—"

BORTH was thinking of Clyde Burke. That gave him a sudden flash of thought. Before Harry caught the connection, Borth shot the question:

"Tell me, Vincent; do you know a reporter named Burke?"

Harry was still somewhat dopey. He tried to phrase a quick answer and slipped. At last, he caught himself; indulged in a puzzled look, as though the name was new to him.

"Answer me!" rasped Borth. "What do you know about Burke?"

Harry tightened his lips, shaking his head at the same time. Borth came to his feet; wagged an accusing finger.

"You know Burke," gibed Borth, "but you don't care to talk about him! Perhaps Burke knows you, and may have something to say. The solution is simple. I shall bring Burke up here and let you meet him."

Yakbar started toward the alcove that held the spiral stairs. Borth stopped the Turk.

"I shall go," announced Borth. "There are others below who can accompany me to Burke's cell. Remain here, Yakbar."

As Borth left, Harry looked toward Diane. The girl was perceptibly pale. She knew what was due; Borth would find Denovar, the scar-chinned servant, guarding an empty cell.

Diane would have been totally lost, if it hadn't been for Harry. The understanding look that he gave was all she needed. Diane's expression tightened. She looked toward Yakbar.

The Turk had noted Diane's falter. His glare was suspicious; he wondered why she had shown alarm. Diane, however, was equal to Yakbar. Cleverly, she started a game that would have failed with Borth but which succeeded with the Turk. Stepping to Yakbar, Diane gripped the Turk's arm.

"There may be danger, Yakbar!" she said, with well-feigned breathlessness. "If this man"—she pointed to Harry—"came here to find Burke, others may be on their way to search for both of them!"

There was a glint in Yakbar's eyes. The Turk showed restlessness.

"Look into the corridor," suggested Diane. "Listen there; make sure that no one has come down from the lodge."

Yakbar stared at the wall, where Harry saw a bell and an unlighted electric bulb. They were evidently the alarm that had sounded Harry's own entry into the abandoned lodge. Yakbar shrugged, as though he thought all was secure; but Diane shook her head.

The Turk decided to go out into the corridor. Remembering Harry, he looked at the prisoner. By that time, Harry had caught Diane's purpose; to aid it, he had slumped in his chair, faking a groggy spell. The bluff fooled Yakbar; he thought that Harry had succumbed to aftereffects of the dope.

To satisfy Diane, the Turk went out into the corridor and made a routine trip to the steel door. That interval was all that Diane needed. She sprang to the desk, yanked open the drawer and brought out Harry's automatic. Holding the gun, she questioned:

"When will Cleeve be here?"

"I don't know," returned Harry. He was on his feet, alert. "But Burke took your message—"

"Then Cleeve will be due tonight. We can't wait for him, though. We've got to capture the place ourselves!"

Harry nodded.

"Yakbar first," whispered Diane. "Listen! He is coming back!"

HARRY shifted behind the door. Yakbar entered; looked suddenly toward Harry's chair. An instant later, the cold steel of Harry's gun muzzle was pressing the Turk's neck.

Yakbar grimaced; his muscles tightened. The Turk was willing to risk one of his quick wrestling moves. Diane called a quick warning to Harry. He jabbed the gun mouth harder, ordered Yakbar to raise his hands. The fellow obeyed.

Diane brought suitcase straps from the closet. Harry beckoned; behind Yakbar's back, he shifted the gun to the girl's hand. When Yakbar next saw the weapon, Diane was facing him with it, and the determination of the girl's expression told the Turk that she wouldn't spare bullets if they were needed.

Yakbar submitted meekly when Harry wrenched his arms behind him and strapped them there.

Action had put an end to all of Harry's dopiness. The constantly changing atmosphere of the air-conditioned room had produced complete refreshment to his lungs.

Diane looked on approvingly as Harry spilled Yakbar on the floor and trussed the prisoner's legs. Harry used a dusting cloth to gag the Turk; after that, he rolled the helpless man into the closet.

There were hasty footsteps on the steel staircase. One man was coming up alone, and Diane recognized his footsteps.

"It's Doctor Borth! Be ready!"

Harry motioned the girl to the desk. He took the gun from her and slumped in his chair, nestling the weapon beside him. Diane smiled wisely. She liked Harry's idea of waiting to see what Borth would have to say.

Arriving, the doctor looked about for Yakbar. Borth was puffing; he couldn't ask where the Turk had gone. Diane gave an answer while Borth stared.

"Yakbar is making an inspection," she told Borth. "He went out to examine the steel door."

"Good!" panted Borth, catching his voice at last. "I bring—bring bad news from below. Burke—Burke has escaped!"

"Escaped?" echoed Diane. "But Denovar was on guard—"

"Denovar has turned traitor! That is the only answer."

"Has he confessed?"

Borth shook his head. His lips framed a hard smile, that promised an ill future for Denovar.

"The other servants are holding him," stated Borth. "He is in Burke's cell. We are going to question him. I want you and Yakbar to be with me, Diane.

Yakbar guarded the cell before Denovar did; and after Denovar took over his duty, he reported to you. Therefore, you are the two who should confront him."

Diane was nodding, as if she agreed. When Borth stepped toward the door, Diane turned her gaze to Harry. Her nod continued. It was meant for Harry. Understanding, Harry came up from his chair, with the sharp order:

"Stand where you are, Doctor Borth!"

A pained expression strained Borth's dryish face. Turned toward Harry, the old doctor let his shocky head droop forward. His look was one of complete resignation. He seemed feeble when he gazed at Diane. His tone carried a piteous reproval:

"You, Diane! A traitor—like Denovar! I see it all—you bribed him—"

"Enough of that," interposed Diane, sternly, "You've said all that Vincent and I need to know. There's no one on the middle floor. That means we're going to the strongroom, and you, Doctor Borth"—the girl's tone was a positive one—"will open the door for us!"

Harry gestured for Borth to turn about. Wearily, his hands upraised, the doctor marched toward the steel staircase. Harry followed close behind him; then came Diane. Their footsteps faded as they descended the stairs.

Complete silence filled the empty office, where Yakbar lay bound behind the partly closed closet door. When The Shadow reached that vacated room, he would learn that others had dealt with Doctor Borth.

Opportunity had arrived before The Shadow.

CHAPTER XIX
TWISTED TRAPS

THE middle floor was silent and somber when Harry and Diane marched their prisoner through the corridors. They reached the door of the doctor's impregnable vault. It was Diane who gave the order for Borth to open it—a command that Harry supported with a gun nudge.

Borth did not stall. All that slowed him was the tremble of his hand. Harry could see good reason for the old man's falter. He remembered Clyde's report regarding the strongroom: that it housed counterfeiting machinery instead of treasure.

It was Diane who had learned that, for she had given the details to Clyde. This was Diane's triumph; she recognized it as she watched Borth fumble with the combination.

"When Cleeve gets here," whispered Diane, to Harry, "we'll have something to show him. He won't have to blow the door to get the stuff he's come for. It will be wide open—"

A final *click* interrupted. Borth tugged the big door. It swung on its silent hinges. Inside, Harry saw a darkened room; it was more than a vault. An ample space, air-conditioned like the rest of Borth's citadel, that room represented the heart of Borth's stronghold.

Borth's hands were raised as he turned about. His words were a dry, bitter crackle.

"Shall I enter?" he questioned. "Do you want me to turn over my own possessions?"

Harry was about to nudge Borth into the strongroom. Diane reached out to hold Borth back.

"We'll go in with him," Diane told Harry. "This door can be opened from inside the vault. Burke was nearly caught by that trick. It won't work with us."

Turning from Harry to Borth, Diane added: "You have missed your last opportunity, Doctor!"

Borth's eyes were steady. His head tilted backward; he crackled an insane laugh, as if something in his brain had broken. He was convulsive, uncontrollable. It seemed that defeat had turned him into a doddering fool.

It wasn't the sort of bluff that either Harry or Diane had expected. That was why they were deceived. As Borth's crazed laughter echoed in their ears; they failed to detect creeping sounds in back of them.

There was a sudden surge of men. Strong arms whipped Harry and Diane back into the corridor. The gun was plucked from Harry's fist. Diane's clawing hands were pinned in back of her. They stared into the faces of Borth's servants, four huskies who they thought were still on the floor below, watching Denovar.

Borth's mad mirth was finished. The white-haired doctor stood with folded arms; his expression was one of dignity and triumph. The change amazed Harry; made him marvel at Borth's strange personality. Harry expected Borth to show the manner of a fiend. Instead, the old man acted like a hero bringing victory to a righteous cause.

"TAKE them below," ordered Borth. "They can share the cell with Denovar. Ah, Diane!" Borth shook his head. "I could scarcely believe Denovar when he confessed that you had bribed him. I came upstairs, hoping that he had lied.

"But I took precautions, also"—keen eyes were glittering, wisely. "I knew that if you were a traitor; you would force me to open the strongroom. That is why I told you that the middle floor was clear. Instead, my men were posted in side corridors, waiting until they heard the laugh that told your treachery was fully proven."

They had reached the end of the corridor that led to the floor below. Borth pressed the switch. The end wall slid back. A sudden spasm of thought wrenched Harry. He looked toward Diane, then at Borth, who was pointing down the stairs. There was something that Harry wanted to say but couldn't.

He'd wait, he decided, until they reached the floor below. He wanted to hear the questions that Borth asked; then frame his answers afterward. It was better to go peaceably, until they reached the cell. The trip probably wouldn't be a long one.

That was a wrong guess on Harry's part.

They hadn't gone down a dozen steps before the captors stopped. One of the huskies turned about, shot words to Borth in a foreign tongue. Borth listened from the top of the stairs. He heard the same sounds as the others.

"Quick!" uttered Borth. "Back—up here!"

The servants tried to shove Harry and Diane ahead of them. They were too late. A flood of flashlights burned from below. Revolvers glimmered in the glow. Harry saw Clyde Burke leading the intruders, with another man beside him.

Clyde's companion was a rangy, dark-haired man whose square face was as firm as his gun fist. Harry knew who he must be, even before Diane shrilled the name:

"Cleeve!"

Borth's men tried to drop the prisoners, to make their own escape. The intruders reached them; they were overwhelmed, carried along by the massed force of Cleeve's followers.

Cleeve broke through to join Diane. The girl pointed toward Borth, as the agile doctor darted away along a corridor.

"That's Borth!" was Diane's cry. "Get him, before he reaches the strongroom!"

Clyde had reached Harry. Together, they followed Cleeve and Diane. Borth was trying to shake his pursuers; but Diane knew these underground passages as well as he did. At the final corridor, Diane shoved Cleeve ahead, gasping that his chance had come.

Harry was almost there when Cleeve rounded the last corner. He saw Cleeve take steady aim. Springing beside Cleeve, Harry spied Borth, faltering as he neared the vault door.

Borth was a dozen feet short of that opened barrier, with the blackness beyond it offering shelter. Cleeve had him covered; he was ready to press the trigger when Harry grabbed his gun hand.

"Don't fire!" panted Harry. "We can take him alive! Look—he's stumbled!"

Harry was right. Borth's legs failed; the old doctor sprawled helplessly on the floor. When he came up to his hands and knees, he stared back helplessly.

Cleeve motioned with his gun. Borth arose and approached. Cleeve shoved him toward the wall; had him stand there with his arms raised.

THE rest of the squad came up, bringing Borth's servants. Cleeve put the rest of the prisoners in line; after studying them, he turned to Diane.

"Where's the Turk who grabbed Burke?" he demanded. "And the other fellow, Denovar, whom you lined up for us?"

"Vincent captured Yakbar," explained Diane, with a smile. "Denovar is a prisoner, down in Burke's cell."

"Who's Vincent?" Cleeve spoke blankly; then turned to look for Harry. "Is this the fellow you mean?"

Diane nodded. She was puzzled as she gazed from Cleeve to Harry. It was Harry who answered for himself.

"I'm a friend of Burke's," he told Cleeve. "I just happened to fall in here, so I thought I'd help things along."

The explanation brought a chuckle from Cleeve. He asked Clyde about it; the reporter nodded. He said that Harry had been looking for him, but he hadn't suspected that his friend had fallen into a trap.

Harry, meanwhile, was reclaiming his automatic from the hip pocket of one of Borth's servants. Turning around, he juggled the gun while he asked Cleeve:

"Anything else Burke and I can do for you, Mr. Cleeve? We've worked with government men before."

"You have?" Cleeve seemed pleased. "I'll tell you what, Vincent. Suppose you and Burke go into the strongroom first. Then we can give you credit for leading us there. How's that?"

"Great!" decided Harry. "Thanks a lot, Mr. Cleeve. Come on, Clyde."

Taking Clyde's elbow, Harry turned him toward the vault. As they took their first step, Harry gritted in Clyde's ear:

"Four paces; steady. Then dive for that strong-room with all you've got in you! Get me?"

"But, Harry, what—"

"Never mind. Do what I say!"

A nod from Clyde. They had finished the fourth pace. Harry gave Clyde a terrific, headlong shove; saw the reporter make a wiry dive for the blackness. But Harry didn't follow. He figured only one could get through; another would have to fight it out, to insure his comrade's safety.

Dropping short of the strongroom, Harry spun about as he came to on one hand and both knees.

Harry was aiming back along the corridor, expecting what he saw. Cleeve and his entire squad were aiming along the corridor, ready to drill both men that they had sent ahead!

FOR the moment, they were forgetful of Borth and his captured servants, who stood helpless and unarmed, not even daring to cry a warning word. The only reason why guns hadn't started to blast was because Harry had outguessed Cleeve.

Harry had shoved Clyde to safety; in his own turn, he was low on the floor, forcing Cleeve's band to change their aim.

All that Harry wanted was the first shot. There'd be a lot more coming afterward; volleys that he didn't expect to be alive to hear. But that first shot would be some satisfaction. Harry thought of that when he was dropping; but before he could even aim, someone else took over the privilege of opening the battle.

Guns roared—not once but with quick-timed bursts. They tongued from the one spot where no one expected them—from the blackness of the strongroom itself. Long spurts of flame sped from above the floor where Clyde had rolled to safety. Jabbing above the level of Harry's crouched shoulders, those stabs sped devastating bullets into the ranks of Cleeve's aiming crew.

Hard-faced men were toppling before Harry could begin his fire. He didn't hesitate; he joined the outburst an instant before Cleeve and his amazed outfit began to use their revolvers.

The echoes of that roaring fire from the vault told Harry who had started the unexpected rescue. Only one fighter could deliver such quick devastation.

The Shadow!

Bullets were ricocheting along the corridor. Cleeve's dropping cohorts couldn't pick the vault door in their hurry. It was Cleeve, himself, who gained the first good aim. Steadying among his failing crew, Cleeve gave a desperate shout. Aiming straight, he pumped three bullets into the blackness of the strongroom.

The Shadow's fire stopped. Its halt came an instant before Cleeve's shots. Triumphantly, Cleeve turned to his fake Feds and called for them to rally. With Cleeve's command came a fierce, mocking laugh, weird, sinister, as it poured its echoes from the depths of the vault.

The Shadow had seen Cleeve's coming aim. He had drawn to shelter before Cleeve's fire started. The Shadow's guns were busy again; they roared the few shots that they still held. Harry fired; so did Clyde.

Madly, Cleeve gave a shout for massed attack. He and his few unscathed followers still had bullets. This was their chance to use them.

Cleeve's attack never started. As he and his few men loomed up from their crouched position, a sharp fire started from the rear of the corridor. The Shadow clipped Cleeve with a final shot. Cleeve spun half about, to see his men being jerked by flying lead. The Shadow had received aid from an added marksman, who had waited at his bidding before opening the rear attack.

Over the sprawling shapes of Cleeve's henchmen, Harry saw Yakbar. The Turk's shots were coolly placed where they did the most good. Cleeve's band was whittled down to a bewildered handful; an easy prey for the last attack that came.

BORTH and his unarmed servants provided that finishing touch—a hand-to-hand grapple, in which they wrested away the guns that wounded thugs were still trying to use. Flat against the wall, Borth and his men had been clear of the gunfire's path, ready to take their coming part.

Diane, too, had found security against the wall opposite. Her thought was escape; but her path was blocked when she darted for the end of the corridor. Yakbar flung out a brawny arm; turned the treacherous girl about, to roll her in among the other prisoners.

The lights of the vault glowed suddenly. Clyde blinked as he saw the actual contents of the strongroom. Doctor Borth had arrived when The Shadow pressed the switch. Borth was opening boxes, showing massed clusters of heavy jewelry. These were the actual treasures that Borth had brought to America, as he had claimed.

There were boxes of cash and checks; deposit books and account sheets that showed the meticulous care with which Borth had handled his funds. Leaving The Shadow with Doctor Borth, Clyde walked from the strongroom to join Harry.

THERE were visitors, later, who arrived at Borth's, summoned by mysterious tip-offs that had reached them earlier. One was Joe Cardona; another, Vic Marquette.

As stocky as Joe, but more dour, Vic was a bona-fide government man. Both the police inspector and the Federal man knew that they had been summoned by The Shadow.

Clyde and Harry were present in Borth's office when he told his story to the visitors. The Shadow's agents pieced in information that made the whole case plain.

"This stronghold was prepared before I reached America," stated Doctor Borth. "When danger threatened, I brought the treasure here, with persons whom I trusted. I never suspected Diane's treachery."

"She bluffed me, too," put in Clyde, "with that counterfeiting yarn. It was my bad luck to fall for it."

"So did I," added Harry. "It wasn't until Doctor Borth had opened the strongroom that I saw through Diane's game. She showed her real self when she thought I came from Cleeve. Before I had a chance to switch to Borth's side, Cleeve showed up."

Doctor Borth smiled a recollection.

"The Shadow learned the deception long before," he said. "He told me that he came here to balk Cleeve. Vincent and Diane had taken me to the strongroom. The Shadow found Yakbar and released him. They heard the scuffle when I broke away from Cleeve."

"The Shadow made for the strongroom," nodded Harry, "knowing that you would head there. I thought I saved you, Doctor Borth, when I made Cleeve hold his shot. What I really did was prevent The Shadow from dropping Cleeve right then."

It was Cardona's turn to voice some explanations.

"Cleeve sent the mob that murdered Fred, the service station man," said Joe. "They were trailing Barsley. They figured Fred knew too much, so they killed him. When I located Barsley, last night, Cleeve decided to scare him away. He called up his thugs and had them cover Barsley's getaway.

"That made us link the thugs with Barsley instead of Cleeve, What's more, Cleeve planted some counterfeit dough in Barsley's closet, to make him look crooked. I'd like to know, though, how The Shadow figured the answer to that one."

Doctor Borth smiled. The Shadow had told him.

"Cleeve joined the chase," explained Borth. "Afterward, the thugs doubled back and boxed The Shadow. Only one person could have told them where to find The Shadow. That man was Cleeve."

Clyde's eyes popped. He realized why Hawkeye had watched Cleeve's. He understood, too, how thugs had bobbed up so suddenly. Cleeve had telephoned them to get rid of Clyde. In preventing that, The Shadow had gained further proof of Cleeve's real status.

Clyde had been safe when he doubled back to Cleeve's, because Cleeve hadn't wanted a murder in his own apartment. The Shadow, however, had stayed near until he learned that Cleeve intended to take Clyde along to Borth's. Since The Shadow intended to be at Borth's when Cleeve arrived, he knew that Clyde would be safe.

As for the crooks at the crossroad, The Shadow had foreseen that Cleeve would have henchmen cover that vital spot. He had been there to polish off the reserves, so that Cleeve could be trapped if he managed flight.

Vic Marquette added a summary of his own.

"Those fake badges never fooled The Shadow," assured Vic. "He figured Cleeve as a smart international crook; and he was right. Cleeve looks a lot like a certain criminal we've been hunting under another name.

"The Delban girl will tell us plenty! She knew Cleeve back in England. She's admitted already that she saw The Shadow here this afternoon and tried to drop him through one of the traps. This whole case is as good as cleared. Only, I advise you to move your jewels, Doctor Borth, before all this news breaks."

Doctor Borth smiled as he commented:

"That matter has already been arranged."

CARDONA and Marquette left with the prisoners. Clyde and Harry followed later, believing that The Shadow had gone long before. They learned differently when they reached the woods just below the clearing. That was when they gained a clue to the significance of Borth's last cryptic remark.

There was a sudden, familiar roar above the roof of the old hunting lodge. Looking back, Clyde and Harry saw a strange plane rising into the moonlight. They recognized the spinning blades of The Shadow's autogiro. They watched the ship lift toward the yellow moon.

This was The Shadow's real departure, with Doctor Borth a passenger. With them they carried a precious cargo, that crooks like Cleeve would no longer have a chance to seek.

The treasure entrusted to Borth was going to a new, unknown hiding place. There, that valued store would lie under the protection of a guardian whose recognized power would discourage other criminal thrusts.

Reclaimed millions lay in the keeping of The Shadow!

THE END

THE MAN WHO CAST THE SHADOW

Walter B. Gibson (1897-1985) was born in Germantown, Pennsylvania. His first published feature, a puzzle titled "Enigma," appeared in *St. Nicholas Magazine* when Walter was only eight years old. In 1912, Gibson's second published piece won a literary prize, presented by former President Howard Taft, who expressed the hope that this would be the beginning of a great literary career. Building upon a lifelong fascination with magic and sleight of hand, Gibson later became a frequent contributor to magic magazines and worked briefly as a carnival magician. He joined the reporting staff of the *Philadelphia North American* after graduating from Colgate University in 1920, moved over to the *Philadelphia Public Ledger* the following year and was soon producing a huge volume of syndicated features for NEA and the Ledger Syndicate, while also ghosting books for magicians Houdini, Thurston, Blackstone and Dunninger.

A 1930 visit to Street & Smith's offices led to his being hired to write novels featuring The Shadow, the mysterious host of CBS' *Detective Story Magazine Hour*. Originally intended as a quarterly, *The Shadow Magazine* was promoted to monthly publication when the first two issues sold out and, a year later, began the amazing twice-a-month frequency it would enjoy for the next decade. "This was during the Depression, so this was a good thing to be doing. I just dropped everything else and did *The Shadow* for 15 years. I was pretty much Depression-proof."

Working on a battery of three typewriters, Gibson often wrote his Shadow novels in four or five days, averaging a million and a half words a year. He pounded out 24 Shadow novels during the final ten months of 1932; he eventually wrote 283 Shadow novels totaling some 15 million words.

Gibson scripted the lead features for *Shadow Comics* and *Super-Magician Comics,* along with a 1942 *Bill Barnes* comic story that foresaw the United States dropping a U-235 bomb to defeat Japan and end World War II. He also organized Penn-Art, a Philadelphia comic art shop utilizing former *Evening Ledger* artists.

Walter also found time for radio, plotting and co-scripting *Nick Carter—Master Detective, Chick Carter, The Avenger, Frank Merriwell* and *Blackstone, the Magic Detective.* He wrote hundreds of true crime magazine articles and scripted numerous commercial, industrial and political comic books, pioneering the use of comics as an educational tool. In his book *Man of Magic and Mystery: A Guide to the Work of Walter B. Gibson,* bibliographer J. Randolph Cox documents more than 30 million words published in 150 books, some 500 magazine stories and articles, more than 3000 syndicated newspaper features and hundreds of radio and comic scripts.

Walter also hosted ABC's *Strange* and wrote scores of books on magic and psychic phenomena, many co-authored with his wife, Litzka Raymond Gibson. He also wrote five *Biff Brewster* juvenile adventure novels for Grosset and Dunlap (as "Andy Adams"), a *Vicki Barr, Air Stewardess* book and a *Cherry Ames, Nurse* story (as "Helen Wells"), *Ann Bonny, Pirate Queen* (as "Douglas Brown"), *The Twilight Zone* and such publishing staples as *Hoyle's Simplified Guide to the Popular Card Games* and *Fell's Official Guide to Knots and How to Tie Them.*

Walter Gibson died on December 6, 1985, a recently begun Shadow novel sitting unfinished in his typewriter. "I always enjoyed writing the Shadow stories," he remarked to me a few years earlier. "There was never a time when I wasn't enjoying the story I was writing or looking forward to beginning the next one." Walter paused and then added, a touch of sadness in his voice, "I wish I was still writing the Shadow stories."

So do I, old friend.

—Anthony Tollin

THE TONG WHISPERER by Tony Isabella

Three tongs are involved in this short adventure of The Whisperer. However, my knowledge of urban gangs of the 1930s, sorely lacking if you must ask, is not why Sanctum Books publisher Anthony Tollin asked me to introduce this story. It's because he realizes that I *am* The Whisperer. Or I could be.

The Whisperer is Police Commissioner James "Wildcat" Gordon... and now you know where Batman co-creator Bill Finger got the name for the only cast member besides Bruce Wayne and his other self to appear in the Dark Knight's first story... while "Wildcat" is the name of another of his DC Comics creations.

Gordon fights especially cunning and violent lawbreakers by posing as a mysterious criminal mastermind. The Whisperer is a quirky character— I'd love to write him myself—but his foes are much more down-to-earth than those who foolishly opt to go up against Doc Savage or The Shadow.

Gordon is almost a prototype Wolverine. He's short, bad-tempered, feisty and dismissive of authority—just like me! He regularly defies the mayor of the unidentified city in which he operates. Every now and then, he punches out his politically appointed deputy commissioner. I not only could write this guy, I could be this guy.

The Whisperer was conceived as Street & Smith's response to the success of Popular Publications' *The Spider*, though his harsh whisper was a throwback to radio's early Shadow, as voiced by Frank Readick over the CBS and NBC airwaves. Occasional Doc Savage ghost Laurence Donovan was tapped to write the new hero. An October 1937 Stock Market crash resulted in the suspension of The Whisperer's own magazine, but "Wildcat" continued to appear in the back pages of *The Shadow*. When Donovan moved on in 1938, Alan Hathway took over the writing of those short stories.

Hathway, whose fiction output also includes four Doc Savage novels, was well-suited to the world of The Whisperer. A newsman with Chicago and New York papers, he knew well the corruption and mean streets of cities. He's been described as a "confrontational unionist," and his "rough-and-ready combativeness" was an essential part of his character. When Alicia Patterson, the daughter of the legendary *Daily News* publisher Joseph Patterson, launched *Newsday* in 1940, Hathway worked part-time for the paper. He became its city editor in 1942 and managing editor in 1944. In 1954, Hathway was the driving force behind the paper's Pulitzer-winning series on labor racketeering. "Wildcat" Gordon would have been proud of him.

Hathway's "The Ghost of Lin San Fu" isn't as richly-plotted as Gordon's full-length adventures, but the stakes are still high. Tong wars aren't generally peaceful affairs and their body counts can be impressive.

What struck me as notable about this tale is its handling of its Chinese and other Asian characters. All Sanctum Books editions have a disclaimer that "the texts of the stories are reprinted intact in their original historical form, including occasional out-of-date ethnic and cultural stereotyping."

There's certainly some of that in "The Ghost of Lin San Fu," but I also find a greater balance than in similar stories with Chinese or Asian characters. There's almost no attempt to have the characters speak in clunky faux-Chinese dialect. Beyond characters speaking in the kind of formal, somewhat exotic speech pattern popularized by the movies of the era, the dialogue between them flows naturally and without the inner groan I often experience listening" to Asian characters in vintage pulp fiction.

Also, while the villains are certainly crafty, their guile is akin to that of other Whisperer adversaries. Another reason I like the series so much is that down-to-earth quality more familiar to Dick Tracy than to Doc Savage.

After you enjoy this Whisperer adventure, keep an eye out for the forthcoming *The Whisperer #5: "The School for Murder"* and *"Murder on the Line."* Both these full-length thrillers were the "inspiration" for early Batman comic-book stories, and you know publisher Tollin and consulting editor Will Murray will have much to say about those "coincidences."

Hmm, I wonder if "Wildcat" Gordon ever had to deal with murderous plagiarists during his career.

Tony Isabella is a comic-book and comic-strip writer, columnist, reviewer and occasional novelist. He currently writes The Grim Ghost *for Atlas Comics. His latest non-fiction book is* 1000 Comic Books You Must Read, *which is still available from Amazon.com and at comics shops everywhere. A contributing editor to* Comics Buyer's Guide, *his "Tony's Tips" column appears every issue. In addition, you can read his daily "Tony Isabella's Bloggy Thing" at: http://tonyisabella.blogspot.com. •*

The Ghost Of Lin San Fu

By Clifford Goodrich

THE venerable merchants put their heads close together. Their tones were guarded, furtive.

"It is to be hoped," the first one breathed, "that the spirit of Lin San Fu will follow his mortal flesh."

His companion's straggly beard hobbled in animation.

"*Aiee!*" he agreed, in a voice filled with fear." It is most earnestly to be hoped! It belongs in the ancestral land."

Both, then, looked anxiously behind them, padded off into the night of China Hill.

Behind them, a figure moved. It had been scarcely discernible in the gloom. The figure glided even more silently than the two elderly Orientals. It showed but briefly as it turned a corner, climbed noiselessly up a rough brick wall.

The man was slight. He wore a quaint, round-brimmed hat. In the gloom, the chin appeared oddly pointed. The eyes were whitish, almost devoid of color, as was the wispy hair. His clothes were entirely gray.

An eerie, chuckling whisper drifted through the night air of China Hill.

"Aye," it hissed. "It is most earnestly to be hoped." The Whisperer was also interested in the ghost of Lin San Fu—the ghost that had killed five men.

That dreaded "supercrook," The Whisperer, who preyed on killers too wily for the cops to catch, pried open a dark window, stepped noiselessly inside a room. He opened a door, glided onto a sheltered inside balcony.

The room below him was large, almost barnlike. The walls were lined with books and paintings. Odd bits of sculpture stood about in corners. It was the studio and library of a man named Jules Goddard, an Orientologist and sculptor of more than a little note.

Only two figures were in the room. One of them was in a rosewood coffin. Anyone who knew China Hill would have recognized those wrinkled features.

When the spectre hovered over China Hill, it was The Whisperer who finally sent him to the land of his ancestors.

Lin San Fu had lived most of his life on China Hill. He had been a harsh and bitter man in life. Five days before, in a distant city, an automobile had struck Lin San Fu. Now, within as many minutes, those remains would be on the first lap of their final journey. A grave in the garden of his ancestors awaited the rosewood coffin.

The other man in the room was young. His shoulders were slightly stooped. China Hill blamed Lee Su Wo for the ghost of the aged man. Lee Su Wo could have saved his father from the fatal accident, wise ones said.

It was vengeance for his son's delinquency that brought the angered spirit back to China Hill. So the graybeards gossiped.

The Whisperer moved cautiously along the balcony. Suddenly he encountered flesh. It was flesh that moved, that acted as silently as did The Whisperer.

The wispy gray man recoiled, shot out a fist. A guttural oath came from the other. Hands as big as dinner plates seized The Whisperer by the neck, propelled him through a door.

But suddenly, a light flashed on. It was a glaring ceiling bulb of more than normal brilliance.

The man before The Whisperer snarled. His mouth was a wide angry gash. The forehead was broad, but low. Black, slanting eyes snapped in anger. This was Kung Ghee, the Mongol, whose purpose in China Hill no one seemed to comprehend.

There was a sudden ear-destroying concussion. The room was a sudden ball of flame. It was as if someone had touched a match to a chamber filled with gas.

The Whisperer used his last ounce of strength to fling himself toward the window. The crash of glass came to his ears as if in a dream. Then there was only blackness.

Kung Ghee he did not see at all.

WHEN consciousness filtered back to The Whisperer, he was wedged in a narrow light well that gave onto a cellar window. He had crashed through the flimsy grating when he fell from the other window high above.

It seemed that the ghost of Lin San Fu had reasons for not desiring investigation; thus the blast—to scare away The Whisperer.

The gray man made his way to the street door of the studio- library. The corpse was gone, on its way to the train that would transport it to eternal rest. Five murders had been committed in China Hill since the ghost of Lin San Fu had been talked about.

Three of the victims had been servants of the man now dead. The other two had been men who knew him well. There was one peculiar thing they all had in common; each of the victims had been found with a tiny object in his hand. They were miniature golden crocodiles.

Somehow the ghost of Lin San Fu was tied to the golden crocodile. And that was no mere matter of personal vengeance. There had been sixteen murders in the Chinese sections of half a dozen cities within five days. And in each case, the miniature of the golden reptile had been found. Chinese tongues were bound by a silence born of fear.

The Whisperer moved down the street. His path was clear. Earlier in the day, he had overheard a remark that told him there was no time to waste. "The ghost of Lin San Fu will speak again tonight," a man had said in Cantonese.

But The Whisperer had heard it through a door that was closed and locked. When he got through it, the speaker had disappeared.

Now, the gray man chuckled softly. He must follow that elusive ghost, find out what made it murder. Three times it had struck on the palatial grounds of Lin San Fu's mansion at the edge of China Hill. With it had come a warning—an eerie trilling cry that had made all the servants flee for their lives.

The Whisperer drifted into the shadows of the night. Soon, he saw the high board fence that surrounded the mansion of Lin San Fu. Then he saw something else that brought a harsh chuckle to his lips.

The broad back of Kung Ghee, the Mongol, went over the fence with the agility of a squirrel.

The Whisperer followed silently. Then he stopped. Icy fingers seemed to play with his wispy hair. This was the thing—the sound—that had thrown chill hands of terror into China Hill.

The sound came from nowhere. Flutelike, fleeting, it filled the night air and was gone. It was the cry ascribed to the ghost of Lin San Fu.

Softly, the gray man crept forward. His eyes stared hard, tried to pierce the gloom. He saw nothing. The night was deathly in its stillness. There was only a faint breath of incense in the air. Incense and the more pungent smell of China Hill itself.

Then it came again—a whirring, whistling cry. It was everywhere about him. It died and again was gone. Cherry blossoms rustled on the trees. Invisible feet seemed to patter near the great house that Lin San Fu had left behind to his mortal heirs.

At that moment, The Whisperer found Kung Ghee.

WITH a curse, the stocky Mongol hurtled from the branches of a high tree above the gray man. He landed astride The Whisperer's shoulders. A snarl rent the gloom and a knife flashed briefly. Gray cloth ripped. Blood trickled to the walk beneath The Whisperer.

A growl rolled deep in the Mongol's throat. The Whisperer twisted free. Kung Ghee may not have known the identity of The Whisperer. It was difficult to guess just what the Mongol did know, or what he was doing in China Hill. He had recently appeared unannounced, from the plains of Northern China. Death had coincided with his arrival.

Kung Ghee raised his knife again. But he wavered. An eerie, hissing challenge issued from the lips of the gray man. A compact fist shot into the Mongol's belly. Kung Ghee grunted, leaped away. The Whisperer plunged toward his assailant. He clutched at the Mongol. A pocket ripped away.

The gray man lunged again. But he was not destined to reach his antagonist.

A sibilant command in Cantonese murmured from the darkness. Guns roared as red flashes stabbed the blackness of the night. Leaden slugs tore through the air, tugged at the gray clothing of The Whisperer.

The little gray man whirled. Queer, oversized pistols appeared in his hands. They spoke with the sound of a serpent's hiss. A high-pitched Oriental scream testified to his accuracy.

But The Whisperer did not shoot again. The concrete walk gave way beneath him, dropped him into a pit of blackness. The heady odor of the poppy swirled around him as he fell—fumes of opium so heavy they would rob a man of consciousness.

The Whisperer looked up quickly, saw the sidewalk trap swing shut. Then he landed on a concrete floor in a tomb of blackness.

THE WHISPERER wondered, as his brain whirled dizzily, if opium were in back of the terror on China Hill. Old Lin San Fu had once trafficked in the brain-destroying drug. But that had been years before. Opium had been stamped out in China Hill. The Whisperer was sure the old Chinese had dropped that rotten source of revenue.

In fact, Lin San Fu had not died a wealthy man. He had left little that was known about to attract the unscrupulous into terrorizing his remaining kin.

A fan whirred dully as The Whisperer lay on the concrete floor. It sucked the numbing fumes of opium from the trap that confined him. A dim light flickered on. Faint, oriental laughter lilted and a door swung back.

Four hard-faced Chinese glided into the cavernous chamber. The Whisperer lay a shapeless huddle on the hard concrete floor before them. A pool of blood spread out from his shoulder.

"The fox in a snare is as harmless as a rabbit," one Chinese intoned in his native tongue.

He stooped over the inert form of The Whisperer. That proved to be an error.

The Whisperer came erect like a striking cobra. He had breathed deeply before the sidewalk trap had shut off outside air, had held that breath even though the lungs felt that they would burst.

He sprang now, seized the loose gown of the Oriental with both hands. The Chinese screamed once, felt himself whirled into the air like a sack of rags.

The Whisperer flung him broadside into the bodies of his three companions. Before they could recover from their astonishment, the gray figure hurtled through the door. His chilling eerie whisper floated behind him.

"When the fox feigns sleep, his bite is more often fatal," he reminded in the dialect of Canton.

A LADDER showed dimly ahead of the gray man. He scrambled up it, out of a trap in the center of the white pagoda.

The Whisperer leaped across the grounds. A great crashing issued from one end of the spacious estate that surrounded the old house of Lin San Fu. The gray man did not know what the crashing was. But he had no wish to tarry here. He could return when he was not expected.

He bounded across the soft grass, skirted a giant white rose bush. The unexpected impact with which he struck another man sent him hurtling to the ground.

The Whisperer twisted to his feet, seized the clothing of the other. He saw the white, strained face of a man he knew.

Jules Goddard was no Oriental. He was an historian and ethnologist, a scholar in the ways of China. He had also been a good friend of Lin San Fu. It was in his study that Lee Su Wo had bid farewell to the remains of his father.

Jules Goddard screamed at the sight of The Whisperer. His thin face seemed to drain of blood. Terror gave him strength his gaunt body did not really possess. He jerked away, raced off into the night.

But other footsteps were crowding close to The Whisperer. Violent curses blasted in good American anger. A police whistle shrilled. The gray man turned. He was surrounded. A flashlight flicked on, and a nasal voice screamed orders:

"The Whisperer! Grab him, boys! You'll all get promotions!"

That voice belonged to Deputy Commissioner, Henry Bolton. Bolton was an unpleasant person who had but two ambitions. One was to catch The Whisperer, the "supercrook" whom Commissioner James "Wildcat" Gordon was steadily unable to apprehend. The other was to replace Wildcat as police commissioner.

Three blue-coated cops converged upon the gray man. The Whisperer exploded into arms and legs. One cop sailed over The Whisperer's shoulder. The gray man darted out of the beam of light. But he couldn't get very far. The place teemed with cops.

The whispering challenge of the gray man hissed into the night. Cops raced toward the sound. At last, the gray marauder was cornered.

Hastily, The Whisperer tore down the concrete walk. His footsteps sounded loudly. He paused in the center of the pagoda. The trapdoor in the walk through which he had fled the underground cavern slammed once.

The bluecoats pounded up, gloated at what they saw. Half a dozen of them crowded down the trap. Others stood above, played their flashlights down the hole.

None of them was looking up in the air.

THE figure perched atop the pagoda had little time. But his transformation was a swift one. The gray clothing was quickly discarded. It revealed a checkered suit that would have made a minstrel man blush.

A quick motion removed peculiar dental plates from the mouth. The jaw became as square as a paving block. A flick of one hand brushed gray powder from hair that was really a reddish hue. Gray spats came from brightly yellow shoes.

Police Commissioner "Wildcat" Gordon was the opposite of The Whisperer in appearance. Wildcat made no sound as he leaped from the pagoda to the soft grass. But after that he was heard aplenty.

"Henry, what's goin' on around here?" Wildcat roared. "Why am I not notified of raids like this?"

Deputy Bolton straightened from beside the trapdoor hole. His anteater nose quivered with embarrassment. He had a small mouth that made motions as if he were blowing bubbles.

"O-one of the men heard shouting here," he stammered. "We almost got The Whisperer."

"'Almost' doesn't make good reading!" Wildcat snapped.

Bolton winced. He was very conscious of possible publicity for Bolton in the public prints.

The cops who had gone down the trap began to clamber out. They growled that there wasn't anything at all down there. Just a big room that didn't go anyplace. And certainly not The Whisperer.

There was a look of relief on the face of the last one out. He was a tall gaunt man with a pate as devoid of hair as a crystal-gazer's ball. Two gray tufts of hair above his ears gave him a slightly funny appearance. But it wasn't funny to crooks who had tried to oppose him.

Retired Deputy Richard Traeger, better known as old "Quick Trigger," was relieved because they hadn't found The Whisperer. He had been the first to go down, in the hope that he might be able to cover up if he found the gray man.

For Quick Trigger was the only man alive who knew that The Whisperer was really Wildcat Gordon. He should have known. A master at disguise, he had made the queer dental plates that created the oddly pointed chin and the eerie, whispering voice of The Whisperer.

He sidled now toward Wildcat. Gordon was paying no attention to his cops. He was examining two small objects in his hand. They had been in the pocket The Whisperer had torn from the clothing of Kung Ghee, the Mongol. This had been his first opportunity to examine them.

The first was a slip of paper. It bore the name and address of the Yat Sen tong.

But that was not the one that bothered Wildcat.

The other was a tiny golden crocodile, a golden crocodile such as had been found clutched in the hands of Chinese murdered in half a dozen cities; in the hands of those who had heard the ghost of Lin San Fu. That miniature struck a chord of memory in Wildcat. But the chord throbbed only faintly.

There was one thing of which he felt fairly certain. He should get information at the headquarters of the Yat Sen Tong. Hong See, the unofficial mayor of China Hill, was a leader of that mighty tong, and Gordon's friend.

Once before, Wildcat Gordon—and The Whisperer—had saved Hong See from a dirty racket. Hong See owed him much. And Wildcat didn't think much would be found on the grounds of Lin San Fu, at present.

"Have four men search these grounds and return to headquarters!" Wildcat snapped. "We will call on the Yat Sen tong!"

QUICK TRIGGER rumbled in agreement.

"I think the newspapers are right about this one, Wildcat," he growled. "It looks like a tong war. And a big one!"

Wildcat Gordon didn't answer. He didn't agree. The police had splintered quite a hole in the high board fence. Wildcat strode through it to the narrow street of China Hill.

Feet pounded suddenly behind him. The commissioner turned, saw a white disheveled figure racing over the grounds. It was Jules Goddard.

Goddard babbled incoherently, moaned that he had been struck on the head.

"What were you doing here?" Wildcat demanded.

"I came because Lin San Fu was my friend," Goddard spluttered. "And because I am a friend of Lee Su Wo, his son."

"What did you expect to do?" Wildcat snapped.

"Explode the story of the ghost of Lin San Fu," Goddard explained. "It is causing great grief to Lee Su Wo. China Hill believes the paternal ghost has returned in vengeance because Lee Su Wo could have prevented the old man's death. Such is the ancestor worship of the Oriental."

Jules Goddard faltered. Fear returned to his face.

"I saw two men who mean no good," he said. "One was The Whisperer. The other is known as Kung Ghee, the Mongol. Kung Ghee slugged me and fled. I do not know where The Whisperer is."

Wildcat Gordon's eyes went hard. He climbed into a waiting police car.

"Come!" he said. "Perhaps we should get to the Yat Sen Tong before Kung Ghee has the chance.

THE Yat Sen tong maintained its headquarters on Poppy Street. Normally, it was a quiet thoroughfare. It was bedlam when Wildcat Gordon drove through it.

Frantic Chinese darted over the sidewalks. Some fled in terror as guns roared. A submachine gun poured leaden death from the windows of the Yat Sen tong headquarters.

Wildcat opened the siren of the police car, whipped to a halt at the curb. He lunged out and up the stairs to the tong headquarters.

Figures loomed on the landing above him. Guns blasted down. Wildcat's Police Positives barked their answer. Two shadowy Orientals lurched forward in death. Then Wildcat was in the room of the tong.

The place was a shambles. Tables, chairs were strewn about. A filing case of records Wildcat had seen before lay on its side. The safe door was open. Wildcat saw one face he knew. Charley Hong was a nephew of old Hong See. He lay on the floor. But his lips moved feebly. Wildcat leaned over him.

"I—tried—warn them—" Charley Hong's breath was labored. He did not have far in this life to go. One hand was clenched tightly. Slowly, it relaxed.

A tiny golden crocodile fell to the floor!

"Tried to warn Hong See away—" Charley Hong muttered. "Will be more murder—They got me—Fan—Fan Li—"

He shuddered once and was still. Wildcat Gordon stood suddenly erect. Fan Li! The Circle of the Golden Crocodile. The gap in his memory was bridged instantly. He saw the thing he had been trying to grasp for days.

Fan Li had never prospered in the United States. It had been a mysterious controlling society in the opium trade years before. Whispered stories said it had died with the dissolution of the legal Shanghai Opium Monopoly way back in 1917. But, in those days, it had been a force that struck fear into the hearts of Chinese all over the world.

Wildcat Gordon whirled on Deputy Henry Bolton.

"Get to the Kai Ling tong immediately," he snapped. "Surround the place. Let no one either in or out until you hear from me!"

Wildcat stamped out, motioned to old Quick Trigger. He remembered that twenty years before, old Lin San Fu had been in the opium trade. Lin San Fu would have known of the Fan Li, perhaps would have been a member. Ideas were forming rapidly in Wildcat's brain.

He saw two things clearly. He remembered a night he had watched the sunset on the China Wall at Old Peking. He thought it told him much about the ghost of Lin San Fu. And he saw sudden possibilities in the power of the Fan Li, the Circle of the Golden Crocodile.

One thing bothered him. That was Kung Ghee, the Mongol. Kung Ghee did not yet fit into the picture Wildcat was painting.

He spoke rapidly to old Quick Trigger. The gaunt retired deputy shook his head.

"I don't like it. Wildcat!" he muttered. "This'll get you into trouble!"

A mirthless grin parted Wildcat's face.

"If the ghost of Lin San Fu speaks again, he will speak to The Whisperer," Wildcat said. "You do your part as a safety check."

Wildcat looked at his watch, drifted toward a telephone. As he did, another figure moved in the gloom of the street. It was a squat figure. Wildcat would have recognized Kung Ghee, the Mongol.

WILDCAT called long distance, spoke to the chief of police in a distant city. He smiled as he replaced the receiver. When he went out of the booth, he found an excited Henry Bolton.

"The Kai Ling headquarters were raided before we got there, "Henry exploded. "Ten men were dead! All the cash and records have disappeared!"

"Go back to headquarters," Wildcat snapped. "Wait for further orders."

Quickly Wildcat Gordon strode off into the night. He found a gray coupe parked in a convenient spot. He climbed in and drove toward the outskirts of China Hill.

The figure who got out of the coupe was that of The Whisperer. The gray man melted into the gloom of night. The high towers of Lin San Fu's mansion lowered behind the wooden fence.

The mansion of Lin San Fu was a masterpiece of weird adaption. Originally, it had been a gem of Victorian architecture in the 1890's. With the passing years, each addition, each repair had been strictly Oriental, Lin San Fu had acquired it when he was still wealthy with the profits of the opium traffic, when his name had been feared by his enemies.

A term in a Federal prison had been the factor that determined Lin San Fu to get out of opium and stay out. He hadn't liked it.

The Whisperer glided silently up the steps. The house was no longer the one Lin San Fu had bought years before. The front door was teak from the forests of Indochina. The Whisperer went in a window.

Searching, he found a servants' ancient stairway. It was a dark spiral leading into darkness. Silently, he crept upward, passed the second floor, and the third. Above him, he knew, was a great flat roof surrounded by weird spires and turrets.

Suddenly, he tensed. For the third time that night he heard the eerie voice of the ghost of Lin San Fu. It welled tunelessly in the air, seemed to come from all directions.

The Whisperer plunged the last few steps upward and burst out onto the flat roof in the center of the mansion. A flutter of wings beat against him. The Whisperer knew he had been right.

Once as he had watched the sun set north of old Peking, he had watched the pigeons wheel in the dusk. The tiny whistles tied to their feet gave weird fluted sounds as they chased away the devils with the setting sun.

The voice of Lin San Fu's ghost was the announcement that a carrier pigeon had arrived!

THE WHISPERER lunged across the roof. Another door opened on the other side. A masked figure shot through it, yelled in high-pitched Cantonese.

Ignoring the other, The Whisperer flung himself at the bird that had just alighted. Tight beside the tiny whistle on the pigeon's leg he found a message. He had no time to read it now.

Angry red flashes stabbed from the other side of the roof. lead knocked The Whisperer's round hat from his head. He ducked. This was no time to fight. His adversary would soon have reenforcements. The gray man dived for the door through which he had come, hurtled down the stairs.

But he did not get far. The stairway was not as he had left it. There was a wall where none had been before. Only one direction was open. Straight along the third floor of the mansion.

The Whisperer took that exit. His supersilenced pistols leaped into his hands. The corridor was queerly twisted. It turned at crazy angles. Patches were illuminated dimly. Others were as black as night itself. Cries welled up all over the building. They were cries of warning, in Cantonese.

Suddenly, The Whisperer saw a man in the passage. It was the squat form of Kung Ghee, the Mongol. Kung Ghee was straight ahead. A knife, half as large as a cleaver was in the Mongol's hands, held high. One quick motion would bring it down, send it straight toward the breast of The Whisperer. Behind Kung Ghee other furtive figures crept. Ugly smiles were on their faces.

The Whisperer squeezed the triggers of his pistol. Lurid blue flame leaped from them. Then glass crashed. The Whisperer was shooting straight into a cleverly placed mirror! Kung Ghee was not actually in front of him at all. But the gray man's shooting told exactly where he stood.

There was a sudden rumble of machinery. The floor beneath The Whisperer gave way as if it hadn't been there at all. His feet struck a steel-lined chute. The Whisperer sped toward the bowels of the weird mansion—then lower.

It seemed to The Whisperer that he fell many miles. The chute ended in a pool of slime. The gray man struggled to his feet, flicked on a flashlight. A long, vaulted corridor of ancient brick loomed ahead of him. The ceiling was round. Even The Whisperer was forced to stoop.

Many years before, the city had built a sewer system that had proved a useless thing caused by graft in politics. It had been used less than a year before a more practical disposal system had been installed.

The Whisperer's nostrils dilated. The dank smell of years underground came mustily to his senses. This must be part of the old, forgotten system. The Whisperer crept down the old brick sewer.

If he could avoid capture for a little while, he might yet solve the rest of his problem. The ghost of Lin San Fu was only part of the maze he had to fathom. Fan Li—the Circle of the Golden Crocodile—was the real deadly menace behind the increasing murders.

Fan Li and whatever it was that the masterminds were after. The Whisperer thought now that he knew what that might be. If he could only stall disaster for thirty minutes—

Wildcat Gordon had given Quick Trigger instructions to wait that long outside the old mansion. Then, if the Whisperer did not reappear, Quick Trigger was to take a picked squad of men and invade the grounds, tear down the mansion itself, if need be.

Suddenly, The Whisperer came to a junction of the sewer. It fanned out into a roomlike cave. Then the gray man felt invisible fingers pluck at his sleeves. He whirled, twisted. But the fingers became many. like a spider spinning its web, stout silken strands were dropped from some unseen place above him.

The more The Whisperer twisted, the tighter the meshes were. He was like a fly in a spider's web. Completely helpless.

Laughter accompanied his distress. Figures materialized from nowhere, prodded him in the back with sharp instruments. The gray man had no alternative but to go ahead. He stumbled along, prodded from behind.

At one point, the old sewer pipe was broken. A rude doorway had been hewn into its walls. The Whisperer was thrust into a great underground cavern. The sight that met his eyes made him blink with amazement,

CRUDE torches flared redly, gave a weird unreal light to what he saw. Against one earthen wall lay the huge figure of a golden crocodile! Massive chains seemed to fetter the monster to the wall. The ugly thing of gilt must have been more than thirty feet in length.

The Whisperer idly thought that it was a remarkable likeness to the original. He recognized it as the *Crocodylus Porosus*, the triangle-snouted menace of the South China waters; one of the types that really are man-eating crocodiles. They will devour anything they can overpower.

Two figures towered in the center of the chamber. They wore the hideous masks of the Chinese war-god. A dozen other figures were in the room. The Whisperer recognized them as law-abiding merchants of China Hill. They were prostrate before the golden crocodile. One of the masked leaders spoke to them in Cantonese.

"You know not how you got here or where you are," he intoned. "Go back with the message from Fan Li. Do as you are bidden, or the golden crocodile will devour you and all your sons!"

The Whisperer was prodded again from behind. *"Aiee!"* a voice whispered in Chinese. "The gray one will make an impressive sacrifice. He and the other two as well. Our power will become tenfold!"

Then The Whisperer noticed two startling circumstances. The first was the gaunt form of old Quick Trigger, huddled near another side of the cavern. Quick Trigger was bound tightly. There would be no reenforcements for The Whisperer! And beside Quick Trigger, and also bound, was Kung Ghee, the Mongol!

The other thing The Whisperer noticed was the golden crocodile. The creature moved! It was alive, no thing of papier-mâché or plaster! The huge jaws clicked hungrily.

An eerie whisper of amazement burst from the lips of the Whisperer. There had once been a story that the Fan Li had imported a crocodile as their horrible emblem. But the society had been stamped out so quickly, it had been given scant attention.

Now The Whisperer wondered if Lin San Fu had kept this beast in the subterranean chambers below his mansion for more than twenty years! It would have been possible. But what force could have motivated him to do such a thing? It was incredible!

Incredible as it may have been, the beast was ready for The Whisperer. The gray man was shoved brutally toward the center of the cavern. An electric motor whirred. An endless belt at his feet began to move. It led to the jaws of the crocodile.

The Whisperer was to be fed to the beast slowly. That would make the maximum impression on those who were there to be impressed.

The gray man was hurled upon the belt. His feet were securely tied and his clothing was searched. One of the masked leaders found the message The Whisperer had taken from the carrier pigeon on the roof.

"You will not need this more," he hissed in Cantonese. "There is nothing for which you will have further need!"

The Whisperer rolled, strained against his bonds. They gave a little, but not enough to do any good. The crocodile opened wide its cavernous jaws, snapped them together with a click. The beast was restless. That was a sure sign of hunger. The creature's legs were linked to the chains that held him by bolted shackles.

The electric motor hummed. The distance to those horrible jaws shrank from six feet to four. Then to three. The Whisperer fought with his bonds.

Dry chuckles came from the masked leaders of Fan Li. Even if he could free his hands, he could not get his feet cleared in time. The ankles were made fast to the moving belt itself.

OLD Quick Trigger moaned.

"Wil—oh damitall!" Quick Trigger was close to calling out Wildcat Gordon's name. But even though death approached, he had sworn not to reveal that identity.

Suddenly The Whisperer's arms were free. The yards of silken cord had given. But at the same instant, the belt that snared his feet bore him relentlessly towards the jaws of the crocodile. The great beast opened its jaws once more, clicked them shut.

The tenseness in the room was electric. Breathing seemed to stop.

Then smoke suddenly seemed to pour from the clothing of the gray man. It billowed out into the room. He was seen to move once. Then the belt took him straight under the jaws of the monster. The smoke obscured him.

Chemicals carried in The Whisperer's pocket could be used as a protective smoke screen when necessary, simply by rubbing them together.

The masked leaders darted forward, then checked themselves. The beast threshed against his chains.

But an eerie, chilling whisper hissed across the chamber.

"The Whisperer speaks but once to warn you!" the voice grated.

There was a *clank* of falling chains.

"The beast is free!" The Whisperer challenged. "Your only chance now lies in flight!"

Immediately, the spell of the Fan Li was broken. Wild screams of fear filled the chamber. Torches fell to the ground. Suddenly, the pall of chemical smoke thinned. The snout of the golden crocodile thrust into the center of the chamber.

One of the masked leaders tripped as he raced toward the door. He stumbled against the gilded sides of the huge reptile. Gilt paint rubbed off. At first, the beast's great snout seemed tightly closed. He swung it in irritation toward the man in the war-god's mask.

In his terror, the masked one sealed his own doom. He struck out at the snout, tried to thrust it from him. Had he known how The Whisperer conquered the beast, he would not have done it.

The gray man knew that a crocodile has no muscles of any strength to force its jaws *open*. With a noose formed of the bonds that had held him, he had encircled that huge snout in a fraction of a second that it had snapped shut. He had drawn the noose tight under the screen of the chemical smoke he had created, had wound more silken strands around it.

But the masked leader did not see those strands. When he thrust out to push the snout from him, he knocked the silken cords from the snout. The huge jaws gaped open, seized the man. The hungry crocodile was fed!

The scream was not that of an Oriental. The crocodile crunched hungrily; the war-god mask fell to the floor. Blood ran in a torrent, as Jules Goddard died in the jaws of the monster he thought he had controlled.

THE WHISPERER was busy. He whipped the bonds from Quick Trigger. Kung Ghee had already freed himself, and disappeared.

"Run!" The Whisperer hissed. "We've got to make time if we're to wash this case up."

Quick Trigger struggled to his feet.

"What's it all about?" he demanded. "It doesn't make any sense to me."

The Whisperer didn't answer. He tore through the ancient sewer until he found a stairway. It led to a trapdoor in the grounds of the old mansion. As The Whisperer raced along, he shed his disguise, became Wildcat Gordon again.

Wildcat's first stop was a phone booth. Again he made a long-distance phone call. His eyes sparkled as he turned away.

"It is as I thought," he snapped.

"What's the racket?" Quick Trigger demanded.

"It's extortion!" Wildcat explained. "The tongs were formed originally for protection of their members in business. It was legitimate protection. Even so, it made them rich. One of the two big tongs alone is worth eight million dollars by actual accounting.

"Lin San Fu had been building toward this for many years. The Fan Li was the only force that could have brought every Chinese in the country groveling with his money. But first, they had to have the membership lists of both the major tongs. They could force Chinese here not only to turn over their own savings, but to steal and murder to get more. The tongs would become defunct, powerless to intervene."

"B-but how about Jules Goddard? Quick!"

"He knew more about China and the Fan Li, probably, than old Lin San Fu himself," Wildcat rapped. "And when I figured out what that whistling sound was, I knew he had been to the mansion for a message earlier tonight. That—and one other thing I have learned."

Wildcat whipped his coupé to a stop in front of the library and studio of Jules Goddard. He slammed through the door. And he was none too soon.

Blam!—Blam!—Blam!

Staccato shots rapped out as Wildcat hurtled into the barnlike room. Kung Ghee was there. He sagged toward the floor, blood dripping from his side.

Two figures waved guns, slammed lead at Wildcat. One was Lee Su Wo, son of Lin San Fu. He still wore part of the war-god costume he had used in the cavern of the crocodile.

The other man was Lin San Fu!

THE old Chinese aimed his automatic at Wildcat. His face was a frozen sneer of hatred. Wildcat's hand scarcely moved. He fired from the hip. A round hole jumped into the forehead of Lin San Fu.

"This time," Wildcat rapped, "he'll really go to meet his ancestors!" Quick Trigger had taken care of Lee Su Wo.

Kung Ghee sat erect, held his side.

"I thank you, honorable one," he murmured. "It has been difficult, not knowing who is friend and who is foe. My country has been enjoying sympathy and support from your countrymen. The presence of the Fan Li would quickly end that. That is why I have been sent here. I was to find out who was behind it, and expose him. Please tell me what you learned."

Wildcat staunched the flow of blood coming from Kung Ghee.

"The ghost effect was to frighten the servants," he explained. "Messages could be received then with greater safety. Lin San Fu did the killing in other cities. He was safe. He was supposed to be dead."

"The old man was afraid of the wrath of his countrymen if he were unmasked in Fan Li. So he conveniently killed someone else, had his son identify the body as himself. The death certificate was made out there, where no one knew him.

"Goddard was a master sculptor. He made a moulage corpse for public display here and to be shipped to the Orient. I had that one intercepted on its way to the coast. The last message the pigeon brought from Lin San Fu was for a rendezvous here with Goddard. They took the message from The Whisperer. But he had read it, and I found out what it said: 'I will return tonight at headquarters'."

Kung Ghee sat erect.

"Ah, The Whisperer, "he said sadly. "I did not know who he was and tried to kill him. He saved the life of this one," and he pointed to Quick Trigger, "and myself. I should like to apologize for my conduct and thank him."

Quick Trigger snorted.

"Don't bother," he grunted. "He'd just get you into some kind of trouble!"

THE END

Coming soon in THE WHISPERER #5:

The Whisperer goes undercover to close down *The School for Murder* that prepares teenagers for crime careers. Then, Wildcat Gordon investigates trucking industry corruption in *Murder on the Line*. BONUS: a magical tale of Norgil the Magician by *The Shadow*'s Maxwell Grant!